969-860-ΠΛ

One of the world's leading science fiction writers, Anne McCaffrey is winner of the Hugo and Nebula awards for science fiction. Brought up in the U.S. and now living in Ireland, she is the creator and bestselling author of the unique Dragon series.

Also by Anne McCaffrey

DRAGONFLIGHT
DRAGONQUEST
THE WHITE DRAGON
RENEGADES OF PERN
DRAGONSDAWN

DRAGONSONG
DRAGONSINGER: HARPER OF PERN
DRAGONDRUMS
MORETA: DRAGONLADY OF PERN
NERILKA'S STORY and THE COELURA

GET OFF THE UNICORN
THE SHIP WHO SANG
DECISION AT DOONA
RESTOREE
THE ROWAN

THE CRYSTAL SINGER
KILLASHANDRA

STITCH IN SNOW

and published by Corgi Books

PEGASUS IN FLIGHT

Anne McCaffrey

CORGI BOOKS

PEGASUS IN FLIGHT
A CORGI BOOK 0 552 13807 X

Originally published in Great Britain by Bantam Press,
a division of Transworld Publishers Ltd

PRINTING HISTORY
Bantam Press edition published 1991
Corgi edition published 1991
Corgi edition reissued 1992

Corgi Books are published by Transworld Publishers
Ltd., 61–63 Uxbridge Road, Ealing, London W5 5SA, in
Australia by Transworld Publishers (Australia) Pty. Ltd.,
15–23 Helles Avenue, Moorebank, NSW 2170, and in New
Zealand by Transworld Publishers (N.Z.) Ltd., Cnr. Moselle
and Waipareira Avenues, Henderson, Auckland.

Printed and bound in Great Britain by
Cox & Wyman Ltd., Reading, Berks.

This book is respectfully and
gratefully dedicated
to
Diana Tyler
and
Diane Pearson

*They have been at a great feast of languages,
and stolen the scraps.*
WILLIAM SHAKESPEARE

1

As was her habit, Tirla took a quick look from the alley into the Main Concourse of Residential Linear G. She pulled back instantly, flattening her thin twelve-year-old body against the plas-slab wall. Public Health Officials were swarming all over, rounding up the early morning crowd of able-bodied workers who had been scanning the Employment Board for a day's work, the mothers with their handicapped kids making their way to the Rehab centres, and the legal children on their way to the linear's physical training facility.

Cautiously she took another look, to see what the PHO were setting up on their tables: vials and the big, compressed air bottles that operated the hyposprays. She withdrew, having seen sufficient to recognize another wholesale vaccination effort. Strange, she hadn't heard of any new 'mune plagues. To give them their due, PHO were swifter than rumour to avert disaster.

Rapidly Tirla ran through her head her current list of those mothers of illegal children whom she should inform: first, those who'd pay her for warning them to

9

hide the kids; second, those who could afford to pay her for stealing whatever vaccine was being administered today. She counted on her fingers: Elpidia, certainly, the old bouzma, Pilau, Bilala, and she'd better ask Mama Bobchik if there were newborns for they'd need the Five-shotter, Zaveta, Ariesan, and Cyoto. She'd need one for herself, whatever it was, and could possibly finagle a box, depending on how this current stuff was packaged. It all depended. Mirda Khan, yes, she'd best tell that old wagon right after she'd warned Mama.

Then she'd better change into clean clothing issue: she'd washed but this week's issue was five days old and looked eight. Public Health were quick to notice details like that. Mama Bobchik was always good for fresh wear, especially if Tirla went to her first with this news. This could be a very good day, Tirla thought with a rise of spirits, and slipped back down the alley for the centre shaft emergency stairs on her way down to Mama Bobchik's pad.

Most of Tirla's twelve years had been spent in scrounging a totally unofficial living in this multi-ethnic, thirty-storeyed community. She couldn't afford to miss a single trick, like today's unexpected Public Health round-up, to escape the stringent controls, the clever obstacles and little traps ingeniously set up by the Jerhattan Complex Administration Council, and the Law and Enforcement Organization to identify and control each member of the restless population of the linears.

Nations might be obsolete but ethnic groups were not, and although everyone could now understand and answer general questions in a pidgin Basic, subsistence level residential linears were multi-lingual. Tirla owed her survival to that.

Officially there had never been a record of Tirla's birth: she was, however, the fifth child born to Dikka – only the first, Tirla's brother, Kail, was legal. (*They* tied a woman off when she gave birth to a second child.

10

Consequently, Firza, Lenny, Ahmed and Tirla had all been born in Dikka's single-parent squat with the aid of Mama Bobchik who had had an illegal child every year until her womb had dried up.) Kail had been official until Dikka had sold him at ten. Firza had had the use of Kail's wrist ID for two years until she was profitably disposed of. In the next year, Dikka, Lenny and Ahmed died of one of the immune plagues that sporadically flared up to decimate the linears.

Two ID bracelets were a fine legacy in Tirla's mind for, in the haste and confusion of body disposal, Dikka's death had not been officially noted. So Tirla, self-sufficient and resourceful, managed to retain the squat, drawing two subsistence rations until Dikka's ID was cancelled after her failure to appear for a routine medical examination.

Wise in the ways of her society, Tirla had not been caught short by the lock-out. She knew tenancy articles, paragraphs and subsections by heart, so figuring out the cancellation date had been no problem. Two days prior to the eviction, she moved her few possessions – hotter unit, the best of the sleep sacks, the 'corder and the pretties Dikka's men had given her from time to time. She did miss the all-night informational programmes on the squat's Tri-D. The big public Tri-Ds on the Concourse stopped 'casting at the midnight curfew. Everything that Tirla heard or saw was retrievable from her clever, shrewd and organized mind. While she'd had Kail's ID, she'd even logged into school. One of Dikka's men said that you had to know the rules before you could break 'em.

Tirla's new quarters were five levels below the Main Concourse, in the maintenance segment of Linear G, right beside the charged security grille which protected the engineering section from unauthorized entry. Only a slight and agile person could reach the eyrie, where massive ducts formed a broad platform before bending up the inner wall. Tirla patched her hotter and 'corder

11

wires into the overhead cables, certain that her small use of electricity was unlikely to be discovered.

Tirla had the curious moral values of people who lived by their wits. She knew when to be ingratiating or stand firm. She knew what courtesies were due whom and never failed in performing them. Everyone who knew Tirla knew very well that she was 'illegal'. Because she was so useful to the residents of Linear G, as she would be today with her warning about the Public Healthers, and because officially she did not exist anyway, there was no profit – yet – in reporting her illicit existence.

She was scrupulously silent about any 'errands' she did. These often brought in the 'floating' credit chips. Floaters were legal tender, *Pay to Bearer*, untraceable chips which changed bearers frequently. Jerhattan Treasury and all the merchant and banking houses wisely ignored the circulation of minor amounts of floaters, just as they ignored the petty traders so long as they made no trouble and their merchandise was harmless.

For another two years, Kail's bracelet supplied his small sister with daily subsistence, weekly clothing issue and other amenities until 'Kail' failed to appear at Evaluation Centre within three weeks of his sixteenth birthday. The cancellation caused Tirla no problem for by then she was well established, almost indispensable to most of the residential clients and gang bosses in the neighbourhood industrial complexes. She could translate any of the nearly ninety dialects and languages, and saved clients hours at official transspeech centres or, worse, misunderstanding.

Linear G thrust thirty massive levels about the squat featureless F and H Commercial Blocks where residents of Linears E, G and I worked. Once, on a Free Day, while Tirla still had her brother's ID, she had gone with Mama Bobchik to the Great Palisades Promenade where thousands upon thousands of people had swarmed to enjoy a brilliant spring day, to overlook the exclusive hives, platforms and great cone complexes of Manhattan Island, and to ooh and aah at the monorail cars, large and small, that zipped along the tracks which garlanded the buildings like coloured tinsel strands. That was the first time Tirla had seen ships floating on water or the great pleasure skycars. There had even been a special issue of holiday food, yards above the standard fare, at dispensing banks. Buril, Mama's son, had a tripper key that he used on the dispers so they'd stuffed themselves before the mechanism's malfunction alarm got triggered. It had been a super day for Tirla. She hadn't thought the world was that big.

That was the same day that Buril explained to her all about the Space Platform which was being built and which needed so many workers. When it was completed, then all the people living on Manhattan who had enough credit and were the 'right kind' would be able to go off into Space and find other worlds to live on. Then all those beautiful buildings would be empty and there'd be enough space for everyone crammed into linear squats to live in proper big apartments with a bedroom for everyone in the family and no more Public Health or LEO men and women tying men and women off, shaming a virile man.

Tirla scratched on Mama Bobchik's door, heard the old woman gasping and groaning as she struggled off the bedshelf.

'*Kto stuchitsya? Perestan'te udaryat'sya. Okh, kak bolit golova!*'

Tirla grinned. So Mama'd a big head this morning, caused by the vodka she's made from the potatoes Tirla had nicked for her. She'd be easy to wheedle out of a credit.

'It's Tirla, and the Public Health are already on the Concourse.'

'*Boje moi! Eto tak?* Have I not enough pain in my life?' But the door was pushed open wide enough for Tirla to slip inside. 'What have you said? The Public Health again? So soon? Why?'

'Another vaccination by the looks of it. They're grabbing everyone, able-bodies, students, handies and their mothers.'

'Ah, we must hurry. Elpidia, Zaveta . . . ' and Mama Bobchik began reciting the names of her usual maternity patients. Tirla tugged her arm. '*Nu, zachem bespokoish menya?* What do you want from me?'

'I cannot help unless I have clean issue,' Tirla said, managing to look piteous and sound efficient.

Buril had fixed the clothing issue slot in his mother's squat so that it could be coaxed to extrude more than it ought. He had had very useful taking ways until Yassim, and Tirla made the warding sign at just the thought of *that* man, had paid Mama a huge sum. Buril had not gone the usual route Yassim's purchases took because Buril had an unusual talent in 'fixing' official equipment. Not a Talent-talent, for Mama would not permit him to be tested and taken away from her: not when she knew that eventually she could sell him for enough floaters to keep her comfortable in her old age.

Mama Bobchik blinked her reddened and bleary eyes and looked at the tiny girl. '*Da, da pravo zhe!* That is so!' She patted Tirla's head before she went to the clothing slot and did something which her heavy frame obscured from Tirla's sight. When she turned back, she had a packet in her hand.

'I washed this morning,' Tirla said, immediately unfastening and stepping out of the old suit. Of course she had to roll up the sleeves and legs of the fresh issue. She neatly folded each roll over wrist and ankle and pressed the edges to seal them, blousing out sleeve and leg to give her apparel more style. She retied the pretty braided rope belt that she'd inherited from her long dead mother and tucked the excess material neatly back. 'Now, I'll tell Mirda Khan, do this level and then up and down.

14

That'll be all I think I have time for. What'll I do for an ID? They'll grab me if my wrist's bare.'

What Tirla wanted most in her life was a genuine, valid ID bracelet that would allow her a squat right, the use of a Tri-D, three meals a day and a fresh weekly issue of clothing. An ID that was hers! And had never been anyone else's. One which would allow her into the school programmes that so few of the kids she knew seemed to care about at all.

Now she cocked her head at Mama Bobchik, knowing perfectly well that an ID was essential with PHOs swarming the linear. Mama Bobchik pretended to consider, giving Tirla just a few moments of anxiety.

'*Eto tak!* For PHOs, we use one.' With a flounce of her skirts, for Mama would not wear the single piece coverall without proper skirts to conceal her limbs, she turned her back on Tirla again. Listen as hard as she might, Tirla could not discover where Mama secreted those precious counterfeit IDs which Buril had also contrived. They were good for one day's use only: one day because, while the band would be accepted by a portable reader such as the PHO would have to record vaccinations, it would show up as a fraud when the day's entries were checked.

Mama Bobchik turned around, dangling the precious ID band. 'You split the take for the warning with me. As usual.' Tirla nodded solemn agreement to the terms, her eyes watching the swing of the band. 'And if you can steal enough vaccine, I will give you thirty per cent of that take.'

Tirla gave an incredulous snort. 'Sixty. I could get caught stealing.'

'Forty, then. No one has caught you yet. After all, I gave you the ID at no cost to you and have the expense of the spray gun.'

'Forty-five!'

The two hagglers eyed each other and then Mama's

broad face beamed down at Tirla's unyielding expression. She spat in her palm and held out her hand which engulfed Tirla's delicate paw to seal the arrangement.

'You are a clever one. You must hurry now.'

The girl was already slipping through the half-opened door and down the hall to spread the warning.

Tirla barely finished her route before the PH Officials began to penetrate the levels, checking IDs of each squat's occupants and herding them out and down to line up for their hypospray.

Tirla soon learned that it wasn't a 'mune plague but a virulent intestinal disease which had started in Linear B with devastating results. All linears were being vaccinated in an attempt to stem the spread of the ailment. Constantly the PH public address system droned on in a short explanation in all the languages registered in Linear G: Tirla did some rapid translations of her own when requested by nervous mothers.

'It's only another food contamination,' she assured the sceptical. 'They've isolated the source which has been heavily fined and they've lost their licence.'

'Huh!' said Mirda Khan, her dark eyes glistening with scepticism, 'that will be gone as long as it takes to send in enough credit to re-issue it. How long will the protection last us?'

'Oh, this one'll do us for a year!'

'A year? They are improving.'

Trudging forward step by step in the long queue, Tirla and Mama Bobchik finally reached the PH, dropped their wrists across the reader and received their shots. Immediately Mama pretended to come over faint and staggered against the table. While the PH woman was coping with that, Tirla swept an entire tray of the vaccine ampoules into the shopping sack Mirda Khan had ready as she, too, came to Mama's assistance.

'*Okh, kak bolit golova!*' Mama said in an appropriately wispy tone, the back of her fat hand against her head.

16

The pain in her voice was not entirely faked considering the hangover headache.

'What's she saying?' asked the PH Official, hovering between concern and annoyance. Side effects in some ethnic groups were not uncommon.

'Her head hurts,' Tirla replied.

'Not from this injection,' was the callous response of the PH-er. 'Now move along!'

Solicitously Mirda Khan and Tirla propped-up Mama Bobchik as she mooched slowly toward the nearest side aisle. Once safely out of sight, Mama immediately reached for Mirda's sack and peered inside it.

'One whole tray? Miraculous, Tirla, truly miraculous. There are more than enough. Run ahead and tell them to come in small groups. The PH-ers have checked our three levels. It will be safe.'

In the course of her errands, Tirla tried her ID bracelet on as many public dispensers as she passed, no matter what commodity emerged from the slot. She tucked each purloined item into the extra material at the back of her coverall, or into a sleeve or a trouser leg. It became harder to move quickly but Tirla managed.

By the end of the day, she had enough small floaters and illegally acquired items to keep her well fed and content for the next month. Maybe even six weeks before she need bother about working again.

2

'There was no aura of menace or threat,' Rhyssa Owen told Sascha Roznine as he stood glaring down at her in her bed. To reduce his threatening glower to a more productive, thoughtful mood, she touched his arm, reinforcing her statement with a mental *See, curiosity. An impingement, not a threat*.

Sascha 'saw' and subsided but he continued to glare at the graph recording of Rhyssa's early morning sleep pattern, where the wide black mark of the spoke showed that she had been roused from an REM dream sequence to full alertness by a mental intruder.

As the Director of the Centre of Parapsychic Talents on the North American East Coast, Rhyssa Owen lived on what had been the Henner estate, a reserve of trees, lawn and mature gardens above the Hudson River on the Palisades. This archaic remainder of the twentieth century residential suburbs interrupted the flow of linear structures that now housed the millions who lived and worked in the massive Jerhattan complex. Rhyssa's quarters were undistinguished from any of the other, almost rustic three-storey apartment blocks set among the gardens and trees. As with all dwellings for the Talented, these were secured and shielded from unannounced entry. In fact, even those who tenanted the linear constructions running on the long sides of the Centre's extensive grounds did not know of its existence, so artful were the screens. No-one should have intruded on Rhyssa, much less in her sleep.

'Awkward, rousing you so thoroughly. You need all the rest you can get.' Sascha projected a vision of himself and Rhyssa curled together in her bed, the double thick duvet tucked around their spooned bodies.

Yes, yes, Rhyssa replied. She responded with a vision of a firm foot pushing the Sascha body out of the bed. *But even if you were physically here, you couldn't've helped, Sascha-bear. It was all in my mind, in my dreams. And that's your duvet, not mine. I never use plaids.*

Rhyssa smiled up at him, fluttering her eyelids to mock his projection. He raised his eyebrows in resignation. They both enjoyed this game. They'd been playing it for years.

Picky, picky. Don't avoid the issue, Sascha said. 'Who, I'd like to know, could knock in on your mind? And why?'

'Indeed!' Rhyssa crossed her arms and stared off into a view of the lowering clouds and dismal rain that obscured a usually breathtaking view of Jerhattan. *That's what perplexes me.*

Don't range, Streaky. You're going to need all your energy to deal with the zealots. He projected the vision of three persons with limbs so entangled they resembled an oriental fetish, each caricatured face wearing an expression of mixed intransigence and scepticism.

Oh, don't! She laughed as she untangled arms and legs and set each person in the image upright, a whiskbroom smoothing tunic, trousers, while emblems of rank were straightened. *I can't remember that when I have to deal soberly with their urgent requests for Talents I don't have. They're laughable enough as it is.*

'Good. That's all they deserve. Shall I have Sirikit check back and see when this phenomenon first registered?' *Sheer impudence!* Sascha snorted his annoyance.

'That's an idea,' and Rhyssa smiled ruefully. 'I only thought of checking my graph this morning. I really do need my sleep.'

'Probably some emergent Talent who doesn't understand protocol. I do wish they didn't always feel required to over-react to their newfound mind-powers.'

'Damned strong one!' Maliciously, Rhyssa's image was of a very young Madlyn Luvaro, mouth wide open and the circle of people cringing away from the waves of sound emanating from her mouth.

Sascha grimaced. Madlyn Luvaro had a mental shout that could penetrate to the Space Station and any of its peripheral dockyards. It had been Sascha's task, as he was nominally in charge of training and development, to teach her how to focus and moderate her mental voice. Madlyn adored him passionately and was embarrassingly possessive of him: an adulation he was finding increasingly difficult to discount and why he assiduously cultivated the notion that he and Rhyssa were on the brink of a total partnership. Kindly, Rhyssa did not disclaim the rumour.

'I'll have Sirikit run a check on possibly emergents.'

Rhyssa shook her head slowly, yawned and sat forward at her desk, kinetically reaching some pencil-files, fanning them out and turning each until the index code side was visible. She selected the one she wanted, and neatly piled the others in front of her, code side outwards as her selection inserted itself in the reply slot. Simultaneously the reader net came off its hook and settled lightly on her head. With one finger, she poked the left contact pad against her temple in a final adjustment.

'We won't find him there,' she said and was as startled as Sascha was that she used a gender. 'Well, I know a trifle

20

more than I thought I did from that fleeting nudge.'

'Your secret lover?'

'Could be,' Rhyssa murmured. #Image of a sly grin and a come-hither expression directed at an amorphous shadow.# Although her tone was light, Sascha perceived that her surprise at making any kind of an identification went deep.

'I'll follow through,' Sascha said and left her office. As he took the anti-grav shaft down from her tower to the vast basement complex where most of the Centre's training and research was conducted, he carried with him a vivid mental image of Rhyssa Owen at her desk, the reader net covering her black hair, a spider-webbing across the wide silver lock which she had carried since her early teens. It grew broader every year and by her late thirties, her hair would be all Celtic silver.

Rhyssa would always have a young face, Sascha thought, as both her father and her illustrious grand-father, Daffyd op Owen had had: young, vibrant, with dark blue eyes that sparkled and gleamed with intelligence, humour and unassailable energy. Rhyssa was nearly as tall as the males in the family; a shade too thin, with long bones which she clothed in elegant, if often bizarre, styles: generally long, flowing garments which set her off in a society that had stripped apparel to the minimum.

She wasn't pretty – her features, though small, were too uneven and mismatched, with her right eye socket canted above the cheekbone which often gave her a gamine expression that no-one who knew her would misjudge. Her nose had a slight bump, giving her a haughty profile and her mouth was too generous above a strong jawline. Still, one forgot such details within moments of meeting Rhyssa Owen. She had inherited the full measure of char-ismatic personality as well as the strong psionic talents of her parents and the subtleties of her grandfather who had battled to secure the position of Talents in the present socio-economic-political atmosphere.

Sascha Roznine, himself a third generation Talent, younger than Rhyssa by three months, preferred his current role as Chief Trainer and Recruiter in the Centre for he had struggled all his life to manage a quixotic temper. Not for him the petty power ploys that Rhyssa coped with admirably. She could ignore the nerve-wracking sessions with Jerhattan's Managers and all the picayune details which would have set him raging in five minutes.

On the other hand, Sascha had immense patience with emergent Talents, coaxing, cosseting, curbing, gently allaying their doubts and building their confidences. When Rhyssa had once pointed out that, in their own way, emergent Talents were as obnoxious as Managers, Sascha replied that Talents learn from their mistakes.

There were so many strengths and varieties of Talent: the pre-cogs, those who could foresee events, generally those which would have a knock-on effect on a large number of other people: those whose prescience was limited to people they knew or were assigned to watch: those whose pre-cognitions had affinities with fire, water, males or females, children, as wide an assortment of focus points as strengths of perception.

Telepathy was the most common Talent: though some people could only receive thought, and others only send it. Telempaths felt emotions and responded to the pervading ones. The trained telempath, however, could either dampen negative auras or reinforce positive ones; alter the tension in crowds, preventing them from turning into mobs.

There were Talents who could 'find' things, given a facsimile of the desired item, or in the case of a human or an animal, a garment or some personal object.

Telekinetics could work on the largest objects or on the most minute levels with particles that could not be seen

22

with the naked eye, or even a microscope, though there had only been one genetic manipulator, Ruth Horvath. Telekinetics were invaluable in so many walks of life that those with this Talent were encouraged to have as many children as possible.

The rarest of the Talents were the pure and double telepaths, like Rhyssa, who could send and receive communications across the world so long as she had met the person she wished to 'speak' to. She could penetrate any mind not shielded by the thin metal caps the nervous wore or by a natural mental shield that very few humans were born with.

Sascha was also a strong double telepath but he lacked the phenomenal range that Rhyssa possessed, nor did he resent the lack. Once her strength had been established by her grandfather, Rhyssa had been committed to a Centre Directorship and all its responsibilities. However, he had developed a few rare tricks of his own so he never felt envious of or threatened by Rhyssa. She was welcome to her Talent.

He heard Madlyn Luvaro before he landed on the shaft cushion at the basement level. She was trying to be quiet and as successful as if she'd been tap-dancing across a sound resonant surface.

Until you learn to damp down your aura, it won't work, Madlyn. Improper flow! Low positive energy is what you need to be 'silent'.

Dammit, I thought that's what I had! And her mental response was contritely discouraged. Sascha pushed out of the shaft and there she was, flattened against the wall. 'I did "hear" you coming.'

Sascha: *Giant step forward!*

He tugged a strand of her tangled mane of black hair as he passed. She fell into step behind him, her large and expressive eyes rueful. Madlyn was a voluptuous eighteen year old with a sensual nature to match her appearance. She, and her Talent, had matured at fourteen

23

and since then Sascha had been struggling to teach her the necessary discipline that any Talent must master, and certainly she would require before her penetrating mental shout could be utilized.

Sirikit's already on it. Sascha had not tried to dampen his immediate concern.

Someone actually intruded on Rhyssa? #Image of Madlyn throttling large amorphous intruder and squashing it into a little ball which she then flushed down the toilet.#

Sascha snorted: Madlyn was quite capable of attacking anything that threatened Rhyssa. Who in the Centre wasn't?

One of the joys of telepathy was that one's needs were instantly understood. Sirikit was already scanning Rhyssa's Goosegg encephalographs for the previous month. Several were paused at the spoking that indicated intrusive wakenings. The Goosegg, initially developed to monitor the odd light flashes experienced by astronauts, was especially sensitive in registering Delta brain waves which were discovered to be the seat of paranormal or extrasensory perceptions. A Talent, trained to recognize his own slight mental alteration prior to paranormal activity, slipped on a net which recorded the brain activity. Many Talents, particularly the pre-cognitives and clairvoyants, wore them night and day. They were lightweight, of a strong fine mesh matching the wearer's hair colour. The net was connected either directly or remotely to the Centre's main banks so that Incidents of paranormal activity could be officially recorded, studied and consulted. It was proof positive to any sceptics that the extrasensory perceptions did occur.

'Look at Rhyssa's recordings, Sascha. There's no question that the Incidents have been increasing,' Sirikit said as he strode to the bank of horizontal spindles used in such comparisons. 'First one three weeks ago, second four days later, then three, and this past week once a night – about four-ish.'

Sascha: *Odd time for a voyeur!*

Sirikit: *With three-quarters of the population asleep in bed.*

Madlyn: *Insomniac?*

Sascha smiled for not only was her mental tone appropriately soft but she had caught the quick exchanges. Madlyn might be a powerful 'sender' but she could only 'hear' those in her immediate vicinity.

Sascha: *An adolescent generally has to be pried from his sleep. Rhyssa thinks it's an emergent Talent.*

Madlyn: *You keep telling me that emergent Talents follow no rule.*

'Any statistics on insomniacs?' asked Sirikit.

'I'll programme it,' Madlyn said, flipping her hair back as she seated herself at a monitor, keying in directories that could access any Bank in the world under the special concessions granted the Centres. She was cleared for normal use although passwords were needed for any sensitive files. Madlyn might be blatant in her sexuality but her mind, open to inspection at all times, was as transparently guileless as a child's. 'Well, this won't be productive. Anyone can have insomniac phases. Anxiety is the biggest cause. There are some people, the elderly in particular, who can get along on only four hours of sleep a night!' #Grimace of horror superimposed on a tossing body in a rumpled bed.# 'I'm wrecked without eight hours!'

Sirikit leaned back from the spools, now all paused to display the tell-tale spoke of intrusion.

Sirikit: *Three-thirty to four, pre-dawn, too early for most shift workers, even air and road-hauliers.*

Sascha bent over her shoulder, studying the reels as if he could glower the riddle into the open.

Sascha: *Rig her net.*

Madlyn gasped and stared at him. Sirikit blinked, sighed and then, rising from her stool, went to the main board to enable that programme.

'Some early morning joy seeker *has* to be overflying the Centre. Set an alarm through her net and we can watch the bugger in the act.' Sascha's voice was vindictive. Madlyn shot him a worried glance. She could feel the wave of high negative energy he exuded.

3

Barchenka, Duoml and His Highness Manager Prince Phanibal Shimaz were prompt to attend their meeting with Parapsychic Centre Director Rhyssa Owen at the Jerhattan City Manager's Tower, a massive structure in the centre of Central Park, the last vestige of nineteenth- and twentieth-century Manhattan. The tower rose above the tallest of the mercantile buildings and it was crowned by ziggurats of communication dishes, giving it an appearance from any distance of a grotesque bunch of stiff daisies, rammed into an immense glass brick. Skycars of varying sizes at the landing level stuck out like a fringe of angular multi-coloured leaves.

Ludmilla Barchenka entered first, her odd bouncing gait indicating that she was wearing her anti-grav boots. A career as Space Station Construction Manager made the Exalted Engineer's infrequent visits back to surface gravity a severe trial – for those she confronted. The woman's appearance did nothing to mitigate her abrasive personality: she was stocky, big-boned though not fleshy, with a flat broad face and the usual features in undistinguished shapes; the short cropped hair of the Spacer added to the image of a tough persona. Pale blue eyes increased the general impression of cold, inflexible tenacity. To top that off, Ludmilla invariably wore a thin metal skull cap shielding device – almost an insult to Rhyssa in her capacity as Director of the Eastern Centre. The Exalted Engineer's dedication could not be faulted but she proved sadly lacking in any social graces or tact.

Rhyssa wasn't sure if Barchenka was merely so security conscious that she 'shielded' or whether she was pathologically wary of the Talents whose services she desperately needed even as she deplored their abilities. Sascha was convinced that Barchenka had some sort of Talent, even if it could not be scanned, and that she refused to acknowledge the possibility. Padrugoi Station was due to be completed, and on budget, at the end of the current year. Considering that the first Laboratory Station had gone over budget by trillions and had been five years late in completion, the Exalted Engineer's achievements were considerable. With interstellar voyages now possible and habitable planets located in two 'near' systems, the pressure to implement the colonization programme was incredible. But first, the Padrugoi Station, the essential springboard to the stars, had to be completed. The Project had world-wide priority and the enthusiastic support of every political and economic faction on Earth.

Though not a well-publicized fact, Rhyssa knew that the Exalted Engineer was perceptibly falling behind schedule despite all her efforts. It was rumoured that the woman slept no more than four hours a night, that daily she accomplished a prodigious amount of work but she expected the same dedication from everyone on the Project. Unfortunately she did not have the personality or basic tact to generate either loyalty to herself or to the Project. Initially the Talents had volunteered to assist but, one after another, they declined to renew contracts. The many enticements to return with their unique capabilities to work on Padrugoi Station had met with failure.

Personnel Manager Per Duoml, coming in behind Ludmilla, moved with the heaviness of someone accustomed to lighter gravity but he managed without anti-grav assists. A Finn, as capable and dedicated as Barchenka, he was slightly easier to deal with. The Talents had liked working with Duoml: he was fair, competent, and had persuaded a few Talents to return for special, short-term assignments. The vast pool of world unemployed had been dipped into time and again to supply the sheer muscle that did much of the construction of Padrugoi: work that could have been completed more handily, and with less hazard, by some of the Talents available. But, while some Talents had worked short contracts on Padrugoi constructing the framework of the immense facility, they declined to extend their employment and they could not be conscripted. And though Rhyssa had dutifully asked the Directors of every Centre in the world, she had no takers to offer Duoml.

Programme Manager Prince Phanibal Shimaz ponced in behind Per Duoml and his presence was neither essential nor welcome to Rhyssa. He used any excuse available to press his suit on her. Peculiarly arrogant and impervious to her continued, and lately overt, distaste for his company, Phanibal was ubiquitous, seized by an unbecoming lust for her which she found particularly repellent from its onset when she was still personal assistant to her grandfather. The Prince was a computer genius – some said he had thought in binary codes in his crèche and teethed on chips – but, barely out of his teens, he had mastered the use of the Josephson Junctions in what he termed as an 'idiot proof' application to regulate with complete safety the vast flow of skycars and drones in and out of major linear depots and over densely populated areas. He was now applying his efforts to creating a similar basic and safe flow of spatial traffic.

Rhyssa composed her face and her mind, smiling with a warmth she did not feel as the three settled themselves.

'You do NOT,' Ludmilla began with no preamble, her deep voice guttural with only that trace of her natal language, 'have the required personnel.' Her pale eyes accused Rhyssa.

'As I have told you repeatedly, Manager, I cannot and will not order the Talented into Space.'

Ludmilla brought her fist down, a wince telling Rhyssa that, in her frustration, the Exalted Engineer had forgotten the gravitational differences. She brought the bruised hand up in a gesture that, in the Space Station, would have been flamboyant but here was less graceful.

'You MUST insist . . .'

'I can insist but they can resist,' Rhyssa replied equably.

'How can I maintain schedules without the personnel to perform the necessary tasks? Day by day we fall minutes behind: minutes which your diffident workers could make up in seconds. I will not fall behind the Schedule. We will make our completion deadline. We must have the suitable personnel. You told me that you have them and I have here the proof,' and Ludmilla extracted a pencil-disk from her tunic, brandishing this at Rhyssa.

'In that reply I said that I would certainly approach all Centres with your specific requirements. I most certainly did not promise to fill the vacancies.'

Barchenka narrowed her pale eyes into a basilisk stare. 'You recruit constantly. It is public knowledge that you find new Talents . . .'

'It does not follow,' Rhyssa inserted her reply smoothly before Ludmilla got wound up, 'that those we recruit are the kinetics that you specifically request. Certainly I could not ask untrained Talents to go into the hazards of Space . . .'

'Why not?' Ludmilla dismissed this consideration with a broad wave of her hand, inserting the pencil-file back into its pocket at the end of the gesture. 'We will train them on the job, to be useful, to be careful, to be specialists. They will love Space. They will make many credits and be wealthy.'

'The Talented do not accumulate wealth, Manager,' Per Duoml stated in his flat, nearly toneless voice, his patient eyes never moving from Rhyssa's face.

'Nonsense! Everyone acquires wealth.' Ludmilla had more than the usual contempt for altruists. 'In the beginning we had many Talents working for us.'

'We wished to assist the Project,' Rhyssa said. 'But you would not accept their stipulations when their contracts came up for renewal.'

'Stupid clauses, untenable for us. Shifts of no more than six hours when we work twenty-four on the Platform. Special shielding for noise. There is NO noise in Space.' Her scornful gaze rested hotly on Rhyssa.

'No noise which is audible to you, Madame Engineer, but which is extremely unpleasant to sensitives . . . '

'Bah! Sensitive!' Once again Barchenka summarily dismissed that consideration. 'Spoiled, pampered, catered to.'

'No, Madame Barchenka, not pampered or spoiled but yes, catered to,' Rhyssa flashed back. 'The Talented are skilled personnel and require some minor considerations to enable them to perform at their best in the hostile environment of Space.'

Barchenka ploughed on as if she hadn't heard. 'It is incredible that such a minority can exert so much influence on the economic life of our world. In the airport, in the spaceport, in industry where, while I order materials, I see the very Talents I must have to complete the most important Project of the world: a Project which has universal approval: which means mankind may reach beyond the limits of this solar system and explore the very star themselves. Yet you and the other Centre Directors do not permit me to hire the specialists I need.'

'It is not the permission of the Centre Directors that

is required, but the consent of the employed,' Rhyssa reminded the Engineer. 'Centre Directors negotiate the individual contracts with the necessary safeguards.'

'I can buy the contracts.' Barchenka's challenge was also a threat.

'Such contracts cannot be sold, Engineer Barchenka, and if you would accept the necessary safeguards, you might be more successful in attracting Talent!' Rhyssa replied sternly, beginning to lose patience with the woman's dogmatic pursuit.

She could ignore Per Duoml's mournful expression: even keep her gaze averted from Prince Phanibal's hot eyes, his slightly wet lips and nostrils which flared slightly from his rapid breathing: but all three glaring at her were an unnerving combination. She kept a smile on her lips, deliberately increasing the flow to her limbic system.

'You can insist,' Ludmilla repeated. 'It is in all your contracts that "it can be voided at the discretion of the Centre in emergencies".'

Rhyssa suppressed a rush of anger that Barchenka had been given access to a parapsychic contract but she reminded herself that such contracts were public knowledge.

'My fellow Directors do not consider that you have a true emergency, Engineer Barchenka.'

For the first time Barchenka flared angrily. 'I say this is an emergency! I say I must have a larger workforce to complete this World–Priority Project.'

'You have unlimited access to the conscriptable pool of workers.'

'Bah! They are useless. Sterile, uneducated, untrainable grunts! I cannot build a Space Platform only with grunts. I will have the kinetics I need. I promise that, Director!'

With that she wheeled and, in a dangerous imbalance, made a lurching exit, Prince Phanibal following her.

Per Duoml took one step forward, bowing slightly at

the waist. 'Even half a dozen kinetics would improve the situation tremendously.'

'As I have explained repeatedly, Per Duoml, ensure the Talents shielded quarters and a six-hour maximum shift and they will be amenable. Surely if there's credit enough in your budget to support the number of trips back to Earth that have been made for the purpose of recruiting Talents, the funds can be found to supply their basic needs on Padrugoi!'

'Engineer Barchenka must adhere to the budget. No alterations can be made to existing staff accommodations.'

'Then Engineer Barchenka is stuck with the result.' Rhyssa fervently wished that Per Duoml would relax his mental shields long enough for her to place directly in his mind the information her words patently did not convey. 'You require kinetics to shift objects of mass proportions in the assembly of Padrugoi. You also need kinetics who can assemble chips of the most complex delicacy in the total vacuum of Space. The kinetic energy required by both tasks is the same and exhausting. They need quiet to restore their strength: they are sensitive to the metallic vibrations of Padrugoi itself, the inhumanly close quartering, the lack of privacy and the appallingly bad rations which are insufficient to replenish their bodies and minds.'

Per Duoml nodded impassively and then shrugged, unwilling to comment before he, too, turned to leave. His departure left Rhyssa with an uneasy sense of foreboding.

Rhyssa directed a query to Sirikit on duty in the Control Room of the Centre. *Any pre-cogs in just now?*

Sirikit: *None. You're expecting one?*

Rhyssa: #Image of Ludmilla Barchenka's grim visage.# *Possibly!*

4

The boy blinked three times, and the channel on the ceiling screen changed again. He sighed. Yet another oldie which he'd already seen often enough to have memorized the good parts. He blinked the switch signal again, through enough of the channels to realize that there was nothing to catch his attention. Not even an educational programme unfamiliar to him. The first few weeks he'd been in the ward, it had been lots of fun, watching the Tri-Ds all through the long nights. Kept his mind off – 'things' after his headaches had eased. Sometimes he almost missed those headaches because, at least then, he'd been feeling *something* in his body.

He sighed. He could do that, too, he reminded himself, thinking positively as Sue, the therapist, said he must. He didn't understand a lot of what she told him, like imagining himself walking and running, thinking hard of how he used to do it – before he ran alongside the ruins and a brick wall had collapsed on him.

Why? The agonizing question made him gasp. He had thought he'd stopped *that*! Asking 'why' was definitely negative and always depressed him terribly. *Why* had that wall come down just as he, Peter Reidinger, ran past it? Had he kicked a stone that had been enough to trigger the collapse? Had one of the boys chasing him lobbed a stone at the wall? *Why*, since it had been standing for fifty or a hundred years all by itself, WHY had it picked that moment to come down? Three seconds later, he'd have been safe – safe from the wall and the boys chasing him. *Why* had he turned into the forbidden area, anyhow? He'd had a choice at the end of the alley: over the wall – only it had seemed very high to him and nothing to give him a leg up; to the right, only that took him back into the Alley Cats' territory and they might have had an ambush laid; or to the left, weaving his way through the ruins, making it more difficult for them to know which way he'd go. WHY?

Negative! Negative! Peter screwed up all his face muscles and then made them relax, group by group. Then he smiled, slowly and consciously spreading his lips and bringing the corners of his mouth up, stretching them until his cheeks lifted, his chin dropped and his lips parted over his teeth, willing the nerve impulses in his face to change the limbic system. As Sue had taught him, he pulled his most happy moment out of his mind: his eleventh birthday when his father had come home on leave from the Space Station in time for the party.

Planting that memory firmly in front of 'why', Peter rehearsed the details of that experience, that happy experience, until he could relive the entire scene from the moment the door chime had announced that his father had made it home until Dad had tucked him into his bunk. He had got so he could even feel the touch of his father's hand on his forehead.

Good thing Dad had touched him there. The only place he had feeling. Peter sighed again, re-felt the

35

touch. Closed his eyes and 'heard' his father leave the room, 'heard' the muffled sounds of his parents' talking, laughing. He expelled another deep sigh.

He was lucky. He could breathe on his own now. Sue had been so proud of him when that autonomic reflex had returned. He filled his lungs, knowing that his chest was rising, his diaphragm was tightening. He *could* feel the air in his windpipe. He held his breath as long as he could, until spots came in front of his eyes, then expelled it.

Immediately he heard the steps of the duty nurse. Miz Allen didn't like to be disturbed, especially when he knew that they had a critical case on Pie 12. He counted ten steps and then she was peering down at him, making eye contact. She then peered at the wall panel which gave out intimate readings.

'Was there a respiratory fluctuation, Peter?'

'Aw, I was just doing my breathing exercises.'

'You were not,' and Miz Allen glared at him for a moment, and then her long thin face relaxed. She laid a light hand on his forehead and then drew one finger down his cheek to press it against his lips. 'You were fooling. Don't fool with your breathing, Peter. Your brain needs oxygen. And it needs sleep, too. It's quarter of four. You should sleep. You know how to achieve relaxation, Peter. Do your progressives, there's a good boy.'

They both heard the sudden whimpering of the burn girl on the other side of a circular ward.

Miz Allen, reproving smile and all, disappeared and Peter counted her steps, twenty-one, to get to the critical case. Peter counted to thirty now, and then the whimpering ceased. He knew burns hurt. He wished he felt *something*, even burns!

He immediately put his mind to the few progressives available to him, the relaxation of every muscle in his face, head and neck. He couldn't move his head but he

36

had sensation in his neck. He reached total slack and thought carefully of HIS place, feeling the spring of grass under his feet, hearing the shimmer of leaves as a wind soughed through them, the smells of the garden, the sky above, the sun warm on his back. He began to float again. He had the sensation of floating up, out of the supine body resting on its cushion of air, amazed and annoyed at the various tubings and wires shunted into him that he never felt.

The garden of his dreams was miles away from Jerhattan. It had been part of the vacation farm to which his parents had taken him when he was eight. For someone raised in linear Jerhattan, surrounded constantly by the noise and smell of people and maintenance machineries, he had been totally entranced by the difference. Peter knew that there were small 'green belts' throughout the Jerhattan complex: he'd been to several, trying to relive that vacation. None had evoked the same response in him, being too small and cramped to close out the eternal noise of the city.

He had found a place, though, to which he could float when he got to the proper state of relaxation. It had grass and trees, barely visible in the eerie pre-dawn light. And he was strangely attracted by other inexplicable strands, comforting wisps of thought, enticing him to linger. One in particular intrigued him and he hovered as close to it as he could, tantalized by a sense of tranquil familiarity.

All of a sudden he was nearly blinded by powerful lights that flooded the scene. A moment of terror. He could not suppress his scream, steadying only when he heard Miz Allen's steps. He didn't open his eyes until he felt her hand on his forehead and KNEW he was safe back in Bed 7 of Pie Ward 12.

'What's the matter, Peter?' Miz Allen always knew if you were shamming. Her eyes flicked to the wall panel. 'Bad dream?'

'Yes, bad dream.' Despite himself, his voice quavered and her expression softened. She didn't tolerate false alarms.

'Yes, your endorphin level shot up. I think you'll have to have some sleep.'

Peter nodded, relieved at her decision. 'I've got VMR tomorrow . . .' He wasn't certain how much of the caution he managed to say before darkness overwhelmed him.

★   ★   ★

You scared him off! Rhyssa accused Ragnar, fuming that someone had triggered her net to alert the Centre's security forces if her pattern spiked during the night. The field lights had blazed up. Moments later she'd heard the thrumble of the skycars, shooting off in all directions. *Sascha!* she roared. He was the only one empowered to set surveillance on her!

We'll catch the bugger!

NOT that way! Rhyssa forced controls to disperse the white-hot fury. Sascha had exceeded his authority – even the bonds of friendship.

I have not!

Rhyssa inhaled deeply, aware that she was trembling with reaction. She expelled the breath right down to her toes, continuing to press downward until her belly muscles were taut.

There was NO threat! she said.

There WAS intrusion! She felt the break in his mental pattern as he responded to an exterior stimulus. *That's bloody strange. There WAS no intrusion. Not a physical one. Not a blip on any screen that can't be accounted for. And nothing – read that – nothing in our air space.*

An emergent! Rhyssa coloured the thought with satisfaction. *That is, if you haven't scared him out of his Talent!*

#Image of herself turning back on to her stomach, hauling the duvet in its pastel print tightly around herself, and dragging a pillow, also in a pastel printed slip, firmly over her head.# Which was what she did.

* * *

'An emergent from where?' was the question that circulated the Control Room.

'Who's awake at four o'clock in the morning?' Sascha asked.

'I can do a probability curve,' Madlyn suggested, 'eliminating all the obvious shift workers.'

'Why eliminate them?' Budworth asked.

'If they're working, they're not doing O.O.B.'

'And who says this is an out of body job?' Sascha asked, turning on Madlyn with surprise.

'What else could it be?'

Sascha grinned. 'You may very well be right, Madlyn, and it's so obvious I wonder none of us thought of it before. OK, who would go O.O.B.?' It was a leading question to which he already had an answer.

'Someone who doesn't like the bod they're stuck with,' she replied.

'But oobing *is* Talent,' Budworth said, 'and all of 'em are registered so they have better things to do than O.O.B.'

'*If* they're registered,' Sascha pointed out.

'I see, so we run a check on new ones.'

'That's right. With the hospitals.'

Madlyn groaned. 'D'you know how many hospitals there are in Jerhattan?'

'Not intimately,' Sascha said with a grin and pointed an index finger at her. 'Think of it as a survey question in your training. Ask for paralytic cases, teen, pre-teen, insomniacs . . .'

'Why blame the teens?' Madlyn asked, bridling.

39

'They won't have been scanned for Talent yet. OK,' Sascha added graciously, 'try anyone faced with a sudden lack of mobility. I'll add the prison systems, too . . . ' He grinned at Madlyn's groan. 'One of the most famous was a guy escaping a sadistic jailor.'

'Can the Centre get prisoners released?' Madlyn's eyes widened.

Budworth chortled. 'Don't you remember your Centre history? This place was started by rejects from prisons and mental institutions . . . ' And the man shot a sly look at Sascha, 'and all kinds of otherwise asocial and/or eccentric personalities.'

'If my brother were here . . . ' Sascha waggled an admonitory finger at Budworth.

'Huh!' Budworth snorted. 'I'm not afraid of your brother even if he is the high and mighty Law and Enforcement of Order Commissioner.'

'I would be,' Sascha replied. 'Which reminds me, I'm late for that appointment. Get the programme started on checking hospitals, prisons. And Buddy boy, you can do the mental institutions. I appreciate the reminder.'

'Ha!' Madlyn said at Budworth as Sascha left the control room.

*　　*　　*

How can there be that many illegal children in the Residentials?' Jerhattan City Manager Teresa Aiello demanded of Medical Chief Harv Dunster. 'Your people are supposed to tie off after a second pregnancy.'

Harv's angular face was grim. 'Only if we get to deliver 'em. You know that some ethnic groups still refuse to practice contraception. Until we have the right to use infertility drugs in subsistence-level food, there'll be unreported births – and continued traffic in preadolescents for sexual perversions, or cheap labour in illegal factories. And the ones with the right blood factors and healthy organs will still be stashed away by the very rich for transplants as needed.' He gestured at the fax sheets on Teresa Aiello's desk.

'And ruthless people will still dispose of the used ones,' added Boris Roznine, commissioner of Law Enforcement and Order. 'Even illegal kids have rights.' He glanced obliquely at the faxes scattered on the worktop.

Teresa inadvertently glanced down. She was a tough-minded woman, but she had a ten-year-old daughter, and the fax of the bloated bodies discovered as flotsam off the North Shore of Long Island spared no one's sensibilities. She averted her eyes. The coroner reported that the oldest had been twelve, the youngest five.

Boris Roznine had contacted her the moment the appalling discovery had been made. The temper of Jerhattan was always uncertain when faced with such news, and Teresa had called an emergency meeting of her commissioners to prepare for a possible eruption if the news was leaked to the media. Boris's twin brother, Sascha, was due to arrive with the Parapsychic Center's suggestions. To insure the tight security around the tragedy, the four were meeting in the shielded privacy of the city manager's tower office.

'Ah,' Boris interrupted what Teresa had been about to say, his right hand lightly touching his temple in indication that he was receiving a telepathic message. 'Positive ID of one, the Waddell girl who was kidnapped six weeks ago . . . '

Teresa winced and let out a groan. The Waddells were acquaintances of hers, high-tech executives; the child, bright and extremely pretty, had been a school friend of her daughter. Teresa had put a top priority on the abduction, and had officially requested that Rhyssa Owen assign her best finder to the case.

'Two others are listed as runaways, reported missing two months ago. Of the others . . . ' Roznine shrugged, glancing at the medical officer. 'The best the lab can do is genotypes, and it's all-sorts.'

Every citizen of the United World was permitted – provided they did not carry the proscribed genetic recessives – to produce a replacement. One parent, one child. Two parents, two children. ZPG was stringently enforced until the pressure of Earth's population could be released on the new habitable worlds, identified but not yet attainable. The Propagation Laws were easier to enforce in rural communities than in the huge residential warrens of cities like Jerhattan, with its population of over thirty million.

Teresa turned to the LEO commissioner. 'You haven't stopped the spot checks, have you, Boris?'

'Hell, no, but we're still not locating the early pregnancies no matter how we try. If I had the personnel to mount simultaneous level searches, we'd catch more.' Boris brought his clasped hands together as if closing a net. He gave a ghost of a grin. 'We did pretty well at the Residentials, six weeks after the last big power outage, but that was a once-off.' Then he spread his hands wide, matching Dunster's resignation. 'You know our situation. We manage to keep a lid on most of the trouble – if we're all sitting down as hard as we can. It isn't as if we need more bodies.'

'The ones that ignore the legal control,' Harv said dejectedly, 'are exactly the ones educational and hygiene programmes don't reach – in any language.'

Teresa grimaced. 'So there's no indication where the rest of those poor kids were snatched?'

Roznine shook his head. 'Could have come from any subsistence level.'

'In the last gruesome chucking, three months back or so, only four were recognizable ethnic types,' Harv Dunster said grimly. 'Near Easterners – Lebanese and Arabic. Two were Tay-Sachs, ten were dark-skinned, and one was an HIV carrier – which may well be why they were all . . . disposed of.' The medic sighed heavily. 'I suspect Lab may also find anti-body positives among this latest—'

'Spare me, Harv,' Teresa said firmly, and called up the main Jerhattan map on her screen. 'We've just had a go-round of the Residentials with Public Health. We haven't got the funds available for another. Exactly where were the bodies found, Boris?' Her fingers hovered over the terminal as she waited for an answer.

'Washed up out by Glen Cove, not far from some of the more exclusive residential hives bordering the Sound.'

'Great!' Teresa's frustration came out as sarcasm. 'No Incident logged?' she asked Boris, though that would have been included in the initial report.

'The storm, yes. The flotsam, no.'

'Shouldn't your brother be here by now?' Teresa frowned, glancing at the clock ticking off the seconds in the corner of the main screen. 'We need all the help we can get on this.'

The focus of Boris Roznine's blue eyes locked briefly as he linked minds with his younger brother. 'Traffic snarl's breaking up. But he says' – his voice suddenly deepened as the Talent peculiar to the twin brothers allowed one to speak through the other – 'Look, I want to save time – yours and mine. These murders go deeper than the loss of thirty juveniles. Forget the HIV factor – it's irrelevant here. They were disposed of because we'd got too close to them, but not close enough, soon enough. Teresa, Carmen's been on search-and-find duty ever since you handed us the Waddell kidnap file. She got a whiff or two of terror, but never enough light to pinpoint. Except that she got a hint of water.' Boris's wide mouth quirked briefly, reflecting his brother's chagrin. 'Most of those children had to be illegals. We all know that that group of pederasts is active – and supplied – despite international efforts to eradicate that sort of traffic. We know that kids are bought as cheap labour and shipped

43

who knows where. And that some are also secreted as possible transplant donors.

'We haven't been idle,' Sascha's voice continued. 'This could, in fact, be the break we've been waiting for. We got too close. It'd be nice to know,' and at that word the door to Teresa Aiello's office swung open and Sascha Roznine strode in, smiling at everyone. As he gave his brother's shoulder a grateful squeeze, he continued, 'where exactly we got so close. We're working on it, and with your assistance, Harv and Teresa, I think we have a line to throw out to those sharks.' His smile took in each of his listeners, but he cocked his head at his brother and winked.

Slowly a smile began to lighten Boris's face as he read the detailed thoughts in Sascha's mind. 'Tag kids with strands through the school system? That might just work! We might even catch the bastard child-stealers this time.' Boris leaned forward across the table. 'You are all familiar with the restraint filaments that were recently developed? Sometimes those we tangle with the strands escape before they can be secured. A second application has been made with a slightly altered formula, and now the altered strand can be traced for up to six months. There're certain anomalies to be resolved, but it's worth the effort to tag every child in the vulnerable group.'

'You mean, this side of the river?' Teresa waved at the panorama visible from her tower office, and the uptown cluster of beehive, cone, and single-tower Residential buildings clearly visible on this bright morning. 'But statistically, it's the illegals in the Linear Residentials who are more at risk.'

'If we could catch Linear kids to strand 'em,' Boris said, raising his hands palms-up in resignation, 'we'd be way ahead. Meanwhile we'll strand as many kids as we can on both sides of the river and hope.'

'Hope?' Sascha asked softly.

5

Rhyssa! She recognized the mental touch of John Greene, the Talented bodyguard of Secretary of Space Vernon Altenbach.

Rhyssa: *We got problems?*

Johnny: *Girl, you really deserve all the headaches of administration if you can guess that much from just hearing me speak your name.*

Rhyssa: *No pre-cog needed, JG, because you never bother me unless there's political pussyfooting. What is it this time?*

Johnny: *A Bill to draft the Talented into whatever position the Gov'mint needs them!*

Not again? Rhyssa's response was half-amused, half-irritated.

Concerted attempts had been made in the past by government agencies to circumscribe the freedom of choice originally granted to the Talented. That was prior to the point at which government agencies began to appreciate the applications of Talent. After the days when Daffyd op Owen, her illustrious grandfather, abetted by Senator Joel Andres had fought to gain legal immunity for Talents exercising their abilities.

Immunity had been particularly vital for clairvoyants because, when they warned of disasters which were, by those warnings, averted, they had been subjected to expensive and time-consuming lawsuits. There had been attempts since then, from the ridiculous to the deadly serious, to regulate, restrict, or regiment all manner of Talents to military, civil service or mercantile uses.

But the Talented had always managed, quite legally and with no untoward exercise of their particular abilities, to circumvent such attempts. Many Talents had willingly sacrificed personal freedoms to serve in the public sectors, some on a lifelong basis, to preserve the right for their peers to choose. Rhyssa's parents had done that, to give her the opportunity to achieve the position she now held.

Again and this isn't funny, Rhyssa, Johnny Greene went on. *Space is in a bind. The Platform has to be finished on schedule before the sheer weight of numbers on Earth becomes more unmanageable than it already is.*

Rhyssa: *So Ludmilla's been lobbying?*

Johnny: *She's got some hefty help and Space's got tremendous pressure on him. I'm the loudest of the Washington/Luxembourg voices so I'm making the contact with you for the rest of the minders. We've been excluded from far more sessions than we ought to be: sessions that have been attended by some of the most antagonistic right mutes that have ever been lined up against Talents. And when you think that I helped Space develop his shields against unauthorized peeking, I could spit! The nerve of him closing me out!*

One of the more sensitive professions open to empathic Talents was that of 'minding' vulnerable top-ranking officials. Terrorism was still a fact of political life: fanatics who had access to sophisticated devices and the capability of striking down key figures emerged sporadically, often on behalf of the unhelpable. Although the problem of the displaced and the minorities had been somewhat eased by the mass resettlements and the institution of the linear developments near every major urban area, and the incidence of assassinations had been drastically reduced, empaths were still employed to 'mind' top-ranking officials who might be targets for the fanatics who still emerged.

World governments had long ago given up any response to emotional blackmail. Crack units had time and again successfully freed hostages: units often composed of previous hostage takers. By and large, though, the protection of vulnerable people was ably managed by Talented minders. Like Johnny Greene.

Rhyssa could hear the hurt in Johnny's voice that Vernon Altenbach had been shielding his thoughts from the man who personally and professionally was also Vernons' best friend as well as his brother-in-law. In his official capacity, Johnny served an Under-Secretary in the Space Secretariat. Prior to that he had been a trained EtoP (Earth to Platform) pilot with twenty successful launches: the twenty-first had grounded him forever. His Talent had saved his crew from death but not himself from losing both left leg and arm. Despite state of the art prosthesis, a new career had seemed advisable. Johnny was extremely useful in both new capacities. He had already prevented four attempts to kill or kidnap Secretary of Space Altenbach.

Johnny: *I shoulda been included in these latest talks but I wasn't.*

Rhyssa: *Which means that Talent was being discussed. Barchenka and Duoml want more kinetics on the Platform in the worst way. I'm doing my best to help . . .*

Johnny, in an uncompromising tone: *Anyone thought of telling Barchenka that she's the reason why Talents won't work up there?*

Rhyssa: *Lance Baden did. He thinks she has selective amnesia. Can't even get her replaced, not with the performance record she's got!*

Johnny: *Vernon's tried! She's so bloody good at what she does . . . it's only how she does it. I'll keep in touch but we felt you ought to be forewarned.* There was a hint of criticism in his voice.

Rhyssa: *Nothing has come up with any pre-cog, Johnny.*

Johnny: *I know, I know. That worries me as much. This thing could be very, very big and not even Mallie's got a whiff!*

Amalda Vaden was one of the most sensitive pre-cogs the Centre had ever produced and her lack of foresight – if Johnny's reading of the situation was correct, and it should be – was surprising.

Rhyssa: *Then obviously the matter is solved before it reaches critical.* She tried to sound firmly optimistic even as a little shudder rippled down her backbone. Someone should be sensing something!

I'll be in touch, Johnny assured her. *I'll even see what the ghosts think. You know how they'd like to see our Talented noses out of joint.*

I think I'll try a frontal attack, Rhyssa said. *Might jog a few brain cells loose.*

When'll I see you then? Johnny's tone brightened.

If possible, today. Run me through Vernon's schedule. When Johnny did, Rhyssa stopped him at the lunchtime engagement. *I like the food there. I'll just drop in!*

*   *   *

Rhyssa always experienced a mild shock when she encountered Johnny in the flesh, for his mental voice was at variance with his physical appearance. He was medium tall, kept himself physically trim and one would never guess his serious injuries from seeing him walk or manage eating utensils. Some latent kinetic ability had proved to be an asset with the amputations. He rose as he spotted Rhyssa approaching the table where he, Secretary of Space Vernon Altenbach, Exalted Engineer Ludmilla Barchenka and Padrugoi Personnel Manager Per Duoml were seated. Johnny's broad smile welcomed her and they exchanged touch and a kiss.

Would you have dared look so stunning if the amorous Phanibal had come, too? Johnny's amber eyes with the little green flecks in them twinkled with devilment.

Rhyssa: *Why doesn't that odious man go back to the Pacific Island that spawned him and attend to the family's plantations?*

Johnny: *All you need is a strong handsome man who'll scare him off. Right now you've got this lot embarrassed by your appearance and yet they haven't said a thing out of line,* he added, all in the split second of the greeting.

'Just the people I hoped to see,' Rhyssa said, giving Altenbach a genuinely glad smile, nodding politely to Barchenka who was scowling fiercely and Per Duoml whose expression was suitably bland. 'When I saw you were to be in Washington, Madame Barchenka, I realized that I should put in an appearance before matters get out of hand.'

'Now, Rhyssa,' Altenbach said, signalling a waiter to bring a chair and set up another place for his unexpected guest, 'you can't disrupt the established procedure of lobbying. That's not the way to play the game.'

'Nor is going behind my back,' Rhyssa said, smiling to take the sting out of her criticism. She turned to Barchenka. 'You have a schedule to keep. What you will not appreciate is that one cannot schedule Talent, nor lobby it. The kinetics you so desperately need cannot materialize to help you meet your schedule. That many kinetics don't exist. Talent is a random and highly individual trait, not an imposed one. No-one can dictate to a Talent and expect the person to perform to the best of her or his ability. That dictation inhibits the Talent as surely as seasickness inhibits appetite. There is no legislation in the world that may chain the mind.'

'There is legislation that will recruit those needed to do the job which the entire world has decided must be done.' Barchenka's stolid words complemented her uncompromising expression. 'The Platform *will* be finished as scheduled. The kinetics *will* participate.'

Rhyssa caught another strong emanation: this time from Per Duoml who nodded solemnly to support Barchenka's statement.

'There are ways,' Barchenka added, her cold eyes scanning Rhyssa's whole appearance − her elegantly coiffed hair, subtle make-up, the couture outfit.

'Legal?' Rhyssa asked with a slight smile, expressing ineffable superiority over the blocky and unfashionable Ludmilla.

The Secretary cleared his throat and handed Rhyssa a menu. 'I'm still of the opinion that this . . . impasse . . . can be negotiated to the satisfaction of all concerned.'

Barchenka made a monosyllabic noise of disbelief and resumed her perusal of the menu which Rhyssa's appearance had interrupted. After only seconds, she tossed it negligently to the table. 'I would prefer nutritious food to this . . .'

Johnny Greene beckoned to the *maître d'*, who was famous for his poise under the most trying situation that Washington could produce. 'D'Amato, Manager Barchenka requires the *other* menu.'

A snap of D'Amato's fingers produced an underling, carrying a slim folder which he presented to Barchenka with a flourish. She gave first him, then Johnny, a sardonic look which turned to agreeable surprise as she scanned a menu composed of the foodstuffs available on the Platform.

'Five, twelve and twenty, taken with tea,' she said in a voice that vibrated with controlled anger.

Watch it, Rhyssa! Johnny cautioned. *Did you catch that flash? She's poison-sure she's got us where she wants us.*

Simultaneously from three other telepaths dining in the same room with the personages they minded, Rhyssa was sent similar warnings.

Fine! Now discover what? Rhyssa said mentally as vocally she chose her luncheon of soup – the restaurant was known for its cold fruit soups – and salad. *Gordie, are you available for some quick scans of obsolete statutes that could cover such a contingency?*

Been driving myself and my clerks all hours trying to find one, Rhyssa, replied Gordon Havers, the youngest Supreme Court Judge ever appointed. *There's nothing in our constitution but since the Soviets won the contract for Padrugoi, there may be something in the Russian section that does! Their legal system is as convoluted as their grammar!*

'You can of course invoke some forgotten but still active statute,' Rhyssa remarked all too blandly, waiting for reactions, 'to conscript Talents . . . ' Both Barchenka and Duoml registered a startled reaction to her blunt words.

Bingo, Gordie cried. *I'll concentrate on the Russian end of Spacelaw.*

' . . . but,' Rhyssa continued soothingly, 'it has always proved unwise to force Talent to perform in an area that is either personally or professionally distasteful to them, and under punitive conditions.'

'We have been too lenient with your temperamental tricks and traits,' Barchenka said, leaning across the table in her anger with Rhyssa. 'You will do this, you won't do that!' She affected a child's petulant tone. 'Many concessions were made to cater to the whims and fads of your Talents, and still no significant numbers will volunteer for the most important Project of all history. Your attitude is unacceptable.'

'I am protecting my colleagues, not being obstructive. I must repeat,' Rhyssa continued smoothly as both Barchenka and Duoml could not completely dampen their reflexes, 'it has always proved unwise to force Talent to perform duties unacceptable to them and under punitive living conditions.'

'That will change! Will be changed! The Platform will

be finished on schedule!' Her voice had risen with each sentence until it stopped conversation throughout the opulent dining room. Now she pushed herself from her chair, wobbling slightly as her movements, more suited to half-grav, brought her stocky body ponderously to an upright position. She kicked the chair away from her. 'I do not tolerate insubordination!' And she clumped away from the table.

'I was doing my best for you,' Vernon Altenbach said to Rhyssa, his face and manner resigned as he rose from the table, his chair moved by a hovering waiter.

'You do not understand our position, Director Owen,' Per Duoml added, but he made no move to leave the table. 'We are forced to use unpleasant alternatives to avert far more serious disasters overtaking the world!'

'I'll see if I can calm her down, make her see reason,' Vernon said and gestured for Johnny to remain. 'D'Amato, send my meal and hers to the private room. I'll be there.'

'Do you believe, in your own heart, Per Duoml,' Rhyssa asked, leaning across the table to the man, 'that we are *evading* our duty to the world?'

He shrugged, his shield tight to his mind – as tight, Rhyssa thought, as his unwillingness to understand the nature of Talent. 'It is the opinion that this – reluctance – puts the whole Platform project in jeopardy.'

'It is Ludmilla Barchenka who puts it in jeopardy,' Rhyssa said with more heat than she'd intended. She smiled quickly, hoping to repair the damage of her candour. Per Duoml might not be Talented but he was scarcely stupid.

'Ah! My esteemed colleague was correct.'

'I am NOT standing in her way. I am protecting my professionals even as she is protecting her project.' Rhyssa regretted that little flair of candour.

Well, she IS why Talents won't work, Johnny said in swift reassurance. *And we all know it!*

Gordie: *Yeah, but she stays! This will be an interesting power struggle, speaking from a purely legalistic viewpoint.*

'I admire Barchenka's unquestionable abilities as a spatial engineer. I would prefer that she returned the professional compliment,' Rhyssa said amiably. 'This soup is excellent, Per Duoml. Let us enjoy it.'

6

Bingo! Gordie Havers told Rhyssa the next day and there
was absolutely no joy in his tone.

You mean Barchenka CAN conscript Talents? Rhyssa felt
a cold paralysis grip her, spine, belly and mind.

*You've got it! I've been over the statute – and it is Russian,
from the pre-Glasnost days and should have been repealed long
ago it's so archaic. In the good old Bolshevik days, it was
illegal – get that, illegal – to be unemployed. The State was
the only employer – not the employer of last resort – but the
ONLY employer. Ergo, everyone worked. Consequently, the
only employer in a system that makes it illegal to be unemployed
can certainly do whatever is deemed necessary with its work
force. Legally, it gives Barchenka the right – under Padrugoi's
International Charter – to draft any technicians, professionals
or workers required by the Space Effort. The Space Effort in
terms of the original law being the Russian one. But the statute
is still in effect and, by legal crook, she can apply it to Talents.
We can fight it, of course!*

And . . . she prompted when he stopped abruptly.

With a glib-tongue attorney like Lester Favelly, we might

just win. But the trial would take years, and could be construed by Barchenka to prove her contention – that the Talents are obstructing the Good Work. He paused significantly. *We could just give her enough rope to hang herself?*

The Talents will be miserable and they won't perform well . . . That was what rankled Rhyssa's fine sense of integrity. Talents did the best they could no matter what the circumstances. To give the slightest suggestion that they skimp was against the most stringent of tenets for the parapsychic. But, in Space, worn down by punishing hours and psychic static they couldn't avoid, inevitably their performances would suffer.

Exactly. Ask the other Directors. You must appear to be accepting the inevitable.

The sort of press this could give Talents would undo the work of the last century, Rhyssa said despairingly.

I know. Although to sweeten this very bitter pill, Rhyssa, Amalda Vaden sees nothing going wrong.

Whose side is she on? Rhyssa could not keep the bitterness out of her tone.

Ours as you well know, was Gordon Havers' crisp reply. *Ergo, it has to work out by our compliance. Consult, Rhyssa. Quick action might shift public support to us.*

7

Some of the fourteen other Centres' Directors were not best pleased to be roused by her urgent request for conference in the middle of their night-times and there was some grumbling. As soon as all were attending, she explained the situation.

And from what equally critical positions does this Russian think we can draft these essential kinetics? Baden, the Australian Director, demanded. Rhyssa always found it odd that his mental tone was devoid of the Oz accent. *We sent everyone we could bribe or blackmail up there. Sheer bloody mindedness keeps some of 'em in place, but my staff's down to nubbins or feather-movers.*

I have told Ludmilla Ivanova, said Vsevolod Gebrowski of the Leningrad Bureau at his most apologetic, *time and again that there are few kinetics not already doing double, triple work in order to supply essential services in the Soviet. Believe me, I have tried to educate her to the practicalities . . .*

We do believe you, Geb, we do, was the mass thought that reassured him.

What's the levy, Rhyssa? asked Miklos Horvath, the West Coast Director.

She's demanding one hundred forty-four kinetics! Rhyssa said grimly and threw up a buffer against the cries of outrage. The number of registered Talents in every Centre was open knowledge to every Director. Transfers shifted key Talents at need from one Centre to another.

We don't happen to have a handy gross of kinetics, Brazil said angrily. *And I spent six months up there, in the most godforsaken barrio I've ever seen. Constant noise! Dreadful food – nutritious food could at least have a distinctive flavour. How can she expect us to function . . .*

If we use the discretionary clause, we can remove the required number from Commerce and Industry . . . Max Perigeaux of the large European Bureau began in his slow thoughtful way.

Ignoring the howls . . .

Under the circumstances, at least we're not liable to penalties . . .

That's a real comfort to those forced up to Padrugoi . . .

Well, Commerce and Industry want this Station, they'll have to suck lemons along with the rest of us . . .

Max went on, his message weaving inexorably among the asides, *. . . put the trainees where at least they can be overseen, we could just about manage it. But how can we expect our people to endure the conditions up at the Platform and still perform creditably? To do less than our best reduces our reputations but how can anyone operate at his best in that milieu! And the noise!* The tall aesthetic man imaged a convulsive shudder of revulsion.

But SOMETHING must be done to give those who are conscripted some surcease!

Barchenka believes we set up the conditions of shielded quarters and short hours to be obstructive! Rhyssa said. *I was informed that there is no noise in the vacuum of Space and, because there is also no gravity, there is less physical stress and longer hours can be worked, not fewer.*

The woman is utterly without a shred of understanding or empathy, Africa North said.

Has anyone ★TRIED★ to adjust her thinking? asked Hong Kong Jimmy.

You've never met Barchenka, have you? Shields tighter'n a chastity belt! Baden said in an acid tone.

What's a chastity belt? Hong Kong Jimmy flicked back in genuine innocence.

Images from nine helpful telepaths enlighted his ignorance. Rhyssa was grateful to him for easing the growing tension in the linkage with that by-play.

We are compelled to comply, are we not! Perigeaux said at his most mournful. *And without delay, so that we can bargain on the best possible conditions for those who must sacrifice themselves. A rotation scheme, perhaps . . .*

If she's after the gross, that makes rotation impossible!

I can try to insist on some sort of short-term stretches, Rhyssa said.

Let us also issue some publicity, Miklos Horvath suggested, *about conditions up there . . .*

Of dubious value when she needs to recruit so many grunts. You know she has to go to the Shelters for anyone below Civil Service 8.

But the public must see that Talent's objections to working in Space are valid . . .

The most valid being Barchenka herself . . .

Can NO-ONE lean on her?

It's been tried . . .

Who's the best we've got?

What about her associate, Per Duoml? Any chinks in him?

It isn't that we don't want to help with the Project, but SHE is her own worst enemy.

Did she specify kinetics only?

No-one's told her that some kinetics are also telepaths!

Don't anyone mention that! Lance Baden said with unusual vehemence.

Wouldn't dream of it!

You mean, she doesn't KNOW?

Ludmilla Ivanova knows what she wants to know, Vsevolod said wearily. *She only hears the explanations she wishes to hear.*

In twelve minutes of rapid fire exchanges, the Talents arrived at a grim but workable course of action. Maxim, Baden and Jimmy would do the actual selection of suitable kinetics. Some Talents could be excused on grounds of infirmity, pregnancy or unsuitable skills – though two of Baden's 'feather-dusters' were well able to perform the fine tunings. Rhyssa, Miklos and Dolores of the Brazilian Centre would attempt to achieve shielded quarters and work-shifts six hours maximum; four for the less experienced kinetics. Barchenka might be running her operation twenty-four hours a day but eight hours of telekinesis were impossibly draining, even in Space and in 0.5 grav conditions.

What we must also organize, for ourselves, Kayankira of the Delhi Centre said as the main issues had been resolved, *is an emergency system in a disaster situation.* In her mind churned images of the last year's catastrophic floods in the north-eastern sections of the Indian subcontinent, mitigated only by the rapid mobilization of hundreds of kinetics when the pre-cog had come in.

Kayan, you've had far more experience with that sort of thing than anyone needs, Baden said with unexpected humility. *Advise us and we will comply.*

You always do! We'll have to strip all non-essential industrial firms and reduce port authority staff to a dangerous minimum. But we shall be very short of those we most need.

Weather permitting! was Hong Kong Jimmy's droll remark. *When are we going to find a weatherman?*

If we weather this one, Miklos said, *we can all apply!*

The mindlink was dissolved: and despite the massive task ahead, the Centre Directors were much encouraged by the contact. Rhyssa informed Gordie Havers of the results and he gave a loud mental huzzah! for solidarity.

They're going to be some mighty unhappy kinetics! Rhyssa told him. *Every Centre is going to be stripped and I'm steeling myself to endure the slings and arrows of outraged businesses.*

Machinery predated kinetics and men used their muscles before that. Let 'em go back to traditional ways. It'll make 'em appreciate us more than ever. Gordie imaged an archaic block and tackle to move material usually 'hoisted' by a kinetic. *Who's handling the publicity?*

Rhyssa: *We're going to have to be careful about that . . . don't want Barchenka to say we're giving her schtick . . . interfering with her on-going employment drive . . .*

Gordie: *The man I have in mind is not a valid Talent but he's a brilliant publicist, Rhyssa. Let me get Dave Lehardt to wave the flag for us.*

Rhyssa: *Dave Lehardt?*

Gordie: *He put our honoured President in the White House . . .*

Rhyssa: *And he's NOT Talented? That's unfair! That campaign was sheer genius!*

Gordie: *We have to allow the mutes a few prerogatives, you know. Shall I approach him on this delicate matter?*

Rhyssa: *Please do. I'll give him all the help I can.*

Gordie: *By the bye, did you realize that most of what you do is totally illegal in Scotland which still has anti-witchcraft laws on the books?*

Rhyssa: *Spare me!*

Gordie: *I had, and look what it got us. I'd been working up to the Russkis by way of the British Isles and Scandinavia. Sorry about that! You never know where to start in nullifying age-old bigotry, do you!*

When Gordie had broken their mental link, Rhyssa spoke to Sascha.

You got touched again? he demanded.

In the head, but not by my peeper. She put in his mind all that had happened in the past half-hour.

He whistled in a descending scale. *We're going to get a lot of flak from Commerce and Industry!*

Rhyssa: *They can't have it both ways. They're the group that gave Barchenka such punitive fines if she doesn't deliver on time. That clause is just coming home to roost where they didn't expect it. They'll have to dust off their machinery and toughen up their muscles. We've made it far too easy for them . . .*

Sascha: *What if they like the old-fashioned ways and don't want to rehire our people?*

Rhyssa snorted derisively. *Just consider how much money kinetics save industry every year in equipment and maintenance costs – the arguments we used to get them to TAKE kinetics in the first place!*

Sascha: *Yeah, but how do we explain it to our kinetics?*

Rhyssa: #Image of her on her knees, tearing her hair out, pleading to amorphous faces, offering jewels and ingots of gold.# *Enlistment has always been preferable to conscription. And we can INSIST on shielding and short shifts. We can't if she implements that blue law. We're also over a barrel and every Talent will realize that!*

Sascha: *Vsevolod can't help us there?*

Rhyssa: *He was appalled, apologetic and all but apoplectic that one of his nationals was doing this to us.*

Sascha: *Nothing mentioned about getting the law wiped off the books?*

Gordie's working on it! Rhyssa did not bother to lighten the grimness she felt.

8

The fury of the Talents was equal only to the despair Rhyssa felt at summarily re-assigning her kinetics, some of whom had already endured a shift on the Space Station. She funnelled both fury and despair into the critical negotiations with the Space Platform Managers. In these, she had the very able assistance of Dave Lehardt, Gordie Havers' talented publicist.

Dave Lehardt swung into her tower office at the Henner Estate within an hour of the Talents' reluctant acceptance of the inevitable.

'My God, do you have wings?' said Rhyssa as the energetic Lehardt shook her hand. He was a full two metres tall, athletic in build and emanating a competence and geniality that could only come from a secure, well-adjusted personality. He was handsome enough, with mid-brown hair, blue eyes, regular but not remarkable features, and he dressed with conservative elegance.

'Not wings! Vanes! More reliable,' he said with a charming grin. He began sorting through the papers in his attaché case. 'Gordie said it was urgent, and I watch the news. What's the matter? Did I break out in spots?' he asked when he noticed her baffled expression.

'No, but you haven't an ounce of Talent, and you ought to.'

'Why?' Dave Lehardt shrugged. 'I've never needed it. Astute student of human psychology and keen observer of body-language.'

He also had an impenetrable natural shield. With all her skill she couldn't have read his mind.

'Now,' he said, hauling a spare chair up beside hers, and spreading out hardcopy of advertisements and graphics, 'we get in there before Barchenka even thinks of crowing in triumph so the public will see that Talents are graciously mobilizing all available personnel to be sure Padrugoi Platform is finished on schedule . . . with phrases that imply she can't make it on her own without Talented help.'

'That's true enough,' Rhyssa said grimly.

'Ah, but there are ways and ways of saying the same thing,' Dave Lehardt said with a truly malicious smile. 'I tangled briefly with the Barchenka Stonewall for another client and, believe me, I'm on your side!'

Rhyssa smiled to herself. Dave Lehardt did have a Talent – a self-confidence that radiated from him like an aura. She'd never met anyone like him before: some-one whose mentality she couldn't delve into, however discreetly. It was a new experience and she found her-self watching his expressive face, noting that his hands emphasized points, and occasionally he added a shoulder movement that reinforced what he said. He also kept glancing at her, his clear eyes meeting hers as few non-Talents would. He was not the least bit in awe of being in the presence of one of the top telepathic Talents.

Oblivious to her reactions, he went on. 'I've been yearning to score on our gracious 'Milla.' A flicker of some quickly suppressed emotion shot across his face but for all Rhyssa's sensitivity, she couldn't decipher it.

'All-out Talent assistance, even at the expense of long-established links with the Public Sector, at considerable personal sacrifice – 'Milla doesn't pay the going rates since hers is a priority contract and has world-wide backing . . .'

'She will not believe that money is NOT a consideration . . .'

'Are you aware of the size of her bonus if she gets the Station fully operational on time?'

Rhyssa grinned. 'One of the best kept secrets of the Talents. We also know the percentage she has to cough up if she doesn't.'

'You are well informed!' He paused with a hopeful expression and then sighed as she merely smiled. 'No, I didn't think you'd tell me.' He snagged the corner of a graphic sheet from the pile and spread it out. 'To address your two points – six-hour shifts and shielding . . . very alliterative, I'm going to be able to use that as a slogan, you know . . . have you *demonstrated* the problem?'

'How do you mean *demonstrated*?'

'Time and motion studies, energy expenditures, that sort of recordable data – remember, I've seen your kinetics in action, but I doubt that Ludmilla or even Per Duoml have taken the trouble of watching them work. They've been too busy bitching about weightlessness and the silence of Space to appreciate the effort kinesis actually takes. I thought you might not have thought of that gimmick. So I had a chat with a Talent I know who was up on the Platform and he gave me some remarkable insights into the actual shift mechanics. If the day's material was properly organized, the kinetic could "put" everything in place for the grunts to lock on and weld.

'Then, the noise element. Samjan ran some of the "noises" past me,' he grimaced and crossed his eyes in sympathy, 'and I think if we constructed a tape of what a sensitive hears in unshielded quarters and played it back . . .'

'Not to Ludmilla. She insists there is no noise in Space . . . '

'She's more of a mute than I am . . . '

'But I take your point. I hadn't thought of a trick like that.'

'No trick, my dear, just presentation and that's where I'm the expert.' His grin was a mixture of impudence and malice.

For the first time in her Talented life, Rhyssa found herself fascinated by a mute and half of that fascination was due to the fact that she couldn't predict what he'd do or say next. It was fun matching wits with him during subsequent interviews, giving the onerous task an unexpected exhilaration.

Dave Lehardt was at her side for the initial meeting with a Barchenka who oozed smug satisfaction which she made no attempt to disguise. Rhyssa was hard put to remain civil. Dave Lehardt talked so fast that the engineer had to listen attentively to catch his points. Per Duoml was, as usual, with her but Rhyssa had been spared another confrontation with Prince Phanibal.

'All we have had is talk, empty talk,' Ludmilla Barchenka said when Dave had explained the two problems – short shifts and shielding. 'Even the physically impaired are able to work proper shifts in Space: no gravity, no sound!' She shot an accusatory look at Rhyssa.

'Ah, but it is not gravity which is a problem, nor the vacuum. Ludmilla Ivanova, I have arranged a demonstration . . . '

'I have no time for demonstrations.' The Exalted Engineer dismissed that. 'I must return to the Platform. Already there are delays which must be rectified.'

'Understood, Engineer Barchenka,' Dave said soothingly, with just the right amount of respect and understanding. 'Perhaps Per Duoml will attend. This demonstration is likely to put the basic problems into proper perspective, and thus help us all resolve the main problems to the maximum benefit to your Project.'

Duoml would be much easier to deal with: his mind was not totally closed although he was as dedicated to the Project as Barchenka. If they could *prove* their points to him, they'd be halfway to victory.

'I think she's disappointed she didn't have to invoke that wretched statute,' Rhyssa told Sascha after that interview.

'D'you think we gave in too easily?' he asked. 'The news quotes Barchenka calling it the "cowardly capitulation of the effete".'

'Let her. If we can just swing Duoml to our side.' Rhyssa frowned. 'I don't see what else we could have done. Dave Lehardt is running public opinion polls. One point is clear – *everyone* wants Padrugoi to be finished, *everyone* wants someone else to work up there and *everyone* thinks people who volunteer for anything are crazy.'

The next day, Dave Lehardt and Rhyssa Owen took Personnel Manager Per Duoml to the most prestigious exercise complex in Jerhattan: a facility that occupied the first nine floors of a residential ziggurat near Central Park. The largest gymnasium was set up with three sets of stress-monitoring paraphernalia and technicians, three pyramids of standard size packages, a forklift, a bevy of impartial observers and the Complex Director who had been a multiple Olympic Gold medallist four times running.

Per Duoml was suitably impressed by OGM Menasherat ibn Malik. So was Rhyssa for the man exuded physical vitality and competence. He also had no more Talent than Dave Lehardt who appeared well acquainted with him. Dave stood by, a slight smile on his face, while Menasherat accepted Per Duoml's homage and conversed amiably with the Personnel Manager.

'Now, Manager Duoml,' Menasherat said, gesturing to the three men who entered from the side. They were stripped down to shorts, all festooned with wires which were hooked up to the machines. 'Let me introduce you to Pavel Korl, Bronze Medallist in heavyweight boxing, Chet Huntley, a forklift operator with International Canning, and Rick Hobson, the kinetic.'

Rhyssa was almost as bemused as Per Duoml as Menasherat made the introductions. Korl and Huntley were big men, towering over Duoml and certainly making Rick Hobson, who was average in height and build, look insignificant.

'Now, if you would care to check the movables in each pile, Manager Duoml, to assure yourself that they are equal in weight . . . ' Duoml had to struggle to lift any of them, 'then, since our guinea pigs are wired up, we can start the test.

'Which is rather simple. By muscle, by machine, by mind, our subjects will transfer their pile across the floor. The energy levels required, the stress factors, the calories consumed will be displayed on the monitors. Now,' and ibn Malik moved to the big screen set in the wall, used for sporting events, 'on Padrugoi, three men will be doing exactly the same in Q hangar. If you're ready up at Padrugoi?' He spoke into the collar mike and the big screen lit up with a scene not dissimilar to the one around them, except that all the men wore Spacesuits. 'In Space, our hand shifter is Jesus Manrique, the lifter is operated by Ginny Stanley and the kinetic is Kevin Clark. Are you all ready? On your marks,' the Gold Medallist raised his arm, 'get set, GO!' His arm came down and the activity on the gym floor and in Q hangar commenced. 'This test will last an hour,' he informed Per Duoml and gestured for the observers to take seats to one side.

After the first few minutes, Per Duoml stopped watching the burly figure of Korl manhandling the packages down the floor, or Huntley zipping back and forth on the loader. He kept his eyes either on Rick who had seated himself at a table and, with no visible effort, kept a steady stream of packages flowing or on the Platform kinetic who was leaning against a stanchion. Occasionally Duoml flicked a look at the monitors chattering out their hard copy.

Both Talents had worked their way through their piles in half the time it took the others. The instrumentation proved that they had expended half again as much energy and used up twice as many calories.

When the test had been completed, Dave Lehardt stripped the hard copy sheets from all six printers, for the Padrugoi tests had been relayed to the gym. Neatly folding them, he handed the sheaf to Per Duoml who took it without a word.

The test subjects were all thanked and left the gym, Rick Hobson throwing Rhyssa an impudent wink as he walked by.

'You will, of course, wish to analyse the results of this test with your own motion experts, Manager Duoml,' Dave Lehardt said, 'but I'm sure you recognized the fact that weightlessness grants no bonuses to the kinetic. As to the noise factor,' and the publicist took a compact recorder from his hip pocket and thumbed it on.

At the babel of squeaks and metallic groans, Per Duoml covered his ears in defence and stared in shock at Rhyssa.

'THAT is what a sensitive *hears* on the Station,' Dave said, spurting phrases in between the worst of the 'noise'. It was a fair selection – the stream of consciousness of eighty mentalities: resentments, complaints, shouts, pains, angers, and myriad metallic noises that some of the kinetics endured. 'With ten thousand people living up there already, the "mental" noise is constant, twenty-four hours. So all that garbage is a constant secondary drain on their nerves, reducing their efficiency if they have no respite from it in shielded quarters.'

Having set the decibel rate herself, Rhyssa knew that Duoml covering his ears was a frail protection but she didn't reduce the volume until Dave had finished his little speech.

'I see that you hadn't realized just what we meant by noise,' she said. 'But the cost of shielding personnel quarters for the kinetics is going to be less than the cost of material lost or damaged due to tired minds.'

'You have made your points,' Per Duoml said with a grim expression. 'I shall present them to Ludmilla Barchenka.'

'Present them and ensure their implementation, Per Duoml, and you will have the kinetic assistance you require. Oh, and one other minor point,' she added, smiling to take the sting out of this condition, 'Barchenka is to relay all orders to the kinetics through the regular channels. We will have no more of her rousting Talents out of their quarters at inappropriate hours and insisting on "extra duty" because her schedule is two minutes out of line! Have I made myself clear on that point?'

He nodded, his expression solemn.

Rhyssa hoped he could now convince Barchenka.

9

'No, *please*!' cried Peter Reidinger as the electrician was about to disconnect the Tri-D in the ward. His cry was echoed by the other children.

'Look, kids, there's some kind of freaky drain on the hospital's power supply, and we've finally traced it to this ward. I gotta fix it or some of your support systems will go down when they shouldn't,' the electrician said with a hint of exasperation in his tone.

'No, wait, please,' Peter said. 'The programme's all about the Space Platform and the Talents . . .'

'Huh?' The electrician took a better look at the monitor.

'It'll only be a few minutes! Just the newscast!' Peter pleaded.

'Wal, I guess . . .'

'Shhhh,' Peter interrupted him, straining to hear the commentator. Not that he really needed the voice-over to identify this as the estate of the late George Henner, one of the earliest supporters of the parapsychics. As the camera panned across the trees, the lawns, the place had an eerie familiarity that startled the boy. *This* was the place he had sought: a place of tranquil greenery and huge old trees and vine-covered buildings. The place that had scared him away. And now he knew why. *They* wouldn't want to have their precinct invaded. *They* needed their privacy to do all the wonderful things they did. Like help to finish the last three spokes of the Padrugoi Platform so that mankind could, at last, reach for the stars.

'It's not only the Talented who are making a sacrifice,' the commentator went on, still standing in that marvellous oasis, 'for Industry and Commerce have granted leave of absence to their Talented employees to assist this final push out to Space. Platform Manager Ludmilla Barchenka announces that the most ambitious World Project yet undertaken will be completed on schedule. And now to other news in the Jerhattan district . . . '

'OK, mister,' Peter said, relaxing against his frame. 'That's what we wanted to see.'

'You're not looking for a career in Space, are you?' the electrician asked, half-teasing. He was always a little nervous around kids who were so badly injured.

Peter cocked his head at him. 'Why not? With no gravity, I wouldn't be stuck in this frame and a push of my toe or my little finger . . . ' he waggled the two extremities which were, after months of therapy, all he *could* move, 'I could float about.'

'Yeah, I guess you could. Now, Nurse, can I start with this frame?' the electrician asked, gesturing to the multiple-tasking device which gave Peter what independence he had in his condition.

'Yes, it's time for Peter's body-brace session anyway,' Sue Romero said. 'C'mon, Peter.'

'Aw, do I have to? Couldn't I watch what he does?'

'No, the moment for positive thinking has come. Let me see that limbic smile on your face.'

Peter hated the body-brace and the morning's 'torture session' as he mentally categorized the therapy. He felt 'heavy' in the frame, his body more lifeless than ever.

'But see, I can move my big toe and my index finger. Please . . .'

'Hey, what the . . . ?' the electrician exclaimed for the diagnostic reader he had just hooked up had unexpectedly registered a blip.

While Peter gamely concentrated on his body-brace drills, the electrician checked out the bed's wiring against the schematics of the equipment. Except for that one brief blip, he could find no short, no dysfunction in any of the circuitry. By the time an exhausted Peter was back in his bed, the electrician had done a thorough test of all the specialized treatment electronics. Baffled by the continual surges on the ward's circuits, the man left a small monitor attached to the one piece of equipment that had registered an abnormality, slight though it had been, and left.

Peter knew by her face that Sue Romero was disappointed in him. He did try to make his body remember how to move. The frame sent electrical impulses into his atrophied muscles: the theory being that the little jolts would restimulate neural and muscular activity. He hated that intrusion into his body, worse than he hated being paralysed.

'Peter, if you would only stop resisting the mechanism,' Sue said, and Peter could hear the reproach in her voice. 'If you would only go with it, instead of denying the help it could give you. You could, you know, even get to the Platform. Your school work is excellent: there'd be no problem with the educational end . . . ' She trailed off, fighting her own dispiritedness. Sometimes with these very badly damaged children, she felt she was pounding at the well-known immovable object – generally, as in Peter's case, the child itself.

The boy was exhausted now, eyes closed, arms and legs sprawled just as he had been rolled out of the body-brace. Sue Romero could not afford to pity him:

it was unprofessional and helped neither of them in his rehabilitation – but she did. As she turned away, she thought he slept. She would have been amazed to learn that he was reviewing that vision of the Centre, with its trees and lawns and . . . Rhyssa Owen.

10

That night, Rhyssa was wakeful anyhow, going over and over that telecast. It had had a very good feel to it as it was being filmed. Dave Lehardt had done his job well. They would, of course, have to wait until opinions had been sampled but Rhyssa felt that Barchenka was coming out a poor second at the moment, despite her apparent triumph at the cowardly capitulation of the effete Talents. She had, and she hadn't. The line was thin and depended on one's point of view. But then, that was the way of most compromises: it was knowing *when* to compromise that was important. Rhyssa fretted that she had somehow weakened the consolidated strength of Talents and wondered how she could rectify what was still, in the minds of most Talented, an untenable position with Barchenka getting her way.

She felt then the gossamer touch, envious, yearning, wistful and so terribly sad that a sob clogged her throat.

Wait, little friend, Rhyssa murmured in the softest of tones.

Say what? Startlement/sense of apology-denial-rejection/an astringent smell. The touch was gone – timorous and reluctant.

Rhyssa tried to follow, her touch was feather soft but the retreat had been too swift: a flicker of shadow across the moonlight outside her window. She made a quick note of the time – 3:43. Then she lay there savouring that touch, examining it, letting her perception analyse it.

A young mind with that swiftness, no old thoughts or experiences to slow the instantaneity of action. A boy on a prank . . . a boy? Doing an out of body manoeuvre? A boy in a hospital – yes, a hospital would account for the astringent odour – his movement constrained so that only his mind could travel?

That fitted the pieces together so perfectly that Rhyssa got out of bed and paced over to the console.

'Bud, I want a call out to all hospital Talents,' she said, unable to keep the elation out of her voice.

'The peeper caught you again?'

'That's right. An adolescent boy, quite likely crippled or paralysed. I want to see who was awake on the wards at 3:43 this evening.'

'The last thing you need tonight is some pimple-faced nerd rousing you.'

'On the contrary, Bud, I think that's exactly what I did need. A youngster able to go out of body? He's got to have a fantastic potential.'

'For what?' Budworth wanted to know.

'*That*,' Rhyssa said with a surge of hope, 'is what we'll have to find out.'

As she climbed back into bed, she had a lot to think about before she could compose herself for sleep. How long had it been since a new Talent that strong had been identified? And what sort of a Talent was it? A new type of kinesis? Very few kinetics could move themselves! Inanimate objects, yes, but animate ones, no. Most out of body experiences were the results of traumas and useless in a commercial sense.

Just remember, my dear, that it was the commercial applications of Talents that has provided them with legal immunities, good jobs and special status for the past four score years. And let us get marvellously complacent. Maybe it wasn't really 'noise' that even kinetics heard in Space but some other form of interstellar communication, a multi-lingual garble, which they were picking up? Open your mind up, gal. Look around you. Look at Dave Lehardt. He has to be Talented, even if it won't register on a Goosegg graph.

Why, Rhyssa Owen, does Dave Lehardt *have* to be Talented?

And that was the quandary she fussed over as she finally slipped back into an uneasy sleep.

11

'I have discovered some interesting new facets of employment on the Platform,' Dave Lehardt told Rhyssa in her office two days later. 'Came out in further talks with my Platform contact, Samjan, and a few judicious enquiries.' He gave her a humourless grin. 'The casualties.'

'Yes, the total is horrific,' and Rhyssa shuddered. 'But working in Space there were bound to be some.'

'Some?' and Dave Lehardt raised his eyebrows. 'Some, yes, but when I checked with Johnny Greene in Altenbach's office, we found there are several sets of figures on the casualty rate.'

Rhyssa straightened. When Dave Lehardt had arrived unexpectedly, she'd been reshuffling the rotas of Eastern Centre's kinetics, steeling herself to endure their understandable reproaches and arguments. Any interruption was welcome.

'Then I got JG and Samjan together and they both did a bit of research,' he went on, 'and, using their security clearances, they came up with what we think are the real statistics.' His expression was bleak and there was a stillness about his body that forewarned her. 'You know how the unemployed are terrified to be conscripted to Padrugoi? They may not be Talented but they got an instinct about baaaaaad situations. They have good reason not to want to get conscripted. She loses grunts at a frightening rate, far beyond the allowable. The major reason is because Barchenka's so bloody-minded about keeping her sacred schedules, she won't interrupt a shift to retrieve drifters!'

To be sure she understood his meaning, Rhyssa un-consciously tried to 'read' his mind. It was like stubbing her toe on a stair riser and she blinked.

'Run that past me again, please, Dave,' she asked, struggling with confusion at her inability to 'read' him.

'Surely you've seen the promotional footage,' he said, 'with the grunts suited up and pushing gi-normous sections of a spoke with the tips of their fingers or a spare foot?'

'Yes . . .'

'In the *real* working situation, not that mockup they did for recruitment, a worker'll push too hard and, with every action causing a reaction in Space, the poor sod goes spinning off into the dark deeps.'

'Yes . . .'

'Well, Barchenka doesn't stop work to rescue them. Oh no, anyone that stupid has to wait until the shift is over before his buddies are allowed to go after him. That is, *if* a skiff is available and *if* the bod's been tracked.'

Appalled at the vivid scene his words evoked, Rhyssa stared at him. 'Is this public knowledge?'

He gave her a cynical look. 'Why do you think the grunts never take surface-leave? It's not the fact that they're paid so little that they can't afford surface leave, or that there's no available space on shuttles for mere grunts or that they're unlikely to have any family to visit on Earth: it's that they're plain not allowed back down to tell *anyone* what's happening. The grunts are also segregated so that even the observant among the more élite employees don't know exactly what's going on. It took both JG and Samjan and some long programme analyses to pick fact out of the publically available fictions.'

'But all the recruitment films show safety lines and . . . ' Part of Rhyssa crowed with delight at discovering Barchenka resorting to very questionable tactics while another part baulked at the enormity of the crime.

'That's *promo* footage, my dear Director. The theory is great. In practice, Barchenka dispensed with safety lines: they kept getting tangled in equipment – slowing down her precious work schedule. So safety lines are a Space myth.

'And Barchenka has such saving ways. For instance,' and Dave Lehardt perched his lean frame on the edge of her desk, 'we discovered by an analysis of records that a suited grunt is given only enough air in his tanks for that shift and maybe a sniff or two left over. Oh, there's plenty of safety regs for the engineers and supervisors and skilled technicians but not for the grunts. She doesn't care what happens to them. There're plenty more where they came from.'

Rhyssa was outraged. 'You just validated my instincts about that woman. Law be damned, I won't ask my kinetics to face such risks!'

Dave gave a snort. 'They're far too valuable to be *risked*. There'd be too much of a stink kicked up if a drifting Talent wasn't retrieved right then. Overworked, yes. Samjan confirmed the notion that eight-hour shifts are another Platform fallacy.

'On top of that conspicuous savings of consumables, I uncovered several other little anomalies: grunt suits have limited-range com units. They can't be heard shrieking for help! Might disturb their fellow workers.'

Rhyssa stared at him aghast.

'There's also a high incidence of agoraphobia among

the grunts and genuine Space *cafard*. But ailing grunts are never transferred down. They just disappear! Accidental death! Never suicide! Always accidental. After all,' and his voice altered to a mock Russian accent, 'everyone knows how dangerous it is to ignore safety warnings and procedures. And then there appears to be a neat little system which causes unexpected casualties during the routine drills they so conspicuously hold from time to time on the Padrugoi.' Dave paused again. 'Checking through medical records, it becomes apparent that the unfortunate victims of those drill "accidents" are always either the injured or the headcases.'

'Oh, my God, Dave,' and Rhyssa propelled herself from her chair to pace agitatedly up and down the tower room. 'WHY haven't any of the pre-cogs caught this?'

'In your brief summary on Talents' capabilities, pre-cogs usually latch on to large numbers, Rhyssa. There are never enough . . .'

'Numerics is not an excuse . . .' Rhyssa was surprised by a vehemence that answered the despair in his voice. Dave might not be Talented but that didn't keep him from being deeply sensitive on many issues. She wondered if his mind was as filled as hers with faceless forms, twisting and turning in Space, further and further from the network of lights that was the oasis of air and warmth in the blackness, and a violent shudder seized her.

A warm hand cupped her shoulder. 'Easy! Talent spreads itself thin enough as it is. You're not God, or gods, to mark each sparrow's fall.'

She blinked her eyes open and looked up at Dave Lehardt. Though his mind was as closed to her as ever, the sympathy and understanding in his warm blue eyes was obvious. She wouldn't tell him that Talents disliked tactile contact: she liked him touching her.

'Armed with this information, however, you can spread Barchenka over a barrel.' His voice was soft and teasing. 'If you see what I mean. Or, maybe

80

you Talents are too simon-pure to lower yourselves to outright blackmail.'

'Not when the lives and safety of my Talents are at risk, I'm not,' Rhyssa declared stoutly. 'Not to mention those poor sods who've not even been given half a chance to survive. I'll insist on short shifts and shields and we'll increase that ante to safety lines for everyone working on the Platform and the deployment of rescue skiffs. Or do skiffs have limited power and air on them, too, so as to save costs?'

He crossed his arms on his chest, grinning at her. 'Your Talents wouldn't be at risk anyway, unless I've misunderstood their capabilities. There's no way Barchenka can pull the same tricks on *them* that she does with the poor grunts. And unless your response is unique among your ilk, I can't see your folk standing by for some of her tricks, once they know what to look for. Some of the kinetics are telepaths, aren't they?'

'Quite a few.' Rhyssa gave a sardonic chuckle. 'A fact we haven't actually mentioned to Barchenka whose understanding of Talent is severely limited.'

Dave let out a bark of laugh. 'Not the whole truth nor even half the truth, huh? Good girl, Rhyssa,' and he playfully knuckled her chin. 'Is distance a problem? Or the vacuum of Space?' When Rhyssa shook her head, he went on. 'Well, you guys could sure be popular with the grunts because *you*,' and he waggled his finger at her, 'could be *their* insurance. A Talent could haul back a drifter, couldn't he? Without asking permission during his shift, or waiting for a skiff?' He gave her a broad smile. 'That'll help a lot. Damned good PR, too. The best because it proves that the Talents will help the ordinary grunt where Barchenka just simply hasn't!'

Rhyssa suddenly hid her face, not wanting Dave to see her expression. *Sascha?* she called. *I've just found the perfect job for Madlyn! Tell you later!*

Sascha: *I can read your evil mind and she's NOT even on the list for the Platform.*

Rhyssa: *She is, as of right now. How often have you said that Madlyn could be heard at the Space Platform. We'll just put it to the test!* Rhyssa smoothed her expression and looked up at Dave Lehardt who was eyeing her keenly.

'Who were you talking to just then? And don't hold out on me. I'm getting used to your ways, woman!' His voice rippled with an odd emotion and the gleam in his eyes intensified.

Rhyssa's grin was half embarrassment at his scrutiny and half delight with her inspiration. 'We've got a telepath with an extraordinarily loud voice. We'll send her up in an administrative capacity. Put her on a radar scope and she'll locate and reassure any drifters for the nearest kinetic to haul back to safety.'

'Lady, you don't realize what a difference that could make to morale up at the Platform.' Dave Lehardt's grin was so infectious that Rhyssa had to grin back. 'Not only is Barchenka unaware that she's her own worst enemy, but her ignorance about Talent in general will prevent her from realizing that she's just hired a battalion of undercover agents.'

'*That's* the beautiful part!' Rhyssa said, grinning more broadly. 'Does Duoml? Or Prince Phanibal?'

Dave Lehardt considered this briefly. 'Prince Phanibal might but he's not on the Platform as much lately: some crisis in Malaysia that occupies a lot of his time. Besides, I read him as being just ornery enough not to tell her something as crucial at this for the sheer pleasure of watching her squirm. Now what's this emergency clause Lance Baden wants added to the contracts?'

'In case of a major emergency, we must be able to bring Talents back down. You remember the floods last monsoon on the Indian subcontinent and that major shake in Azerbaijan? We knew about them ten days before so we could muster help and reduce the effect of the catastrophe.

Sending her a hundred and forty-four kinetics has wiped out our disaster squad organization. We want a twenty-four hour clause – to bring key personnel back to Earth in time to cope here.'

'Can't you teleport 'em down?'

Rhyssa laughed. 'No, more's the pity. But we're working on it. Our Talents are finite, definite, and nowhere near such a fantasy application as instantaneous transmissions. That takes more power than a human brain can generate.'

'I thought the moral code on legitimate bio-engineering permitted . . . '

'Hold it right there, Dave,' and Rhyssa held up a warding hand. 'Read the code: congenital defects yes: manipulations no. And I doubt any bio-geneticist would monkey with the brain yet . . . even a monkey's brain.'

'If you can find one. Though don't you think it's likely that someone has been doing illicit experimentation, the world being what it is these days?'

'That's cynical of you, Dave.'

'Sometimes saying "no" is registering a challenge,' he replied with a shrug. 'I wouldn't rule out the possibility.'

'Meanwhile,' and Rhyssa brought the discussion firmly back to relevant matters, 'I'd very much like to see a full report on what JG and Samjan have been discovering about Platform personnel problems.'

Dave grinned, taking three diskettes from a breast pocket. 'I thought you might. Gives you a stronger bargaining position for shields, short shifts . . . '

'Safety lines and skiffs,' Rhyssa finished, taking the diskettes but letting her fingers linger on his a little longer than the transaction required. 'I thank you, sir.' What on earth was happening to her in Dave Lehardt's presence? She felt as giddy as . . . as Madlyn could be in Sascha's company.

12

When Per Duoml, Prince Phanibal Shimaz and two
other minor officials, one of them the Accommodations
Officer, arrived to settle the 'minor details', Dave Lehardt
had another presentation that altered the proceedings.
Rhyssa, sitting with Max Perigeaux, Gordie Havers and
Lance Baden, found the meeting eminently satisfying.

Showing the accurate fatality statistics – figures that
bleached all colour from the faces of Duoml and the
Prince, Dave Lehardt talked knowledgeably of some of
the 'minor' problems which the Talents would be willing
to undertake – such as the retrieval of any suited workers
experiencing 'malfunction of suit jets', and telepathic
contact 'with those using short-range com units', plus
monitoring systems, and the inclusion in the Talents of
two with broad diagnostic capabilities. Dave pointed out
that the savings on skiff fuel and man-hours required for
retrieval would more than compensate for the cost of
shielding required in Talent accommodations, and quick
diagnosis of agoraphobic tendencies would reduce lost
worker hours.

Nor was there any discussion about the emergency clause. Lance Baden announced that he was to be Talent Liaison with the Engineering Staff and that was that.

Lance: *And what were they saying about cowardly capitulations?*

*   *   *

Rhyssa was so weary from accumulated stresses that she experienced no elation at having forced every single concession out of the Padrugoi officials. She wanted nothing more than a quiet supper and some mental peace. Per Duoml had been naturally shielded, but the other Project representatives hadn't. When their initial euphoria at coercing Talents on to the workforce was burst by hard facts and figures and compromises, their emotions, sentiments and angers had been hard to deflect.

Sascha: *I've cleared everyone out of the first floor. Relax!*

Rhyssa: *Oh, you are a pet!*

Sascha: *Lot of good it does me!* But she knew he was only teasing.

Rhyssa entered the Henner house, appreciative of the deep silence in the elegantly appointed rooms. Very little had been altered from the days of George Henner, the parapsychics' first benefactor: all had been lovingly preserved in his memory. The subterranean offices, the annexes, her 'tower', were modern, with state of the art technology, but the main reception rooms reflected more leisurely times. She walked through to the kitchen where modern appointments were hidden behind old-fashioned cupboards. This workroom also exuded a very comfortable aura, being spacious, with an archaic, but working, fireplace, a huge table and comfortable chairs. The dining portion faced on to the gardens at the rear of the main house, bright with blooms and bushes.

Some thoughtful kinetic had activated the kettle. It was

on the boil as she entered, and so she made herself a cup of tea, found sandwiches in the crisper and, kicking off her shoes, curled up in one of the wingchairs.

There was something amazingly restorative about looking out on to the garden, watching the flowers move in the light breeze. She set her mind adrift, savouring the quiet, despite the deep-seated nagging presentiment.

'I'm not a clairvoyant,' she told herself and sipped her tea. 'What I am feeling is just a reaction to the last few hectic days. A quite natural depression.'

Then she felt the touch, once again coloured with wistfulness and a deep sadness that pierced her to the heart, making her own malaise seem insignificant.

She didn't dare reach out for fear of startling the boy. Boy, he was, and despairing. Had her transitory unease triggered a response from him at midday? Or was it his need seeking consolation? What could so desolate a young person? One can endure detached misery – tragedy happening at a distance to people one has never met – but to 'feel' the palpitating misery of another person, as she did now, was an intense experience.

Delicately she impinged on the boy's mind, hoping to gain some clue as to his whereabouts. He was dreading something, and the yearning for trees and lawn and flowers, and some*place* that was not hospital, had precipitated this nebulous contact. And her mind, less controlled in its weariness, had attracted his. Dreading what? She inserted the question.

The body-brace! Rhyssa hadn't expected an answer. She tried to keep the lightest of contacts though, oddly enough, he 'felt' very close at that moment.

Isn't it meant to help?

It doesn't. It hurts. It's artificial, it's awful. It's a cage. The bed is bad enough. I don't want to. I . . . don't . . . want . . . to!

86

A wail from the depth of a forlorn and comfortless mind reached her and was abruptly cut off.

*   *   *

'We got another one of those surges this afternoon – usually we get 'em at night,' said the hospital's maintenance man as he held up the print-out to the consultant engineer who the concerned hospital administration had finally called in.

The engineer peered at the peak, a sudden sharp deviation lasting seventy-two seconds. He asked for the other anomalies and was presented with further examples.

'Shouldn't be any drain on the systems at 3:43, 3:03, 3:52, 3:13. You've checked all the equipment.'

'I put meters on several floors. Got a blip on PedOrth Ward 12 when I was installing it. So I took everything apart on that ward and there wasn't nothing malfunctioning. Craziest thing I've ever seen. And you know how Admin is when you got outages and anomalies with all them life-support systems hooked up. Funny though, nothing in the ICUs.'

'OK, screen me your schematics for all the equipment used on PedOrth and see what's being used there.' The engineer sighed heavily for he could see this was going to be one of those days.

13

A stir around the beds in the circular ward alerted Peter Reidinger and he blinked away the screen which blocked his view. A very old lady stood in the doorway, Miz Allen hovering with her 'you'd-better-behave' look on her face as she glanced around the ward to be sure everything was in order for this visitor.

Instantly Peter's attention was riveted on the lady. She was different. That became more apparent to him as Miz Allen began to introduce her to the kids in the ward. Cecily even smiled. She answered the lady and that was another minor miracle. Cecily was spina bifida who 'ought' to have been corrected in utero but hadn't been. She'd had to have one leg amputated from osteomyelitis and was awful slow to recover from the operation. She kept feeling the missing leg something terrible. A Talent had been working with her, not Sue Romero, but a specialist. Peter was in a sweat of anticipation by the time the lady reached him.

'This is Peter Reidinger, Ms Horvath.' And the way Miz Allen cocked her right eyebrow told Peter that he had better behave himself.

Ms Horvath just smiled down at him, her eyes twinkling and they weren't at all old, or rheumy or hard. He wondered she let herself 'look' so old.

I promised my husband that I would grow old gracefully, she startled him by saying. *That way I wouldn't startle people so much when I don't act my age.*

Peter goggled at her. She hadn't moved her lips and yet he had heard her voice clearly in his mind.

'Peter . . . ' Miz Allen prompted him.

'Pleased ta metcha!' Peter managed to get out. Miz Allen cleared her throat warningly at his tone of voice.

'Thank you, Mrs Allen, I'll just chat a bit with Peter,' Dorotea Horvath said, pulling a chair to Peter's bedside and dismissing Miz Allen in a manner that astounded the boy. *Miz Allen doesn't really believe in telepathy and Talents. And we just haven't had the chance to go round pediatric wards lately. So we missed you.*

'Missed me?'

Dorotea smiled again, a smile that was magical because it seemed to envelop Peter with such warmth and caring. The hard knot of self-pity and resentment that had been building up at the thought of another body-brace session dispersed.

'That is, until you started visiting Rhyssa.'

'Rhyssa?'

Into his mind came a touch. *I'm Rhyssa. I sent Dorotea to you because you run away from me. Dorotea says you can't run away from her right now, Peter Reidinger. Please come live with us where I know you long to be.*

'Now that you've had an official invitation, will you accept?' Dorotea asked, brimming over with amusement at his stunned reaction.

'But I can't. I'm crippled. I can't go anywhere . . . '

Ahahahaha! Dorotea chided him, still smiling. *A boy who can go out of body on tours of Jerhattan at three in the morning is no cripple!*

'But I can't *use* the body-brace,' and Peter was horrified

to hear himself blubbering, to feel tears streaming down his face. He hadn't cried in months.

Crying's a natural release for emotional pressures, said Dorotea and she blotted his cheeks matter of factly. *All that manly repression has also been blocking Talent. I do believe that the brace also posed an inhibition. I think it short-circuited natural ability. We'll sort it out. Of THAT I'm positive.*

And suddenly Peter had no doubt at all.

'First, of course, we have to get your parents' permission.' Dorotea was always practical. 'Do you think they'll mind?'

'Mind?' Peter nearly shouted. He knew the hospital fees, even with the huge compensation the City was forced to pay since he'd been injured on City-owned property, had been a terrible financial drain on his parents. His mother came to see him regularly but his father's visits got fewer and shorter. His mother always had some plausible explanation for Dad's absence but Peter hadn't been fooled.

Suddenly Dorotea's eyes widened in pleased surprise. 'I don't think you'll need much training after all,' and she pointed at him.

'What?' Simultaneously Peter realized that he was hovering above his bed and an alarm just beneath it had gone off.

RHYSSA! Dorotea's mental shout was a very welcome diversion for Rhyssa.

The Eastern Director had not been able to make that first contact for several reasons – the foremost one being the Padrugoi priority. The other reason was that Dorotea was still the most accurate Talent diviner in the entire world, with the deftest touch to allay fear and suspicion.

Dorotea: *Rhyssa, Peter Reidinger reeks of Talent. I can't imagine why the resident didn't tumble to it a long time ago, despite the fact that Peter's been suppressing his natural feelings* to be considered a brave boy. *Being in a hospital situation, he'd have to blank out all peripheral static or get wound up in everyone else's pain. Though he's not your common-garden variety kinesis or telepathy. In fact, I've never touched anyone quite like him. One thing's sure, he no more needed a body-brace than you need a videophone.*

Rhyssa: *Can you expedite his release to us?*

Dorotea: *In my best granny mode! I don't anticipate any trouble with the family — they've been struggling under the medical costs. I gather the father has trouble visiting his 'crippled' son. They should regain some perspective now that Peter'll be able to pay for his own way from now on.*

Rhyssa: *How medical is he?*

Dorotea gave a mental snort: *With a little help from his friends, he won't be medical past the gate of the Centre. Whoops! We've just been charged by an irate electrician and a stupefied consultant . . . and — My God!*

Dorotea broke off contact, startling Rhyssa for Dorotea had no trouble double-talking. Rhyssa waited for Dorotea to come back and explain her abrupt disappearance. After three minutes with no further word from the telepath, Rhyssa reluctantly resumed her immediate task.

Worried about Dorotea and the boy, it was difficult for Rhyssa to keep her mind on the reassignment of kinetic Talents, but the matter had to be cleared up as soon as possible. The Eastern Centre would be left with just ten to do the work of thirty, and five trainees who could be slotted into some of the less exacting 'hoist' work. Airshuttle clients, passenger or commercial, were just going to have to wait longer to collect their luggage: all construction firms would lose kinetics save those on two nearly completed projects where kinesis was the only way to safely install heavy equipment on the uppermost storeys.

She and Miklos Horvath, Dorotea's grandson, on the West Coast also had to arrange 'fetch and carry' teams, telepaths with kinetics who could work in tandem and at long distance. But such skills were exhausting and would have to be reserved for emergencies.

Dave Lehardt had come up with yet another valid suggestion which might not improve relations with Barchenka and Duoml but would certainly be a more effective use of the four-hour shift of each kinetic.

'I looked at some of the motion studies,' Dave had told her, 'and some videos of an actual working day. Samjan mentioned that he spent a good portion of every shift on Padrugoi doing nothing. Waiting until material was organized from the storage yard or bins, or while the engineers sorted out minor discrepancies. So I got Samjan and Bela Rondomanski who was Space Lab Designer together with Lance Baden who's a trained engineer. Bela said a lot of the delays on Space Lab were caused by a chronic disorganization in Supply. Lance said that the problems hadn't been completely solved when he did two tours at Padrugoi but one of Barchenka's strengths is her organizational skill. Take them one more step forward, and, in a four-hour shift, a kinetic can get everything in a spoke section lined up so that all the grunts need to do during the next twenty hours of shift time is give a tiny shove and the elements will fall into place.

'Of course, it'll mean a good deal of reorganization in the stores and material already up at Padrugoi, and maybe some shipment rearranging, lighting a fire under the tardy suppliers, but the time spent doing *that* will cut down on the man-hours upstairs.'

'Duoml's returned to the Station,' Rhyssa said.

'We'll just borrow hangar Q again for another handy little demonstration. I'll work out the details. Hey, you're looking mighty good today: new hair-style? Sure shows off your skunk streak.' Her screen diffused on another of his famous confidence-inspiring grins.

Skunk streak indeed, she thought, her fingers smoothing it back. At least he'd noticed. With a sigh, she went back to her analyses, Until she realized she hadn't heard another squeak from Dorotea.

Then, as abruptly as the contact had been broken, Dorotea returned.

Well, I said I'd come back as soon as I could. It's too soon to be sure WHAT he does do, Rhyssa, but he apparently taps into electrical sources. He's been glitching the hospital circuits fit to drive the electrician AND a high-priced consultant barmy. And it also explains WHY he couldn't cope with the body-brace: the impulses which were fed directly into his synapses were short-circuiting inherent abilities so the poor lad was trying to cope with an overload. Sue Romero is in bits, thinking of all she's been doing to Peter and he's in a state because he had no way of explaining why the body-brace was all WRONG for him . . . and the Head Nurse, Miz Allen, is one of those by-the-bookers and compounded the problem. Oh, his family are delighted, especially to know that Peter will not be 'handicapped' – but their heads read 'crippled, useless, financial drain'.

It'll be standard contract until he's sixteen and fully trained. Here's one kinetic Barchenka won't get her space gloves on!

Rhyssa: *When can you bring him home?*

We're on our way! And the triumph in Dorotea's tone permeated the entire Centre. *Get Roddy's room in my house ready.* #Image of Space-Force posters on every wall, models of spaceshuttles, mass passenger hotels, stealths, space labs and generation ships depending from the ceiling and a bunk bed with desk space below, sleeping space above.# *Nothing could be more distant from the antiseptic environment he's been living in for months.*

14

The physical meeting between Rhyssa Owen and Peter Reidinger was not quite an anticlimax. Dorotea had warned her that Peter's mother and older sister were accompanying him in the heli-amb, excited but slightly apprehensive at his new circumstances.

Ilsa Reidinger was a 'nice' woman, terribly concerned for, and certainly extremly proud of, her Petey. She struggled with a less than congenial job in order to help meet the medical bills. The sister, Katya, at sixteen was what Dorotea called 'pushy', trying to figure out how her brother's good fortune might spill over on her: disgruntled that Peter had Talent and she had none. Dorotea said that Katya resented Peter because the cost of his hospitalization had kept her from having many of the things which she, the elder child, ought to have been able to enjoy. *Perfectly understandable reaction,* Dorotea told Rhyssa as the women deftly manoeuvred Peter's gurney into Dorotea's house and into Roddy's room.

Both telepaths could feel Peter's spirit lifting as he saw the unmedical furnishings and artefacts.

'But how'll you do all that has to be done *for* him all the time?' Ilsa Reidinger began, surprised at his new quarters.

'Oh, Peter'll only need a little help in the beginning, Mrs Reidinger,' Dorotea said. Her *allez-oop* was the signal for Rick Hobson to 'lift' Peter up into the bunk bed. 'Now, let's all clear out and let him settle himself in. And,' Dorotea added as she shooed everyone before her, 'the heli-amb is waiting to take you and your daughter home. Here's the vid number. As you saw, Peter has a set in the room. Call him any time. Unlike the hospital, you can see what mischief he's getting into. All right?'

Dorotea's positive manner made refusal impossible and soon the heli-amb was thrunking its way up out of the Centre's grounds.

Dorotea: *Rick, hook me up a line from the 4.5 k.p.m. generator in the garden shed and bring it right into the room with Peter.*

What IS this all about? Rhyssa demanded as Dorotea started firing orders left, right and centre.

I told you, Dorotea said, then added aloud since they were now alone as well as face to face, 'he seems to tap into the electrical system and use *that* for power. Some sort of a gestalt. I want some of our engineer Talents to link with me when he's rested enough for us to do some testing. But it'll have to be you and me for a while, Rhyssa. He's had such a terrible time.'

Dorotea's eyes welled with tears and automatically Rhyssa gathered the older woman into her arms, smothering her with love, affection and admiration.

'I'm sorry, dear,' Dorotea said with a little sniff, pulling herself away. 'You've had a lot to cope with now and you don't need me turning into a watering pot but . . . ' And directly input in Rhyssa's mind the jumble of pain, despondency, anguish, guilt, self-accusation and the soul-destroying terror that Peter had been enduring.

Easing Dorotea to the couch, Rhyssa sat beside her,

shaken by that account despite years of dealing with the bizarre mental states of emergent Talents.

'I think a spot of tea would go down well right now,' Dorotea said and Rhyssa gave a weak little laugh at Dorotea's ever practical mind. *Peter? A cup of tea? Lemon, milk, sugar?*

Yes, please was Peter's answer, surprising Rhyssa.

You see, he needed only a little help to project his thoughts instead of squashing them down. Dorotea's face wore an exaggeratedly smug smile.

They were all enjoying a cuppa when Rick Hobson bounced in, festooned with an electrician's belt and heavy duty cable.

'I don't know what kind of an outlet or receptacle you need, Dorotea,' he said, winking at her, nodding to Rhyssa and then waving a hand at Peter who was watching all this from his bunk.

'Well, Peter, what do you think you need?' Dorotea asked. 'He's just been sort of hooking in to the electronic gadgets of the bed.'

Both women caught Peter's hesitation and concern.

'Oh, well, it's as easy to sort the specifics out later,' Rick said, easily, catching Rhyssa's warning look. 'T'any rate, the generator's right outside and powered up. Any time you need it, it's there.' With a cheery wave to all, he left.

'It's all a bit much, isn't it, Peter?' Rhyssa said gently.

'I don't know what I did that makes you think I'm any good at all,' Peter said in a voice as pale as his complexion just then.

'Dorotea thinks you used available electrical power to assist those dawn visits you made to me,' Rhyssa said. She gave him a mischievous smile to reassure him. 'I'm honoured that it was my mind you linked with to bring you where you wanted to be.'

'You are?' Peter turned his head away from the drinking straw in his teacup so that he looked down at Rhyssa.

'I don't get many men invading my bedroom, I assure you.'

Subtly Dorotea was supporting her, increasing for Peter the sense that his intrusion had been clever and original. Both women generated subliminal thoughts to bolster his perception of himself, reversing the low self-esteem which was currently inhibiting any forward progress.

'I didn't *mean* to intrude.'

'You will soon understand that among telepaths a midnight knock on the door isn't considered an intrusion . . .'

'But all those lights . . .'

Rhyssa let her thoughts echo the annoyance she had felt at that proprietary supervision. 'You didn't hear me chewing them out for scaring you off either.'

'Ooooh, Rhyssa was angry,' Dorotea added.

'You were doing what many have tried, and failed at miserably,' Rhyssa went on.

'I was?'

'It's what we call an out of body experience,' Rhyssa went on. 'Very few people ever achieve that degree of mental control.'

'They don't?' Peter was wide-eyed in awe now. 'But it's not hard.'

Dorotea and Rhyssa exchanged amused glances. 'Nothing's hard when you know exactly how to do it, Peter,' Rhyssa said, 'and you've apparently mastered the art. Dorotea and I are both hoping you can teach us. I don't have much kinetic ability . . .'

Sascha: *And aren't you glad of that right now.* #Image of a suited Rhyssa whirling about Padrugoi chased by a whip-wielding Barchenka.#

Rhyssa: *Don't you dare interfere, Bearman! This is tricky enough as it is without you in my mind! OH, my GOD!* And suddenly Rhyssa began to realize the extraordinary potential of young Peter Reidinger, and just how his

97

kinetic abilities could be utilized. Why his Talent was as far from spoon-bending as modern pre-cognition was from priestly auguries divined from ox intestines.

Sascha, Dorotea, Sirikit, Rick, Madlyn in instant response: *Damp it down, Rhyssa. Have a heart!*

Dorotea: *Well, you've all got the picture now, so leave us alone with the boy. We can't mess this one up.*

Rhyssa had to take a deep breath, hoping that the sudden revelation she had been unable to keep from other strong telepaths in the Centre had not also been picked up by Peter Reidinger's still emerging skill. He was certainly not reacting.

Dorotea: *I blocked him, Rhyssa. Get a hold of yourself.*

Rhyssa managed to go on ' . . . So, Peter, if I could get the hang of what you're doing with the generators, it could be an extremely valuable added whammy.'

Dorotea: *I couldn't have put it more discreetly myself.*

Rhyssa: *Thanks.*

'I don't know what I'm doing,' Peter said sadly.

'It's the sort of thing you don't *think* about doing, Peter. You just *do* it – because you want to, because you need to. And Dorotea and I will help.' She grinned at him. 'Communication is where telepathy excels. The spoken word sometimes isn't as clear as it should be: words can be misused, inappropriately assigned muddy meanings. You're accustomed to a word meaning one thing: someone else will think it means something else entirely and misunderstand what you just said. Speaking mind to mind clears up a lot of such confusions. Or have I just confused you more?'

Peter began to smile suddenly. 'Like how I couldn't explain to Miz Romero just WHY I hated the body-brace.'

'That's a very apt example, Peter. You just didn't have the words for the concept of that sort of interference.'

'But how'll I move without a brace?'

'By the power of your mind alone, which is exactly what you did when you were going out of body. Only we'll teach you how to take your body along with you! AND manage most of your daily care. You won't be dependant on nurses or orderlies or anyone. In one sense it was what Sue was trying to get you to do — make your mind motivate your body to remember what it once could do. Only you took it one step beyond that, and neither of you knew you had latent kinetic ability. So, of course you couldn't do what she wanted. You were a good jump ahead of her.'

He was still sceptical. 'I'm kinetic?'

'Do you know what the word means?'

'Sure. But I didn't think I was.'

Rhyssa rose. 'Well, you are. So *think* about it because you're also a telepath.'

Dorotea retrieved the cup. 'You take a rest now, dear. Then I'll show you about the house so you'll know where everything is when you want it.'

15

Although Sascha usually handled training, the affinity established between Peter and Rhyssa made it sensible for her to guide his initiation.

'I'll help as much as I can,' Dorotea told Rhyssa, a look of resigned disappointment on her face, 'but I am eighty-four and I've slowed down a lot.' Then she smiled with bright mischief. 'Of course, I've always liked cooking for a male appetite. And he'll be able to do most things for himself in short order. I'm sure of it. I know a strong Talent when I bump minds with it.'

So Rhyssa, Dorotea and Sascha made a little ceremony of adding Peter Reidinger's name to the Registry of Talents at the Eastern Centre. Peter was still not quite certain of his great good fortune. Rick Hobson who was empath as well as kinetic monitored the kinetic aspects; Don Usenik, the Centre's versatile medic, kept a close check on the boy's physical condition and the boy resided in Dorotea's house.

'I can still handle the mothering bits,' as she said

staunchly, 'especially since Rhyssa has enough to administer.'

By the end of the first week, Peter was able to handle all his intimate problems, a success of immeasurable proportion for a sensitive boy. The morning he managed to take a shower all by himself was celebrated by his mentors as the achievement it was. The first time he had attempted a shower, he nearly scalded himself and then overcontrolled and had to be rescued from icy water by Dorotea.

It also took time, and finesse, to descend from his bed without hitting the floor in a heap. Or reel around Dorotea's house, colliding with furniture. Gradually he achieved a delicate control of the gestalt and 'walked': only the really observant would notice that his feet never actually touched the ground and that the bend of his knees only approximated to a normal walk. He could not grasp things but he arranged his hands in appropriate positions so that he appeared to be carrying objects. With such accomplishments, he was a different boy altogether and the change astonished his mother on her next visit.

'There's never been any Talent in our family, on either side,' she confided in Dorotea at one point. 'I just can't imagine where he got it from.'

'Necessity, Mrs Reidinger,' Dorotea said at her most grandmotherly. 'The accident has forced him to transfer motor functions to another part of his brain. Even the best of us only utilize about two-fifths of brain potential.'

Ilsa Reidinger did not really understand Dorotea's explanation, but she accepted it because Dorotea spoke with such authority.

'The human body learns to compensate, Mrs Reidinger,' Dorotea went on soothingly. 'All Peter needed was a chance to train in new ways. Which, I must say, he has done extraordinarily well. We're very pleased with his progress.' Dorotea beamed placidly at her guest.

'Yes, but what will he *do*?' Ilsa Reidinger asked plaintively.

'Why, Peter will do very well here at the Centre, helping other youngsters – and adults, too – who have to learn to compensate for drastic handicaps.' When Dorotea 'heard' the woman's reservations on that score, she added, 'Oh, the work pays very well. He's on a training scholarship right now, of course, but his profession pays very well indeed. He's all set for a fine career at the Centre. You're going to be very proud of him.'

Dorotea chose to ignore Ilsa Reidinger's other dominant thought: that, if Peter was Talented, Katya must be, too. The girl was being ever so difficult, wanting to know why Peter got all the luck and she was stuck in a boring school, doing boring studies while Peter was getting everything his way just because he'd got lucky.

'Can he read minds?' is what Ilsa Reidinger asked out loud. She was uncomfortable believing that Peter could do that any time he wanted to.

'Peter has a very limited range,' Dorotea replied mendaciously, intimating regret. The mother was having a hard time accepting any part of her son's new abilities. 'He can hear very strong thoughts but his projections are short range. His Talent lies in kinetics. Do you understand that word?'

'Yes, it means people can push things about without having to touch them. Like the ones going up to Padrugoi Station to help get it assembled so we can colonize the stars.'

That glib phrasing came from Dave Lehardt's clever publicity campaign on the Tri-D.

Then Ilsa asked more timorously, 'Would Petey go into Space?' In her very audible public mind, Ilsa decided that whatever the answer she wouldn't mention *that* to Katya.

'Quite unlikely. The Platform will be finished before Peter's received all his necessary training.' The very thought of Barchenka conscripting Peter Reidinger made Dorotea queasy. Ilsa Reidinger was disappointed, however, suffering from the usual maternal syndrome of wanting *her* son to be unique, which he was, and famous which the Centre would not wish on him, and perhaps rich, which Peter would also be, in that, as a Talent, he could purchase through the Centre anything he really desired. 'He shows a truly unique Talent.' Let that be a sop to her pride.

'Yes, but what exactly *does* Petey do?'

'Well, you saw him walk, and serve us tea quite by himself. That is all accomplished by his kinetic Talent. So you see, he is no longer dependant on mechanical or prosthetic devices to conduct normal activities. When he's surer of his abilities, we'll add more complicated tasks.'

'He'll be able to hold down a job?'

Mrs Reidinger really had not even grasped the basics, Dorotea thought, or comprehended the obvious achievements. She had barely grasped the fact that Peter would no longer be a financial, or an emotional, burden to his family. She was just a nice woman who had certainly been devoted to Peter during his convalescence but the strain had taken a toll on her, too. Dorotea ventured to wax more enthusiastic about Peter's potential.

It suddenly occurred to Dorotea to wonder if the testing routines, established by Daffyd op Owen, needed to be updated, or made more sensitive. Hospitals were usually well staffed with Talents of all descriptions. Why hadn't someone spotted Peter? She really ought to discuss that notion with Rhyssa – when she'd finished up with the mess Barchenka was causing.

'I shouldn't think there'd be much young Peter can't do if he sets his mind to it.'

'Being a kinetic, you mean?'

'A rather special one, at that, since he's had to overcome severe physical limitations.'

Still slightly puzzled by the fuss being made over her Peter, but immensely relieved by his future prospects, Mrs Reidinger departed.

It never occurred to Dorotea that her remarks — meant to allay a mother's natural concern — would have unexpected repercussions. Certainly she and Rhyssa were beginning to realize the boy's immense potential but, even to colleagues, they had been discreet.

'It's a case of make speed slowly, Lance,' Rhyssa told the Australian Director who seemed to spend more time on a Spacehotol and in the Jerhattan area than arranging matters in Canberra for his leave of absence on Padruogi. He had dropped in to see her on his way from yet another long scheming session with Dave Lehardt, Samjan and Rondomanski.

'I've seen some fair dinkums, dealing with the Aborigines and the Maoris, Rhyssa,' the Aussie replied in his distinctive drawl as he slouched on a chair in her tower office, 'but this lad takes the peach. If he's come on this fast with only a li'l 4.5 k.p.m. generator for him to play with, think what he could do with *real* power.'

'All the more reason to make speed slowly. Control is the most vital part of his training.' #Image of Peter, head first, zipping around Jerhattan on a whirlwind tour, with a 'tail' of detritus, people, small vehicles and oddments caught up in the wake of his passage.#

Lance grinned, his teeth very white against his perpetual Ozzie tan, his sea-green eyes glittering. 'Too right, mate. I get the drift. But with a Talent like his and a proper generator, we could bleeding near shift drones all the way to the nearest planet.'

Think that in your most private mind, Lance. Don't let a whisper of it escape your shield.

Lance propped his angular body upright, his expression completely serious. *I was funning!*

Rhyssa nodded her head slowly once. And he let out a long whistle.

Yeah, but just imagine the look on Barchenka's face if we could tell her that precious Padrugoi Project has just turned obsolete.

'Not quite,' Rhyssa said with a vindictive grin for she'd entertained a few very satisfying fantasies on that very theme herself! 'A facility like Padrugoi is required for any number of valid reasons apart from a jumping-off point to the stars.'

Lance: *How many ★know★ about Petey boy?*

Rhyssa: *About his potential? Main staff know he's unusual. I was too excited when I realized the possibilities inherent in his gestalt but they only know I was excited about the boy. There are just three of us, myself, Dorotea and Sascha who have extrapolated his potential. Rick Hobson thinks the boy is inordinately quick but we had to have a kinetic in on his initial training. Like you, Rick's got to go to Padrugoi so we're cramming as much technique in as possible. He and Peter mesh well. YOU are my choice for his more advanced training so don't do anything stupid up on Padrugoi, will you?*

No way! That's a mean carrot to dangle in front of me for six long months! Lance rose. 'Pure shame that Dave Lehardt's not a real Talent. He's wizard at handling the Finn and that slimey little Neester bloke.'

Rhyssa gave a little convulsive shudder at the mere mention of Prince Phanibal.

'You don't like him, do you?'

'No!'

Lance chuckled. 'Always knew you were a woman of good sense, ducks.'

16

Rhyssa did worry about Peter: so did Dorotea, both keeping their concerns from Peter whose telempathy was steadily improving along with his kinesis. He was not limited to receiving, or sending emotions, but was developing a true telepathy and able to send and receive both abstract and lingual messages. Nor did Rhyssa or Dorotea call attention to those moments when, in sheer ebullience, Peter didn't 'draw' on the generator in kinetic exercises.

Dorotea enjoyed cooking for his now eager appetite and once Peter was able to perform routine tasks, she fine-tuned his kinesis with food preparations. He could pare apples and potatoes, scrape carrots, cut up vegetables, string beans, all kinetically. He ate anything and everything and his body began to fill out with good firm flesh: Rick showed him exercises for muscle tone and hours spent in Dorotea's garden tanned his skin to a healthy glow. Peter no longer looked the wasted paralytic with atrophied muscles. Extreme care was needed in all Peter's activities since he still had no feeling in his extremities or lower torso and would be unaware of cutting or burning or bruising himself in some of his perambulations.

When Rick finally had to leave for his tour at Padrugoi, Peter took it hard, moping about the next day.

'Rick will be back, Peter,' Rhyssa said, joining them that evening at dinner. 'He's taught you about all he knows. Now, you have to teach yourself. That'll be hard . . .'

'Teach myself?' Peter was so shocked that his good manners briefly deserted him. His fork hovered above his plate. He and Dorotea had an agreement – he could get the food to his mouth however he chose if he was alone, but he was to observe proper etiquette with anyone else.

'Yes, teach yourself,' Dorotea replied as if this were the normal routine.

'Rick has given you the basics,' Rhyssa added with a warm smile. 'Certainly you're now able to do everything for yourself and help in the house and the garden. Now, you begin the next step – testing yourself. Don't worry. Rick left a long list for you to complete by the time his tour of duty is over.'

'But he didn't tell me how . . .' Peter was clearly floundering.

'You know how,' Rhyssa said, separating the words and acting surprised at his reaction. Dorotea nodded a sharp seconding. 'All paranormal Talents come from an instinctive level. Sharpen your instinct.' She smiled at him, patting his arm soothingly. 'That instinct led you right to the Centre, didn't it? Don't worry about the "how"! Rely on your instinct. Use it by sending different types of inert objects to destinations further and further away. First to places you are familiar with. Then by memorizing Tri-D visuals, and maybe even using mathematical co-ordinates. For example, that forkful of mashed potato. Where would you like to put it?'

The fork's burden of mashed potato disappeared.

Sascha: *What is going on down there?*

Rhyssa: *Does it concern a portion of mashed potato?*

Sascha, somewhat disgusted: *It does!* #Image of a white glob in the middle of his desk.#

'And where did you send it, Peter?' Dorotea asked in a non-committal tone.

'Sascha's desk. But on the wood, not ON anything important,' Peter assured her.

'I won't require you to eat it, but do bring it back!'

The well-travelled forkful reappeared on the side of Peter's plate.

Sascha, sarcastically: *Thank you!*

Peter: *You're welcome!* Then he giggled like any youngster succeeding with a practical joke.

Sascha to Rhyssa and Dorotea: *We just get Madlyn housetrained and now we have Peter! Sometimes . . . I suppose, if he's up to tricks, he's adjusting to Rick's departure.*

Peter was also up to work the next day, this time using the gestalt with the generator to shift many items about the Centre. Dorotea started him with small objects, moved from one room to another, emphasizing accuracy of placement, picking locations with which Peter was familiar. They finished off the morning by having him shift heavy bales of computer paper from storage to the Control Room, getting his placements from squares crayoned on to the floor. Budworth finally signalled that Peter's aim was perfect. And asked him to remove the trash barrel.

'Weight seems to be no object,' Sascha said, reviewing the achievements at lunch. 'How much did he have to rely on the gestalt?'

'Not much. We've got a graph on its usage,' Rhyssa replied. 'His need is verging on the psychological.'

'Ah but that doesn't alter the fact that he does use it,' Sascha said, thoughtfully. 'Can and *does*. By damn, Rhyssa, he's extraordinary! Once he can really lean on generator power, there isn't anything he can't shift, is there?' Sascha's eyes were shining with excitement. 'If only we could figure out just how he achieves the gestalt?' Rhyssa shook her head, with a rueful smile. 'Could Rick?'

Rhyssa sighed. 'Rick did just the basic kinetic training exercises with him. He didn't have more time. Damn Barchenka. Wouldn't you just know that we'd have an emergency that required the very kinetics that she's yanked out of our reach. Why didn't we have an earlier pre-cog of this?'

Sascha leaned back in his chair, regarding his good friend and Director with an uncharacteristically solemn expression. 'Rhyssa hon, could you follow his mind?'

She gave a short laugh. 'I'm an adept at telepathy but Peter's going where no man has gone before in his own head. Maybe another kinetic could follow. I'm going to dragoon Lance Baden as his advanced trainer as soon as that wretched Padrugoi is finished.' Rhyssa blued the mental air with assorted images of her frustration. Sascha nodded sympathetically.

'Then we'll just have to continue doing kindergarden stuff with him until Lance is free. And build him up physically. Does Don Usenik see any chance of exercise re-stimulating those damaged nerves? Now that . . . '

'Trouble!' Budworth's voice rang through the special alarm speaker in Rhyssa's office.

What kind?

'Goddamit, I want to speak to Director Owen NOW!' said a voice on the room address system as Budworth patched the call through.

'You are,' Rhyssa replied coolly. 'Please identify yourself.'

'Damnit, didn't they tell you? Bob Gaskin, Jerhattan Port Authority. You took our kinetic away from us and now we've a container pinning three men down and no bloody way to lift it quick enough to save their lives. Right now only the safety bar on the forklift is . . . '

'Do you have the area on video?'

'I do . . . the whole yard . . . '

'Relay it to this screen immediately.' *Dorotea, bring Peter to my office. We've got to try to help. They're patching through the image.*

Dorotea: *Dare we?*

Rhyssa: *We'll never know unless we do. Lives are at stake. He's got the potential and he's done well enough already with bulky, heavy things.*

Dorotea: *That's halfway across the City . . . Peter, we've got something a little trickier than bales of paper in Rhyssa's office. Move along now. See if you can beat me walking!*

Sascha and Rhyssa kept their eyes on the screen now aimed at the container, the hoist cables at one end of it still whipping in backlash. It had come down askew, across a small forklift, the sturdy frame of which was keeping it from crushing the driver and two men who'd been working near him. The Talents could see the dangling arm of one man pinned at one side, the feet of a second protruding under one corner, nothing of the driver.

'Why did that hoist cable part, Mr Gaskin?' Rhyssa asked calmly. 'Surely you checked all your equipment before you put it in use again.' Rhyssa deliberately sounded censorious.

The office door opened and Dorothy and Peter entered: Peter's eyes went immediately to the screen.

'If your goddamned Centre hadn't pulled our kinetic, this wouldn't have . . . Holy hell! How'd you get someone here this quick?'

The three adults held their breaths as they watched the long unwieldy mass of the container slowly rise off the crumbled forklift, the driver slumped across his controls, another man sprawled flat on the ground while the third staggered to his feet, holding his injured arm. They were also aware of a humming which they could feel through the floorboards of Rhyssa's office. The hum died away as the container was lowered carefully to the waiting lorry loadbed.

'Bravo, Peter, beautifully done. Magnificent,' Rhyssa said and saw him crumpled on the floor. 'Oh, Lord! Did you strain yourself, love?'

Sascha reached the boy before she did, lifting him gently and depositing him on Rhyssa's conformable chair which instantly altered to fit the boy's limp body.

'Will the men be all right?' Peter wanted to know, his white face contorted with anguish. *They were hurting bad.*

'More to the point, young man,' Sascha said, frowning, 'are you all right?' *Don, get up here on the double!*

'By God, ma'am, how'd you do that?' cried Bob Gaskin. The Port Authority Manager was mopping his face with hands that were shaking.

'You haven't been completely abandoned by Talent, Mr Gaskin. We have a skeleton crew . . . ' #Sascha's image of Peter's frail form, bony structure emphasized, made it very hard for Rhyssa to keep her features composed.# ' . . . which we can throw into gear for emergencies of this nature. Do please now overhaul your equipment. We don't have the manpower for unnecessary accidents, you know.' She ignored Sascha's exaggerated grimace as she saw medics rushing to assist the injured men as a Southside heli-amb landed nearby. 'Good morning, Mr Gaskin.'

'We'll check in with Southside General Hospital later, Peter,' Rhyssa told him.

'After Don's checked you out, young man,' Dorotea added, 'though your concern for the men does you credit.'

I know we had to, Rhyssa, Sascha said on a tight band to Rhyssa, *but should we have?*

Rhyssa made a face. *Hobson's choice, Sascha. We maintain an official position of the skeleton crew. By the way, don't do that to me again real soon, huh?*

Sascha rolled his eyes, expressing remorse but no reassurance. *I'm not sure how long we'll be able to hang that lie, so would you get all uptight if I tried to follow his mind's thrust when he's lifting?*

No, after this exhibition of Peter's ability, I was about to ask you myself. If we could duplicate the gestalt, even our feather-weights could move containers.

'OK, who's done what to whom now?' Don Usenik wanted to know, looking around the room before he spotted the wan Peter on Rhyssa's chair. 'What have you been doing? Moving mountains?'

17

'Which do you want first? The good news, or the bad news?' Dave Lehardt asked Rhyssa a week later.

She could tell nothing from his expression: the look of his eyes was curiously intent on her face. He might not be a Talent but he was unusually astute at picking up minute body language signs. She really didn't care what news he brought since she was so glad to see him, but she followed his cue.

'The bad!'

'Barchenka is certain you've been holding out on her. She's heard that you have a team of kinetic Talents that are not on your official register. She's about to create stink. And I have to tell you that I've heard some mighty peculiar rumours circulating.'

Rhyssa laughed. 'We're not holding out on her: Talents can't. Tell her to ask her own Russian telepaths. She ought to trust them. What's the good news?'

Dave Lehardt raised one eyebrow in a sceptical arch. 'The polls are again favourable to the Talented. When businesses employing them had to cope with old-fashioned ways, Talents popularity hit a fifty-year low – worse even than after the Hawaiian volcano disaster – even though everyone was pro-Padrugoi and everyone – meaning the Talents – doing their share. Seems that this non-existent team of yours has provided emergency services. Only no Talent has been observed on the scene.'

'It's a remote technique that we've been developing for emergency situations,' Rhyssa said, schooling her face. Not for any lack of trust in Dave Lehardt, but to protect Peter. 'And the one reason we felt we could strip all our Centres of Talents to help Padrugoi.'

'A remote technique?'

'That's what I said.'

'No Talent I've spoken to knows anything about it.'

'I said it was remote,' Rhyssa repeated, struggling to keep amusement out of her voice. She was certainly playing the truth like a big fish on the end of a long line. 'Not something we want to go public on just yet. I'm sure you can appreciate *that*!'

'So Ludmilla can't get her hands on it?'

'She's coerced almost every kinetic we have onto Padrugoi. She's got sufficient numbers and skills right now to finish her work on schedule. She shouldn't get greedier!'

'She wants to come in under schedule and the way your Talents are working, she could.'

'Is a bonus involved in early completion?' Rhyssa was annoyed. Damn the woman to a disintegrating orbit!

'Didn't you know?' Dave Lehardt seemed surprised.

'I heard a great deal about penalties and a completion bonus but strangely enough, nothing was said, nor even hinted, that early completion was her goal.'

'I'll do what I can to squash the rumours. And, if I may be so bold, keep that new team out of operation if at all possible. No more cavalry charges to the rescue without warning me, huh? Please?'

That was very sound advice which Rhyssa intended to

follow. Since that emergency lift, she had been chary of using Peter's skill. It just took too much out of his not so sturdy body. He was strengthening himself daily: it was becoming almost an obsession with him. But his Talent was rigorously restricted to life-threatening situations in the Jerhattan area which, fortunately, were few. In the on-going training sessions using fax placement photos, Sascha linked minds with Peter when he 'lifted' items to other Centres.

'I can follow his thoughts all the way,' Sascha told Rhyssa after a week of these exercises, 'I can even feel the vibrations of the generator in his cerebrum, but *how* he effects the gestalt is still beyond me. And, as nearly as I can tell, he's relying less and less on the power. At least for light stuff.'

'If he keeps on this way, maybe Lance's right,' Rhyssa remarked, when Sascha queried her. 'Plug him in to a powerful enough source and he could probably obviate the need for Padrugoi.'

Sascha blinked. #Images of Barchenka's expression! Images of the consternation on the faces of the Station's major supporters! Images of egg-splattered features. Images of one small boy sending out starships the way children his age launched paper planes. Last and largest image of Sascha with an elongated mouth wide open, chin to his chest.# 'Could he?'

Rhyssa laughed, rolling her eyes at such exaggeration. 'I won't say he couldn't. But you know as well as I do that all Talent has limitations. Now is not the time to put any sort of pressure on Peter. He's such a happy boy.'

'We can thank God he is!' #Image of Sascha patiently controlling the love-lorn Madlyn Luvaro, huge wads of cotton wool in his ears.#

Rhyssa imaged back stray forkfuls of potato festooning his office. 'A kinetic has far more options than a telepath!'

'He's easier to keep happy than Madlyn ever was, too,'

Sascha said, stretching his long legs. 'The odd traffic snarl or two a day and he feels he's worth his keep. Which reminds me, I've had some pretty pointed remarks from industrial VIPs lately about this remote team of ours. My answer is that we've managed to combine the trainees with an experienced feather-weight to achieve the necessary heft, but the application is limited due to the extreme youth of the participants.'

'Oh?' Rhyssa sighed. *That old tangled web routine, huh?*

Sascha quirked an eyebrow. 'Favouring Shakespeare? Thought your family ran to Popery.'

Rhyssa laughed, #imaging her illustrious grandsire, Daffyd op Owen, as she remembered him, tall, silver-haired, slender, with the face of a poet and the chin of an Italian prince.# 'Sometimes the Bard fits better. Which industrialists have asked?'

'Nail on the head, girl. Everyone of them supplies something to Padrugoi! And, as you know, there've been delays in getting material up to the Station, weather problems mainly with all those freak storms messing up launch windows.'

Rhyssa frowned and, in an uncharacteristic show of nervousness, flipped a stylus end over end. 'Life-saving, yes: and with the technique he's been showing over distances, I think he probably could launch a drone up to Padrugoi through any sort of weather. But there's no way Peter's going to help secure her bonus or prevent her fines.'

Sascha grinned. 'I won't mention the possibility of such fun and games to him, you spoilsport.' #Image of him hastily raising a solid barrier against the barbs emerging from her eyes.# 'She couldn't hire him anyway. He's only fourteen. Underage, even under existing Soviet law!'

Rhyssa let out a low whistle, then grinned. 'Yes, he is a minor, isn't he? And Dorotea reminded me that he's been working pretty hard with you. Tomorrow he has a day off. And I've got all these files,' she gestured resignedly at the stacks on the edge of her desk, 'testing reports to go through.'

'Why don't you take a night off?' Sascha suggested, grinning drolly. 'With Dave.'

Rhyssa sat bolt upright, closing her mind.

'Honey, I don't have to peek.'

Rhyssa groaned. 'He's not a Talent.'

'There's no law in the charter that says you have to marry Talent, you know.'

'But that's the way to increase . . . '

'Yeah, and where did Peter Reidinger come from? I think sometimes, my dear friend,' and Sascha leaned over the desk towards her, 'we have to look with our eyes instead of our heads. Just thought I ought to mention it. Dave's the best friend Talent's got.'

'It's not up to me, Sascha,' Rhyssa added, feeling uncomfortable for the first time in her old friend's presence.

'Could be. Maybe not. Lehardt's clever enough to do his own promo work.' With that Sascha left her.

18

Today, as Tirla entered the Main Concourse of Linear G, she sensed an aura of excitement, but a suppressed one so she knew that something was about to happen to relieve the tedium of linear living. Most of the little groups of people were composed of women. Some general workers were scurrying to the Plaza to see if the Work Board scrolled out jobs for able-bodieds. Aye-bees were more concerned with getting enough day work to keep out of Conscriptive Work Services than listening to idle female yattering. No self-respecting linearite wanted to be sent on a hard-labour tour or worse, Spaced-out to the shipyards around the Big Wheel. Few CWs ever earned a return ticket. And now even the Talents weren't exempt.

Tirla edged close enough to one of the groups – Hispanics – to pick up the drift.

'He lay hands on . . . '

'Church is always *le mismo* . . . The singing is bad.'

'My Juan now . . . when he is reminded of the purity of the Virgin, he doesn't beat me for a day or two . . . '

'The true man of God provides food for the soul . . . '

Tirla snorted to herself. Food for the soul was not high on her priorities when her belly was empty.

'I have heard,' Consuela Laguna said earnestly, 'that if he lays hands on the lame, he cures.' Consuela's son was handicapped beyond remedy or repair. Tirla was always being asked to translate the medical bulletins for the woman who remained positive that somehow, sometime, her Manuelito would be restored to health by some new miracle treatment.

So, Tirla thought, a Religious Event had been un- expectedly scheduled for Linear G. That was odd. Only four weeks ago there had been a Public Health meeting. She'd nipped in as she usually did – carefully – and lifted vials of the new vaccine they were offering. That was how she kept herself 'mune and earned a modest profit by selling the remaining dosages to parents of other illegals. It was true, Tirla thought, that there hadn't been an RE in a long time but something aroused her suspicions. TWO specials within four weeks?

She moved on to the next group, all Neesters from the Levant, and they were babbling about how could they get their men to attend tonight, instead of adjourning to Mahmoud's squat to see his new belly dancer. After such a session, the men returned home in a lustful condition. Neesters didn't care how many illegals they had, just so long as their virility was unquestioned. If the kids could somehow be raised to their tenth birthday, they could be sold for enough to make the risk pay. She slipped around to an Asian gaggle and they were chattering excitedly about cures and whether it would be bad for business. Asians provided ancient remedies for the many minor ailments that beset those in the warreny residentials.

'He has come as promised . . . ' she heard as she slid up to old Mama Bobchik whose black eyes were wide with elation while her cheeks were a mottled, glowing red of excitement. 'You come, too, *dushka*,' she said, catching

119

Tirla's arm. 'You must tell us his words, exactly. The last time I could not hear what was said and my soul is black with sin.'

'*Nakonetz,*' Tirla agreed easily. Most Religious Interpreter Groups generally said nothing in the most ornamented phraseology. Tirla could amuse herself by anticipating the trite phrases and flowery words. 'So the extension was granted after all?' She must maintain her reputation of knowing all that went on in the linear.

'*Da, eto tak!*' Mama Bobchik happily reassured her. 'My man was sent word to prepare late last night.' Argol Bobchik was one of the linear's sanitary engineers. 'The word is that this Religious is all-seeing,' Mama babbled on, 'with an excellent back-up group. They were well received at Linear P. Early as it is, already this morning many traders have booked space. It will be an occasion. We have not had religion here in G for some months. We are all in need of guidance. The souls of many are dark with sin and must be purged.'

Tirla nodded solemnly. Mama Bobchik was certainly old enough to be facing a mystic accounting of the sins on her soul. Too bad no LEO man would be there to hear it.

But how had Tirla missed such a juicy rumour? Maybe it had been decided very late last night. At any rate, the presence of traders would make it easier for her to wash the 'tied' credits for the Yassim man. She shuddered, using his name even in the privacy of her head. She didn't like to hold on to *his* money too long. Not that *he* had any reason to distrust Tirla. She just wanted to make certain *he* never did. Especially if *he* suspected she was close to saleable age. She was small and thin enough to pass for the seven years she admitted to. Someday, someone would count fingers on her. From time to time, she thought about what to do then. And tried to keep enough floaters stuck inside her blouse at all times so that she could flee to another linear. She had even managed to get her hands on a highly illegal copy of the cargo train schedules and had found her nearest access points to the subterranean concourse to eyeball escape routes.

Now she deftly disengaged herself from Mama Bobchik's fat fingers and moved on to the Pakis who were chattering about bringing in some relatives from Linear E and arguing over the advisability of such a move. Some insisted that, since the extension was legit, there would be no risk. Then Mirda Khan – a personage Tirla was always careful to please – came up and quickly dismissed such stupid generosity.

'The blessings of such a lama would be few,' Mirda muttered in an intense and angry tone, just audible to those around her, 'for he cannot waste his holy strength on the trivial. Such as he would be gracious enough to dispense must be for us, here, in Linear G. For us,' and she poked her thin breastbone with a broad flat thumb, 'the true believers, his faithful in Linear G.'

'The Very Revered Pontis Prosit has been at Linear P,' one of the other women murmured reverently. 'Pandit heard of the miracles he performed.'

Tirla was sceptical of miracles for, on close inspection, there were always alternate explanations for healings and savings and revelations. But they were fun to delve.

'Then we save such for ourselves!' Mirda replied fiercely, defying contradiction. Suddenly she spun round, somehow aware of being the object of scrutiny but Tirla was quicker and she flattened herself against the Concourse pillar. She'd heard enough anyhow and left.

So this Religious Interpretator, this RIG, had a reputation? As Tirla was quite aware, it took a real clever talker to keep from violating the variety of complex doctrines in a linear. This . . . Pontis Prosit . . . might well be worth listening to. And watching closely. In her precarious situation, Tirla was open to pointers.

If the whole thing was legit. She mulled over the probables as she ducked into side-aisles before coming out again on to the Main Concourse, far enough away from the Pakis to be screened by other groups. Then she glanced up at the nearest publi-text screen. She watched through usual notices and announcements until it scrolled down to 20:00 hours.

The full details were being vividly proclaimed, complete with fanfares of brass instruments and snippets of the Respected Venerable Homilifier Pontis Prosit smiling beatifically at vast audiences. A chorus was promised – and a short blast of five-part harmony and high soprano descant was presented as an enticement to attend the full show. Tirla liked music, good foot-stomping music. This V R and Holy Religious Interpretation Group purportedly had only recently returned from the eastern cities of faith where he had endured fasting meditations of great length and illumination. Linear G was fortunate in the extreme that he was able to fit this evening's assembly into his busy tour. So, he hadn't had a booking in a while, Tirla thought cynically. Well, Religious Interpretations were popular in linears, better than fights sometimes, and often more showy. Tirla liked shows. And legal extensions.

There had been a Public Health round-up recently so a second covert one was unlikely in her experience. Also while a RIG could be staged to mask more illicit operations than washing tieds in public, having PH'd Linear G so recently, there might not be any undercover LEOs. There would certainly be crowd controllers. That was standard procedure and Tirla now knew most of them despite the way they altered their appearances.

The important thing was that she had the Yassim tieds to change. She should never have agreed to, but Bulbar had been insistent and the 'talker' – a hitman that she would not willingly offend – had told her that she was being given this opportunity in reward for services already rendered. Having consented to a professional engagement with Mama Bobchik who was not only another person it was unwise to offend but someone who would defend Tirla because she had received her newborn from her mother's womb, Tirla was committed on two counts to attend.

Reassured and making several contingency plans, Tirla began her usual morning routine – bargaining for the day's meals, getting a bath and a clean issue of clothing. Her old threads were so worn that she couldn't have hidden her emergency floaters, much less the tieds, adequately.

But as she proceeded, she was stopped by various female clients, each wanting her company during this RIG because the featured lama-shaman was reputed to speak in 'tongues', had meditated on holy eastern islands and places and Tirla was absolutely the only person who would faithfully tell them everything he said. There was a manageable limit, however, to how many people Tirla could adequately represent. Surrounded by very insistent, vocal and physically active prospective clients, none of whom she cared to antagonize, Tirla organized them.

'Bilala, you and Pilau must come together . . . Anna, you team up with Marika . . . Zaveta, Elpidia comes as well . . . Chi-shu, Lao Wang with you . . . Cyoto, Ari-san is your partner.' And so she grouped them. Twenty pairs were as unmanageable as they were un-avoidable. Before she got into any further difficulties, Tirla discreetly removed herself from public view. She must get the tied credits out of their hideyholes and secreted about her for easy access.

19

'We have an Incident,' Sirikit said, her light voice crisp and carrying to Budworth who was Duty Officer in the Parapsych Control Room.

'Who?' Budworth sent his gimballed chair spinning across the tiled floor to her station. Seeing him manoeuvre so rapidly around the Control Room made people forget that his spine had been crushed in an accident and that he had only minimal movement in his head and two fingers.

'Auer,' and Sirikit's surprise was reflected in her voice.

'Really!'

'And Bertha!'

'That's an unusual combination.'

'Not if Pontis Prosit the Great Flimflam is involved. I caught the PA for Linear G.'

'It is very true she would have his guts for garters,' and Budworth grinned wryly. Bertha Zoccola was generally a relaxed and tolerant individual but mention of that particular RIG was enough to enrage her. Budworth set himself for her fury in reporting a pre-cog involving the man.

Whenever a pre-cognitive Talent responded to an Incident, they would flash the Centre, alerting Control to receive a verbal description of what they had pre-viewed. Budworth positioned his chair at the fingerboard next to Sirikit. He scratched his chin on the rim of his head support. He felt the surge of excited anticipation which he always experienced at these moments.

'C'mon, you net-heads, report!'

Sirikit glanced away from her screen, to grin at him. A bleep startled both, though they were expecting an entry.

'Auer here,' the emotionless voice announced and the pre-cog's face appeared in one of the response screens. 'A real messy one. High panic, screams, mobs, kids trampled, the usual thing. Why don't you grab Pontis and Space him to the shipyards? I'm tired of protecting that scuzfart.'

'You saw Flimflam himself, Auer?' Sirikit asked encouragingly. At Budworth's nod, she took over the routine questions. She was one of the most deft at post-Incidental debriefing and Auer always responded well to her. Budworth busied himself with tapping out a query for scheduled public events. More crowd control would now have to be assigned to Linear G.

Auer shrugged with an indifference both observers knew was false. 'He's prominent. All coloured lights and glittering hands. Then running away. As usual. Never stays to calm the audiences he excites to riot pitch.'

'Where?' Sirikit encouraged him.

'Your typical residential assembly hall. Usual Pontis backdrops. Nothing unusual – except,' and Auer paused, frowning down at something, 'except – that's odd!'

'What's odd, Auer?'

'All over a scrawny girl?' When he looked up, his eyes were haunted.

'Yes?'

'I feel . . . and her danger is acute. It doesn't end

125

tonight. She's Talented!' That was said in a surprised voice, then Auer passed a hand across his eyes, scrubbing downwards. 'It's gone now. It's gone.' The screen blackened.

Another screen brightened.

'You shouldn't allow that man a PERMIT at ALL!' Bertha Zoccola was bristling with indignation. 'You've caught him dealing time and again! Those people don't have the credits to spend on mystical cures and miracle healings. He spouts the most appalling sort of pantheist tripe. AND in the worst language!'

'What did you see, Bertha?' Budworth asked the plump little woman who still cherished a worn deck of Tarot cards that her great-grandmother had once read with a high enough degree of accuracy to earn a significant credit balance.

'I keep telling you that man is nothing but trouble.' Her double chin quivered and her expression was troubled. 'I don't care if the Domestic Satisfaction Index does rise after he's played a residential. Why should we Talents protect a quacksalver, a faker, a pharisee, a hoaxer, a gyp! An arrant carnie!'

'We're not protecting him! Now, what did you see, Bertha?'

'Halfway through that . . . that gibberous effort of his . . . you never can tell WHAT he's saying in that mumbo-jumble of his, there's a movement, to the left of the platform . . . ' She jingled her left hand, her many wrist bracelets clacking noisily . . . 'or do I mean, his right?' She raised the other hand, splaying fingers crammed with rings. 'There's a commotion. It has to do with a large group of women.' She waggled her hand again, frowning. 'Then everything goes wild! A name! They're all calling a name! And I can't hear what it is! Oh, wouldn't that cause a saint to swear! The one vital detail! And I *thought* I heard it so clearly . . . ' She stopped, pursing her lips in concentration and then slowly shook her head, sighing. 'No, it's gone. I'm so sorry.'

'Thanks, Bertha dear. You've filled in some details.'

'Who else?' Bertha always wanted to know.

'Auer.'

'Him?' Bertha was incredulous. 'Well, what'd'ya know about that? Do keep me screened, Buddy.'

'You bet.' Budworth was punching Sascha's office as her picture dissolved. 'Sascha, we got an Incident.'

'There's only one crowd controller assigned to the RIG, Budworth,' Sirikit murmured to him. 'Residential Linear G is listed as blue, calm.'

'Well, it's about to change colour unless we can neutralize. Sascha, something's going to bust wide at Pontis' meeting at G tonight.'

'Linear G?' The large blue eyes in Sascha's slavic-cast face widened with surprise. 'We'd nothing planned *there*,' he murmured in an aside. 'Who saw it?'

'Bertha and Auer.'

'What?' Sascha raised his eyebrows. 'That's a first. I'll be back to you, Buddy. I'll have to organize our infiltration with the Bro. I've just been informed by Rhyssa, our revered Director, that she and Peter are too deep into gestalt techniques right now to stop, so this is in my lap.'

Budworth grunted, absently scratching his jaw as the contact faded. He hoped there'd be remotes. And if Sascha's LEO brother, Boris, was involved, there would be. Vicarious or not, Budworth appreciated being involved in these unexpected spectaculars. You never knew what would happen during Incidents. He was honest enough in the back of his mind – the only safe place to think in the Centre – to realize that he hadn't been a physically brave person even before his accident. Still and all, he found this breathless anticipation and stimulation to be very pleasant sensations for one husked by a mobility chair.

Sirikit was making rapid entries, documenting the

Incident. Although the Talented now had immense credibility and the meticulously kept daily files might generally be scanned only by Research, the procedures outlined by the Parapsychic Centre's first administrator, Henry Darrow, were scrupulously followed. The full spectrum of Talent was far from being known and certain facets of Talent not at all fully developed: witness young Peter Reidinger's Talent for an electrical gestalt.

20

Tirla did not dare be late to the meeting, but she also
didn't want to arrive too soon, to be hassled by even more
people, demanding her particular service. No matter what
baksheesh was offered, she could translate for only so
many at a time, especially with the other, and more
pressing matter, to complete. *That* had to be managed.
She chose to arrive with enough time to do a quick survey
and identify the best vendors as well as any undercover
LEOs or PHOs. The fortuitous scheduling of this RIG
still bothered her.

Unless . . . the thought occurred to Tirla that maybe
there would be some Treasury persons in the crowd,
checking up on vendors. That 'laundering' itself was the
target of this occasion. But the Ts were easy to spot.
They were always so . . . obvious . . . about blending
into the crowd.

Having arranged to meet the women at the main
south-east entrance, Tirla entered the assembly atrium
from one of the side north-west gates. Someone else
had already disabled the entrance-eye that read IDs

and counted attendance so she didn't have to. The petty vendors had their booths up and merch displayed: mainly trinkets and synth clothes, stuff that could be quickly shifted. But there were air-cushion carts being angled through the wider doorways, proving that some serious trading could be done. She felt somewhat easier in her mind. The big traders wouldn't risk themselves or their merch at a risky-disky.

She took note of prices as she wended her way through the gathering crowd. She hoped there'd be some fresh produce – well, fresh in that it had been recently nicked from the underground warehouses that supplied Jerhattan's markets. She'd treat herself to a nice crisp pepper, carrot or apple from today's baksheesh. Something to sink her teeth into instead of the subsistence mush or compound protein loaf. She wanted to get a stick of real chewing gum, though, to keep her mouth moist when she started translating. Translating to a group always dried up her mouth until she couldn't even spit words out. She spared only a glance for the activity on the platform where hands were rushing about, draping curtains and swags, and hauling lighting and sound equipment about with much advice and counter-advisings. She was never impressed by packaging – just the quality of the contents. She found gum at Felter's stall and made him launder one of the smaller tied notes.

She was just savouring the minty flavour of her gum when she caught sight of an all too familiar profile in totally unfamiliar synth issue clothing. Yassim was actually here? She ducked behind a large man in a stained robe which had once been the height of fashion. He was holding up both arms, wigwagging at someone on the staging. The smell of him nearly made her swallow her gum but his outline completely obscured her.

What was *he* doing *here*? Tirla wondered. Didn't *he* trust her? As her camouflage dropped one arm to cup his hand to his mouth to shout a direction, Tirla chanced a second look.

Yes, it was *him*. *He* was unmistakable. He'd done something subtle to his face, altering its shape — probably pads in his cheeks and lower lip but he hadn't, couldn't, alter his long thin hooked nose and the sloping forehead. Nor anything about the way he walked, as if he owned the place, strutting about in a loose overrobe that hadn't suffered much cleaning in its long life. His headgear was also appropriately worn, torn and stained. It was a creditable attempt to blend in, but Tirla's sixth sense once again aided her self-preservation. There *he* was, sauntering about, inspecting trinkets, pausing to ask questions of vendors, appearing to go from one group of friends to another. Groups whom she quickly identified as some of his multitude of ladrones, hitters and sassins. Well and discreetly guarded though he was, why was *he* here?

Her odorous blocker moved and she moved with him, keeping him as cover. When he stopped, roaring out instructions, she too did. And saw *him* talking to three Neester mothers who had young children with them. Suddenly Tirla knew what *he* was doing here. With equal certainty, Tirla did NOT want to be anywhere in *his* vicinity while child-buying was on his mind. She did, however, make a mental note which ladrones and sassins she knew among his followers. There had to be one she could trust to give *him* the tieds she'd exchange into floaters today. There was no way she could avoid that chore.

Subliminal music had started and the lighting in the Assembly Hall began to alter subtly, heralding the beginning of the Religious Interpretation. Tirla ducked behind the nearest vendor's shillboard and slipped to the south-east entrance.

An agitated Mirda Khan seemed to have eyes in the back of her mirror-adorned headdress for she swung, her

131

face as sharp as a predatory bird's, as Tirla approached. She hooked her fingers painfully into Tirla's grasp and hauled the girl to her.

'Where were you? Where were you?' Mirda shook her, her eyes sparking with anger. The old woman showered her with spittle and sour breath so that Tirla pulled back as far as she could. The other women who had commissioned her to translate the RIG's words formed a close circle around her. As this circle also shielded her from *his* notice, Tirla did not resist.

'I was pricing the merch,' she said, unrepentantly.

Bilala and Pilau were trying to edge around Mirda and pull Tirla to their segment of the circle. Mirda jammed Tirla tight against her angular body while Mama Bobchik somehow got a hold of Tirla's free arm, effectively pinning her between the two formidably large women.

'*He*'s here,' Tirla said to Mirda, squirming to give herself a little space in these unloving grips. She repeated the phrase until all her customers knew.

'*He*?' Mirda stretched body and neck, and peered over the heads of their little knot. She gave a snort. 'Yassim'll roast in hell before I sell him another child.' Her fingers tightened convulsively on Tirla's shoulder. 'You stay away from him. You hear me good?'

Tirla nodded enthusiastically. If Mirda knew Yassim, was there a chance she could inveigle the woman to pass on the laundry? Not with any sure knowledge that all of it would reach *him*.

'He gives a good price,' Elpidia whined. She had a girl-child old enough to spin off. She also had a drug habit to keep for which she exchanged the yearly fruits of her womb. She fretted about whether or not to go back to her squat and bring down a child for him.

'I would not sell to such as him!' Mirda's black eyes flashed scornfully. 'Price or not. Even selling to the Station is better.'

132

'What did she say?' Elpidia demanded of Tirla for Mirda had used her language.

Tirla shrugged. 'I am hired to translate the speaker, not settle disputes between clients and she is not one to annoy.'

Elpidia scowled at Mirda Khan who hauled Tirla around, nearly wrenching her left arm out of Mama Bobchik's hand.

'Come,' Mirda said and, her outer 'best' robe billowing its musty folds across Tirla's face, she led the group forward, acting as a spearhead through the still thinly scattered gathering. She halted right under the stage where no-one could thrust in front of them to block their view. She was about to push Tirla forward when the girl wriggled free.

'I must be able to see him. I will stand here, where I can see, and where all of you can hear.' She repeated this until it was clearly understood by all her clients.

She felt safe from *him* within the circle. She began to relax, and even to enjoy the music despite the patchy sound of the shrill replay as it ground through a multi-ethnic repertoire. Where were the famous live back-up performers? This had been publicly billed as an occasion! Tirla took note of activity on the stage, the draperies billowing suddenly here and there from movement behind them. She could just catch a glimpse of the right-hand wings and people milling about, waiting to go on. So, there was a chorus. She much preferred live singing.

Out of the corner of her eye she caught a glimpse of a big man to her right, wandering with all too apparent indifference. Under the brim of a battered peak cap, she sensed a penetrating assessment of her companions and she leaned surreptitiously into Mama Bobchik. She felt something else, a soothing brush across her mind which caused the high sharp chatter of the women to fall off into a less excited pitch. She wasn't sure what *that* was all about.

The man wasn't Treasury. She followed his progress, was aware that he was in contact somehow with two women who gave every sign of being oblivious to him as they chattered and laughed together, jostling through the early comers to find a good position near the stage. She peered suspiciously at the two, faces painted with careless hands, one of them obviously pregnant, though she wore the gear of a prostitute. Their faces weren't familiar to her and Tirla was beginning to wonder if the meeting really had been staged by an authority like Treasury or PH when a third woman, well known to Tirla, greeted them effusively and stayed to gossip. Reading from their lips the commonplace remarks they exchanged soothed the girl. It was seeing *him* here that made her so nervous. What had happened to his stock? He wasn't often caught short enough to brave a public affair. She didn't owe him so much that he'd come after her. She wasn't even overdue with the laundered credits. She touched the little pouches of tieds in the clever vest she wore for the purpose under her issue suit and reassured herself that all were in place.

A fanfare blasted for attention and the excited babble died down to eager anticipation. Not a bad flourish, Tirla thought, quite willing to be carried along by a good show.

Then the choir stalked out self-consciously and arranged themselves with some poking and pulling on one side of stage centre. As close as she was to the stage, Tirla could see that their costumes were neither clean nor new. Not all of them managed to find the right pitch from the final note of the recorded blurt of brass. Tirla knew the song they sang, a really old good one so the fact that they sang it badly was inexcusable. She only had to translate it for Cyoto and Ari: everyone else mumbled along in their own languages. She was somewhat consoled for the sloppy rendition by the fact that if Public Hygiene was involved, the show would've been a lot better than this.

Then the emcee came out, falsely bright, and started the pitch, waffling on about the training and merits of the Revered Venerable Pontis Prosit. As he was merely repeating all the claptrash about mystical training in Asia from the Public Announcement, Tirla didn't start to translate it until Bilala hissed at her to earn her fee.

There was another rouser song, one which slipped from one musical ethic to another with no respect for tonality or rhythm. Perversely, the singers managed to perform this travesty competently. Tirla identified six who were spaced out on something. That they could sing at all might indeed be a minor miracle of this RIG.

More flourishes of recorded instruments and rolls of drums which stirred even Tirla's cynical pulses. Drums could be so exciting! A great crashing of cymbals – some of the singers had them hidden in their robes – a painfully glaring display of assorted lights and narrow beams, an ear-blasting crescendo of bugle synths accompanied by fragrant smoke bombs and the Revered Venerable Religious Interpreter arrived, his robes artfully gleaming.

Her clients were suitably impressed by his 'magical' appearance but Tirla had caught a glimpse of the square aperture in the floor before he shot up through the densest veil of smoke, to hover on his column above the stage and the awed spectators. She preferred something more dramatic; she'd seen that sort of entrance so frequently it had lost any impact. Clearly she was in a minority. Even Mirda pretended to be afraid, covering her face with a fold of her head cloth.

The Religious Interpreter went into his act immediately, face upturned so her best view was of a waggling chin and dark holes of nostrils. The light show dazzled, taped music supported his mouthings, for that was what they were, syllables meaning absolutely nothing, with random words from every language she had ever heard in a linear tossed in to confuse.

'What does he say, the holy man?' Mirda demanded.

'Tell me what he say?' Mama Bobchik pulled Tirla to her. Bilala and Pilau were equally insistent: one kicked Tirla's shin and the other transferred a substantial amount of her weight on to Tirla's undefended toes.

'Nothing,' Tirla replied disgusted. 'He says nothing!'

She was poked, pushed and pulled.

'He's saying something.'

'He speaks mystically.'

'Tell *us* what he says.'

'Ah, I understand that word for myself! I will pay you nothing, bitch.'

Tirla was furious at that threat. Furious at the RIG. She'd translate when he said something translatable. She was pinched and tweaked and slapped now. In self-defence Tirla caught the pattern of his babble, and involuntarily mimicking his stance and delivery, she rattled off the nonsensical sounds in an undertone, translating the occasional real word into as many languages as she must before picking up the gibberish again.

Then the man stopped talking, spread his arms, his beatific smile radiant in the flood of light picking him out, seemingly afloat in the air above the stage. Then Tirla realized that he was staring in her direction.

In a gesture that startled her as well as her clients, he lunged forward, eyes flashing, face contorted, his accusing finger pointing straight at her.

'Unbelievers, profaning a sacred moment with chatter. Hear, learn, obey, repent your evil uncaring ways. Be taken into the light of the world. Be admitted into the holy sepulchre. Be one with humanity and all loving caring creatures. Be purified. Be saved! BE!' His accusing hand lifted and spread open as a beam of light caught his fingers and spilled down his raised arm.

Tirla, translating as rapidly as possible in the dramatic pause, was thankful for some coherent phrases. Her clients might be listening to her but their eyes were on him. He had the crowd's rapt attention now. Tirla didn't think anyone outside the circle could see her but she didn't dare stop talking. Most of all she was regretting the taste of crisp green pepper which she had hoped to purchase when the women had paid her.

The lama-shaman assumed another dramatic pose, this time arms out, palms upturned in entreaty.

'Bring me your sick, your weary, your wretched souls. Let me heal them. A touch will ease the tortured mind, the fevered body, the twisted limb, the blurred sight. Approach! Be not afeared. All things come to those who deserve. All creature deserve Love. For it is Love, Love, Love that heals!'

Tirla rattled this off easily, trying to peer through the shielding bodies to see who would be working the scam. Barney with his lizard eyelids: one blink and his eyes were milky white blind, another and he could 'see clear once again, hallelujah!' Maybe Mahmoud with his double-joints all twisted out of shape and one touch of the lama-shaman's healing touch and they'd straighten. Maria with her weeping sores?

The lama-shaman threw back his head, his hands now turned gold in the narrow spot-beams, glittering from some sort of paint he must have used. Her clients, however, inhaled with awe at the sight, their faces rapt as he made mystic passes with his magical hands. Glistening strands and bits whirled from his fingertips, disappearing in brief sparks as they left the light beams. That was a new trick, Tirla thought. Not bad. Pilau tried to catch a strand but it disintegrated, leaving no trace in her grubby fingers.

Just then another strand, stronger, shot from the stage and fell on the head of a bemused man. He was less bemused when, with another grand flourish, the lama-shaman began to reel him in.

'You have been chosen, brother. Come to me! Embrace me!' A ramp extruded from the stage, straight towards the 'chosen' who glanced about with apprehension but

137

was pushed on to the ramp by those behind him, and propelled forward by those on either side. 'Kneel, brother,' intoned the lama-shaman and appeared to glide down the air.

Tirla could feel the faint vibration of the stage mechanism which supplied this effect but she didn't pause in her translations. It was a pretty good gimmick. She wondered where the control was. The mark appeared genuinely stunned at being 'chosen'. He knelt obediently, a dazed expression on his eyes. 'Rallamadamothuriasticallig omahnozimithioapodociamoturialistashadioalisy mquepodial – Omathurtodispasionatusimperadom usigenalliszweigenpolastonuchevaliskyrielisonand ia. Mosspirialistusquandoruulabetodomoarigatoim ustendiationallamegrachiatus . . . ' the Revered Venerable intoned, holding his hand above the mark's head.

More syllables and almost words which Tirla couldn't anticipate enough to mimic. She could appreciate and admire the Venerable's truly respectable breath control. Why, he sounded as if he could go on forever!

'What does he say?' Mirda pinched her sharply.

'How can I hear when you babble at me,' Tirla replied and made up suitable phrases which she then translated. 'Whoops!'

Strange things were happening above the 'chosen's' head. How did the lama-shaman DO that with sleeves so tight at his wrists, Tirla wondered. Hair, face and throat of the mark were now shimmering with gold, which paused at a very dirty collar. The expression was first ludicrous and then ecstatic. Tirla wondered what this Venerable pray-man could be using. She was beginning to enjoy this.

The Revered slowly turned back to the audience, his face also golden-hued, the white of his eyes visible.

'The power is with me. Whom else will it touch?'

Raising his arms again and extending his hands forward, he gave the audience sufficient time to see the effect the 'power' had had on the first 'chosen'. With a twist of his wrists, his palms turned over and strands shot out in all directions. Before Tirla could duck, one of the filaments landed on her head. Whatever it was stuck tightly in her hair despite quick efforts on her part to get rid of it. Her hands were caught by the adhesive, bound to her head now. She began to panic. There was no way she wished to be hauled up in public. Not with *him* in the hall. Not with 'tieds' on her – credits she had no right to possess under any circumstances.

The choir began to chant for the chosen to come forward, to receive power. The audience caught it up and the sound of it had an ominous overtone of envy from those who felt themselves more worthy of such an honour.

'She's been chosen!' Bilala and Pilau shrieked as they tried to push Tirla forward toward the ramp nearest them, bursting into an ululation that shot panic through Tirla's heart.

'No, she's got to stay. She's got to tell us.' Mama Bobchik and Mirda Khan were not to be cheated. They pulled Tirla back.

'Break it, Cyoto. Help me, Lao Wang. Elpidia! Zaveta!' Tirla struggled in earnest now, terror beginning to chill her guts.

All the other 'chosen' were making their way up to the stage. The strand tightened, pulling at her hair. She twisted. Then suddenly she was snapped free. She caught the glint of a knife blade as she fell back against the solid Mama Bobchik. Zaveta and Mirda locked with the screaming Bilala and Pilau who were attempting to regain control of Tirla.

As she had done before in such situations, Tirla dropped to the floor and plunged to one side, tripping someone up who fell heavily on her left foot. Tirla ignored the stab of pain and crawled on, her breath now coming in sobs. She rolled free of her encircling clients and scrambled to her feet, ploughing through the chanters. Someone saw the dangling golden strand and grabbed it, nearly jerking her off her feet. To free herself she wrenched the tangled hair from her head, leaving the bit of scalp dangling in the man's hand.

'Grab her!' The chant was interrupted to set up the cry. She squeezed past several grasping hands, frantic to get to the lobby and the nearest emergency exit.

'Here, I gotcha!' She was encircled by massive fore-arms. She lifted her arms and slithered down, was kicked in the belly but, despite being winded, she rolled, too ac-customed to such dirty tactics not to have self-preserving instincts. She had a glimpse of one of *his* sassins, face wreathed in a witless grin of success, before she landed against the far wall, and suddenly two pairs of trousered legs shielded her.

She was helped to her feet by kind hands, made con-scious of soothing thoughts of assistance, understanding and sympathy. She recognized the aura just as her splayed fingers felt the door frame. This close to known safety, she eluded the hands, whipped out the door and sped across the foyer, paying no heed to pleas to stop. An incredible multi-toned bellow rose behind her, an angry frustrated noise which gave impetus to her pumping legs. As she pounded down the access aisle, she heard a familiar thumping-thud in the air above.

LEOs! Had they been on hand? Or had they been called? But it took time for LEO ships to assemble. She found the small square duct she needed, whipped off the cover, crawled inside and, with some difficulty in the restricted space, snapped it back in place. She crouched in the dirt and grime, tilting her face away from the light as her lungs fought to repay her heart for the strain.

She heard people racing by, heard their exclamations as they reached the dead end, heard them turn and come back, heard their steps continue past her refuge. Despite the noise, Tirla fell asleep.

21

'RHYSSA!' The alarmed voice of the Duty Officer was accompanied by an impulse through her headnet that roused her instantly.

'Yes?'

'Major disaster pre-cog,' Budworth said. 'Recorded all across Asia. Looks like Kayankira's going to get another monsoon overload. They haven't repaired the restraining dams from the last one. How're we going to cope with all the strong kinetics on the Station?'

'Is there time to bring any down?'

'That's the panic! There's time enough but weather conditions all across the world are freaky. Even if a Padrugoi shuttle launched, the nearest clear landing site is Woomera. The kinetics have to be on site to be effective.' What Budworth didn't say, 'if Barchenka would allow 'em to leave the Station', flashed like a neon sign in Rhyssa's mind.

'Get Sascha up for me, will you, Buddy?'

He did. Are you considering Peter? Sascha asked. His mental tone was mixed between an eagerness to try and the multiple risks involved.

Rhyssa: *I must consider Peter's unique capabilities in a situation as critical as this.*

Sascha: *How? Without compromising Peter's security!*

They both slapped up internal shields as they felt the arrival of other thoughts.

Kayankira: *Rhyssa, I've got to have all the kinetics you have left. I understand there's no chance of getting any of them down from Padrugoi?*

Rhyssa: *That's my understanding.*

Vsevold Gebrowski: *I shall insist! I shall take this to the World Council. They have deplored the situation in India. Let them put words into action. Reducing the density of population in that area of Bangladesh also diminished the available workforce and the necessary work has not been completed on time. Now we pay for that.*

Miklos Horvath: *Not if we draft the kinetics on Padrugoi down to help. And the clean-up effort will be reduced by kinesis now!*

Rhyssa: *If we can force the weather to give us a break!*

Bessie Dundall at Canberra: *The pre-cogs all indicate the worst flooding ever in Bangladesh. The new levees haven't been completely restored so flood waters will drown this year's harvest: the barriers won't work for some reason — I suspect their erection will prove that once again corruption and bribery have been widespread. We have to do something!*

Alparacin: *Rhyssa, what about that team of yours I hear about?*

Rhyssa: *They're not well enough trained for a disaster of this magnitude, dear friend. They'd be burned out.*

Peter: *No, I wouldn't.*

Sascha, Rhyssa, Dorotea: *QUIET!*

Peter: *I was. Just to you.*

Rhyssa held her breath. But no Talent queried the unknown 'voice'.

Rhyssa: *Naturally Eastern will do whatever we can. May we have copies of the pre-cogs? But I assure you that highly skilled kinetics are going to have trouble coping with this sort*

*of thing and all I have are a handful of fourteen-year-old
trainee kinetics.*

Madlyn: *Madlyn here . . .*

Sascha: *Honey, you're the one voice that never has to
identify. What have you heard?* #He imaged to Rhyssa a
vision of Madlyn Luvaro, hands to her mouth to make
a megaphone, leaning out of an airlock, shouting down
to a wincing Earth.#

Madlyn: *Lance has been arguing with Barchenka since he
got the pre-cog. She absolutely refuses to risk a shuttle or a
pilot. You gotta admit the weather's pretty freaky all over
right now. I can see it clear as day: lots of turbulence and
not just over the Indian subcontinent. Lance says there has to
be one safe place on Earth they can land and they've got to
help. He's citing her for contractual violation. She says it's
too dangerous to risk so many Talents: now she's doing the
matriarchal, protecting-you-against-your-own-altruism. Ha!*

*And there isn't a pilot we've talked to who'll risk a drop into
the soup kettle down there. Wait! Lance says,* and Madlyn's
mental tone altered to a rote recital level, *now's the time
to try. He says you'll know what he means. He accepts that it
could be a risk but, if ever to put it to the test, now's the time.
Have you got all that?* Madlyn sounded mystified.

Sascha: *You've come through loud and clear, Madlyn,
and we copy.*

Madlyn: *Lance says that the pre-cog indicates even more
horrendous damage than the last monsoon flood caused so Talent
has got to give kinetic support. He's dragooned a pilot into
coming, but the guy's scared of attempting to land anywhere.
Lance's assured him that all the kinetics on board will do the
landing OK. Is Lance gone Space-crazy? All right, I'm telling
them. He says he, and a contingent of the heavy duty kinetics —
enough to effect flood control — will be on the shuttle* Erasmus
*in hangar G at 08:00. They're OK in Space but they'll need
the help landing. That doesn't make sense to me but that's what
I'm supposed to tell you.*

Sascha came storming into Rhyssa's room. He'd pants

143

on but carried the shirt in his hand. He really did have a superb body, Rhyssa thought privately. Why isn't there the necessary chemistry between us? We'd make beautiful children. He looked so magnificent angry.

'Lance is out of his wig if he thinks Peter's up to a controlled landing in Dacca weather. Landing pallets in a warehouse is a considerably different can of worms to a shuttle full of live folk we can't afford to smear across a gale-struck concrete runway.'

Rhyssa fed a direct repeat of Lance's earlier conversation on Peter's potential and a similar situation into Sascha's mind. 'He was only joking at the time,' she said ruefully. 'Quite a legitimate extrapolation.'

'We just can't risk it,' Sascha said, pacing up and down the room while Rhyssa untangled herself from her pastel covered duvet and started dressing. 'As neat a solution to the lack of kinetics as it is.'

Rhyssa, with ineffable sadness: *Sascha-bear, you're half-way to figuring out just how he can do it!*

They were both startled by a timorous tap on her door.

'Yes?' She and Sascha exchanged glances for no-one they knew 'tapped' on doors.

'It's Peter. Can I come in?'

Sascha threw his arms up in a dramatic reaction to Peter's arrival.

'Yes, yes,' Rhyssa said, shooting a comprehensive warning at Sascha who nodded his head energetically.

In his distress, Peter floated rather than walked into the room.

'No-one bothered to channel their thoughts,' he said, both apprehensive and defensive. 'I couldn't help hearing.'

'No, of course, you couldn't, Peter,' Rhyssa said.

Is Peter there? Dorotea's anxious tone startled them.

I'm here!

Young man, if you ever leave me again in that abrupt fashion, I'll tan your bottom!

144

Rhyssa and Sascha had never heard that particular note in the telepath's voice before.

I was trying to explain the problem to him, when he teleported.

I know the problem, Dorotea, Peter said in a very patient tone. *To land the shuttle safely at Dacca. And, with enough power, it'd be no more difficult than that container was, or the steel I sent to San Francisco.*

'The turbulence of a monsoon is totally unpredictable . . . ' Sascha began.

Peter's expression was one of abused patience. 'It'd be the same principle in spite of turbulence. And better because the shuttle won't be powered so that won't throw off the snatch and grab of my gestalt.'

'Simple when explained in that fashion,' Sascha said at his driest. Then he flung up his hands in exasperation and turned to Rhyssa.

Rhyssa took a reasonable stance. 'The distance, the mass involved, even the turbulence are not factors you've dealt with before. We can't, and won't, risk burning you out.'

Peter grinned. 'You wouldn't. Though I'd need much more than 4.5 k.p.m. To be safe, I'd need some real power – like the City's turbos. They might seize up . . . but I wouldn't.'

'We don't *know* that, Peter,' Rhyssa said gently, permitting him to sense her anxiety.

'But *I* know that about me,' Peter said and levitated to the bed where he perched beside her, upright enough, but with his arms and legs draped in unnatural positions. He made adjustments when he caught Rhyssa's look. 'Instinctively!'

Then she hugged him, feeling tears of pride for the shining self-confidence that had emerged in the past few weeks. She held his lax, narrow body for a long moment, then, sensing his embarrassment at her emotional gesture, she ruffled his hair and released him.

145

'Peter,' Sascha said, hunkering down by the boy, 'this IS different from the exercises we've had you do. And this gestalt ability of yours is unique! We just can't risk it.'

'Dorotea said I should trust my instincts,' Peter said so firmly that both Sascha and Rhyssa regarded him for a long moment. 'I also read the pre-cog report. If there aren't kinetics, many people will lose their lives as well as everything they've been struggling to build over the past two years. There'll be massive ecological damage, more plague, starvation. You keep feeding me all this stuff about the responsibility we Talents have to the rest of the world, how we're supposed to reduce death and damage. If I'm willing to take a little risk, I'd be a real Talent.'

'I also heard what Madlyn said to you,' and Peter grinned ingenuously, wincing as if avoiding a loud noise. 'Mr Baden means me, doesn't he? That it's time to really try me.'

Sascha sat down on the bed on his other side and looked helplessly at Rhyssa.

'As I see it,' Peter went on, clearly more in charge of the situation than his adult mentors, 'we Talents don't have any option. We need the ones with Mr Baden in the *Erasmus*. Sascha, when I shifted that steel the other day, you said I had graduated into a really useful category of kinesis. With enough power in the gestalt, I *know* I can land the shuttle.'

Sascha slowly shook his head. 'There's another major consideration, son . . .'

'I've been studying schematics on power generation,' Peter continued blithely ignoring any considerations, 'turbos in particular as they're more reliable.'

'You have?' Rhyssa was constantly being surprised by the turns of Peter's avid studying.

'Well, I thought I ought to get some sort of basic concepts from which to work . . .' He saw their expressions and gave them a little smile. 'I used to watch a lot of college level vid courses. They were a lot more interesting

146

than most of the late-night recreational garbage. Having to think hard took my mind off myself for a while. Engineering was a good think.'

Sascha and Rhyssa were reduced to nodding in belated comprehension.

'Especially,' and now Peter's eyes twinkled, 'as no-one really seemed to *know* what to make of my gestalting. And that's the other consideration, isn't it, Sascha, keeping gestalt kinesis under wraps?'

'He's got us there, Rhyssa,' Sascha said, with a chagrined expression.

'That's what you're *really* worried about, but look, if the pilot brings the shuttle down far enough, I know I can get it safely through the turbulence and land it. And even the pilot doesn't need to know it wasn't Mr Baden and the other kinetics who steadied the shuttle.' When he saw that they were seriously considering his suggestion, he added, 'It isn't as if I'd be bringing the shuttle all the way down from Padrugoi by myself, you know.'

'And you think the City's power system will supply the necessary gestalt for you?' Sascha asked in a wry tone.

'The East Side Power Station's turbos should be enough.' Peter's eyes glowed at the prospect of all that power at his disposal.

Rhyssa and Sascha began to laugh at the sheer impudence.

'You know, I really think that'll work,' Dorotea said, entering the room. She still wore night clothes, hers a fetching pale lilac that set off her lovely white hair and porcelain complexion. 'Since eavesdropping is in general order today, I've been following the conversations with great interest. There won't be time to talk that idiot of a Power Resources Commissioner into agreeing to anything of such an experimental, and highly confidential, nature. The fewer people who know what we're doing the better.' Then her face took on an exceedingly sly look, totally uncharacteristic. 'Let's invoke a G and H!' She chortled, looking exceedingly pleased with herself.

'All we have to do then is call Boris, have him clear the power station and use his official capacity to get us in.'

'Invoke G and H?' Rhyssa stared at the elderly telepath as if she'd never seen her before.

'What's a G and H?' Peter asked just as Sascha began to guffaw, but his look of respect for Dorotea's percipience was not lost on Rhyssa.

'Why didn't I think of that!' she said in exasperation. To the mystified Peter, she explained. 'That's our Mayday Code, for George – that's George Henner who once owned this house – and Henry – meaning Henry Darrow, who established Talent as a verifiable paranormal skill. If a Talent invokes a G and H, he gets immediate and unquestioned co-operation from every other Talent.'

Sascha rubbed his hands together. 'You know, I've always wanted the excuse to invoke that Mayday code.' *Brother, it's a G and H: we need escort to the East Side Power Station, and it's to be cleared! Shouldn't be difficult with only a minimal night crew on call.*

Boris: *A G and H? Fascinating. I'm up to my ears in a riot and you elect this moment in time to call a George and Henry?*

Sascha: *All we need is you and a LEO heli?*

Boris, sarcastically: *Just me?*

Sascha, agreeably: *You to get us the co-operation we need.*

Boris, in a sly tone: *And I can expect return co-operation from you?*

Sascha: *It's a George and Henry Mayday, Bro. You can't refuse.*

Boris: *Quid pro quo, Bro. I was about to request your presence!*

Sascha: *For a riot?*

Boris: *This one certainly requires your particular Talent.*

Sascha raised his eyebrows enquiringly at Rhyssa who reluctantly gave an assenting nod.

'Did you follow that, Peter?' Rhyssa asked because the boy's face still registered surprise.

'Yes,' he said tentatively.

'You don't really need me, Peter,' Sascha said encouragingly, 'if you've got Rhyssa . . . '

'And Dorotea . . . ' the lady added stoutly.

'To buffer your mind,' Sascha continued. *Don as well, I think,* he added to Rhyssa. *Why does Boris have to need me at this moment in time?*

Dorotea: *Boris always did have an awkward streak in him. Comes from being a LEO by temperament.*

Rhyssa turned briskly to Peter. 'Now, you'd better get dressed. Fetch your clothes here, Peter. And what should he get for you, Dorotea? You can change in my bathroom.'

'I'll get down to Budworth for the vital statistics we need,' Sascha said, 'the weight of the shuttle, a radar link with the shuttle, repros of Dacca – in good weather – weather reports.' *If I really think about this in any detail, I'll go crackers!* he added on a very fine thread to the two women.

Rhyssa and Dorotea replied with equal fervour: *You'll have company!*

Rhyssa added: *If Peter *thinks* he can do it, I prefer to think he can. After all, it's the thought that counts.*

Dorotea: *That's what does the trick.*

The necessary equations, based on Peter's established use of the gestalt plus distance, weight and optimum speed of the shuttle, atmospheric conditions and turbulence at the landing site were all completed by the time the LEO heli arrived to transport them.

'I thought you were having a riot of a time and we'd get a deputy,' Sascha said, but he was exceedingly relieved for his brother's support.

'I am, but I'm the best authority you have for whatever's going on,' and Boris smiled with white-toothed malice. 'You'll really want to be in on this one, Bro. We've got a lead on the kidnappings.'

Sascha swore with great ingenuity on several levels.

That's as important as this, Sascha, Rhyssa conceded. *With Dorotea and Don to help me buffer him, he'll be fine.*

I wouldn't interfere with a G and H if I didn't have to, the LEO Commissioner said, even as he reached down to assist Dorotea into the heli.

Sascha, the kidnappers must be stopped, Dorotea said, so sternly that her tone startled all the telepaths. *There! That's settled!*

'And this is Peter Reidinger?' Boris said, as Peter reached the steps in his treading-water gait. 'Hi!'

From the stunned look on Peter's face, Rhyssa suddenly realized that no-one had thought to mention that Sascha's twin brother was the LEO Commissioner.

'No, you're not really seeing double. I'm older by five minutes,' Boris went on amiably, deftly taking Peter under the arms and hoisting him aboard. *We'll both see them safely there before I abduct you, Bro, for my less nefarious purposes. The boy's the G and H?*

Sascha waggled his finger at his brother: *Naughty, naughty!* He swung aboard and started stowing the medical equipment Don Usenik handed up, ignoring Boris's grumbling. When Don climbed in, Sascha slid shut the door and the big heli-bus glided upward and south-east.

Boris had strapped Peter into a window seat and, utterly entranced, the boy gazed down the black canyon of the Hudson to the mass of lights that glowed from every ziggurat and ribbonway of Jerhattan.

'Rather breathtaking no matter how often you see it,' Rhyssa said to Peter who nodded, not taking his eyes from the view. By the time they landed on the roof of the facility, all the Talents were subtly aware of the emptiness of the massive structure.

'Well done, Boris,' Dorotea said. 'This way, Peter!'

'I hope you know what you're doing,' Boris remarked drily. 'My Office is on the line in this!'

'Thanks, Boris,' Rhyssa said. 'Can you retrieve us when we shout?'

'If I can't spare Sascha, I'll send one you can trust,' the LEO Commissioner said as he handed Don his monitors. Then the big heli lifted away from the heli-pad.

Rhyssa took one equipment case from Don as he hauled open the roof door. As soon as Peter glided inside, he began to emanate excitement, his eyes sparkling with anticipation while he manoeuvred down the stairs. They entered above the great turbines which were humming slightly as they served the needs of the great metropolis. They turned into the control room that overlooked the turbine floor, a room lined with the equipment that registered the flow of electricity to the various sub-stations. With an ineffable air, Peter assumed the conformable chair of the Duty Engineer, swinging it idly from side to side until the adults organized the monitors and started hooking him up.

Above the windows overlooking the turbines were sufficient vid screens to display what Peter needed to see. Rhyssa began entering the appropriate programmes, bringing up on one screen a high resolution fax print of the *Erasmus*, on another, a display of its specifications, then weather simulations, and finally linked the Station's communications grid to the main NASA board to follow the shuttle's descent. The *Erasmus* was already in flight, having begun its descent promptly at 08:00, Station time, 01:30 Earth time. The power station clock read 05:50 as the deep radar net began to show the shuttle's spiralling descent. The final screen pictured the Dacca airport, lashed with rain, whipped by fierce gusts of winds which shifted tree trunks, parts of cars, crates and all sorts of debris across the concrete runway where Peter was to bring the *Erasmus* safely down.

When Don Usenik had completed the equipment check monitoring Peter, Rhyssa and Dorotea took seats behind them, the mind of each lightly touching the boy's. He seemed not to notice, so intent was he on the *Erasmus*'s

151

course. Just as it hit the atmosphere, the generators began to whine.

Rhyssa shook her head, as unable as the others to reach that part of Peter's mind that had now linked with the enormous power of the turbines below them. The whine built, the decibels increasing to an almost unbearable pitch. Dorotea scrunched her features up, unashamedly covered her ears with her hands. Rhyssa was staring in disbelief at the wildly altered readings on the control console. Don Usenik kept his eyes on his medical monitors. Peter remained outwardly composed. Rhyssa noticed the slightly condescending smile on his face and just hoped he wasn't about to overreach himself.

Simultaneously both she and Don noticed the perspiration on his forehead but the smile remained in place. The generators reached a frenzied peak and maintained it. And the touch of Peter's mind altered! It became hard as stone. Peter hadn't locked mental contact out, but he had suddenly restricted the contact area, indicating intense concentration. Rhyssa caught Dorotea's eyes, but the older woman merely pointed to Don's patient and unalarmed watch of the monitors. The descent of the *Erasmus* visibly steadied and slowed.

HE'S DONE IT! Rhyssa, Dorotea and Don said in muted congratulatory tones.

Rhyssa hoped someone was recording for posterity what was unquestionably the most dramatic moment for Talent since a Goosegg registered Henry Darrow's Delta wave pattern during that first recorded pre-cognitive Incident. Her mind still in contact with that part of Peter's which was accessible to herself and Dorotea, she watched the *Erasmus* landing, coming to a gentle stop, regardless of the battering wind that the shuttle seemed to ignore, at the passenger terminal. Peter gave a little chuckle and suddenly the turbulence between shuttle and terminal abated, an eerie storm eye of absolute calm. Passengers hastily disembarked, paused in astonishment as they became aware of the surrounding lull. One, his face indistinct on the small screen, lifted clasped hands above his head in a victory sign, and then hurried into the dubious safety of the wind-battered terminal.

'Where should I send the shuttle, Rhyssa? Once I let go, that turbulence will just flip-flop it all over the place.'

I hadn't thought that far ahead, Rhyssa admitted on the quiet to Dorotea.

'The weather charts suggest that Woomera would be the safest place, Peter, but . . . ' Dorotea said, quickly scanning the world-wide met report.

Only a slight increase in the generators indicated the effort involved as the *Erasmus* slowly turned and started back to the main runway.

'I think we'd better warn the pilot where he's going,' Rhyssa said and spoke urgently to Sirikit at the Control Centre.

We've had the most unusual brown-out here, Sirikit answered her.

Get Main Aircontrol to warn the Erasmus *pilot asap that he's being diverted to Woomera.*

Erasmus? *Diverted?* For once the tranquillity of the Thai woman slipped into astonishment. *Of course! Immediately!*

Preferably before he wets his britches, Don added under his breath, making both Rhyssa and Dorotea grin.

None of the three adults could feel any stress in the mind of the boy who was totally wrapped in the curious process of gestalt. Physically he looked more frail than ever, and the bones of his skull seemed to expand under the thin skin of his head. They could all feel the tremendous power surging through him but they could not deduce how he effected the control.

Slowly, against all the tenets of aerodynamics and in spite of the prevailing turbulence, the *Erasmus* sped down the runway and achieved a perfect take-off.

'I don't believe this,' Rhyssa muttered softly. 'Who taught him to fly planes?'

'Every boy in this generation understands shuttle craft,' Don remarked, but his expression was no less bemused than theirs. He watched as the *Erasmus* climbed slowly up into the swirling rain and cloud and out of sight. They followed it up to the supersonic level.

The generators wound down from their busy pitch.

'There!' Peter said suddenly with a note of complete satisfaction in his voice. 'He's firing the engines and he should know what to do now. I told him to land in Woomera. That was fun!' he added with less vigour. He was extremely pale and still perspiring heavily. 'That was a lot of fun!' His eyes gleamed and he grinned at Don Usenik who shook his head with incredulity as he pointed to an almost normal pattern on the bio-scan screen.

'Fun? You called that fun, Peter?' Rhyssa exclaimed almost angrily, realizing that she'd been under a tremendous strain of worry even if Peter had not.

'With power like this, I could lift the shuttle much easier than the pilot,' Peter said in a voice that was suddenly hoarse with fatigue.

Dorotea, very privately to Rhyssa: *'How're you goin' keep 'em down on the farm, after they've seen Paree?'* Dorotea rolled her eyes expressively.

'Marked fatigue, low energy level but even that's within what I'd call the normal range for a Talent,' Don announced in a baffled tone. 'You did great, Peter,' he added proudly.

Clearing her voice, Rhyssa said wearily aloud, 'I don't think Ludmilla's going to believe that on-board Talents ALSO 'ported the shuttle out again.'

'Well, I couldn't leave it on the runway, Rhyssa, now could I?' Peter asked with weary irritation. 'Those shuttles cost billions.'

Suddenly all the telepaths were aware of other touches, vying to reach their minds.

Kayankira: *Oh, thank you, thank you. HOW did you manage?*

154

Rhyssa, Dorotea and Don exchanged glances.

Dorotea, on a very thin thread to the other two: *No, Rhyssa, we didn't think this whole thing through very carefully.*

Rhyssa gulped and replied with an evenness in her mental tone that Dorotea applauded. *Lance's right there. It was all his idea. A real G and H. Wasn't it, Lance?*

Lance: *I'll tell her. I'd rather shout 'Eureka' but accept the caveat.* #Image of a large crocodile, jaws wide in amazement, followed by a kangaroo bouncing from a pictorial map of Australia to the moon.# *You never know till you try, do you, cobber?*

'Enough!' Dorothea said suddenly. 'Let's get Peter home to bed. Don't you try to move a muscle, young man.'

For one brief moment, Peter looked as if he was going to disobey. Then his expression turned woeful. 'I don't think I could right now.'

'Nothing a good night's sleep and a hearty breakfast won't put right in next to no time,' Dorothea said briskly but the fierce glance she gave Rhyssa suggested that a lot more recuperation time might be required in spite of Don's optimistic interpretation of the monitors. 'Now, how do we get him back to the Centre? Boris and Sascha are apparently up to their eyeballs in their riot control.'

The Centre vehicle's coming, Sirikit said and there was a ripple of amusement in her voice. *Just stay put!*

Even through the heavy roof sheeting of the power station, they could hear the vibrations of a heli. The roof door opened and a figure charged through.

'You all right down there? I got told to come pick up the pieces!' cried Dave Lehardt, descending three steps at a time.

Rhyssa nearly wept with relief. What had Boris, the sly mutt, said? 'Someone you could trust!'

'Hi, Peter,' Dave said, 'what have you all been up to that your PR man gets called out of his bed in the wee small hours of the morning?' Then he knelt down by the boy, his expression very gentle. 'You look done in. Tell me later, huh?' With tender solicitude, he gathered up the exhausted boy and moving with exquisite care, started up the stairs with him. Rhyssa followed, immensely grateful for his unexpected presence.

22

Within minutes of the Event, an Incident Room was in place on the wide mall in front of the assembly atrium. Crowd control Talents and LEO specialists had quickly defused the volatile temper of the incipient mob. Although a number of attendees had managed to evade the LEO back-up, in mall aisle and emergency routes, the rest were being systematically IDed.

The focus of the Incident, some twenty women of various ethnic groups, had been immediately sequestered in one of the rehearsal rooms behind the atrium and, despite their loud lamentations and protestations of innocence, were being adroitly questioned by a special Talent team.

By then Boris and Sascha had arrived in the big heli. Already the tapes from the hi-eyes, discreetly set in the high ceiling of the hall by two industrious electricians who had come with the RIG set-up team, were being viewed in the Incident Room by the original pre-cogs, Auer and Bertha Zoccola. Boris and Sascha took up observation positions. The portable's walls were packed with analysers keyed in to the LEO mainframe. Debriefing reports by crowd control Talents were being made at the various stations while LEO personnel avidly read rap sheets spewed out by churning printers as the wrist ID scans were processed. Frequently the LEO Commissioner was interrupted in his viewing to initial warrants. But the main meat of the Incident eluded all. Revered Venerable Pontis Prosit had once again flitted off in time.

'So my pre-cog centred on the women,' Bertha was saying, studiously avoiding eye contact with Auer. The dour man was pulling at his lower lip, oblivious to her as the replay continued. 'While his was for Flimflam. When are you going to bust that guy? He's obscene, a miserable maggot of a man, leeching off emotions – you know that's all he is! An emotion leech, growing fat whenever he has a mob to suck! The bigger the bunch he manipulates, the bigger his hit.' She waved her arms in exaggerated circles.

'As I've explained before, Bertha, he inadvertently serves a purpose,' Boris explained patiently. 'He works them up, yes. He may get a vicarious pleasure to "hold them in the palm of his hand" but his histrionics defuse a lot of pent-up garbage in a catharsis not generated by passive watching of the Tri-D fare. Occasionally he runs pretty close to dogmatic insult but usually he's innocuous and says nothing . . . '

'Says nothing is right!' Bertha muttered indignantly.

Boris went on. 'He had registered sponsors for tonight, some East Indian Mystical Concept Group which is properly registered and screens as legit. We had no grounds to deny them, or him, the right of Religious Assembly.'

'Religious Assembly!' Bertha was outraged. 'Religion he ain't got. And religious assemblies are supposed to be uplifting, not downtreading. He's a rouser, a leech, a spewer of blasphemy. He's dangerous.' She waggled a finger violently under Roznine's nose. 'There're laws against inciting to riot and he caused one tonight.'

'Unfortunately, Bertha, your pre-cog absolves him of primary blame.' Boris tried to exude pacification even when he knew that, superb pre-cog though she was, she 'received' nothing. Her voice was getting louder with each denunciatory remark and she had never been noted for tact.

'Who gave him strands, Commish? You can't tell me he didn't use 'em with criminal intent!'

Boris's patience snapped and he sent a crisp summons to Sascha who was outside, helping the telempaths keep control. 'On that count, we've a search and find warrant out for him right now.'

'It was me twigged Flimflam, Bertha Zoccola,' Auer said, entering the argument and glaring furiously at the little woman. 'He's none of your business.'

Sascha arrived and deftly rendered her speechless long enough to escort her to a debriefing position at the opposite end of the room.

'We got another wild one manufacturing that strand stuff for Flimflam?' Auer asked Boris in a low voice.

'Could be, Auer,' Boris replied unhappily. 'That's the only way fringe fanatics like Pontis Prosit could obtain strands.' The 'tangling' substance was a recent LEO invention, produced from an aberrant chemical compound to provide a fast-drying mid-range restraint. Top secret, its formula and processing were of a complexity that ought not to be duplicatable. 'There's a real smart head out there, somewhere.' Unlike predecessors in the job of LEO Commissioner, Boris did not regard wild Talents as perverts, but as misguided, undisciplined errants, to be straightened up into useful channels. 'Forensic says the stuff is pretty damned close to our formula. More toxic which is bad, and less durable which is fortunate. You've a good feel for technical matters, Auer. Keep your mind open for us, will you? Report even the slightest twinge.

We've got to find this bozo as soon as possible. I don't care what sort of Talent emerges from residential genes but, whatever it is, it should be registered with us.'

'I can't imagine Flimflam having enough credit to hire that sort of smarts. Yassim's got himself a new ladrone?' Auer asked cynically, pointing at the replay.

Boris regarded him with approval. 'You caught that one frame of Yassim?'

Auer shook his head but pointed to the tape being played over and over on the screen. 'I keep up to date on the LEO visitors' list. Every ladrone, hitter and sassin known to be connected with Yassim was here tonight. He had to be, too. Didja get many?'

'A good crop but no-one of particular importance,' Boris said and then grimaced. 'You know those new indestructible door-eyes we've been installing? It could have been Yassim's people, or maybe the new Talent who supplied Flimflam with strands, but every one of them was disabled. Very cleverly, with a bit of wire, a hairpin, even a twisted length of foil: nothing irreparable but enough to cloud the count. We're IDing everyone who didn't have a chance to leave after the Incident but we're shy counts on exactly who, and how many, came to the party.'

Auer nodded again, sympathetic in his own sour way to the Commissioner's frustration.

'I'll keep it all in mind, Commissioner. Leave you to it.'

Boris spoke to the head of the team 'questioning' the focus group, *Norma, any luck?*

Norma: *No sir, they're still on the boil. We're getting anger, frustration, envy, some anxiety and worry over being detained, mainly maternal, but really, sir, we can only get the dominant emotions. They're angry at being 'done'. And not by old Pontis Prosit Flimflam. Trouble is, none of 'em speak much Basic. Could we have a linguist down here? Someone who's got Neerest, Paki and Asian languages? Ranjit, maybe?*

Boris: *I'll send him along presently. Anything else?*

Norma: *Yes, sir, nine of them are involved in some kind of feud. We've had to separate them twice already to keep them from scratching each other or pulling hair. Something about being chosen and it wasn't right to intervene. Doesn't make any sense.*

'Being chosen?' Boris spoke aloud as well as mentally.

Sir?

Thank you, Sergeant, you've just triggered a thought! Boris turned to the screen as yet another replay of the Incident began. He forwarded it quickly and then reduced the speed, his eyes on the screen.

You've got something? Sascha was at his shoulder.

Boris: *If my theory that Flimflam was fingering people for someone — Yassim, since his men were there in force — I want to know what the common denominator of choice was. Most of them were males except our focus group which were . . . ah, here we are!*

The two brothers watched as the reduced speed clearly showed the strand falling in the centre of the focus group.

It didn't hit a woman! Unless she was a midget, Sascha said, pointing to the thin hands clawing up out of the mass. Boris tapped out an enlarge, sharpening the definition in the centre of activity. *A child? No child in the group being held. Twenty women. I can count that many heads.*

Sascha: *Are some tugging?*

Boris: *Yes, and some resisting.* Norma said the women are contentious and in an overlay of thought, Boris repeated Norma's exact words.

Sascha: *And feeling cheated. Look! Knife severing the strand. Now all hell breaks loose.*

'OK, who were the nearest crowd controllers?' Boris asked.

Cass Cutler and Suzanne Nbembi were summoned, still wearing their undercover gear although Cass had peeled off the heavy make-up and discarded the tangle

161

of cheap jewellery. Boris spun the tape back to the relevant scene.

'Cass, Suzanne, good, strong damper work today.'

'It was very close, Commissioner,' Cass said, rolling her eyes. 'Could have been a bad one without that pre-cog.'

'Either of you two see a child with our focus group?'

'No,' Cass replied quickly and then frowned. 'At least, I don't think she was with *them*. We first noticed her trying to get away from Bulbar.'

'We would have intervened,' Suz added, 'No girlchild should be caught by that scuz – but she freed herself. Knew well enough how.'

'She dodged behind us for a moment, on her way to an exit. Just then the Incident erupted. Funny about that . . . ' Cass faltered, frowning. 'I felt *something*, Commissioner, when I touched her. A shield solid as a wall and that's odd enough for a linear kid.'

'Could she have come out of that cluster?' Boris tapped the monitor and the focus group.

Cass and Suz obediently regarded it. Boris speeded it up, stopping where the sight of the hands, looking more balletic in slow motion than frantic as the slender fingers splayed in panic; then the sequence went on, fingers clutching at the strand, the flash of the knife, the scrimmage of the women.

'Can you get the perimeter of the scene just before they started to boil?' Cass asked.

Boris tried every combination of review, but the hi-eye had been fixed on the pre-cogged site of the Incident and, although the definition was sharp, the angle obscured what Cass wanted to see.

'Ranjit Youssef reporting as requested, sir,' the young LEO officer presented himself a respectful distance from the absorbed cluster around the screen.

'And what did the search of the assigned quarters reveal, Lieutenant?' Boris asked formally.

162

'Commissioner, the count of illegal children under the age of ten is eight hundred and three, including five newborns. In fact, all the children apprehended are under ten.'

Although the LEO Commissioner was not actually surprised, the total was considerably higher than estimated. He propped himself against the desk edge and folded his hands over his chest, rubbing his jaw pensively.

Eight hundred? Boris said.

And three, Sascha added, his mental tone equally grim.

Boris: *And all to be sacrificed to produce more underfed disposable kids to be abused one way or another. HOW can the traffic be stopped when people blindly follow an archaic ethnic imperative?*

'Any with legal wrist IDs?' Boris asked aloud.

'The nine year olds, sir, but so far no IDs match the genetic print registered for the number. There are also far fewer pre-teen and teens than a residential population should generate.'

'As usual. How many of the illegals under ten were found in the quarters of the focus women?'

'Thirty-two, some too young to run for it. The older ones had some warning – they always do. But a Clamp is already initiated. No one without a wrist band will move out of this linear,' Ranjid said, 'even through disposal chutes.'

'Ah yes, disposal chutes,' Boris added with a further sigh of resignation. 'And, I trust, the cargo lines? Good.' He tapped a sequence and the screen showed the architectural schematic of Linear G, slowly rotating to display every angle of the immense ziggurat. 'Norma Banfield needs your linguistic abilities, Lieutenant. She's in the rehearsal hall to the left of the stage. She's got a mess of ethnics with little Basic and there are two factions at least willing to pull hair.'

'Pull hair?' Cass sat upright, a wisp of a memory surfacing from the recent explosion.

'Got something, Cass?' Boris asked.

'I'll work on it,' and she sagged into as relaxed a state as the activity in the room permitted. Suz began a soothing massage of her neck muscles to encourage recall.

'I'll do what I can to help Lieutenant Banfield,' Ranjit saluted and left.

Cass stood. 'I wanna check something in the hall, sir, unless some officious moron has sent the cleaners in already.'

'Go to it.' Boris gestured broadly and turned back to the schematic to try and figure out where refugees might hide in the maze of corridors, closets and conduits. *Sascha, get your teams to start searching ducts. Scared kids can squeeze into the damnedest places. I don't want a single illegal to get caught by Yassim's slimy hooks.*

Done. Sascha's eyes blanked briefly as he gave the orders.

'I got it,' Cass cried, re-entering the room. She gave an eerie yodel and held the trophy up. 'Her scalp, by all that's holy!'

With two fastidious fingers, Boris took the hank of hair, the dull severed strand tangled right to the bloody patch of skull skin. *Loufan! Find out all you can about the person who grew this!*

The technician hurried to the Commissioner's side, received the tress without expression and went back to his cubicle.

Commissioner, Ranjit said and, after a polite pause to be sure he was not interrupting, added, *They're hiding something.*

Norma: *Someone. I concur. Someone important to them.*

Ranjit: *I think the reason for the dissension, sir.*

Norma: *I would go along with that. May I nudge them, sir?*

Boris: *By any fair means, Lieutenant.*

Boris grinned to himself, knowing Ranjit's scrupulous sense of honour, and then felt the mental touch that meant Sascha had overheard the exchange. With their mutual concerns, such awareness saved so much time and repetition.

Dealing with the unTalented took heroic efforts, Boris thought. On the one hand, did he really want everyone to have paranormal abilities? Or at least, some minor paranormal quirk, so that there would be less hassle? But that gave rise to envy – envy of someone more Talented than oneself, which only increased dissension and prejudice. No, far better to have a small minority, dedicated – and disciplined – to perform functions that the mind-numb could not. And all of the peculiar and unusual quirks *registered*!

Sir? Loufan paused, *I removed the strand as it interfered with the reading and is certainly irrelevant. The subject is a Eurasian ethnic mix, pre-adolescent female. Good strong genoprint, good immune factors, healthy, unusually so.* Loufan sounded surprised. Linear G subsistence fare was nutritionally adequate, of course, but if the child were illegal, as Boris suspected, how had she managed to be healthy? *And – there's no match of birth ID.*

Boris: *Did you really expect to find one?*

Loufan: *Yes, sir.*

It was Boris' turn to be surprised.

Loufan: *She could have been a runaway or a kidnap.*

Boris: *OK. File the data, Loufan, and give the hair to Bertha. Ask her – in your ineffably polite style – if this artefact sparks anything off in her mind.*

'Oh, the poor thing,' Bertha came storming back to him. 'Hair torn right out of her scalp! Commish, who did it?'

'Possibly Bulbar. Sense anything?'

Bertha had the lock pressed against her ample bosom, closed her eyes and concentrated. 'Not a thing, but it's there in my mind now.' She grimaced in sudden revulsion and thrust it back to him. 'Take it away!'

Sascha intercepted the lock.

'Black, good length,' Sascha murmured, ' – some of those women never cut their hair – healthy, and much cleaner than you'd expect. Shouldn't be too hard to find a juvenile with a hunk torn out of her scalp.'

'I'd rather you give it to Carmen.' Boris added a private urging. *Ranjit thinks quite a few of the older illegal kids eluded the search teams.*

23

Carmen Stein laid the lock across her thighs and stroked it flat, using her long fingernails to separate the tangled hairs. For several more minutes she fingered them, softly coaxing a sense of its grower's whereabouts. Carmen always looked so placid and imperturbable when she was evoking her Talent as finder. Better than most, Sascha knew just how much activity her brain was generating at such moments. She was one of the best searchers he'd ever encountered and, because her Talent was intense and exhausting, he protected her as much as he could, limiting her assignments.

'The incident occurred how long ago?' she asked without taking her eyes from the hair.

'Approximately sixty-two minutes.'

'Ah, that accounts for the darkness. She is hiding. I cannot see where. There is no light. A constricted space.'

'A conduit?'

'That's possible.' Carmen sounded dubious. 'I think she sleeps.'

'That's a cool one.'

'No,' and Carmen took him literally. 'Not cool. Tired.' She offered him the hair.

'No, keep it, Carmen, for now. We'll need to know if she moves.' Calmly Carmen leaned forward, took a clip from the brightly enamelled jar on the table, and fastened the tress, the scalp end now coated with a protective film, high on the right side of her head.

Sascha had relayed Carmen's comments to Boris.

A conduit, huh? There're so few of those in a linear. The LEO Commissioner's mental tone was facetious. *We're flushing kids out of every available space. I hate this, Sascha, I hate it.* Sascha sent quick, soothing thoughts to ease the turmoil in his brother's mind. *The miracle of life should be a blessing, not a curse. How CAN people be so irresponsible as to produce countless unwanted children and WASTE them?*

Even illegal kids have rights, Sascha responded, gently quoting his brother's own words. *See that even the least of them get that much.*

Illegals go to the Space Station. Boris sounded defeated.

They don't go as grunts. They're trained to DO something a lot more constructive than their parents ever did. Leave it, brother.

Mutual support system? Boris's mental tone was wry. *I'm putting in an appearance to scare some sense out of those flipping focus females!*

No-one better. By the way, when you have a spare moment, listen to a news update. Then you'll know why we twisted your arm with a G and H.

I congratulate the triumph I sense in your mind but I'll have to wait on a replay of the event . . . and Boris entered the rehearsal hall, thinking what a scarce commodity 'time' was right then.

He crossed the threshold, assuming his most awe-inspiring official manner. Tall, handsome, the strength in his powerful frame shown off even by the bulky action uniform, he succeeded in scaring the gaggle of women silent; a silence which did not last too long but the bursts of argumentative crosstalk were considerably subdued.

I just got something, Commissioner, Ranjit told him. *A flash from the woman fourth on the left, the plump young one with the caste mark. 'It's all Tirla's fault.' Tirla is, I think, a feminine name.*

'Translate for me, Lieutenant,' Boris said, striding imperiously in front of the women, his tone haughty. 'I am LEO Commissioner Boris Roznine. Where is the girlchild you had with you this evening?'

Boris had no trouble picking up the reactions of resentment, envy, anger, dismay and fear as he gave Ranjit time enough to repeat the three phrases in the various languages. The women had had time to realize that they were in deep trouble with authority. Several had vivid worries about their children, left too long alone in their squats. Others concentrated on nursing their sense of grievance. He caught occasional variations on the phrase Ranjit had twigged but no-one else volunteered a name. 'It was all *her* fault.' They contented themselves with impersonal malice.

'Let me reassure you that the children in your homes are being cared for until you can return to them,' he said, smiling kindly.

As the import of his sentence was understood by each linguistic group, the wailing, breast beating and pulling of hair began, and more recriminations were spewed. Boris was well aware of fury, loss, resignation, relief in one case, but not the actual linguistics used in the varied emotional reactions.

Ranjit: *This Bilala says that it is all* her *fault for resisting the lama's choosing.* Ranjit was now restraining the plump caste-marked virago from rushing at the haughty, hawk-nosed older woman on the other side of the room. *She says Mirda Khan brought all this on herself. Mirda Khan replies that — ah, the name again, Tirla — would not have been able to translate for any of them up on the stage. She had done little enough to earn baksheesh, a tip.*

Boris: *Lieutenant, ask them who is Tirla's mother?*

The question was basic enough to be understood by most of the women. It shut them up and briefly closed down their mental perturbations. Then they all launched into personal lamentations again. The answer was also quick. None of them was Tirla's mother and without exception, just as Boris had hoped, everyone of them flashed a quick mental image of the girl in question.

Got it, Ranjit and Norma told him in unison.

As I did, and, with a gesture to signify that the women could now be processed or released as their condition warranted, the LEO Commissioner hurried back to the Incident Room.

Loufan awaited him there in front of the graphics pad, stylus ready. For this sort of transference, Boris grasped the thin shoulder of the Asian and concentrated on the vivid image of the Tirla child. Loufan sketched quickly, capturing in a few clever lines the intense face – remembered by most in its panic at being stranded – the wide-set, slightly tilted, huge dark eyes above prominent cheekbones, the abundant waving dark hair framing it, the fine straight nose, the small cautious mouth, the long sweep of a determined jaw line, the odd cleft in the chin. A charming face if one discounted the fright, an intelligent one despite fear. This Tirla looked no more than six or seven but some wisp of thought – from the fat old woman – suggested that she was older. The woman's memory of her went back quite a few years.

'Is that her?' Loufan asked, transferring the sketch to the screen.

The LEO Commissioner allowed himself a good long look, matching the image on the screen to the consensus in the minds of twenty women.

'Yes, that's it. Print it, circulate it to all officers and Talents. I think we need that child. She's a . . . ' Boris hunted for the appropriate designation for her ability and failed. 'Well, she's raw Talent and needs our help,' he concluded. *Sascha, would 'instantaneous' be more correct than simultaneous translator?*

Sascha rooted briefly in his brother's mind. *If she was employed by ten different ethnic groups to translate, she's unique enough right there. I suppose it has to be a Talent to switch so easily from one language to another. First we'll have to find her. Then we can assess exactly what she is.*

24

Tirla!

Tirla woke suddenly, jolted out of her exhausted sleep by someone calling her name, softly, appealingly. Tirla did not move, nor so much as open her eyes.

Clever little trinket, isn't she? Call her again.

Won't work, Boris. She's alert now.

It had to have been part of a dream. She often thought she heard her mother calling her name. It had to be a dream because no-one could know where she was, despite LEOs searching the main conduits and sending drone units down the smaller ones. On her way home from the débâcle of the meeting, she had escaped all types of earnest hunters. She had seen the numbers of children being flushed from hideyholes.

Her hunch about the meeting had been correct. It had served as an excuse to sweep down on the pads, collect illegal children and check all IDs. No-one, absolutely no-one, had ever known where she squatted. She didn't even think to herself where she was. And no-one was likely to discover it even in this intensive search.

Somewhat reassured, Tirla nestled back into the warmth of her sleep sack. Suddenly she heard noises nearby and froze. She heard the doors into the closed section being opened. This search was unusually thorough. Not even she had been able to get into the engineering space and yet it was being checked.

[*It's dark wherever she is. That's absolutely all I can tell, Sascha.*]

[*Keep with her, Carmen. She's got to turn on a light or come out sometime.*]

Not even *his* men could find her and they knew all the ducks and dodges that any subbie had ever figured out. She'd been so lucky not to be caught by Bulbar. He was wicked dangerous. Her head still throbbed where the hair had been torn away. She had dabbed on some dis-wipe. Bulbar could have been carrying any kind of 'mune to infect her – scabby old scuz.

Her problem with *him* remained. She hadn't washed the tieds. How would he expect her to when he, and every trader, had been lucky to escape the bust. Not that *he* took excuses. What awful luck to be singled out by the lama-shaman! Which of the women had he really been after? And why? It made no sense to Tirla. None of 'em was pretty or young, or even on the lay – not with *their* husbands!

The noise of search was diminishing and carefully Tirla reached unerringly for the water jug and food that she kept for such emergencies. Chewing the dry-eat made terrible noises in her head. She'd heard about the wide-range ultra sensitive gear that was said to pick up breathing in a radius of five klicks but there should be enough minor noises from the generators and air-conditioning units to mask her chewing and she was real hungry. Thirst and hunger assuaged, Tirla snuggled deeper into her sack and went to sleep again.

25

'Take a break, Carmen,' Sascha told the finder. 'She won't venture out until night. If then.'

Carmen rubbed delicately at her temples and sighed. 'You're right. I'll rest. She's unusual, isn't she, Sascha?'

'We believe so, even if we don't know specifically why.'

Carmen regarded him with some surprise. 'It's a lovely clear mind. Like a bell. When she's asleep. She's wary and cautious awake, that one. I can touch her but not read her. And with her in the darkness, I can't even help you home in on her.'

'She'll come out in good time.'

Carmen shot a look that suggested Sascha Roznine might – this once – be wrong. He grinned and winked as he turned to leave her quarters.

★   ★   ★

'Frankly, Sascha, we've run everything we got on the people Flimflam fingered for Yassim,' Boris Roznine said, tossing a sheaf of hardcopy to the desktop, 'and we can't find a common denominator. They're mostly able-bodies, doing enough work to keep away from Conscriptive Work Services, only minor misdemeanours on their sheets, none of 'em known to gamble or dip.'

Sascha smiled knowingly and felt his brother poke at his mind but he kept his shield in place. He could do that to Boris whereas Boris could not keep him out at all.

'You've had a hard thirty hours so I'll tell you. They were all fathers.'

'What?' Blood suffused Boris' face.

'Flimflam had accessed ordinary info on residents of the linear. Mind you, it was so simple we didn't see it at first. Bertha's sensitive to females and children: Auer to the blacker side of life.'

Boris scrubbed at his head. 'Sometimes it is the simple things we miss. So Flimflam was fingering fathers with likely youngsters and the girl was a bonus?'

'I guess, and we're still in the dark about her,' Sascha added, aware of his brother's next query. 'Carmen's latched on but the girl's cautious and hasn't moved since she went to ground.'

'Scared?'

'Strangely enough, no. I'd hazard that she's had to keep a low profile before. She's a pre-teen and illegal.'

'That will sharpen the senses.'

'How're you doing with Yassim's operation?'

'We figure he picked up at least nineteen children, maybe a few more.' Boris grimaced. 'We collected eight hundred and three illegal kids from Linear G. If what Harv believes is possible – that every one of the related mothers has been having a kid a year – we're minus a possible forty. We located eighteen of that forty in a storage basement but they've got the entry jammed. We're working on it.' Boris shook his head. 'They really will be better off in hostels.'

'And in Space?' Sascha asked wryly.

'Even in Space they have a better chance than stale-mated in a linear.'

'But they won't be able to reproduce themselves.' Sascha had never approved of the law that required the sterilization of illegal offspring.

Boris raised his hands in resignation. 'I don't make the laws, Sascha. I only enforce them.' Then he leaned forward and tapped up a new programme on his big screen. 'All right. Now, we have to find Yassim in *his* warren and save nineteen kids or more from him.'

★　★　★

'She's moved, Sascha,' Carmen told him, her tone half triumphant, half anxious.

'This time of day?' Sascha consulted his watch.

'Linear will be crowded with those coming off work.'

'Keep as close as you can to her.'

'It's very difficult, Sascha. It's almost as if she isn't "seeing" the things she's looking at. I can't get a real fix, except that there are people all around her. Wait! She's stopped. No, that's no good. All I get is a mass of standard issue clothing. She's still in a crowd.'

'I'm in touch with our teams on the main levels of G. Just give us a direction, Carmen. Any direction.'

Sascha to Cass and Suz: *Alert to our quarry!*

★　★　★

Tirla was relieved that it had been Mirda Khan she first came across. Mirda was full of the whole affair, her black eyes snapping with indignation and a certain sly malice that she had not suffered at the hands of the Public Health – it had been a long time since her womb had borne fruit. But she had the grace to mourn the losses of her friends, both their children and their hope of more.

'They will see how hard it is for those of us who have no children to sell.'

'Was that why Yassim was there? To buy children?'

'Why else?' Mirda lifted her shoulders in an eloquent shrug. 'He would have no interest in spiritual things.'

'Did he get them all?' Tirla was aghast. Yet, if a big score put Yassim in a very good mood, he would be easier for her to deal with over the matter of the tieds she had been unable to wash.

'No, *they* got most of them. Yassim cannot have many but he got them for nothing!' Mirda was indignant. 'No price was paid to their grieving mothers and fathers. They ran into his arms to escape the LEOs. Ran! And no credits exchanged, not even a bargain made. Oh, he will not dare to enter G again.' Then suddenly Mirda latched steely fingers on to Tirla's shoulder. '*What* was the lama–shaman saying? You didn't tell us. Aiyyee, and to increase insult, you did not even have the grace to accept the strand that chose you. You have earned the undying hatred of Bilala and Pilau for not accepting his choice.'

Tirla wrenched herself free. 'Choice? I am nothing, why would he choose me? I think he missed. Tell Bilala that I think he was aiming for her and missed. But, as for what he said, you missed nothing. That lama–shaman spewed stupid syllables only. Not a proper word in any language. Even in his head he wasn't using real words. He didn't mean to. He is a sham man, not a shaman. It was all set up for the Public Health to raid Linear G.'

'How could that be?' Mirda was startled. 'No, it could not be. Not with traders there with all their goods and some of it not things the LEOs should discover on them. And certainly not when Yassim, and every ladrone, hitter and sassin he employs, were also present. THEY would have known. Perhaps the strand was meant for Bilala as you said. She felt that it was proper for her, too, you understand, for she has been worthy. A woman who has borne a child every year for her husband. Aiyyee, and

177

they have taken that from her now, and his pride from him. He will reproach her until the day of her death.' Mirda beat herself across her breasts and Tirla used the distraction to slip away.

So, Yassim had children from G and had not paid for them. And she had tieds which she could not deal for him, which she had better return. If he had enough children, then he would not steal her.

It was wrong of Bilala to hate her. Tirla wished that she had asked Mirda if any more of her clients did. It was essential for Tirla to stay on good terms with everyone in Linear G. She was just as illegal. Bilala or Pilau could be spiteful enough to turn her in, as a token revenge for the loss of their own children. Unless . . .

Unless Tirla could get a price for the children who had run into Yassim's clutches. She knew where he kept such merchandise. It would depend on who he'd got.

Tirla skipped down a side aisle and, looking around to be sure she was not observed, she yanked at a conduit grille. It resisted and she saw that that screws had been replaced. She felt inside the grille to be sure there were no wires or 'eyes' but this was a small opening, one only a very small or thin child could have used. She got out the vibro-blade she had earned for some long-forgotten favour and sheered off two screws. Then climbed into the dark conduit.

*   *   *

Just when I had a good placement. Carmen was exasperated. *Or thought I did – she's gone into the dark again. No, wait, Sascha, there's light around her now. She's in some sort of a cramped tunnel.*

Sascha: *Uses the bloody conduits like a subway. I'll have the schematic of G on my screen for the next year at this rate.*

Carmen: *Think how well you'll know the innards of a residential by then.*

Sascha: *Thanks. Keep track of our mole.*

Carmen: *Why didn't you set a bug on her first?*

Sascha: *If you'd corner her for us, we will.*

Carmen: *Finders keepers! Wait a minute, Sascha, I think she's moving out of G.*

Sascha: *How can she?*

Carmen: *She's in the underground. Red light. The freight subways are the only tunnels illuminated in red, aren't they?*

Sascha: *Omigod, which direction has she gone?*

Sascha, Cass here. Mirda Khan was just seen talking with our quarry. Khan insists that the girl escaped from her. I'll believe that when pigs fly.

Sascha: *What were they talking about?*

Cass: *The meeting, Flimflam, Yassim. Khan has gone into panic and isn't making much sense. She's afraid, there's suddenly a real big dollop of guilt, anxiety, mainly fear. For herself and just a little for Tirla.*

Sascha: *Boris, our quarry may be venturing into one of Yassim's industrial territories. Alert your surveillance.*

At his desk in the parapsychic tower, Sascha Roznine experienced the sort of frustration that plagued few Talents. Hardened criminals were easier to apprehend than one pre-adolescent child who looked nearly half her actual age. And what on Earth was the child doing in Yassim's territory? She'd've done better to crawl back into her very secret hideyhole. He was tormented with memories of the pix of vivisected child bodies.

26

Barchenka was furious when informed that she would be deprived of her strongest kinetics for the week it would take to mitigate the monsoon flooding. She first cried mutiny, then grand larceny but was brought up short by her own Station Authority who pointed out that the Talents had a legal right to attend a major disaster which undeniably existed in the Bangladesh flooding: the pilot was an off-duty volunteer and there had been no damage to the *Erasmus* which he had returned to Padrugoi as soon as Woomera cleared him for a launch.

Massive efforts in shoring up the levees and careful manipulation of the barriers and dams prevented the Ganges from turning the lower portion of Bangladesh into a vast lagoon from Bogra to the sea. Still, whole towns had to be evacuated and necessary supplies shifted, difficult enough even kinetically in the apalling conditions. The force of the channelled flood did inundate Chittagong and coastal towns below it but not as disastrously as the pre-cog had predicted. Talent once again had reduced the impact of a major natural catastrophe.

Peter Reidinger, on the other hand, slept late into the next morning but when Don Usenik checked him over, he seemed none the worse for his major gestalt effort. But there was no doubt that his achievement had altered him: he neither floated nor essayed to walk: he strutted, chin high and a slightly superior smirk on his face.

'What was the saying? "Power tends to corrupt, and absolute power corrupts absolutely"?' Sascha asked Rhyssa, peevish in his frustration over the lost girl. 'He's insufferably smug this morning.'

Dorotea gave a snort. 'Don't overreact, Sascha! He's got a right to crow. Perfectly natural in anyone, especially a fourteen-year-old boy whose only available movement until recently was tonguing a switch or blinking his eyes at Tri-D to change channels. Pretty heady stuff to save a country. I scanned him pretty deeply at brunch while he was still sleepy and there's nothing in his mind that smacks of corruption.' She grinned. 'A bigger generator, more derring-do, and plenty of self-satisfaction.'

'Lighten up, Sascha-bear,' Rhyssa said, smiling encouragingly. 'Or don't you remember some of the tricks you and Boris pulled at that age?'

'A telepath can't get into quite the same sort of trouble a kinetic can,' Sascha said, grimly thinking of a girl fumbling in red-lit freightways. What was her Talent?

'Peter's got a fine sense of integrity, Sascha,' Rhyssa said. 'He's sensitive and sensible. We have to think *how* to bring him back to cruel reality after his minor miracle.'

'A diversion usually helps,' Dorotea remarked with a gleam in her eyes. 'I used that ploy often with my lads.' She wrinkled her nose and sighed. 'All too often.'

'It's going to have to be pretty good to distract him from the *Erasmus* ploy,' Sascha said with uncharacteristic gloom.

Johnny Greene: *Rhyssa, you guys called a G and H. Did it have something to do with the spectacular landing and take-off of the* Erasmus?

Just then one of the phones on Rhyssa's desk rang and, being nearest, Sascha picked it up.

'Yes, Dave? No, Rhyssa's got a call on her mind. Can I help?' Sascha listened for a moment and then replaced the handset, his face grimmer than ever.

Rhyssa: *Johnny, it's very complicated.*

Sascha: *You haven't heard the half yet, dear. Dave's got bad news for us, too. Ludmilla's claiming that we've perjured our immortal souls and deliberately falsified our register.*

Johnny: *Vernon's had all kinds of flak from NASA, the Space Authorities, the Padrugoi Authority . . .*

Rhyssa, fiercely: *Remind Vernon what kinetics are doing on the Indian subcontinent. Sascha, tell Dave that his public pitch is that, despite all odds, Talent has kept its covenant of disaster assistance. And both of you get up here as fast as you can. Particularly you, Greene.* To Dorotea, she said, 'I think Peter's immediate illusions of grandeur are going to be heavily dampened.'

Boris, entering the telepathic conference in a plaintive tone: *The Power Resources Commissioner is also demanding an explanation for a G and H that caused last night's brown-out and wiped out all his power reserves. The City Commish wants a lot of answers. Sascha, you heard anything?*

Sascha, savagely: *No!*

Vsevolod Gebrowski, urgently: *Rhyssa, Barchenka is out to get you! And there's nothing I can do to distract her. I told her G and H. Her telempaths have explained that this is a Talent emergency code which needs no elaboration. She does not accept that.*

Rhyssa: *You tell Ludmilla from me that she's had plenty of secrets she doesn't share, like early completion bonuses, as well as fines on delays. I don't question her: she doesn't question me.*

Vsevolod: *She does. I warn you.*

Dorotea, helpfully: *Amalda Vaden sees nothing untoward.*

Rhyssa: *Why did you bring her in on this?*

Dorotea: *I think we need all the reassurance we can get.*

Sascha: *Dave Lehardt, Gordie Havers and two top NASA generals are on the same heli with Johnny.*

Rhyssa remembered how Peter had looked after dealing so beautifully with the *Erasmus* crisis, replete with a sense of real satisfaction. She groaned. 'He's only fourteen.'

Carmen: *Sascha, I've got a fix on her.*

Sascha was out the door as if he'd 'ported. *Good luck!*

Rhyssa: *Right back at you!*

'Peter's far more mature than most fourteen-year-olds I've dealt with,' Dorotea mused. 'Including you,' and she favoured Rhyssa with an admonitory glance. 'And he's got all the right instincts for being Talented.'

27

Tirla did NOT like using the freight subways. The red light was off-putting. However, a cargo train servicing the automatic industrial complexes all along the riverside was the only way to get to the secreted holding place Yassim used to stash his merchandise, a train going into the J Industrial. Then she'd have to walk to the correct shunt. There were emergency alcoves all along the right-hand side at intervals so she could avoid being crushed by any passing cars. Dead unthinking things like tram trains didn't frighten her. Live unthinking things like some of Yassim's sassins and hitters did.

She waited a hundred metres from the yawning red-and-black mouth of the G shunt for nearly an hour before a J train arrived. It would have to slow as it reached the junction so it was no problem for an agile person to drop on to the first segment, catch a good hold of the flange and settle down for the trip. Flattened on the top, she was small enough to have several centimetres clearance from the ceiling curve of the tunnel. She reset her grip as the train picked up speed again, vibrating under her.

The fetid wind, a noxious combination of overheating metal, grease and the acrid stink of electricity, roared down across her body and she angled her face, and nose, down.

When the J train finally slowed with screeching brakes and made the left-hand turn into the cargo docks of its destination, she readied herself to jump off. She had to land clear of the coding machinery which opened and sorted out the goods to be delivered from the load. But she'd done it with no problem before and did it again, dropping lightly down and running up the narrow ledge by the various chutes and moving ramps which began the unloading.

When she came to the first curve in the narrow tunnel and the last of the red light was gone, she used her handlight, glad that she'd filched a fresh charge for it only the previous week. With this to show her way, she trotted along in a half-crouch until the muscles in her legs and back ached. She dropped to her knees, then rested a moment before continuing on.

Yassim kept his merchandise in a room hidden behind a false wall of barrels at the back of an automated factory. With her keen sense of self-preservation, Tirla had once taken the precaution of investigating his holding cell. The noise of the ill-tuned machinery drowned any screaming. Purchasers could view the children kept there on a closed circuit so they had to be reasonably cared for. Disabling the archaic scanner would be no problem for Tirla. There was also a ventilator hatch in the ceiling.

The kids had been in there nearly two days now. They'd be rested, feeling pretty good about their new conditions – a considerable improvement over squats. They might not want to leave. She wished she knew who Yassim had grabbed, then she could figure out how to stir them. Well, leave Yassim's hospitality long enough to force him to pay their parents proper compensation.

She reached her objective, loosened the appropriate

wires on the ancient scanner so that the static would snow the visual. Gaining entrance through the ventilator hatch, she was dangling from the ceiling to the excited clamour of voices.

'Hey there, cool it way down!' she ordered in Basic, repeating the message for those who might be slow to translate or need to be reassured. 'Yushi, pull a mattress down so I can land soft. It's a drop.'

While Yushi and his younger brother complied, she did a quick estimate. Yassim must be real pleased – twenty-four prime kids to sell. There were the remains of a recent meal which relieved her of one obstacle: the guards were not likely to check soon again even if the visuals were snowed. But it meant that the kids would have one less reason to *want* to leave such a cushy set-up. Why, there were only two kids per bunk. They all had new gear on, and the girls were tarted up like their mothers.

'Yassim take any of you yet?' Tirla asked, imbuing her voice with trembling urgency and widening her eyes with real fear. 'I got here as quick as I could!' she added, implying that maybe this hadn't been quick enough.

'Huh?' Yushi was good at taking orders but not at thinking.

'They took my sister,' and suddenly little Mirmalar's painted face screwed up into tears. 'They took her an hour ago. And she had on the prettiest things . . . orange and brown with gold, and new earrings . . .'

'Oh, I'm so sorry, Mirmalar. I did everything I could to get here in time,' and, as Tirla lavished sympathy on the now weeping seven-year-old, she could see panic beginning to spread to the others. She got madder than ever at Yassim. Ten years old was soon enough but not seven-and eight-year-old *babies*! What kind of pervs did he supply?

'Whaddya mean?' Tombi asked, his manner slightly aggressive: he was Bilala's eldest son. He was nibbling at a sweetbar – from the smears on his face, one of a series.

'We gotta git out of here,' Tirla said, releasing Mirmalar with a reassuring pat. 'This place has a baaaad stink.'

'It ain't got any at all,' Tombi replied, though he turned his head immediately to the rudimentary sanitary unit in the corner.

'They take Raina already, you all are in biiiiig trouble. I'm gonna get you all out. Now. Before more bad men come. You girls know what I mean,' and she waggled a stern finger at them. Tombi and Dick snickered. 'Same thing happens you guys, too, and you know you too small for that carry-on yet.'

Tombi stopped nibbling the sweet and looked apprehensively at the door.

'Sure they feed you up good. Sweet stuff coming out your ass, giving you a bellyache,' and she dismissed the remains of the recent meal. 'This place's good to keep you from crying much. You cry plenty soon and no-one hear you ever. Stick it up you good, every which way and that's the best of it. You know what your mothers tol' you. You know what to watch out for.'

She was scaring them, the younger ones were beginning to weep. She didn't want them so scared they couldn't move.

'Yushi, Dik, Tombi, help me move the bunks. We make a stepstair. There's room up there to stand.'

'I ain't goin',' Tombi said, glaring defiance at her. He was heavier and taller than Tirla but she kicked him so hard where it hurt that he doubled up.

'You're going 'cause your mother sent me to get you.' Tirla knew how scared Tombi was of Bilala. 'So you're coming. Now, move! And crying won't do no good so stop. You need your breath for climbing and walking.'

Just then the enormity of moving twenty-four scared and perhaps unwilling kids sank in. Tirla allowed herself only a moment to reflect on it. She had to do it, somehow, because otherwise she would have to leave G and she didn't want to. Linear G was home: she'd made herself a place there, she had a business, she was safe. Well, safe enough if she laid low for a while.

She chivvied and bullied all the kids up into the ventilation shaft, kicked the telltale bunk over – no-one would pay any attention to the crash – and replaced the grille. Someone might think that the kids were small enough to escape through it but where would twenty-four of them GO?

She led the way, grouping the kids so that there were bigger ones holding the hands of the smallest. She made Tombi rearguard to give him some responsibility and put Yushi in the middle. He'd always follow orders.

The unloading platform with its eerie red light gave her no comfort for she just knew that some of the kids wouldn't be able to manage the acrobatics needed to get on one of the drones. They could, of course, straddle tracks all the way back to G but it was a long, long walk and there'd be danger every time one of the speeding trains went by.

Well, maybe they could all make it back one station to I, and get lost in that industrial complex. It was safer than staying here in J. Or was it? Maybe she should just take the older ones who would be in more danger? No, they were all in danger because whoever was left could be made to tell who had rescued the others. Maybe if she put the younger ones in a safe place . . . and went back for help. Mirmalar's father adored his daughters. He'd do anything to save the remaining one. And Yushi's father was one of the strongest men in G.

The vibrations that told her a train was on the tracks beyond the shunt alerted her. How much time did they have before they'd know if its destination was J?

'Hide in the tunnels! Quickly! Stand on the ledges!' She took Mirmalar herself for the little girl was puckering up to cry again.

'Ah, there's never anyone on goods trains,' Tombi said.

'Yeah, and how d'you think Yassim's people get back and forth? Dumper cars are big enough to hold a dozen people.'

That shut Tombi up and lost him more face in the eyes of the other boys. Tirla shoved him towards a tunnel as she pulled Mirmalar after her.

The screech of distressed metal announced another goods train being shunted into J from the north. She hadn't counted on one quite so soon. She'd never get the kids on this one even if it was going in the right direction for them to get home. Unless there was a dumper car.

Something odd here – Tirla realized with a sinking feeling in her heart that there wasn't any cargo waiting on the platform to be loaded on to the arriving train. If one was coming in here, what was it coming *for*? Could Yassim have someone in the main dispatch office? Could he know that she had emptied his cage?

There were five cars on the double-ended train. Two looked like empty dumpers. Without waiting to question such great good fortune, Tirla hauled Mirmalar out on to the platform.

'Quickly. It won't stop long. We must all get in.'

They were, therefore, all on the platform when the train stopped. So none of them escaped the sleep gas that suddenly spewed out, catching them all in its mist. They fell like wilted flowers on to the plastic-coated loading surface.

28

'She's some kid,' Sascha said as he and Carmen carefully placed the object of their intensive search on a blanket pad and covered her. 'Christ, but she's a bit of a nothing.'

Carmen smiled slowly and turned the sleeping child's head to one side to see where the lock had been wrenched. Her other hand went halfway to touch it, but cancelled the gesture. 'She's nothing but skin and bones, Sascha. We'll have to improve her.'

Sascha frowned a bit, looking around to see the rest of the team attending the other children.

'We may not want to, Carmen. Boris and I have a feeling about this one.'

'So do I.' Carmen smiled at him with her most mysterious smile.

Boris: *Did you catch her?*

Yes, brother dear, her and them. She'd sprung the lot of 'em. She must have known exactly where to go. Sascha spoke aloud. 'I'm wondering how.'

Boris swore with frustration. He and Sascha had followed Carmen's lead and while Tirla was haranguing the kids, a team had been cautiously organized, aware that Yassim had 'interests' in Industrial J.

Boris: *What the hell possessed her?*

How about we find out where they were kept? Sascha asked.

Boris: *What good will that do now? He's not likely to reuse a holding area that's been breached.*

Sascha: *He would if he thought the kids had escaped on their own.*

Can you manage that? Boris's tone leaped to hopefulness.

Sascha: *I can try.*

Boris: *If you could, and rigged it, we'd have one more bolthole filed on Yassim. WHY did she do it?*

'Let's wake Tirla up,' Sascha said to Carmen, reaching for the oxygen. 'If she can show us where, we can get some good out of this operation.'

'We already have. We've found more than we hoped, haven't we?'

'Yes, and no. Bear with me, Carmen. There's a lot more than this valuable young girl at stake.'

Revived, Tirla went immediately on the defensive, wary, contained, her dark eyes darting around, taking in the unconscious bodies, noticing the medic who was daubing scrapes and bruises with nu-skin. Carmen offered a restorative drink – deliberately taking a long swallow of it before handing the cup to Tirla.

Sascha, lightly trying to get inside her mind, could only sense her fierce thirst. With great restraint, she took a very small sip, rolling it around in her mouth before drinking more deeply. Her bright, dark eyes challenged him. He sat down beside her in a relaxed position, hooking his hands around his knees and leaned back against the wall.

'Tirla,' and he saw her visible start of surprise. 'Oh, you're well known in G. And your bravery in releasing the children will be appreciated, and not just by their grieving families.'

'How could you find me here, with them?' She glanced enquiringly from him to Carmen and then saw the lock of her hair which Carmen still wore as a talisman. Involuntarily her hand started to the scabby patch on her head. Her shoulders sagged around her narrow chest, but any emotional reaction was carefully guarded in her mind. 'I've heard of people like you. You found me because you had my hair.'

'It's not witchcraft, Tirla,' Carmen said gently. She handed the strand back to the girl. 'I have a Talent which allows me to find lost people and things.'

'I wasn't lost.'

'No,' Sascha said conversationally, with an approving grin, 'but you found what was missing from Linear G.'

'He hadn't paid for them.'

Carmen gasped. 'You mean, once he's paid for them, he can have them again?'

'Sure. The parents live on subsistence. They need the money for extras only floaters can buy.'

Sascha was well aware that the girl's seeming callousness distressed Carmen who had seen the child in a much different light.

'Also puts you in well with your clients who were rather upset with your abrupt departure from the meeting,' he said amiably.

Eyes never leaving his, Tirla nodded once.

'They're all illegal, aren't they?'

Tirla's thin shoulders lifted in an indifferent shrug. 'Sure, so it's no credit out of your stash what happens to them.'

'Oh, no,' Carmen said, pained. 'They're alive. They have rights!'

Tirla gave her a quick look before resuming her scrutiny of Sascha. 'Illegals don't have rights.'

'Only their births are illegal, Tirla,' Sascha said. 'They're alive. They *have* the right to shelter, food, clothing, training and useful occupation. They do not

192

have the right to reproduce themselves.' Sascha was about to explain the legal anomaly in simple terms when he realized she understood perfectly. She was mature far in excess of her chronological age, and well conditioned to the realities of residential life. She was not a romantic like Carmen. 'But they do not deserve the occupations Yassim had in mind for them.' Sascha caught that instant spurt of fear, followed by the hardening of the young eyes, the flick of hatred. 'You don't like Yassim either.'

Again one of her indifferent shrugs.

'Would you by any chance help us disable him?'

She had been wary before, now she appeared to Sascha to coil in on herself. 'You're not LEO. Why do you want to queer Yassim?'

'No, I'm not LEO myself but we have a connection. Especially against someone like Yassim.'

Tirla gave a snort. 'Someone like Yassim buys himself off every time LEO collars him. He has powerful friends. LEO can never make it stick.'

'You wish that LEO could?'

She hesitated briefly, then gave him a candid look. 'There will always be men like Yassim, but I could do without *him* very much, thank you.'

Sascha would have given a great deal then to have been able to read her mind, to delve that reply. Tirla was far deeper than they'd had any reason to suspect. She sat there in front of him, cross-legged, completely composed, alert and . . . bargaining just as if she could get up and leave the scene at any moment.

'I want to get rid of Yassim, too, Tirla. Will you help me?'

A glimmer of a smile touched eye and mouth. 'What's in it for me?'

Carmen inhaled in surprise. Sascha sent the finder soothing thoughts, urging her to let him handle this his way. He flicked his fingers, fanning out crisp new floater notes.

'How did you manage that?' Her eyes widened in surprise and indignation.

Sascha did not often employ his kinetic ability but this trick was always effective. 'You help me now – and we must be quick about it before Yassim discovers his birds are flown – and these are yours.'

She eyed the notes. Casually she scratched about her ribs. Sascha kept his grin to himself, knowing that she was checking on the tied notes hidden there. She considered his offer with all the solemnity of a computer analyser.

'There's the little matter of your legality, Tirla,' he added gently.

Boris nudged him mentally. *C'mon, brother, we don't have time for amiable lipflap.*

Sascha: *On the contrary, we have all the time we need, brother. This is a strong personality and a deep one. I'm not rushing her.*

Boris: *Get on with it then.*

Tirla gave him a wide-eyed, bright smile. 'I am the only child of my mother.'

'But not her legally registered issue.'

'How would you know?'

Sascha touched her hair. 'That told us. But it is a small matter that can be quickly remedied.'

She regarded him from narrowed eyes. 'A small matter?' The twist of her lips was cynical. 'You must be in real good with LEO.' She considered, obliquely watching Carmen's expression. 'And I get to keep the floaters as well?' Her tone was ingenuous.

Sascha suppressed a grin. Legality would be the most valuable reward he could offer and still her fingers itched to relieve him of the money as well. Not that he had offered a large sum, not to a street-wise child like Tirla, but the amount would keep her in extras for several weeks.

'If we get a move on – now!' he said, drawing out his acceptance.

She spat in her right palm and held it out to him.

Without a second thought, he accepted the deal in archaic ritual. Her grip was unusually strong for the delicacy of her bones. Physical contact with the now conscious and vibrant personality startled Sascha with an odd jolt – a sense of pre-cognition that was gone too fast for him to pin it down.

What did she do to you, Sascha? Boris caught the edge of it.

Sascha: *I'm not sure, brother, but this one we handle very, very carefully. I want a special ID for Tirla when we get back. Hear me?*

To hear is to obey! Boris sounded facetious but Sascha was relieved by his compliance. *Keep the bargain, but I want this wild one under control.*

The deal struck, Tirla rose with lithe grace to her feet, her head barely coming to Sascha's belt. She tilted her head back, appraising him.

'So how do we disable Yassim?'

'Can you lead me to where he kept the children?' When she nodded, he went on. 'We want to fix it so that he will think the children escaped by themselves.'

Tirla snorted contemptuously. 'I had to frighten them to make them leave at all. Such things I had to tell them. Though it was all very true.'

'How would Yassim know that they were all docile? It need only look as if they had broken out. That one of the guards had been careless locking them in.'

She considered that. 'Yes, that could have happened. They had only just brought food.' She gave him a shrewdly appraising glance. 'You will have to crawl.' This amused her.

'Up this tunnel?'

She nodded, then looked over her shoulder for the first time betraying some apprehension. 'What happens to them?'

'They can sleep on until we get back,' he replied. 'We've got to move now.'

She led him into the tunnel and he did have to crawl, wondering how she had managed her initial trip until he saw the small circle of light which guided her steps. She had the courtesy not to go faster than he could follow. He had time to reflect on this amazing raw new Talent. She might not have an ounce of telepathy, or was perhaps too wary to let down the shield which had protected her so long in her young life, but there was no question that she possessed considerable Talent.

She halted at the end of the tunnel and turned to him. 'You wouldn't fit down the hatch I used, but if you know how to open that inspection door, that's an easier way to get to where *he* held the kids.'

Sascha took the scrambler from his belt and decoded the door. He opened it cautiously, aware of the hissing intake of her breath. He listened – on another level than Tirla who was kneeling at the lower half of the opening. The level and complexity of noise in the main industrial complex was appropriate for an automated factory. He 'heard' nothing human, but it was Tirla who first slid through the door. He opened it enough for his larger frame and closed it carefully behind them.

Though the industrial space was lit only by occasional green lights of operational machinery, Tirla moved confidently forward. Sascha would have passed right by the false wall but she went unerringly to the double drum and pinpointed the lock mechanism with her pencil light. She glanced questioningly at him.

'Electronic, I hope?' he murmured and she nodded.

He scrambled the circuit and the door swung back to reveal the deserted room, the overturned bunk bed, the table with the empty food packages. She pulled the door shut behind them, shooting him a disapproving look for his careless entry.

'How did you get them out?'

She pointed to the darker square of the grille in the ceiling.

'Good work.' He righted the bunk bed, pushed it back into its former position, managing to stick a miniscule device on the wall behind it. Then he looked about the place. It stank of many things, not all tangible. 'I think you'd better mastermind this escape, Tirla. Make it look like a kid had done it.'

Tirla's upper lip curled in derision. 'None of them would have!'

'Point taken, but for Yassim's benefit it should *seem* so.'

With her eyes half veiled, Tirla considered the problem. Sascha waited patiently, wishing he could have been in her head, noting her thought processes.

'OK,' and she was across the room to the corner where pieces of clothing had been discarded. Deliberately she tore strips from several garments, her hands clever in finding the break in a hem or seam that would rip. 'There'll be a fight . . . ' She hauled mattress pads off two of the lower bunks, the soiled blankets off the upper ones. She went back to the corner and, using a shirt, gathered up some of the containers and the remaining food before she knocked over the makeshift table. 'Now, we open the door just enough to let kids out, and start leaving trails. Come out, I'll just close the door over a bit. Now, you drop stuff halfway to that wall. Then circle around. I'm going this way. I'll meet you at the maintenance door.'

He did as she directed and they met again in the chucking, clanking dark of the automated manufactory.

'Lock it?' Sascha held the door ajar.

'Yes.'

'But how will Yassim know how they got out?'

'They're not there, are they? The cage door is open.' Sascha saw her shrug and felt, rather than saw, her malicious smile. 'Why should I make it easy for him?'

By the time they reached the loading dock, Sascha's muscles were protesting their abuse. The team had loaded the children into the cars and the dock was now full of cargo to be transshiped.

'You cut that fine, Sascha,' the team leader told him. 'There'll be a goods train through here in two minutes. We're not supposed to disrupt the service.'

Tirla tugged imperiously at his sleeve. 'My floaters.'

With one hand he passed them to her, with the other he grabbed her wrist. 'No tricks now. There's more business we can do together. We'll discuss it back in G.'

Sascha didn't know whether it was her surprise that allowed him to capture her or if she willingly co-operated with him. But she entered the car ahead of him as he tried to keep his grip from breaking fragile bones.

Go! he told the driver and the starting pressure of the special train pushed him against the padded end of his car.

'Are you taking us all to G?' Her tone was casual.

'That's what you wanted, wasn't it? To get the kids back to G.'

'I kept our bargain.' Now her voice held an element of antagonism.

'So will I. Back at G. Then we deal again.'

She was silent for a long time, thinking that over.

29

Peter tried to follow the Tri-D meteorologists's report on the latest freak weather conditions that seemed world-wide, Bangladesh being the worst example. It was difficult to concentrate when he felt 'problem' hovering in the air. He *knew* he'd done nothing wrong: in fact, he knew that he'd done something most extraordinary, about which he felt very good indeed. But it was hard not to be. He could also sense the nebulous anxiety emanating from Rhyssa, Dorotea and Sascha. He shouldn't have asked Dorotea about a bigger generator. The moment the words were out of his mouth, he knew it was the wrong time. But he'd *proved* what he could do with enough power to increase the gestalt and that 4.5 felt 'puny' kid's stuff now.

Kid's stuff! Peter grinned to himself and gave the 4.5 a little shove: it whined obediently. Like a dog. And who was he kidding? He was still only a fourteen-year-old boy. He had already absorbed enough Talent discipline, seen enough examples of the sort of people Talents were to realize that he'd rushed the gate. You don't climb mountains when you can't walk. Rhyssa, Sascha and Dorotea had supported him throughout the entire *Erasmus* incident, ready to help him, ready to keep him from burning himself out. And he hadn't. But had it been *because* they had been right there to protect him? Think about *that*, Petey boy, and get your swelled head back to normal. There are a lot of things you *can't* do right yet.

He poured himself another glass of orange juice and brought it to the living room as the broadcaster announced that once again supply shuttles for Padrugoi had been grounded by weather conditions. The screen depicted the rank of four perpendicular space vehicles, locked into their gantries, waiting for lift-off conditions with urgently needed material so that this first World Project would be finished on time.

Talents were helping to do that, Peter thought with a little thrill of corporate pride. He had just started wondering how big a generator he'd need to send a shuttle safely through the foul weather when the programme switched to coverage of the flooding in Bangladesh. There were no scenes *showing* the Talents at work although teams of doctors and rescue workers were filmed rushing about. There'd also been no mention of exactly how the *Erasmus* had landed so safely at Dacca. He hadn't really *expected* to be mentioned publicly. But you'd think there'd be some comment that Talents were risking their lives in the appalling monsoon conditions. What they'd *done* was shown, right enough, but that somehow didn't seem fair.

Rhyssa and Dorotea were always subtly mentioning how important it was not to rub Talent into people's noses. People resented differences. Talent must always be discreet. The way his mother looked at him had demonstrated *that*! Peter grimaced. His own mother was scared of him now. When he'd been totally helpless, she's been so good about coming to see him, hugging him, kissing him, always bringing him something: a fax clip about his favourite ball team, a couple of her special cookies, a few flowers, so natural. Now when she visited, she wouldn't hug him and she sat bolt upright in the chair and tried not to look at him when he wanted so much to show her what Talent allowed him to do.

When Mum was here, he redoubled his efforts to appear to *walk* normally and *carry* things properly so it wouldn't freak her out. How often had she said she prayed every night to see Petey on his feet and walking around. And she never *looked* at him now. She never once mentioned his ball team. Not that he'd ever play sandlot baseball again . . . Then Peter grinned, thinking what homers he could whack, how fast he'd run the bases. Maybe now he could be the pitcher he'd always wanted to be . . . His fast ball would be *something else*. Even if he only used the 4.5!

But he'd gone past that sort of *ordinary* thing, hadn't he? If you can zap shuttles about like gameboard pieces, *ordinary* accomplishments didn't satisfy.

He drank his orange juice. Not *all* ordinary things, though. Some very ordinary and extremely homely actions – like getting himself an orange juice when he felt thirsty for it – were, in a special way, far more important than what he'd done with the *Erasmus*.

He sent the empty glass back to the kitchen, rinsed it out and put it upside down on the drain board.

You had to keep things in perspective. It WAS more important to have the freedom to do *little* things and the *option* to do bigger ones. But, jeez, it had been a wonderful feeling to have all that power and do something no-one else could have done with it . . . just when help was needed.

The Tri-D was showing floodwater flowing obediently away from a small town and its surrounding fields. The sandbags and barriers along its torrent would seem to be containing it but Peter could now recognize the subtle signs of kinetic force. He wondered which Talent was at work. Rick Hobson? Mr Baden? Now, if he'd had access to a generator, he'd've been able to do that. He settled down to learn what he could about flood control from the programme. Next time he'd be ready to help. The 4.5 k.p.m. was portable, wasn't it?

Rhyssa: Peter, would you come up to my office please?

Sure! He leaned briefly into the generator and sped through the air, in through the front door, slowing to manoeuvre the staircase, and got his feet to the ground as he reached the carpeted hallway leading to Rhyssa's office. No effort!

Show off. Rhyssa stood by her office door but she was smiling. 'We don't have any mountains for you to move today but there's trouble in the wind, dear boy, there's trouble in the wind.'

Peter stumbled in his forward motion and corrected himself. *Trouble? Why? We didn't do anything* wrong!

Her touch reassured him, as it always did. Dorotea was great: she treated him casually as she would any of her grandchildren and that relaxed attitude made many things easier for him. But Rhyssa was different: her mind had so much depth, not that he'd disobeyed the prime rule of mental privacy: he could sense the depth and purity that was there. She was also the most beautiful woman Peter had ever seen, on or off the Tri-D. And she was so *good*! Everything about her was shining and brilliant. She made him feel whole and strong.

'We did something a shade too right,' Rhyssa said, 'and we have not been quite as discreet as we should have been.'

Momentarily afraid, he reached out to see exactly what they'd done wrong.

Peter!

'Sorry.'

Rhyssa, more fiercely than Peter had ever *heard* her: *Damn that Barchenka woman!*

'Was I *supposed* to hear that?' Peter was confused.

'Yes, and double damn Barchenka!' Rhyssa said aloud

and waved him on through to her office, closing the door behind them.

He halted, sensing the aura of crisis. Dorotea, who was rarely perturbed, was brushing imaginary threads from her slacks. Things must really be bad. He zigged sideways, aware that Rhyssa just missed bumping into him.

Dorotea: *Well done, Peter!*

'This is a strategy council, Peter,' Rhyssa said, gesturing for him to sit as she resumed her chair in the tower bay window.

Peter floated over to the comfortable seat, grateful for its automatically adjusted support.

'Don't ever forget just how proud we all are of you,' and Rhyssa's gesture included the entire Centre. 'You've added a brand new dimension to Talent.' She gave him an impish smile. 'And reminded this Centre's Director not to get too complacent.'

Without violating etiquette, Peter could hear what she wasn't saying aloud. Talent was very happy: the unTalented were not.

Dorotea: *The unTalented always resist a new Talent which we haven't carefully led them to expect. In this instance, you!*

Rhyssa: *We don't do something right, Peter, without doing something wrong!* Peter sensed a second qualification behind the thought and remembered his manners.

Dorotea: *AND we've got to figure out how to improve our testing methods!* She cleared her throat in a businesslike manner. Then winked at Peter.

He thought, very privately to himself, that something bad was definitely about to happen but they loved and approved of him and that was all that mattered to him.

'If your main desire right now,' and Rhyssa smiled with that special twinkle in her eye which she saved for Peter, 'is to have the biggest generator on the planet at your disposal,' and Peter flushed, looking hard at his bony knees (that wasn't what he'd asked Dorotea – exactly), 'the main desire of half the industries on Earth AND in

Space, is to have you using theirs, and theirs alone.'

Space? He could get into Space? He looked up in surprise, staring at her. She didn't mean *his* way.

'How do they know about me?' He felt suddenly very defenceless. His father was always talking about the Managers working a man to death with no consideration for him as a human being, only how productive he was, a cipher in a gigantic programme.

'They don't know it's *you*,' Dorotea said.

'That's the problem,' Rhyssa went on.

'Why?' Peter asked, thinking of *big* generators.

'Candidly,' Dorotea said, 'you're fourteen, you're only just beginning to understand your Talent and premature exposure could . . .'

'Burn me out,' Peter finished for her, though privately he didn't think he *could* burn out – if he had the right power source for anything he wanted to shift. 'But I didn't burn out . . .'

'Without in the least diminishing your achievement, Peter, we were closely monitoring you the other night,' Rhyssa went on. 'What *they* have in mind for you is another can of worms altogether. Speaking as Centre Director, it has never been the policy of the Centres to assign trainees even part-time work until they're at least eighteen.'

'Even I . . .' Dorotea put in, her hand gracefully sweeping her chest, 'wasn't permitted to do much until I was eighteen!' She made a face. 'As a child, I thought I was just playing a game, guessing which ones in the room could hear me . . . People who *thought* they might be Talented.' She shot Peter an image of herself as a five year old, prettily dressed – and her early beauty was still apparent in her face and manner – walking through the Centre's crowded reception area.

'But I've *proved* what I can do,' Peter said. 'And I was the only one who could land the *Erasmus*.'

'The situation is not about right or wrong, Peter,'

Rhyssa said, leaning forward to him, a sad expression in her eyes and face, 'or even a moral obligation to reduce suffering and mitigate disaster.' Then she opened her mind so he could directly assess the current problem.

Peter had known, of course, that the parapsychic Centres had had to send the best kinetics to Padrugoi to help complete the Station on time. He hadn't realized all the undercurrents beneath the carefully contrived public image of Padrugoi, much less the machinations of Ludmilla Barchenka who forced the capitulation of Centres, ruthlessly stripping kinetics in what was basically a face-saving operation. He fumed when he *saw* that this Barchenka woman was threatening *his* Rhyssa with all kinds of offences when it was now patently clear to him that Barchenka was at fault. And he was part of the problem. No, at the moment, he was ALL of the problem because Barchenka was out to add him to her force of Talent.

'And I used to think working on the Station would be the most special thing you could do.' It just wasn't fair!

'No, not fair, Peter,' Rhyssa replied, 'but Talent recognizes that completing the Station is far more important than individual personal considerations. Completing it on time is obviously Ludmilla's personal goal. I can't deny her that, only her means of achieving it, since by her achievement, mankind has made another giant step to the stars. Don't be deflected too much by the skeletons in the space lockers. There's been no major forward progress in all of human history that has not been accompanied by some problems . . . '

'Like letting people float out into Space and die because rescue would put her behind schedule?' Peter was aghast.

'That's been taken care of,' Dorotea reminded him.

'By Talents, and now she thinks she can conscript me?' Peter was so agitated that he floated above the chair.

Dorotea, prosaically: *You're drifting, dear.*

Peter settled down. *Well, I just won't work for a person like her. And you're not going to ask me to!*

'Indeed and we're not,' Rhyssa assured him, 'but first,' and then she grinned, her eyes twinkling, 'we have to prove to *them* that you're *you*! We've been trying very hard to keep you sheltered until you've more control . . .'

How much control do I need if I can move a shuttle about the world?

'Peter!' Despite the sharpness in her voice, Peter knew that Rhyssa was amused by his outrage, proud of his achievement, concerned for his future. He subsided. 'Thank you. Now, we were warned to expect visitors of high rank and great prestige. We wanted to brief you since you are the cat we are about to let out of the bag.'

'I rather think he's the cat among the pigeons,' Dorotea said with a sarcastic snort.

'Pigeons? War hawks, Dorotea,' Rhyssa corrected, settling into her chair, as she capped the metaphor. Then, although the office was shielded to mental intrusions, they all heard the unmistakeable thrunking of a big helicopter landing on the X outside Henner House. 'Peter, don't let the fuss get to you. There's bound to be some bruised feelings and outraged sensibilities. You just pay them no heed!'

Just now he couldn't help but heed the fine but controlled aura of apprehension. They were worried. About him! FOR him.

Ragnar's voice came through on the intercom. He was Duty Officer and twenty years in the Centre made him impervious to rank and prestige. 'Rhyssa, there's a bunch here to see you. Do I send 'em up?'

'Yes, I'm expecting them, Ragnar.'

His 'humph' came over the speaker and Peter noticed Rhyssa's little smile. He also noticed that she was nervously running the stylus through her fingers. Dorotea sat even straighter in her chair and managed to look not only larger and more imposing but very . . . very queenly.

There was a polite knock on the door and Rhyssa pressed the release button. The first man in the room was a telepath, Peter realized, and he was directing tight private warnings at Rhyssa. The second man, very tall, thin and sort of wise, looked directly at Peter and nodded. He *knew* who Peter was even if Peter didn't know him. He was also a telepath.

Peter knew the third man, Dave Lehardt, who immediately moved to stand by Rhyssa's desk, facing the others as they filed in. He made his partisanship very clear. He exchanged a glance with Rhyssa and gave an almost imperceptible nod of his head. She had a slight smile on her face now and Peter sensed that she was very glad to have Dave Lehardt so close by. But Dave Lehardt wasn't a Talent, Peter knew, and was surprised by the intimate exchange. Dorotea had said that he was a public relations expert for Talents and the Centres.

The next six men to enter were obviously important people, four were in uniform and only one of them was Talented. He appeared very nervous and kept looking from Rhyssa to Dorotea. The last man to enter made Peter shudder. He gawped at Rhyssa in a fashion that made Peter very uneasy: his eyes, his manner made Peter wonder if he was one of those perverts his mother used to warn him about.

As Rhyssa asked them all to be seated, Peter picked up names: Vernon Altenbach who was Secretary of Space, the Russian officer was General Shevchenko, Padrugoi Liaison Official and, even with the shield he wore, he was bristling with aggression. The telempath was Andrei Grushkov and Peter felt sorry for him: he had to be truthful to his employer, the General, but he felt obscurely that he was betraying Talent. There were two NASA officers, a General and a Colonel and this pervert was the world famous Josephson Junction specialist, and a Malaysian Prince besides, who did such fantastic programming of air and Space traffic. Peter didn't like him any better once he knew he was such a genius, not when the man kept ogling Rhyssa in that sloppy way. The man who came in first was Colonel John Greene and Peter watched in some awe as the most successful EtoP pilot of the early days of the Padrugoi Project placed a chair next to him, Peter Reidinger. And smiled quite pleasantly at him. Colonel Greene seemed to be the only one who was smiling. Even Judge Havers looked solemn.

'It would be pointless for me to deny that I was aware of the reason for your visit. Shall I call up the Eastern Centre Register for you to check on our memberships?' Rhyssa asked composedly. She placed her fingers over the keyboard.

Peter regarded her with pride. She even had a little smile on her face. And that pervert kept smarming at her.

The Russian General cleared his throat. 'We have already seen it, Madame. But we believe that you have not honestly declared your full kinetic strength.' He crooked his head to see his telempath's face.

'Andrei can certainly assure you that our declaration is honest and complete. We have nothing to hide. No Talent does.'

'Andrei has also assured me, Madame Owen,' the General continued ponderously, 'that no kinetic anywhere could have successfully landed the *Erasmus* . . . not even the twenty-two on board her . . . OR,' and he paused dramatically, 'assisted its take-off from the Dacca field in the weather conditions prevailing that day.' His chest seemed to deflate slightly once he had delivered his accusation.

'It was me,' Peter said. He wanted to get this all over with, and get that smarmy-faced man out of the same room with his Rhyssa. 'I mean, it was I.'

The stunned silence was worse than noisy disclaimers.

Then Colonel Greene started to chuckle and then Dave Lehardt began to laugh. He also winked approvingly at Peter. Not one of the other visitors appeared to be the least bit amused.

'And tell me just how, young man,' Vernon Altenbach asked – Peter knew he didn't believe him – 'you accomplished such a feat?'

Rhyssa, laughter rippling her tone: *Stick to the facts, man, the facts.*

'Well, the *Erasmus* needed help landing at Dacca because the kinetics *had* to be there to reduce the disaster potential. So Rhyssa called a G and H – that's a Talent Mayday – and I got to use the generators at the East Side Power Station,' Peter replied. He kept his face straight but he was enjoying the incredulity of his audience: the non-Talented, that is. The Russian telempath was admiring and Peter sat himself even straighter in the chair.

Dorotea: *Well said, Peter!*

Gordon Havers: *In times of doubt, honesty is the best policy.*

Johnny Greene: *You better believe it because they're not!* Unobtrusively, he patted Peter's knee.

'You have, I must assume, a kinetic Talent?' Vernon continued.

'Yes, sir. I'm in training as a kinetic, but I can't do as much as I'd like because the people who should be training me are all up on the Station.'

Rhyssa: *Don't spread it on too thick, Peter.*

Johnny: *Nonsense. They deserve that kick in the shins.*

'How much training have you had then?' the General wanted to know.

'Well, Rhyssa and Dorotea do the best they can but they're telepaths . . .'

Rhyssa dryly: *Thank you!*

Gordon: *He's sticking to the truth.*

' . . . Initially Rick Hobson was helping me, but we'd

only just got past the necessary stuff when he got conscripted to the Station . . .'

'Talents were NOT conscripted,' General Shevchenko objected forcefully. 'They volunteered to assist in the completion of the first great World Project.

Peter gave a contemptuous little snort. 'If you're not given a choice, you've been conscripted.'

'And you expect us to believe that a frail boy manipulated the *Erasmus*?' Prince Phanibal Shimaz shot out of his chair and stood belligerently in front of Peter, shaking his finger at him. 'I, Phanibal Shimaz, Prince of Malaysia West, know that this would have been impossible from such a source! Tell us the truth, little boy!' and he made the adjective pejorative.

'He IS telling the truth,' Johnny Greene said, rising to his feet to look down at the much shorter Prince. Dave Lehardt and Rhyssa shot to their feet with angry exclamations for Prince Phanibal's behaviour.

'As Andrei confirms to me,' General Shevchenko said in a hard voice. 'You exceed your authority, Your Highness.'

'And I shall prove it,' Peter added, glaring back at this Prince. Just because he could do games with Josephson Junctions and traffic flow patterns that no-one else could do didn't make him an authority on Talent. And he was a coward for he wore a metal head shield. Almost an insult in itself. 'Look!' And Peter raised his right arm, wishing he could just make his fingers point, but they wouldn't.

Actually it was easy enough with power diverted from the Centre's equipment to raise and hold the big helicopter just outside Rhyssa's bay window so that all could see it. And see that the huge rotor blades moved idly in the breeze of its ascent.

'Do be careful with it, Peter,' Johnny Greene said amiably, one of the few in the room enjoying the moment, 'it's Government property.'

'I'm always careful, Colonel Greene,' Peter replied,

feeling the euphoria of potency. He was almost sorry that he couldn't think of an even more convincing demonstration of his kinetic Talent. Dorotea was glaring at him significantly in her enough-is-enough look. He returned the vehicle gently to the ground.

'How old are you, Peter?' Colonel Greene asked him, just as if they were the only ones in the room.

'I was fourteen on the eighth of September.'

'And you get about now yourself under your own power? the Colonel enquired and Peter could see in his eyes that the man *knew* the extent of his handicap. 'I was that much . . . ' and his fingers measured a two centimetre gap, ' . . . away from paraplegia myself after mission number twenty-one.'

That was when Peter realized that Colonel Greene was very much on their side and making it very clear to everyone else that Peter's Talent was off-limits.

'I've learned how to compensate just fine,' Peter replied and the Colonel's eyes said that was the right answer to make. 'Rick Hobson really helped me. We were just beginning to go on to tougher things when he had to go to Padrugoi.'

'So you've been Rhyssa's skeleton crew? All by yourself?' Colonel Greene chuckled and looked across at the Secretary of Space.

'I'm not nearly as much of a skeleton as I used to be,' Peter extended his arms and legs, dispassionately regarding them. 'I'll get some muscle on them yet. I've got to build slowly, you see, and it takes time.'

Colonel Greene rose. 'I think that's the answer, gentlemen. It takes time to build muscle, any kind of muscle, and you build slowly to last longer.'

'Now wait just a moment here,' and Prince Phanibal recovered from the surprise and shock he had had, 'that is not the answer I came to find. You have indeed concealed from the world a kinetic Talent of demonstrated ability. He can take the place of those at Bangladesh . . . ' He

211

leaned across Rhyssa's desk and Peter saw her flinch backwards away from such a menacing posture.

Peter couldn't stand it. Kinetically, he dragged Prince Phanibal backwards from Rhyssa, the Prince's face set in a paralysed rictus of amazement. The door which opened to allow his exit closed firmly behind him.

'Peter!' Rhyssa could not quite disguise her relief or her consternation at this breach of courtesy.

'He's got no right to threaten you, Rhyssa! No right at all!'

Dorotea: *Bravo, Peter, though I shouldn't encourage you!*

'Now see here, young man,' Shevchenko took one step towards Peter and stopped, blinking in astonishment, as he could not continue moving forward.

'That's enough, Peter,' Rhyssa said with appropriate severity. *That was rather clever of you, dear, even if you wouldn't realize it.* #Image of Rhyssa suppressing laughter.# 'The General will not intimidate you any further. General, I think Peter has inadvertently displayed another cogent reason why the Centre is unwilling to utilize his unique abilities except in a crisis. At fourteen, he does not always abide by the courtesies that a more mature personality has learned.'

'I demand that the boy apologize to His Highness Prince Phanibal immediately.'

'You may demand all you wish, General,' Rhyssa said sharply, 'but I don't even know why a traffic Manager, royal or not, was included in this gathering.' *Odious little man!*

'Engineer Barchenka insisted on his inclusion,' Vernon Altenbach remarked, attempting some diplomacy.

'I insist that he be *excluded* from any future meetings involving the Centre or myself.'

Peter: *He's a slimeball!*

Johnny and Gordon Havers together: *Where did you stash him?*

Peter: *He's in the helicopter and he can't seem to get*

212

the seat buckle undone. Peter couldn't help grinning. *I won't let him.*

Johnny: *Buckle down, Winsockie, buckle down!*

Dorotea: *I didn't think anyone in your generation knew that old song.*

'Now, gentlemen, you have, I trust, seen to your own satisfaction that we have only been protecting young Peter, not deliberately denying the Platform his Talent. I'm sorry that you had a long trip for nothing,' Rhyssa said, coming around her desk to shake hands with Andrei Grushkov. 'However, when Peter is fully trained and we have a better understanding of the parameters of his potential, we are of course obliged to let prospective employers bid for his contractual services.'

Vernon Altenbach helped ease the disgruntled Russian General out the door, the NASA Colonel and the telempath assisting. But the others lingered until the first group had entered the elevator.

'Ms Owen,' the General began, 'is it possible, given the boy's display of incredible ability, that he could . . . from time to time, that is . . . Well, we do have a serious crisis right now . . .'

'What kind?' Rhyssa asked in an unencouraging tone.

'NASA's supply schedule is at a standstill with the current world–wide weather conditions . . .'

Peter zoomed out of his chair, hovering between Rhyssa and the General. *Please consider it, Rhyssa. Working for NASA wouldn't be the same as working for Barchenka, would it? But it would be almost as good as being in Space.* He exerted all his mind's pressure against hers, begging her consideration. He felt her stern resolve not to exploit him.

Johnny: *It's something to consider, Rhyssa, though we won't be pushy about it. If you say no, we'll go quietly. But it would gall me personally, and professionally, to have Barchenka saying that the Americans couldn't meet their contractual obligations.* He cocked his head at Rhyssa, grinning wryly.

Peter could *feel* Rhyssa beginning to relent.

Dorotea: *Consider it a training diversion, Rhyssa.*

Rhyssa: *But that's it! He's had hardly any training!*

Johnny; *Repetition hones skills, gal, and it sure reduces the glamour quotient.*

Peter didn't understand that but felt Dorotea's approval become more urgent. He sensed that Rhyssa was now seriously considering the suggestion.

'Look,' Johnny said aloud, 'this is so important that Vernon would actually get himself another minder for a few weeks. I know all the technical data that Peter needs to understand if he's flinging shuttles about the stratosphere. Hell, I'd get a vicarious thrill out of it myself, getting back into Space by proxy. And if Peter's working for NASA, Barchenka can't say Talent has been obstructing Padrugoi's timely completion.'

'I know it appears that it's always us who compromise,' Gordon Havers said, entering the discussion, 'but we put a wedge in her works if suddenly we insure delivery of the material she needs.'

'You'd have to go with Peter, Rhyssa. I'm no longer up to that sort of sustained effort,' Dorotea said. 'Once Sascha's sorted out the present crisis at Linear G, he's well able to sit in your chair a while but you'd be more use to Peter than either of us would. *One* of us has to monitor him during the gestalts. I can see you squirming to go, Peter Reidinger. Is it what you really want? Will you behave like a mature Talent?'

Peter managed to curl his fingers around Rhyssa's.

'I'll behave. I'll do just as I'm told. I promise! And I'd learn a lot.'

'You'd call the moves, Rhyssa,' Johnny Greene said.

'I don't think we have any choice in this either,' Rhyssa said and Peter leaned against her, wishing for her not to sound so defeated. She looked down at him and cupped his head with one hand, smiling tenderly at him. 'I'm not defeated, Peter dear, but I dislike intensely being left with no options.'

'Think of the options that you've cancelled,' Johnny Greene said with a malicious note in his voice as he lifted his middle finger skywards.

'Put like that,' Gordie said, grinning, 'we're one up on Barchenka.'

Rhyssa turned to Dave Lehardt, her expression severe. 'And you keep Peter's name out of the 'casts and the fax.'

'Your skeleton crew at work again?' Dave asked, pretending to ward off an attack.

' "Dem bones, dem bones, dem dry bones, and hear the word of the Lord!" ' sang Johnny Greene, doing an intricate breakdance step.

30

The blond man had an air about him that fascinated Tirla.
She had never had much to do with Talents – as people
called them – and she surreptitiously crossed her wrists.
She had heard these folk discussed in the residential often
enough, in fearful awed whispers, but she hadn't believed
half the powers ascribed to them: finders of persons and
things, seers of souls, readers of secrets, prophets of future
things, movers of mountains.

She stole a look at him, head leaned back against the
padded wall, eyes closed and she dared to observe him
more closely. So, she noticed the quick flow of facial
muscles, as if he were having an argument in his head.
His jaw tightened in anger and his lips thinned. He should
be pleased with his day's work, Tirla thought. She was
startled then, when his mouth relaxed into a half smile.
A clever sort of smile and his eyebrows twitched. Had he
won the argument in his head? A strange man though he
appeared no different from others.

He wasn't LEO, and yet he was and she didn't quite
know where he fitted in, nor how he and his teams had

appeared so timely at the J shunt. Especially when she had just realized the difficulty of cajoling scared whiney brats like Tombi into riding cargo pods back to G. Without this rescue, Yassim's ladrones would surely have recaptured them, herself included. She shuddered.

So they had been rescued from Yassim. But not from Authority. She wanted no part of Authority. They had too many conflicting rules and regulations and silly restrictions that only begged to be ignored or evaded. She didn't – quite – believe that he'd be able to produce any ID, no matter how well he seemed in with the LEOs. The prospect briefly dazzled her, to the point where she could feel the narrow plastic strip knocking against her wrist bone.

No matter! She had clean floaters: more than she needed for the tieds she had been supposed to launder for *him*. So she was well ahead in this game. The matter of the hot tieds briefly bothered her, but if Yassim was looking for kids, she didn't want him looking at her. And it was very likely that the LEOs could not collar Yassim. So, morally, she could hide the tieds for a while and discreetly exchange them, especially if Yassim was put out of circulation, over the next several months. This was the biggest hit she had ever made.

But – she was uneasy. She was trapped in the closed cargo pod and she didn't really know where they were going, though she had been keeping mental count of the rail junctions. He could just as easily leave her off at the hostel with the others. Who'd believe that she had an arrangement with him? The train began to decrease speed and Tirla, with a spurt of dread anticipation, waited for the shunt connect. They were going to the G platform. She was both comforted and concerned.

'Where are we now?'

Sascha opened his eyes and she saw that they were an unusual shade of light blue. Amusement flickered from them. 'You know we're at G. So now we return the lost children to their grieving parents. That is important to you, isn't it, Tirla? That Bilala, Zaveta, Pilau, and especially Mirda Khan and Mama Bobchik, know that you helped retrieve their lost ones.'

Now how could he know that? How much did he know about Tirla? Why was he playing her along this way? This one was sharp indeed. What sort of a scam was he running? Not all of this action had to do with that perv Yassim.

She refused to be drawn by what could just be a shrewd guess on his part. LEOs were not above putting surveillance on meetings, even a silly RIG with that lama-shaman. Perhaps there had been 'eyes' on her clients, although why such a gaggle of silly women – unless it had to do with selling kids – would be 'eyed', she didn't know. Anyway, no-one had been there to deal kids – most were too young yet. They had all been looking for 'messages' and 'salvations'. Yet this Sascha identified her clients. He had known that Mirda Khan and Mama Bobchik were especially important. Then she found an answer.

'It just pays to be a good neighbour.'

'Oh, you have definitely been a good neighbour today, Tirla. And a very good citizen!'

Now he laughed softly, throwing his head back and showing large white even teeth. It would be a very nice laugh, Tirla thought, if it didn't worry her that he was laughing at all. Perversely she liked him, for his strong grip and his droll words but she didn't trust him any further than she could have thrown Bulbar.

She gave him a quick stare for calling her 'citizen'. Citizens lived across the river in the beautiful hives, luxury cones, platforms and complexes, not in linears.

'Trust me, Tirla?' His eyes were not laughing, nor was his mouth, and his voice was gentle and entreating.

'I have no reason to.'

'If I give you one?'

218

She snorted scornfully. Just then the train braked to an easy stop and the lids of the pods opened. There were people standing there, ready to lift out the unconscious children. A slim woman in a LEO uniform standing at the edge of the platform spotted Sascha and thrust a narrow plastic case at him.

'Here's a reason, Tirla.' Sascha showed her the ID bracelet in the case. He took advantage of her surprise and clasped it around her wrist.

She stared at it, holding her arm away from her, trying to absorb the significance of having a legal identity and then the slowly dawning knowledge that the bracelet was not banded in the usual residential colours. Green banding meant you could travel between linears but what did the gold and black stripes mean?

'You are now legal, Tirla.'

Just then the four freight elevators reached the cargo level. A mass of women flowed out on to the platform, raising loud lamentations when they saw limp bodies on medipads. Sascha drew Tirla and Carmen to one side as Public Health personnel circulated, establishing the parentage of those Tirla had rescued.

'What happens to them?' Tirla asked. This was not what she had had in mind when she set out on her mad venture. Parents would not be pleased that their children were now in the hands of Authority. Nor would they profit as she had intended. She had an ID bracelet and more credit than she had ever possessed in her life. And what good did it do her? The tenuous position she had carved for herself, her clients, her means of supporting herself were gone: her future was as bleak as that of the children she had saved from Yassim.

A tall young man, very handsome of face, slender of build, and wearing a LEO uniform, planted himself squarely in front of the Sascha person and saluted.

'What do you wish me to tell the women, sir?' he asked.

'That Tirla here,' and Sascha moved her to stand in front of him, his hands lightly – and, she felt, kindly – on her shoulders, 'found where Yassim had hidden their children. She was leading them back home, to their mothers and fathers, when we, also searching, came upon them.'

In a voice that penetrated the tumult of wailing women, Ranjit rattled off the announcement in the required languages – a task which made Tirla restless under Sascha's hands. As each of the linguistic groups understood, they fell to whispering among themselves. When Ranjit had finished, Mirda Khan and Mama Bobchik waded forward, their expressions grim. Sascha felt Tirla's narrow shoulders tense. Surreptitiously she shielded her brand new ID bracelet by moving her arm slightly behind her.

'And the children?' Mirda Khan demanded in Basic, jutting her pointed chin out. She stared pointedly at Tirla, not Ranjit or Sascha.

'The records have been checked,' Sascha said, his voice diplomatically apologetic. 'Their births were illegal.'

His phrasing made Mirda Khan frown so Sascha signalled for Ranjit to translate. The wave of hysterical weeping was punctuated as mothers of now officially illegal children threw themselves across the unconscious bodies, obviously determined to resist attempts to remove them. Sascha ordered the crowd control partners to neutralize the incipient hysterics. He dampened his own reception but he could not remain immune to the intense emotional agitation that battered his senses. Yet these same women would have sold their sons and daughters in a few years.

Sascha: *Boris, it's going to be a lot easier to buy these women off with something.*

Boris: *How about the truth? Isn't a hostel a better fate than the future Yassim planned for them?*

I would think so, Sascha replied, *but I do not think they'll see it in the same light. I'll tap our slushfund if you won't ante up*. Anything, Sascha thought, to shut up the spine-crawling ululations. He was not used to having to deal on this level.

Boris: *Getting soft, brother?*

Sascha: *You're not here and listening. And there's Tirla to think of.*

Boris: *You're taking charge of her, aren't you?*

Sascha: *I'd rather she wasn't jeopardized. Her Talent could be very useful in multi-language groups.*

The noise was fearful, the aura exceedingly unpleasant for any Talents with the least modicum of empathy. Tears were streaming down Carmen's face.

'How much, Tirla?' Sascha asked her. Startled, she twisted in his hands to see his expression. 'How much will stop their tears and relieve their loss?'

'You'd pay?' He saw the leap of astonishment in her eyes, and then a canny veil settling over their velvety brown.

Brother, this one's going to deal for the hairs on our chests.

'For the youngest, you don't have to give much.' She named a figure. 'Add ten per cent for each year they have, and that should be enough.'

'I'd say five per cent for each year.'

'Seven!' she retorted. 'The bigger they are the more it takes to fill their bellies.'

He spat in his hand and held it out. She closed the deal and then stepped four paces nearer to Mirda Khan.

Ranjit, monitor this for me! Sascha told him.

Ranjit: *She's speaking Arabic. She's saying that she has been arguing hard for the grieving mothers ever since they were caught in the tunnel. Only because she has spoken out so forcefully has a way been made to ease the sorrow of the mothers. Illegal children have rights, the big man says, and she believes him. They will be much safer than with Yassim for which every mother should be thankful, knowing perfectly well the fate which awaited the children, despite the grief it causes. For how else can people survive on mere subsistence alone. A price has been agreed, as*

221

they must have seen, and she has acted in good faith. Sascha,
Ranjit added as Tirla turned to face another section of the
women, *this child is amazing. She's speaking Urdu now as
glibly as she did Arabic. Oho!*

There was a commotion and a plump little woman,
her face contorted with conflicting emotions until her
beady eyes were hidden in the folds of her cheeks, pushed
through. Sascha recognized her from her caste mark and
the vindictiveness of her roiling thoughts. She would
have leaped upon Tirla if Mirda Khan and Mama Bobchik
had not intervened. Sascha sprang forward to protect
Tirla, berating himself for not anticipating an attack.

'Unwanted bitch,' the woman shrieked in Basic.
'Illegal, you! The bint is illegal! She is illegal!' She
struggled against the restraining hands. 'Take her. You
take her if you take my Tombi. You take her!' And that
was a threat.

'Of course I am illegal, wasted barren woman whose
husband will beat her morning, noon, and evening for
refusing a fair price that will feed him for many days to
come on lamb and poppadoms.' Tirla leaned with fervour
into the task of returning verbal abuse. She had, Sascha
noted, managed to run her bracelet up under her sleeve,
out of sight.

Sascha now restrained Tirla by her shoulders. 'She is
illegal, woman. She comes with us. Tell them, Ranjit!'
When the Talent had, he added. 'The deal she spoke of
will be good for only three more minutes.' He looked
pointedly at his wrist chrono. 'Then there is no more to
talk about. Let each mother who accepts the offer stand
by her child.'

Then to shut up the renewal of Bilala's caterwauling,
Sascha shot a strong silencing command compulsion on
the hysterical woman. She fell back in the arms of the
women who held her, her mouth working soundlessly.
An awed hush fell over the platform.

The business was quickly concluded then and Tirla

watched solemnly as crisp floaters changed hands. She had never seen so much money in circulation at one time and in front of everyone. It was better so. No-one could claim afterwards that one had received more than another. Some of the women lingered, displaying real distress as their children were loaded back into the front four cars. Sascha propelled Tirla toward the last car, Carmen beside them as the remainder of the Search Group took their places.

Tirla held up her braceleted arm. 'You keep the bargain in fact but not in spirit?' Tirla demanded as the drone cover slid shut. She tugged at the coveted wristband.

'The bargain is kept in fact and in spirit, Tirla, but you can't come back to G, not with Bilala your enemy.'

'Huh! That one!' Tirla snorted derisively. 'She wouldn't find me if I didn't want her to. I'm not afraid of that stupid woman.'

'Frankly, I would be, were I you,' Sascha said. 'She'll certainly make sure Yassim knows what part you had in clearing out his hide.'

That caused her to reflect although Sascha still could not nudge his way past her shields.

'Then what was the point of making it seem as if they'd escaped?' she wanted to know with some exasperation.

'That seemed a sensible safeguard at the time. Up until you'd wanted to be such a good neighbour. C'mon,' and Sascha held out his hand, 'I think I can find you a safe squat for a few days with a friend of mine.' *Dorotea?* Sascha called, *can you spare a moment for this waif?*

Tirla looked at his hand as if it were covered in acid. 'At the hostel? With *them*?'

'You're legal, remember?' Sascha reassured her with a little smile. 'Technically, you're free to move anywhere you want to now. You've got a wad of floaters but,' and he raised his hand in a cautionary gesture, 'you know as well as I do that an unattached kid in a linear right now is in jeopardy. Yassim has got to find replacements and

Mirda Khan and Mama Bobchik wouldn't be there to defend you.'

'Defend me?' Tirla was both indignant and astonished.

'Oh, they did, in their own ways. And if a ladrone doesn't snap you up, the Public Health will as you're underage and should be in school.' *Wow!* Sascha exclaimed to Dorotea. *That opened up an excited crack.*

Dorotea: *Keep working it then!*

'Frankly, I would be wary, were I you,' Sascha said. Tirla's own reaction to the magic word was to finger her precious ID.

'School? I could access Teacher?'

'You've the right to all the education you can stuff into your head – that is, once you overcome the little problem of being an unattached minor. C'mon, get into the pod. It's ready to go and I want you out of this hostile environment.'

Tirla cast a look over her shoulder at the knot of women around Bilala and said, 'stupid cunt' under her breath but she did not resist Sascha's guiding hand.

'Once you've caught up with the grade level, you could even go to a regular school.'

'Me? In a school?' Tirla was sceptical as well as contemptuous.

'I suspect you've got a lot more Talent than you realize, Tirla.'

Dorotea, acidly: *You were never one to understate a cause.*

Tirla hunkered down beside him, balancing her torso between spread knees, hands dangling limply between her legs, her butt against the padded end of the cargo pod, supporting her odd posture. She cocked her head up at him, hauling the strands of dark hair off her face, her dark eyes sparkling with, it seemed to Sascha, a private amusement that, for all his telepathic skill, he couldn't penetrate.

'Talent?'

'Yes,' he said, 'Talent.' And settled down beside her just as the train began to ease forward.

'I'm nothing like *you*,' Tirla said, warily, swaying a little.

'No, you're not. I cannot talk to everyone in their own language as glibly as you do.'

Tirla thought for a moment and then shrugged. 'That's not hard to do.'

'Not for you. Ranjit, who's quite a linguist, was making heavy weather of the translations just now.'

Tirla shrugged again, dismissively.

'In a few years, you could earn a big wage just translating.' He could feel her attention. 'Enough to live at the top of any linear and never have to worry about the Yassims of this world.'

'Working for LEO?' She was plainly unwilling.

'For someone with your gift of languages, there are far better opportunities than LEO. You do need some schooling.'

'I got schooling.' Her tone was both rebellious and indignant. At Sascha's prompting 'Oh', she added, 'I used my brother's ID – as long as I had it. I got schooling.'

Dorotea, would you check that out? The brother's name and ID is on the Incident report.

I caught a glimpse again, Sascha, Dorotea said. *I'm going to need personal contact with her to get past that shield. I gather you plan to bring her to my place and I'm to play sweet frail harmless grandmamma? Boy, this has been a day! In for a penny, in for a pound. Did you get any of the high level interview?*

Caught most of it! Sascha sent an image of him cheering like a mad soccer supporter.

When all the excitement dies down, Sascha, we are going through the testing procedures with the proverbial fine-tooth comb.

Just then Sascha felt the jar as the four forward cars were detached to go on to the western hostel that would accommodate the illegal children. He caught the look of apprehension on Tirla's face and her quick glance at him.

Sascha: *I'll take her to my spare room if you'd rather.*

Dorotea: *Nonsense, I may hate type-casting but I'm far more suitable. Though you're doing rather well.* The admission was grudging.

Sascha smiled and resettled himself.

'It'll be smoother from now on,' he said to Tirla. 'We're being shunted to the commuter track.'

'Where are you taking me?'

'To my grandmother.'

I'm not sure I care to be related to a glib philanderer like you, Sascha Roznine. No morals.

'If she'll have you for a few days until I can find the right residential school for you. That would solve the problem of nosy Public Health Officials and keep you out of Yassim's notice. But, as I said,' he went on casually for the mention of 'school' had briefly opened her shield and he'd seen a fearful startlement – a hunger and a withdrawal – before it lowered, 'you've a legal ID, floaters enough for months, and you can suit yourself.'

Their car had been shunted several times and now the progress became smoother and faster. Tirla noticed it, and she also noticed how the other people in the car relaxed, smiling and chatting with each other on a vocal level.

Residential school, my ass, Boris's disgusted tone echoed in Sascha's mind. *I can just see Fairmont or Holyoke taking in that subbie.*

Sascha: *Tolerance, Bro, tolerance. She's clean and healthy, and that tight mind might conceal a genius.*

Boris: *For scams!*

Dorotea, steel in her tone: *You just let US handle one of our own.*

Boris: *Since when am I disowned?*

Dorotea: *When you're wearing nothing but your LEO hat!*

Sascha had a mental image of his brother withdrawing

quietly, offending hat in hand. No-one took on Dorotea in a crusading mood. He glanced down at Tirla who was deep in thought, staring down at the floor, though her body appeared relaxed. When the cargo pod door came open as they reached the vehicle park in the quiet grounds of the Eastern Centre for Parapsychics, she reacted with amazement and disbelief. As the other members of Sascha's team piled out, laughing and chatting over the successful assignment, Tirla just stood, her large eyes wide and white in their deep-set sockets as she stared around her. Sascha did not hurry her. The old Darrow estate, with its big old beeches, maples and oaks, the wide lawns and the attractive two storey residential units, was unique enough in modern Jerhattan and had to be a revelation to a linear resident. Tirla looked appalled.

'My grandmother lives over there,' Sascha said, pointing to the dwelling which had once been the gardener's lodge. 'There she is, weeding the border.' *You are the most complete ham, Dorotea. Weeding?*

Dorotea: *True enough, but I wasn't going to swathe myself in black subsistence and bedeck myself with bracelets and nose-rings to make her feel at ease. And the border does need weeding.*

Sascha: *What about your arthritis?*

Dorotea: *I always suffer for my art, m'dear. I've recruited Peter, too. He needs to climb down from rarefied atmospheres and something homely will help. Also, he may be older than she is, but he looks young. He's to appear with eats. Refreshments are always a good way to start off a conversation, particularly for someone with a near-east background.* 'Why, Sascha, what a pleasant surprise!' Dorotea hoisted herself to her feet and held out her arms to him. *Kiss me, you lout. Even grandmothers need a ration of passion now and again!*

'Grandmother, this is Tirla . . . Tunnelle . . .'

Dorotea: *Inventive boy!*

' . . . and she needs a place to stay for a few days. Would it be too much of an imposition?'.

Dorotea extracted herself from Sascha's enthusiastic embrace and extended a mud-daubed hand to Tirla. Since Dorotea had been accepted and acceptable from the moment of her birth, she had about her an aura that made rejection from anyone impossible so that Tirla delayed only a moment before grasping the extended hand. *She's got bones like a bird's, Sascha. How could she possibly do all she's just done?*

'Tirla, this is Dorotea Horvath.' *There's nothing frail about Tirla's mind, Dorotea.*

'Actually, I was just about to quit and have something to eat and drink. The sun's warm today. Peter, is the juice ready?' she called, and gestured for her guests to precede her into the little house.

Sascha was glad that he had thought of Dorotea, instead of taking Tirla to the far more daunting manor house and its formality. Judging by Tirla's stunned expression, even this homey room was way outside her experience.

'I expect you'll want to wash up, and I need to,' Dorotea said gently, touching Tirla's arm and pointing to the little hall. 'Lavatory's second door on the left, dear, plenty of towels. Peter,' she said as she made for the small kitchen, 'we have two more guests.'

Peter: *What's she like?*

Sascha: *Scared.*

Peter, in a wry tone: *Know the feeling!*

Dorotea: *Tight shield.*

Peter, earnestly: *I'll be careful.*

Dorotea: *And don't show off. You'll terrify her.*

Peter: *I did all the showing off I'm going to do this morning.*

An apprehensive Tirla re-entered the room, surrep-titiously trailing fingers along wooden surfaces and across the sofa backs. Sascha noticed that she had washed her hands, arms, neck, face and that portion of her bony chest that was visible above the round neck of her rather worn clothing. She had brushed her long hair neatly back over her shoulders. Sascha thought of the cheerless functionality of subsistence living quarters and gave Tirla another full mark for nonchalance.

'Here we are,' Dorotea said, arriving with a large tray laden with all sorts of fingerfoods: savouries, small open-faced sandwiches, wedges of fruit and strips of fresh vegetables. 'Peter, don't drop the glasses!' Fortunately, Tirla's back was to the boy who was kinetically herding four large tumblers because he needed both hands on the huge pitcher of orange juice.

'Hold it while I pour,' Peter said, handing Tirla a glass, a diversion which kept her from seeing that the other glasses slid to positions on the low table near Dorotea and Sascha.

Dorotea: *Peter!*

Peter: *She didn't see it.*

When all had been served with juice, Peter bounced into the chair beside Tirla and took a long drink of the juice, wiping his mouth and exclaiming with satisfaction at the taste.

'Don't inhale the juice, Peter,' Dorotea said as she offered Tirla the tray of snacks. *An uncommon fondness for green pepper,* for Tirla's eyes had brightened at the sight of the slices. Closely watching Dorotea, the girl had closed her fingers about three, then increased her haul to six when there was no reaction. 'The cheese puffs are hot and fresh,' Dorotea said, pushing them toward Tirla. 'You'd better get them now before Sascha or Peter hog them all.'

Tirla let the pepper strips fall into her lap and obediently took a cheese puff.

Sascha, plaintively: *I couldn't make myself some coffee, could I, Doro?*

Dorotea: *Drink! Anything. She won't until we all do.*

'Peter, this is just what I needed. I must have dehydrated in the sun. Sascha, there's asparagus in the breadrolls. I know you like them! And Peter, you are not to eat all the chicken sandwiches. They would, you know.' Dorotea rattled on, nibbling at a cheese puff which she then put to one side and took a bite of a pâtéd cracker. *Well, we've all sampled everything to prove there's no poison or drugs. Ah, good! Oh, my word! She's starved!*

Tirla had indeed started to drink and eat with quick sharp bites and snatched swallows, as if she was torn between eating and drinking, and afraid that this food would suddenly disappear. All three telepaths were aware of a sudden lightening of her carefully guarded thoughts as she made inroads on the snacks. The pastry melted in her mouth, releasing tastes that satisfied unknown cravings with textures that titillated her tongue, from the reassuring crisp watery tang of the green peppers to the bite of sharp cheese and savoury meat fillings.

Food would be a trigger, Dorotea went on wryly, *when you consider she's probably been hungry all her life.* She took a long drink of the orange juice. 'I hope you've more in the kitchen, Peter, because it tastes marvellous. But then, fresh squeezed orange juice always does, don't you think so, Tirla?'

Sascha! Boris' tone was authoritative. *Your waif's in good hands. Someone just snatched one of the Jerhattan kids we stranded three weeks ago.*

'Well,' Sascha said, rising and dusting his fingers of crumbs, 'I'll leave you to it, Tirla. You're safe enough here for a few days, and Peter can show you how to log on to the Teacher. Right?'

As he strode across the lawn to the main house, Dorotea told him, *She paused in her eating when you left, but I fear the snack tray and the orange juice pitcher are of far greater moment than you, honey.*

Sascha wasn't certain, in his private mind, if he liked taking second place to a batch of canapés even with a pre-adolescent.

230

31

'You been here long?' Tirla asked Peter the next morning as they ate breakfast in the pleasant, and to Tirla, amazing kitchen room. Dorotea was preparing eggs, fresh eggs, in a pan at a stove. Tirla did not wish to distract her because she was using a naked flame so she spoke in a low voice.

'Hmm,' Peter said amiably, taking neat spoonfuls of the ripe melon. Tirla also watched to see how he dealt with the food. She'd've sliced it thin and eaten down to the rind. 'Ever since I got out of hospital.'

'Why were you in hospital?' Hospitals were fearsome places to Tirla who had always made a practice of avoiding medics as well as quacks. She also had a wary distrust of 'sick' people, never having been ill or injured.

Peter gave a diffident shrug of one shoulder. 'A wall collapsed all over me.'

'You must have been hurt bad.' In Tirla's experience people did not survive walls coming down on them.

'Couldn't walk for months. Couldn't even feed myself.' His eyes took on an unfocused cast.

'And they let you live?' Tirla was stunned at such good fortune.

Peter regarded her with some surprise. 'Of course, though for a while there, I really didn't want to live.'

Tirla absorbed this remarkable statement as she bent to the task of eating melon. It was really good – not gone off like most of those she scrounged. She flicked careful glances at Dorotea to make sure the fire was under control. Why didn't the woman use the hotter she had right there in the wall? One of the first things you learned in the linears was not to mess with naked flames. Fire was a sure way to get the LEOs down on you.

'Why did you?' Tirla asked, realizing Peter was waiting for her to comment. 'Live, I mean.'

'Rhyssa taught me how to move again.'

'You do move sort of oddly,' Tirla said, having noticed the peculiar gliding motion he had. He didn't in fact seem to 'step' though his legs moved.

Peter snickered, his mouth full of melon. He swallowed and grinned broadly. 'That's because I'm not really walking. I impel myself kinetically.' His eyes glinted with mischief at her mystification. 'I make my body move. It can't.'

Tirla stopped eating, staring at him until she recalled that even in linears a lengthy stare was impolite. 'Your body doesn't move? But you're eating. You're using your arm and your hand. . .just like me. . .' She held hers up.

'I'm pretty good at it, aren't I?' Peter was delighted with the effect on Tirla. 'I've done some other stuff, too, moving. . .' He broke off, with a slightly rueful grin, before he went on, 'I hear you're pretty good at your Talent, too. That was larky – getting the kids away from the pervert.'

Tirla slowly shook her head, dismissing her achievement. 'Nothing like what you do. I don't have much Talent at all.'

Peter snorted with good-natured contempt. 'That's what you think. It's not what Rhyssa said. I'm good at what I do. But you're very, very good at what *you* do. Don't knock it.'

Slightly embarrassed by the sincerity of Peter's tone, Tirla changed the subject, eager to pump him on puzzling topics.

'You said Rhyssa helped you? Is she the dark-haired one who was here last night after Sascha left?'

Peter nodded his head. 'She's the Director here.'

'Not Sascha?'

Peter shook his head, grinning. 'Sascha's the Deputy Chief. He takes over when Rhyssa's involved with someone. Like me! I'm her special project. . .' He broke off, blinking his eyes rapidly, flashed a quick, almost apologetic, glance at Dorotea before he grinned. 'Rhyssa has lots of special duties, being the Director. I'm not the only one.'

Tirla noticed that his cheeks flamed briefly. What could embarrass a boy like Peter? Then Dorotea was passing plates with freshly cooked eggs and bacon, and urging Tirla to sample the hot toast. Tirla ate until she was stuffed. She thanked Dorotea profusely for the effort of handcooking.

'I enjoy it,' Dorotea replied, smiling gently, 'especially for appreciative appetites. Peter, why don't you take Tirla to the study and log her in. You've got to go through some assessments first, honey, but once your standard's been decided, you'll be expected to be present for all the classes you're assigned.'

Tirla nodded briefly, far more interested in the way Peter got down from his chair and, indeed he did glide as he conducted her to the study: the curious fluidity to his movements fascinated her.

'And you aren't really walking?'

'Nope, it's all kinetic. My spinal cord got severed when the wall fell on me. Medical science can't splice

233

that — yet — but kinetic science gives me movement. Better'n being stuck in a support chair,' he assured her blithely. 'Here's your terminal and here're your earplugs. I've got to do my hours with Teacher, too. Can't slip out of that with kinesis!' He made a face as she slid into the chair he indicated. When she had slipped the plugs into her ears, he typed a sequence with an odd finger movement and suddenly the blank screen cleared.

'Tirla Tunnelle, may I, as your personal Teacher, welcome you to this Educational Programme.' The screen showed the school room and a pleasant-faced woman seated at the desk. Tirla knew that this Teacher was a construct, devised to reproduce the old teacher-pupil confrontation, but she had always liked the look of Teacher, someone you could trust: who wouldn't laugh at questions or honest mistakes; who was there to help you learn. 'Sascha Roznine told us that you have had some credits under the name of Kail, Linear G resident, Flat 8732a. Today, if you will bear with me, Tirla, we will just see how much of those early lessons you remember. Now, shall we begin? If you need to be refreshed about the function keys, please type H for help. Or, if you're ready to begin, strike Return, and we'll begin the assessment.'

With conflicting emotions of awe, of someone who realizes a long-held dream, with fear that this miracle might be withdrawn for some capricious reason, Tirla touched Return.

32

'I think,' Dorotea began, drumming her fingers rapidly on the kitchen table, 'Tirla is going into an education-overkill phase. She won't leave the terminal, though Peter has been as slyly devious as you, Sascha, in getting her outside. I also think she finds the grounds daunting instead of pleasant. She sticks to the paths and won't use the playground facilities. But all this study and no play is not an improvement.'

Don Usenik who had joined the informal meeting as medical adviser shook his head, mildly amused by Dorotea's fervour. 'According to the medical reports, she's in excellent shape. Amazingly so when you consider the conditions under which she's lived.'

'Well, I think it's wrong for a child her age to try and absorb two years' education in four days,' Dorotea maintained.

'Any improvement in receptivity?' Rhyssa asked.

'What does Peter say?' Dorotea countered with some heat.

Rhyssa laughed. 'Peter thinks she could if she would.

When she's involved in her studying, he can 'hear' an on-going mental commentary. She has amazing retentive powers, visual as well as auditory. She's answered him telepathically once or twice when she didn't realize it.'

'We have got to make her aware of her potential,' Sascha said, frustrated.

Rhyssa leaned across the table. 'It will take time, Sascha. There's no need to force scope to her Talent.'

'Boris would like a hundred more like her,' Sascha said, frowning.

'But I thought you and Boris had found the Jerhattan child,' Rhyssa said, having followed his thought. She didn't like what she read: that Boris wanted Tirla to work undercover with Cass.

'Oh, we found and rescued her all right,' Sascha replied with no sense of achievement, 'and two others, but there were no leads whatever of any use. Only a minor ladrone who reports by phone . . . another of those conveniently illegal connects. So a dead-end. The girls could tell us nothing: they'd been gassed, blindfolded, stuck in some sort of a smooth plastic cocoon. Their trauma went pretty deep.'

'The psychological scarring of their incarceration is going to be difficult to neutralize,' Don remarked, frowning. 'A new wrinkle in rendering the abducted docile, tactile disorientation. Villainous trick,' and he shook his head. 'You and Peter are off today, aren't you? So that leaves Dorotea and me to come up with some brilliant ideas on sharpening up the tests, huh?'

'And me,' Sascha said, coming out of his gloom. 'I am, after all, Director of Training for this Centre. The trouble with a unique like Tirla is that she doesn't realize she's got Talent in the first place. And in the second, how can you test children that aren't supposed to exist?'

'What training have you planned for Tirla then?' Rhyssa said.

Sascha shrugged. 'Training? She's a natural at what she

does – getting into the communication centre of anyone's brain and adapting to whatever language they're using.' He spread his hands wide. 'How can we improve on that? And she can't explain. Any more than Peter can explain how he does what he does.'

'I'd do this myself but I hate crowds and I can't walk far,' Dorotea said suddenly, 'but Sascha, why don't you start by hauling her away from Teacher for an afternoon? Those issue shoes are useless and while she might feel happy in subsistence issue, I would like to see her dressed in something nicer. Several some-thing nicers.'

'Me?' Sascha glanced first at Dorotea and then at Rhyssa and pretended not to see Don's amused expression.

'You!' And Dorotea pointed a stern finger at him. 'She trusts you.'

'But I've never bought clothes for a kid.'

'No need to panic,' Dorotea replied unfeelingly. 'I'm sure Tirla knows what she'd be comfortable wearing and that's all you need to go by. She's still a trifle young to want to bedeck herself alluringly.'

Wanna bet, Rhyssa said in a tight aside to Dorotea who gave her an unfathomable glance without betraying a mental explanation.

'Take her to one of the good malls. Let her see how the other half lives – the one she's inhabiting now,' Dorotea went on. 'And then treat her to something tooth-rottening and utterly satiating. Spoil her a bit. Show her there's more to life on this level than a square box and a wrist ID.'

'She might know of other kids with unusual aptitudes,' Rhyssa added. 'She doesn't miss much.'

'That's for sure,' Sascha replied heartily. 'Your heli just landed, Rhyssa. I'll just see you all off.'

'Peter!' Rhyssa called. 'Dave and Johnny are on their way. Are you all packed?'

Dorotea snorted. 'He's been ready since before you

237

thought of the,' she paused and grinned wickedly, 'distraction.'

'I'm coming,' Peter called, 'porting his travelcase to the heli-pad, and glided to Tirla's room. 'I'll see you. Keep clocking in the study time.'

She hit the 'hold' and regarded him in surprise. 'You going somewhere?'

Peter grinned mischievously. 'Rhyssa's got a job for me.' He winked.

'Job? For you?'

'Sure, I'm very useful, I'll have you know.'

Tirla gave him a long disbelieving look. 'Doing what?'

'More of what I'm good at.'

Tirla looked her profound disbelief. 'What could you be good at?'

Peter made a clicking sound in his mouth since he couldn't snap his fingers. 'I just wish I could tell you, Tirla. But it's a professional secret.'

'So don't tell me. I got better things to do than guess secrets!' Tirla turned back to the monitor.

'But I'll be gone weeks.'

Tirla wriggled her fingers at him over her shoulder. 'Have a good time,' and she kept her eyes on the screen. The Teacher on hold had her mouth open, hand half-raised as she was making a particular point in the lesson. Tirla tried to resume her studying, but the truth of the matter, though she couldn't let on to Peter, was that she would miss him. Weeks?

He was the first boy she'd ever met who had some sense. She knew he was supposed to be a very clever kinetic: he had talked to her about thought transfer and telepathy, which made her a bit nervous. There ought to be *some* privacy for a person, after all. But he'd also been good about helping her with some of the harder problems Teacher set her. At least Sascha would be around. She wouldn't like Sascha to be gone for weeks.

She was surprised to have her lesson interrupted a second time and by Sascha.

'Tirla! Have you stirred out of this room today?'

'No,' she said, tapping out the answer to the problem on the screen.

'Tirla! Turn that damned thing off! We've got something better to do with the afternoon.'

She rolled over on her side to look up at him. 'What?'

'Buy you some new shoes and clothes.'

Tirla looked down at footwear and her toes visible in the slits that had appeared. 'I did try to find the issue slot but Dorotea doesn't have one.'

Sascha hunkered down and firmly punched the off switch.

'Hey!' Tirla regarded him with astonishment that soon turned to antagonism. She reached for the switch and he caught her hand.

'You can pick up where you left off when we get back. On to your feet,' and Sascha gave her hand a warning pull. 'We don't have issue slots at the Centre. Generally we get ordinary stuff from the remote mall but as I haven't a notion of your shoe size or what colours you like, I think this once, we'll go in the flesh. When we're done, we're going to have a treat.'

Tirla was definitely interested now. She bounced to her feet, her black eyes sparkling. 'What kind of treat?'

'That'll be entirely up to you, my dear,' and he led the way to the transport lot. 'In our malls there's a lot to choose from,' he added in a provocative tone.

Whatever misgivings Sascha might have entertained about shopping for a child were swiftly compounded. First Tirla had to recover from her initial shock at the size of the mall which Sascha chose. Then she led him a dance through every department of the twelve-storey complex, eyes and head constantly on the move as she did an initial reconnaissance.

Back on the first floor, she considered at length the

239

various items that had caught her attention the first time. On the fourth level, fortunately the one dealing with shoes and young apparel, the sole of one shoe disintegrated. ('From the heat of the speed at which she was travelling,' Sascha told Dorotea later.)

When an officious floor walker moved in on Tirla with the obvious intent of removing the waif from the elegant premises, Sascha intercepted him.

'I wouldn't,' Sascha said in a low voice, pushing out his sleeve so the special design of his wrist ID was visible. 'I'm escorting her. Is she acceptable as a patron now?'

'Yes, sir, I'm sorry, sir, but you must admit . . .'

'That's why we're shopping.'

The man walked quickly out of Sascha's vicinity with several anxious backward glances.

'You weren't going to hex him, were you, Sascha?' asked an amused voice beside him.

He turned to see Cass Cutler grinning up at him. 'If I could, I'd put a hurry one on Tirla. We went through all fourteen levels of this place like a dose of salts and now she's settling down for a second tour.'

Cass laughed at his discomfort. 'And they sent you out on your own with your protegé?' She laughed again. 'That's unkind.'

'It's supposed to be mutually instructive.'

Tirla reappeared and latched on to Sascha's hand, regarding Cass very narrowly from her suddenly inscrutable eyes.

'I remember you,' Cass said. 'You ricocheted off me and my partner at Linear G. And you messed up Flim-flam's scam to a fare-thee-well. My congratulations!'

'You're one of him,' and Tirla jerked her head toward Sascha.

Cass laughed again, a throaty, genuine laugh. Sascha could feel Tirla's fingers relaxing. 'Not quite, Chip. We're on the same side but I'm LEO, crowd control. You're Talents.'

'Crowd control takes Talent, too,' Tirla replied generously. 'Peter told me.' She looked about her slightly contemptuous. 'Not much of a crowd here today.'

'I'm not on duty today,' Cass replied, grinning down at Tirla. 'I see you're on a day off, too. What've you found that appeals to you?'

Will you help me, Cass? Please say yes! Sascha pleaded. *I've a hideous presentiment that that child intends to case the entire mall again before she'll even try something on.*

'If you don't mind me saying it, Tirla, you'll be able to walk further with a decent pair of shoes on your feet. There're some good bargains to be had right now. What strikes your fancy?'

With a sense of reprieve, Sascha followed Cass and Tirla to the shoe department. An hour later, after two harried human clerks had replaced the mechanical fitter, Tirla's small, narrow and very dainty feet ended up in soft purple leather boots, the only pair that would fit her feet.

Totally unsuitable for a child, of course, Cass said, *but they do fit.*

And she adores them! Sascha saw how Tirla's face glowed as she strutted from mirror to mirror, regarding her feet.

'Mr Roznine,' the head clerk said wearily as the docket spun out of the teller machine, 'your . . . young companion has a most delicate and unusual foot to fit. May I recommend this concern? They do very fine custom work.'

Sascha read the man easily and what he didn't say was, 'So that we won't have to go through this again.' But he was just as grateful to take the card which could be inserted in Dorotea's mall machine for home shopping.

He blessed Cass with every new purchase for the woman actually seemed to enjoy the looking, the trying, the discussion of fit, style and colour which wearied him.

'The concept of having unlimited funds to spend is foreign to the child, Sascha,' Cass said at one point, 'but you must admit that she knows what suits her.'

Tirla was modelling a one-piece outfit as different from subsistence issue as diamonds are from rhinestones. The main colour was a soft blue with purple accents in seamstitching, pocket trim and fasteners. Once Tirla found that outfit to her taste, and Sascha's – for it was always Sascha to whom she turned for approval – it took the combined efforts of both Sascha and Cass to get her to buy additional clothing.

'Why do I need more? I've boots and this material's hard wearing. It'll do for weeks. Even if I had to catch freights again,' and Tirla's eyes twinkled with mischief at Sascha.

He had to chuckle at her impudence. 'It's a fetching outfit, Tirla, there's no question of it. But even Teacher will get tired of seeing you in it.'

Tirla gave him a long hard look. 'Teacher doesn't SEE me.'

'No, but Dorotea and I do, so do Sirikit, Budworth, Don, and Peter and Rhyssa. You never see them wearing the same clothes two days in a row.'

'Oh, they have lots of clothes. Dorotea has closets full.' Tirla didn't sound envious: if anything her tone was slightly censorious, as if she didn't feel it was proper for people to have so many things to wear.

'A few changes are in order,' Cass said. 'I've got quite a few myself,' she added encouragingly while Tirla merely stared back, her hands plunged into the deep pockets and her shoulders hunched under the smooth fabric.

'This isn't coming out of your floaters, Tirla,' Sascha began, suddenly realizing what might be causing her hesitation. 'Dorotea and Rhyssa want you to be suitably dressed now that you're a Talent. You're not a subbie any more, you know.' He pointed to her wrist ID.

'Oh,' and there was a look of surprised wonderment on

242

the girl's face as she regarded the bracelet with dawning comprehension. 'Is that why those salespersons were so nice to me?'

'Quite likely,' Cass said in a dry tone of voice. 'Everyone in malls like these recognizes the distinctive pattern.'

Tirla twirled hers on her fragile wrist. 'They do?' She settled the band outside the cuff of her new clothes. 'How much can I buy with just this?'

Sascha disguised a choke of dismay with a cough just as Cass caught him in the ribs with her elbow.

'Let's find out, shall we, Chip?' Cass asked cheerfully and held out her hand.

Tirla took it readily enough but her other hand immediately sought Sascha's and then she was dragging them after her toward a rack of brilliantly coloured trousers.

She was not as profligate as Sascha feared but she ended up with 'something different to wear every day of the week.' Then Sascha made good his promise of a treat, inviting Cass to join them in the Old-Fashioned Parlour of Gastronomical Confections and Irresistible Desserts.

Tirla managed to get through three immense rich concoctions that Sascha privately thought revolting.

Cass: *Let her enjoy, Sascha. Ice-cream is something she's heard about.*

Sascha: *What if she comes home sick? Dorotea will skin me alive.*

Cass: *This child has an iron constitution if she's survived subbie slop until now. And look at how much pleasure she's having?*

Sascha, groaning: *I'll be sick!*

It was then that Tirla realized there were other girls and boys enjoying the Parlour and, her spoon now on automatic, she took full note of the other youngsters.

That blonde ought to wear bright colours. She'd look better in pastel shades. Boy, what's he wearing such tight pants for? He'll squeeze 'em dry. Now that red outfit might look good on me. Maybe I can get

243

something like that next time Sascha wants to spend money.

Sascha glanced surreptitiously at Cass who rolled her eyes.

Sascha: *Stream of consciousness and loud and clear. Does she realize she's broadcasting?*

Cass, busily spooning up the last of her treat: *Highly unlikely. That child's had to be on the qui vivre all her life. Frankly, Sascha, I take it as a high compliment that she's relaxed her guard in our presence enough to do some unguarded thinking.*

Sascha: *Good point.*

As nonchalantly as he could, he observed Tirla, listening to her pithy and acute remarks about physical appearances, style, clothing, manners and a range of other subjects that flowed across her alert and fascinating mind.

Then Cass, with apparent reluctance, rose and said that she had to get back to the Centre as she had an evening assignment. Tirla even looked disappointed that their threesome had to break up.

'Look, Chip, anytime you want to have a gawk round some of the other malls . . .'

'There are OTHER ones?' And Tirla shot an accusing glare at Sascha.

'Thousands,' Cass told her with an unrepentant grin, 'but you can't really do more than one at a time or it all gets jumbled up in your head as to what you saw where and which price. Believe me, I know!'

Tirla saw the merit of that and, tucking her hand in Sascha's, was content to return to their transport and the Centre.

By the time they reached Dorotea's their purchases had arrived by express package tube, piled neatly about the room.

'What a charming combination!' Dorotea exclaimed on seeing Tirla's clothes. 'Did you buy the mall out, Sascha?'

'Give her a little time and she probably will. Cass made the mistake of informing her there are a thousand more just like Grafton's and we may never be able to pay her bills.'

Dorotea laughed. 'I'll expect a fashion show after supper, Tirla.'

'Show? Why? I can put on something new every day this week. That'll show you,' Tirla replied. 'What's for supper? It smells good!'

'After all you just finished eating?' Sascha demanded.

'That was the treat. Don't I get supper after a treat?'

'Of course you do,' Dorotea assured her, glaring at Sascha.

If you'd seen the three huge gooey, sickeningly sweet things she consumed only a half hour ago . . . You maybe better not stuff her with supper, Sascha cautioned.

'Wash your hands, Tirla and I'll serve immediately. Are you staying, Sascha?'

'No, thanks,' and he managed to sound polite. *Peter was right about her being telepathic. But she doesn't know she is.*

Dorotea: *Hmmm. You see, you did learn something from her today. What did she learn from you?*

How to spend money, Sascha replied sourly and left.

33

If the official spectators at the launch even noticed the youngster seated to one side in the upper control room, they would have supposed him to be a child on a special tour – his youth according him a treat. The men certainly noticed the woman who sat beside him for she had an arresting beauty and that unusual silver streak in her dark hair. However, her attention never strayed from the boy. Equally involved in him was the tall, dark-haired man in fatigues with a colonel's eagle on one collar tab. So few spared the trio more than a passing glance. The real action was taking place out by the massive towering gantry where gale-force winds whipped the steam from the shuttle's rocket end. All launches recently had been pretty tricky, with the weather causing havoc with any air transport, let alone the critical first minutes of a shuttle launch.

The countdown echoed through the shielded room – at the count of eight, the spectators were jockeying for position for an unimpeded view through the treated slit windows, eager for ignition and take-off. Fingers were surreptitiously crossed for this was the thirteenth successive shuttle flight. Not that anyone was superstitious.

'We have ignition!' As often as that phrase was uttered, it was always said with a ring of quiet triumph.

None of the spectators would be able to hear as the shuttle engines began their full-throated roar, another noise, that of power generators pulsing at ever increasing speed. A subtle whine that built and then levelled off just as the shuttle, one of the majestic new Rigel class, began its first imperceptible upward thrust. The final link to the launch tower fell way. Everyone held their breath. Then, despite the wind howling down the gantry lane and the lashing rain, the shuttle crept upwards from the reinforced concrete without deviating a centimetre from the optimum take-off trajectory. Lift became obvious with increasing acceleration and suddenly the 'bird' was up and running, disappearing except for the radiance of its rockets, into the lowering ceiling of dark-grey swirling clouds.

Immediately all eyes turned to the newly installed infrared monitors that continued to track the shuttle on its unswerving path through the atmosphere and safely above the turbulence, well on its way to Padrugoi Station where its payload was urgently needed.

'The pilot has the comm,' Peter Reidinger said, opening his eyes. He glanced first at Rhyssa and she nodded, smiling reassurance, and removed her hand from his. He liked her to be touching him in these moments even if he couldn't feel it.

'You have the comm, Crosbie,' the controller said, letting out a small sigh of relief. 'Good thrust, Pete. You're working like a charm. Got the whole thing down to a science.'

'It is,' Johnny Greene reminded him, grinning.

'You know what I mean, Colonel,' Jason Murphy said, flapping his hand.

'He's teasing you,' Peter said, turning his attention to

the monitor. He didn't really need it: he could follow the ascent of the shuttle – like a pulse in his vein, a tingle of power running up and down his bones. He could feel that.

'Very economical thrust, Peter,' Johnny said, perusing the printout on the generator control panel. 'That's the third one in a row at that level gestalt. I think we can now establish certain parameters to power usage in bad-weather launches . . . even if I still can't tell how you do it.' He made a disgruntled noise in his throat. The ex-EtoP pilot had been hoping that he could learn Peter's gestalt link by following his mind during a launch. He had only latent kinetic Talent but he and Rhyssa had decided that that might be all to the good – for a pure kinetic might be unable to adapt to Peter's ways.

'Maybe you're trying too hard, JG,' Peter suggested. 'I keep as open as I can . . .'

'I know you do, lad. Wide open. I'm just too clumsy to get through the door. I think it's going to have to be a trained kinetic.'

'Second stage ignition,' the controller said, alerted by his board. 'On its way! You do good work, Pete. Good work.'

'C'mon, time for your swimming lesson, Pete,' Johnny said. 'Gotta keep you fit enough to launch these birds.'

'Can't I stay to be sure it docks OK?' Peter would not admit it even deep in his skull where Rhyssa might see it, but he didn't have enough energy left immediately after a launch to move from the couch. He needed a few moments to re-energize himself so he used any excuse to gain that respite.

'The bird's OK,' Jase assured him.

'Look all you want,' JG said, reseating himself.

Peter wondered if Colonel Greene had guessed but he never let on if he did.

The spectators below were beginning to file out of the gallery, hunching into wet-weather gear, bracing themselves for the stiff winds. With a wink, Jason turned on the intercom.

'I tell you, Senator, it is a measure of the state of the art in Space technology that we're now able to launch despite the weather.'

'If I had a nickel for every hold I've had to wait through, m'boy, I'd be able to buy drinks for the entire base. Just how much did you say this new technology cost us?'

The figure mentioned by the congressman was three times as much as Peter's contract had actually cost. And nearly 100 per cent more than the generator.

Peter grinned broadly, thoroughly enjoying the eavesdropping. He had been appalled at how much a 'big' generator cost (though JG assured him that it was a pittance when compared to other items purchased for Canaveral) and he couldn't believe the contract figure for his short-term services. And bonuses for every successful launch as well. He had been even more delighted when Rhyssa suggested that the Centre increase the 'pension' that was being sent to his parents.

Talents were generally not contracted until they were at least eighteen years old, but the circumstances and his unusual ability had been construed as sufficient to be an exception – a brief exception.

Vernon's advice to the Centre had been that if technology costs, it's bound to be considered more efficient than something in the medium range: the difference between this fact and fiction went into the Centre's Research Fund.

At that, it had taken some finagling on Altenbach's part to get the Canaveral staff to consider the 'new technology', even with the enthusiastic assistance of General Halloway and Colonel Straub. Peter had not been mentioned: the generators had, plus some very odd 'instrumentation'. Peter, in fact, was hidden behind a screen with Rhyssa when the 'new technology' had its first test. He had kinetically flown a drone from

Canaveral to Eglin Field despite winds of gale force 8 and a ceiling of 100 metres. He had landed it right on the target painted on the runway – to show the precision of the 'new technology'. He was then allowed to launch a loaded drone into orbit where it could be retrieved by a Padrugoi–based craft. His precision again was the deciding factor: too many drones had wandered off course so that the drone programme had been drastically curtailed.

Two days later a proper shuttle launch was grudgingly permitted. There was no forseeable change in the terrible weather patterns and shipments had fallen weeks behind delivery. That first morning, Peter had been a trifle anxious and the shuttle had ascended at such an astonishing rate that the controllers thought that a misfire had occurred and were about to abort the mission. Peter, with Johnny telepathically assisting him, had reduced his 'thrust' and the mission continued. The pilot later was heard to mention that his instrumentation had registered a G-force of 11 for the first few moments: he'd been scared shitless thinking he wouldn't even be able to activate the escape pod control on his armrest. And he meant 'shitless'.

The 'new technology' improved in finesse over the ensuing launches and NASA breathed a corporate sigh of relief that it could complete all the programmed supply runs to Padrugoi.

Rhyssa and Johnny watched the expression on the boy's rapt face as he followed today's shuttle's progress. Jason Murphy handed them coffee as they waited through Peter's absorption.

'OK,' Peter said finally, as the screen showed the shuttle nearing its docking rendezvous and he had recovered sufficiently, 'the new technology is ready for its swim.'

He had now recovered enough for a proper descent from his chair, raising his right hand in a creditable wave to Jason as he manoeuvred the steps to the ground exit of the room.

It had taken four launches before Jason, as Mission Launch Controller, was comfortable with 'new technology' and Peter's peculiar part in its schematics, but he had come to like the youngster and had given up trying to figure out how he did what he did – whatever it was.

'Get your slicker on, Pete,' Johnny said.

Peter had discovered that he could kinetically keep rain from soaking him but he now resisted the temptation to show off unnecessarily. Dutifully Peter flipped the slicker over him. Exiting the concrete bunker, they all made a dash for their waiting car.

34

Two weeks after Rhyssa and Peter went to Florida, Boris made one of his rare visits to the Centre to appraise Sascha of the fact that undercover agents believed more children had been sold. The agents had noticed a lot of floaters being spent in Linears A, B, and C. So Cass and Suz were sent on assignment to Linear E. As the two women frequented all the Jersey linears, they were known to the inhabitants. Cass's pregnancy made her even less suspicious and she pretended ill-health to account for Suz's company. So far they had nothing to report, not even a ripple of expectation. Whenever contact permitted, they stuck a locating strand in the hair of the children they encountered each day.

Similar teams were 'stranding' linear children through-out the Jerhattan area. Scan teams worked round the clock, waiting for a strand to show in an unlikely area.

'You know, Bro, we've got nothing but stopgap techniques. Planting a telepath won't stop kids being abducted,' Boris said. Sascha was in Rhyssa's office, attending to routine administration details as he took a break from formulating new testing procedures. Boris stood at the window, looking out on the peaceful scene below.

'No, no, no and no, Bro,' Sascha said without looking up from the monitor. He made a rapid motion, then swivelled about to give his brother a hard stare. 'There is no way in which I'll permit Tirla to be used as bait!'

'But she's a natural,' Boris said. 'She knows how to decipher linear rumours the way no other operative available to us can.'

'You think I,' and Sascha jabbed his chest with his fingers, 'would risk her?'

'Candidly, I don't think Tirla would be at risk,' Boris went on, beginning to pace. 'We could put her in with Cass and Suz, set her up with every telltale known to technology. She *knows* linears, she can speak any lingo, she's clever as she can stare and . . .'

'She's twelve years old and you're not using her as bait,' Sascha roared, not bothering to dampen his outrage and fury.

Boris regarded him with surprise. 'That kid was never twelve! And what's the matter with using the one advantage we've found in dealing with linear abductions? She's got a unique Talent, a natural camouflage and an ability for this sort of thing. Look how she managed in Linear G.'

'Linear G was a once-off. I'm not putting her at risk like that again.'

'She was never at risk. Except maybe from you!' Boris glared right back at his brother. 'And this was Cass's idea. I think it has potential. One thing's sure, Bro, unless we can get at the mastermind behind this despicable traffic, we're going to be losing kids. Kids who might well be Talented, too.'

'You step up your search and seizes, Boris. Leave Tirla out of your calculations. There are other ways, ethical and technological ways, to solve LEO problems.'

'Sascha, if I had the personnel to do it the hard way, I would,' Boris replied, his face reddening in an effort to keep his temper in the face of his twin's intransigence.

'Use some of the Linear G kids as bait then. They'd love a chance to get out of the hostel!'

Boris gave his brother one long look. 'You know, that's not a bad idea. I'll check 'em out.' With that he strode out of the room.

35

Despite the 'work', these last three weeks in Florida had been almost vacation time for Rhyssa, John Greene and Peter. Launching thirteen of the eighteen supply shuttles occupied two or three hours of a day at the most for Peter.

When Johnny Greene started to explain to him the mechanics of lift, trajectory, orbiting and other such matters pertaining to the job at hand, he and Rhyssa discovered that there were woeful gaps in Peter's education. He had not even had bedside schooling during the nine months since his accident. So a telempathic tutor was immediately hired.

Alan Eton quickly discovered that Peter had the usual boyish disregard for grammar, spelling and syntax, though his vocabulary skills were, in technical areas, beyond his age group. His mathematics were well into first year university and his understanding of certain aspects of physics curiously advanced. With the Colonel as his role model, Peter was eager to progress in those sciences. John Greene suggested that he had better improve his computer and English skills even if he was kinetically superior. While Peter understood some chemical and biological concepts – particularly those which had a bearing on his accident, he had, naturally, had no laboratory experience. A course of study was initiated and regular school hours kept, with Alan guiding Peter deftly into independent and non-curricula study of whatever the boy wanted to learn while filling in the more obvious lacks. A university degree, bachelor or advanced, was not at issue for Peter Reidinger: his career was well underway but it was essential for him to have an overall understanding of many disciplines to develop his full potential. Occasionally as he struggled through his lessons, he wondered how Tirla was doing. And what sort of training Sascha was giving her.

Physiotherapy was still a necessity and, without the inhibiting body-brace, Peter had no trouble exercising his limbs which he did religiously, hoping to acquire some muscle.

'There have been instances,' the physiotherapist told Rhyssa and Johnny, 'where even badly damaged neural tissue has been stimulated. That's what we can wish for Peter. To feel and to move normally.'

'What's the probability?' Rhyssa asked.

The physiotherapist had shrugged ruefully. 'Who knows? It certainly does no harm for him to exercise kinetically. Improves muscle tone and fluidity of movement. I'll be honest, I wouldn't have guessed he was walking kinetically when he entered the gym the first time.'

Swimming was Peter's favourite sport. Water supported his body and, with minimal effort, he gave the illusion of swimming. Thrashing his arms and legs about too violently resulted in water up his nose so he quickly found a happy medium. He could even do incredible dives off the board, hovering in the air as he made his body twist, and then enter the water cleanly. There hadn't been enough sun in those weeks to produce a tan but surrogate facilities had given him an excellent colour. And Rhyssa.

'You needed this rest,' Johnny told her as they lounged on the sunbeds while keeping an eye on Peter, splashing happily about in the pool, pretending he was a dolphin.

'You know,' she said with a deep sigh, 'I think I did. It's been pretty hectic the last few months.' She sighed again. 'But that's the rigours of being Centre Director – and I wouldn't be anything else in spite of the negatives.'

'You ever going to marry, or have kids?' Johnny asked at his most casual.

'Johnny Greene, what are you leading up to?' She cocked an eyebrow which warned him that, if he wasn't straight with her, she'd probably winkle the information out of his mind.

Johnny gave her a rakish grin. 'Nothing except that Dave Lehardt's just arrived.' His grin broadened as he saw her reaction. 'Ah! So! You're not entirely immune to his charm after all.'

Rhyssa managed to laugh though she couldn't do anything about the sudden flush of pleasure at the news. 'How do you know? You can't 'hear' him if I can't.'

'I saw him get out of the car. He's coming round through the house.' The gleam in Johnny's eyes was intolerable to her.

'We're just working friends,' she said and heard a mental ha-ha from Johnny as Dave Lehardt strode into the pool room. Johnny chuckled again as Dave's glance rested on her just that moment longer before he greeted the others.

'Hi there, Skeleteam,' Dave called to Peter who had an arm looped around the pool stair-rail. 'Need a hand out?'

'I think you'd better, Pete,' Rhyssa said. 'Your lips are blue and your skin's wrinkled. Hi, Dave.'

Johnny on a tight band: *You'd make a good team, you know. His beauty and your intelligence!*

Rhyssa: #Imaging herself chasing Johnny with an out-sized hunk of wood with the words 'blunt instrument' carved on it.#

Johnny: *Dorotea thinks so, too.*

Rhyssa: *You guys let me do my own thinking.*

Johnny: *Dave will because he couldn't hear you. And that's about the only drawback. He lusts after you, you know.*

'Really impressive launch today, Pete,' Dave Lehardt went on, hauling the boy out of the pool by one arm and deftly covering him with a huge towel.

· 'He gets better every time,' Johnny said, latching on to a spare lounger with his artificial foot and hauling it closer to where he and Rhyssa lounged.

Rhyssa: *You watch yourself, John Greene. I've my own minder and I'll tell him to dunk you if you misbehave.*

Johnny: #Imaging his own wide-eyed innocence.# *Me? Step out of line . . . especially if you threaten to shortcircuit my cybernetic limbs in a lousy pool. D'you know what salt water does to my spare parts?* #Now he imaged a violent shudder that sent bits and pieces spinning off his artificial arm and leg.#

'Actually, the last three shoots have been within a jog of the same power settings,' Rhyssa said audibly to the new arrival.

Dave Lehardt periscoped his lean length to seat himself on a lounger and grinned at Rhyssa. Was she imagining that his eyes were warmer when he looked at her? Damn him for not having a Talent! Damn him for having such a naturally dense mental shield! She hadn't any real clue – except in blue eyes she wanted to drown in – to go on. No wonder the unTalented regularly bungled relationships. And yet . . .

'NASA is delighted with the effectiveness of its new guidance and tracking system,' Dave was saying, looking well pleased, 'and they're quite happy to leave it in the "need to know" category. More queries from Padrugoi, requesting details of this top secret G and T as a possible adjunct to their systems.'

'And?' Johnny queried, flipping over on the sunbed, eyes narrowed to slits and his body relaxing in the warmth.

'General Halloway hems and haws with the best of them about a trial model, with a formidable test schedule ahead of it, by no means a totally proven system . . .'

'I am, too, a proven system,' Peter said, looking disgruntled as he floated over, an eerie-looking manoeuvre since his feet were invisible under the swathing of towel which he was trying to keep out of the puddles around the pool. His teeth chattered.

'On here,' Rhyssa said, making room for him on the sunbed. She would have fallen off if Dave hadn't quickly prevented it with hands and knees. She felt warm where he touched her, a warmth that was not generated by a sunbed. Then she settled Peter beside her, adjusting his limbs. 'You're up to fifteen minutes sunning today, aren't you?'

'Tell you one thing,' Dave went on, still supporting Rhyssa's body, 'I'm going to have to change the nickname, Skeleteam. You don't look so much like one any more.'

'All this good wholesome Florida sunshine,' Peter said, grinning at Dave. He'd finally got over his jealousy of the PR man: it was difficult to be jealous of a guy you liked so much, who could think up neat treats and found the best places to eat. Johnny and Rhyssa often argued – when Dave wasn't around – that the man had to have Talent: it simply wasn't measurable. Then Johnny discussed things like traumatic breakthroughs and psychological reluctances and Rhyssa replied that sometimes it was nice to know someone who could always surprise you.

'If you see any of that wholesome sunshine, let me know, huh?' Dave remarked with some bitterness, for the rain had lifted only briefly in the past three weeks.

'When are you guys going to develop a reliable weather Talent?'

'Look, we just got one minor miracle up and running,' Rhyssa replied, 'give us at least three days!'

'God only rested one day,' Dave said, deepening his voice to a base register and looking pious.

'Three weeks, three months, three years, three decades,' Johnny replied in a sepulchral tone. 'Can't even figure ol' Petey boy out and I've been busting my buns for weeks now.'

'Pete,' Dave began, 'how do you see what you do? Might as well ask the source right out straight,' he added in a broad aside to Rhyssa.

Peter laughed. Dave was always clowning. So Peter pretended to consider the question, knotting his brows and rubbing his chin the way Johnny sometimes did. 'It's like I think that's what I want to do – move the shuttle up – and I sort of lean into the generators, revving them up, and then I sort of,' he shrugged his thin shoulders, 'let go.'

'Like a stone from a slingshot?' Dave asked.

'Yeah, sort of like that.'

'You don't sound sure.'

'I'm not. It needs doing. I do it.'

Rhyssa put a warning hand on Dave's knee for she could sense Peter's distress about being unable to explain adequately. Dave's hand immediately covered hers, keeping her arm in a slightly awkward position. Over Peter's prone body, Johnny grinned at her.

'There are many operations,' Rhyssa went on quickly, 'one accomplishes strictly on an involuntary basis. Like breathing. You don't consciously go through the steps of drawing breath in and exhaling it: it's an involuntary procedure. Or take reaching for a glass. You don't consciously tell your hand to extend the required distance, tell your fingers to encircle it and your arm to lift the light weight. The task is accomplished without much conscious effort. Peter is working on such a deeply involuntary basis that he cannot – yet – analyse the requisite steps. Once Lance Baden is released from durance vile on the Station, I think we'll see progress in understanding what Skeleteam does as easily as he breathes.'

'It's not quite that easy,' Peter said.

'Don't hurt Skeleteam's feelings,' Johnny said in mock affront. 'He'll strike!'

'Not with his contract, he won't,' Rhyssa said feelingly.

'You know, Pete,' Johnny began in a thoughtful tone, 'what you said about something needing to be done and doing it. You really don't stop to think how? You just do it?'

'As you yourself, if I may remind you, landed a badly damaged shuttle on your twenty-first mission,' Dave put in. 'Experts still haven't figured out how you did that!'

John Greene grinned at him. 'Neither have I. Sorry, Pete.'

'You were using kinesis?' Peter asked.

'Nothing else would have got us down that day with one wing crumpled and the tail assembly blown off. Technically it was considered a traumatic explosion of Talent necessitated by an intense urge to survive.'

'What hit you?' Peter asked then. He'd wanted to ask but it had never been quite the right moment and he wasn't sure if the Colonel liked to be reminded of how he'd lost an arm and a leg.

'Some damned fool half-trained clowns, doing aerobatics through the flight path,' and Johnny cursed fluently and inventively on both audible and telepathic levels. Peter's eyes rounded with awe at the flavourful language. 'Fortunately they didn't survive to answer to me, or the law, for their antics.'

'Oh!' was Peter's reaction to John's uncharacteristic bitterness.

'You're not going to waste the pool, are you Dave?' Rhyssa asked to change the subject, and in the hope of regaining control of her hand before her arm fell asleep.

'You're stuck with me for a few days at any rate,' Dave replied. 'Without benefit of the Skeleteam, the airport's socked in solid.' He rose and, whistling a jaunty tune, picked his way through the puddles to the changing room.

Johnny heaved a sigh and resettled himself on the sunbed, hands cushioning his head. The nu-skin sheathing his artificial arm looked real enough except, Rhyssa noticed, that it didn't take a tan. Peter could and was getting a rich brown that made him appear like any other healthy, if scrawny, boy his age. He was also falling asleep, considerably more tired by the morning's activities than he would ever admit. Smiling tenderly down at the boy, Rhyssa eased herself off the sunbed and on to the lounger that Dave had just vacated. She checked the timer: Peter had ten minutes to go. She relaxed on the soft mattress.

'JE-sus CHRIST!'

Dave's sudden expletive roused her and helpless, she saw him flailing with arms and legs mid-air from a slip in a puddle, his long body poised to come down right across the corner of the tiled pool in what could be a serious fall. The sunbed lights went off and the next instant his abrupt descent was halted and he came to rest gently on the poolside, unharmed, unbruised but considerably shaken.

'How the hell . . . ?'

'My God!' exclaimed Johnny Greene. 'Did you do that, Pete?' he asked and the very slightest of snores answered him. 'My GOD! I did it! I did it! I DID IT!' His voice rose in a crescendo as he stared at Rhyssa in a state of shocked delight and surprise.

Rhyssa began to shake her head, grinning so hard at the breakthrough that she thought her face would split.

'That was all you,' she assured him, 'once again Johnny on the spot!'

36

_____

Sascha!

He could not ignore Dorotea's call but it was coming at an awkward moment. He lifted his hand to signal to Budworth and Sirikit for a slight break in their discussion.

Dorotea, vexation colouring her mental tone: *As you showed her how to use her wrist band to purchase damned near anything anywhere, you may now teach her thrift and budgeting. And some sense of order in her own room! There's not an inch of space that isn't stacked ceiling high with 'bargains'.* 'Bargains' had assumed expletive status.

Sascha: *Where is she?*

Dorotea, at the end of her patience: *Trying on clothes while viewing today's lessons!*

'Look, Bud, run those ethnic groupings again. We've at least got a statistical forecast of how many psionic Talents each generation has produced since Darrow and op Owen's time. Now let's break it down into individual Talent manifestations: pre-cogs, finders, affinities, kinetics, telepaths, telempaths.'

Budworth shrugged equably and began to formulate the programme.

'I still don't know *how*,' Sirikit said in her soft, lilting tones, 'that's going to help us discover Talent in the linears.'

'Where there's smoke, there's gotta be a fire or two,' was Sascha's cryptic comment as he exited.

Since that fateful shopping trip three weeks before, Tirla had discovered a new pastime that almost rivalled her hunger for learning. At first, Dorotea had been amused. 'It's hunger of another sort: acquisition. It'll pass.'

Cass had accompanied her on two more expeditions, showing her how to use the subway transport and thought it was fun to watch Tirla slip into the most exclusive shops and boutiques. When she started shopping on her own, she was detained twice by overzealous officials and, to her credit, had waited patiently until someone – usually Sascha – arrived from the Centre to verify her right to the ID bracelet and to make charges against the Centre's account. Not that she bought something every afternoon that she spent in the malls. Sascha deeply regretted that Cass had told her how many malls there were in Jerhattan. Linears only supported one.

Invariably, Tirla ended her afternoons at the Old-Fashioned Parlour. When Tirla announced that she was going to work her way right through the five pages of confectionery selections, Dorotea had laughed.

'It might put a little weight on those bird bones of hers, and she always eats her dinner,' she said. 'I wish she would put on weight. What must those shop attendants think when that child looks half-starved all the time?'

Dorotea was standing in the living room when Sascha arrived in answer to her summons, and pointed sternly toward Tirla's room. Sascha tapped on the door and Tirla's cheerful hum broke off.

'Who is it?' There was always that note of apprehension

when Tirla was caught unawares. Once she could break into the telepathic mode that Sascha was certain she possessed, she would 'know'.

'Sascha!'

'Just a minute.'

For just a moment, Sascha thought he caught a stray coy thought and then the door opened, in stages, because Tirla had to rearrange things to get it wide enough for him to enter. Sascha looked in and groaned.

'Tirla, what happened to the kid who had to be coaxed into buying more than one outfit?' It was the first thing that came into his head, and was probably not at all the way to handle the situation.

Dorotea, in disgust: *Hamhanded twit!*

Tirla blinked at Sascha. 'But you told me I could shop whenever I wanted to. Just look what I found today?' And she held up a pair of stiletto-heeled sandals with jewelled straps. 'And they fit. They didn't cost much because the shopkeeper had had them around for decades and practically gave them to me. Aren't they lovely? D'you want to see them on? They make me much taller.'

'I'm sure they do, Tirla but, to be candid, they're not the sort of thing a girl of your age should wear.'

'They fit!' she repeated as if that were the most important aspect.

'Tirla! Is there no place I can sit down in here? And that's what has Dorotea so upset. You know how neat she keeps everything in the house . . . '

Dorotea: *That's right. Blame me.*

' . . . While Talents may have what they need, and also what they want, within reason,' and he stressed the words, 'that's the operative phrase. This . . . ' and Sascha gestured broadly, hooking a hanger, and its layers of clothing, off the door. The pile tumbled to enlarge a mass of colourful blouses lying beside the door. 'This is no longer reasonable!'

Tirla merely looked up at him, her face expressionless

but he sensed so deep a hurt and disappointment that he relented instantly. 'I don't think I can send it all back. I've tried everything on.'

'Look, Chip,' and he used Cass's affectionate nickname for her, 'sending it all back is not the answer.'

Dorotea: *It's a start!*

'Learning to buy wisely is. Some of this stuff . . .' and Sascha pointed to items of intimate apparel in lace and gauze that were far too sophisticated for even a twenty year old, '. . . can be packed up and stored . . .'

Dorotea, acidly: *Where?*

'In the vaults.' He began picking up other inappropriate garments. 'And we'll get the clutter down to manageable proportions.' In doing so he exposed a small hill of shoes, all colours, in a variety of styles that astonished him and all of them small enough to fit Tirla's dainty feet.

Dorotea: *Cinderella complex.*

Sascha: *Pairs, every single one of them.*

Dorotea: *Then how can they be pairs?*

'Five pairs of shoes, no more, Tirla.' He saw her sulky expression. 'Five pairs at one time. And ten different outfits in the closet. None of this . . .' and he held up an emerald-green ballgown with exquisitely detailed beadwork in silver and a leaf green. It was exceedingly stylish and the colour was perfect for Tirla but not until she reached twenty. Eighteen at least. Tirla's basic dress sense couldn't be faulted. 'I'll have some trunks sent over so you can put everything away. Then we're going to sit down and work out a budget.'

'Budget? Like they do for cities and projects?' Surprised, Tirla came out of her sulk.

'Yes. The Centre has a budget, I have a budget, Peter has a budget . . .'

Dorotea: *All God's chillun got budgets!*

'Then I won't be able to go shopping again?'

Sascha was not impervious to her broken voice and her sad expression.

'Shop all you want. Look in every damned mall on Manhattan, Long Island and the Jersey Shore. Just don't buy anything. Windowshop to your heart's content.'

'Never buy anything again?'

Dorotea, mimicking a nostalgic violin air: *La da da, da da da dah!*

Sascha: *All right and how would you curb a kid who's never had much in her life and suddenly can have anything she wants?*

Dorotea: *More or less as you're doing. Just don't waver at the sight of tears in her big black eyes!*

Sascha caught an undertone in Dorotea's voice that puzzled him.

'No, Chip, not never. Just not so much so constantly, things you don't really need right now, because you've got enough. Of practically everything as far as I can see.'

She sank to the edge of her barely visible bed. 'But it's not fun to windowshop unless you've got someone with you. Where's Cass? She loves to shop.'

'Cass is out on assignment.'

Tirla cocked her head up at him, no longer a disappointed and confused twelve-year-old. 'More kids missing?'

'Not yet,' he said mendaciously. 'We want to keep it that way.'

'Is she in a linear?' Excitement brightened her expression. Sascha nodded.

Dorotea: *For the love of little apples, don't tell her where or she'll track Cass down.*

'Why don't you let me work undercover with her? I could be her kid and . . . '

'NO!'

Tirla rocked back on the bed at the vehemence of his response. She looked hurt and confused again and even younger than her chronological age.

'Sorry, Chip,' and Sascha ruffled her now sleekly

clean and shining hair in an effort to compensate for his tactlessness. 'Give yourself a little break. We didn't catch Yassim and if he spots you, he'd have you wasted so fast, none of us could help you.'

Dorotea: *Well, she's still afraid of Yassim!*

She was so afraid that Sascha gathered her up in his arms and rocked her.

'Yassim can't get you here in the Centre, Tirla. You're safe here. I want to keep you safe so you can grow up and use that rare Talent you have . . . to earn enough money to pay for all you've been buying.' He tried to make a joke of it. He felt her stiffen in his arms. 'No, not your floaters!' And he had to laugh. The little witch. Her hoard was precious to her, never to be broached. 'Just think how little you'd have left if you HAD spent your stash. Think of that the next time you want to buy something. Pretend you're spending YOUR money.'

'I *wouldn't* spend MY money,' she mumbled against his chest.

With the slender little body trustfully curled in his lap, Sascha permitted himself just a few moments to caress her hair and savour the feel of her in his arms. Why Tirla? Of all the women in the world, how could this little waif, streetwise and precocious, become so entangled in his emotions and heart? She couldn't possibly understand how much she meant to him. She was far too young for that aspect of maturing to have touched her. And yet . . . she responded to him as she did to no-one else. With a final little hug, he put her from him which he did as gently as he could. One day, eight or nine years from now . . .

Dorotea had no comment to make. To his surprise, Tirla obediently began to fold up her possessions, neatly and carefully. Sascha watched for a few more moments and then, looking where he put his big feet on the cluttered floor, went to arrange for trunks.

37

The moment Dave Lehardt entered the kitchen that evening as Rhyssa was clearing up the debris of their celebratory meal, she knew 'a moment' had come. Over the last few months of their close association, she had learned to pick up the subtle hints of his body language. She felt her heartbeat begin to speed up and she tried not to crash dishes about or drop things: that would have been too much of a give-away. And with this lover, she could extract no helpful clues from his mind. Perhaps that was why Dave appeared to be so much more romantic than any of her Talented associations.

He came right up to her so that she had to look about, to acknowledge his proximity.

'The hardest thing in dealing with you Talents is to catch you when no-one else is listening,' he began. His blue eyes held a very intense look. He took the saucepan away from her and put it firmly back into the soapy water, put both hands on her arms and turned her slightly, but decisively, toward him. 'Pete and Johnny are so involved in a rehash of my pratfall, they couldn't be paying attention to anything else.' With a little pressure of his hands, he pulled her against him.

Johnny: *Don't you dare be coy!*

Rhyssa: *Get out of my head, Johnny Greene.*

Peter: *Ah, just when it's getting interesting. How'll I ever learn how it's done!*

Rhyssa: *Break off! Both of you! If I feel so much as a tendril of thought . . .*

Johnny: *I think she means it!*

Peter: *I KNOW she does!*

Her mind was filled with a deafening silence.

'They're not,' Rhyssa assured him.

'I've been told and warned, obliquely and to my face, that I've no right to ask a woman of your obvious Talent, and talents, to marry a man without an ounce of the right stuff in him.'

Rhyssa felt a surge of anger flare deeply inside her mind. She wondered who had been inhibiting this wonderful, caring man. Especially when he'd done so much to aid and save all Talents. Then she willed him not to stop talking such marvellously romantic stuff and tilted her head up encouragingly. He could stop talking now and maybe try to kiss her. She shivered with anticipation.

'But I think such a decision is up to you, and me. And I'm so totally besotted with you that I can't think straight when you're in the same room with me, and I don't think of much else but you when we're apart. Rhyssa Owen, would you even consider marrying me?'

'What took you so many eons to ask?' she said, folding her arms about his neck, grinning up at him.

With a gladness that seemed to emanate from every pore of him, he clasped her firmly in his arms and kissed her with a great deal of entirely satisfactory expertise, just as if he'd read her mind.

38

Peter and Rhyssa returned in quiet triumph the day that Cass Culter reported to Boris that three Neesters and two Hispanics in Linear E were suspiciously more affluent than they had any right to be. Boris decided that he would not darken the happy return with such news and did not even inform Sascha of the event.

Dorotea and Tirla both exclaimed over how well Peter looked, tanned and healthy, moving with more confidence while Rhyssa listened, an oddly soft smile on her face. Dave Lehardt had had to remain behind in Florida to finalize his PR campaign, setting the stage for Colonel Johnny Greene to assume the role of Skeleteam.

In his turn, Peter took full notice of Tirla's new elegance and was amazed that she had shopped in the malls herself.

'Well, Sascha took me the first time . . . '

Dorotea, privately to Rhyssa: *And said Open Sesame and in a week Tirla's room was as full as a bazaar.*

Sascha: *I heard that. Knock it off!*

Rhyssa: *Did she pick that outfit herself?*

Dorotea: *She picked out everything herself and a lot of things a twelve-year-old girl has no need of . . . yet.*

Rhyssa: *She's got good taste . . . in what she's wearing now.*

Dorotea: *Good taste all round. Just a trifle sophisticated.* Dorotea was aware that Sascha was seething and changed the subject.

Peter and Tirla slipped out of the room.

'How come you're allowed to go to the mall all the time?' Peter asked Tirla, envious of her freedom. *He* was never allowed to go anywhere on his own.

Tirla shrugged. 'Oh, they tried to tell me how dangerous it was.' She giggled. 'As if I didn't know how to take care of myself in any old Linear. Particularly one as straight as the ones here in Jerhattan.'

'And you go whenever you want?'

'Nearly every day.' She cocked her head at him. 'You ever been to the Old-Fashioned Parlor of Gastronomical Delights?'

'Me?' Peter thumped his hand against his chest, then grimaced. He still didn't have the small-muscle control needed to use just a thumb or a finger. He was feeling aggrieved on several counts. 'Oh, I heard about the Parlor.' He pretended indifference, but then his pose faltered. 'Is it really that good?'

'Good?' Tirla's enthusiasm bubbled out of her. 'It's spectacular. You wouldn't believe the concoctions they serve. "The most" ' she quoted from the menu, ' "scrumptious, delectable monstrosities of confections you'll ever experience." ' Sensing Peter's longing, Tirla deliberately encouraged it. 'Any kind of flavor of ice cream, all homemade, every topping known to man . . . '

'And you just go?'

'Sure. Why not? It's only four stops away on the subway.' She jerked her thumb at the murmur of adult voices coming from the living room. 'Who'd miss us for half an hour, anyway?' When she saw the hesitation on his face, she added almost challengingly, 'They're busy. We'd be back before they'd know we'd gone!'

That decided Peter, though he knew perfectly well that his physical circumstances were far different from Tirla's. Nevertheless, she was younger than he was, and if she was allowed, he was, too.

They left the house by the side door, Tirla skipping beside Peter in delight at his company. It was going to be such fun showing him just how well she knew her way around.

39

Peter could sense how pleased Tirla was to be able to take him someplace which she had frequented but would be new to him. So he just smiled as they took their seats on the subway from the Centre platform. Other Talents on the same car grinned at the two, telepathing greetings and congratulations to Peter who had learned to assume a modest demeanour in public, even among other Talents.

Tirla was describing in great detail which gastronomical delight was her favourite, with four kinds of ice cream and four kinds of toppings, and four kinds of nuts and cherries, coconut and multi-coloured sprinkles.

'My mother took me to a place like that,' Peter said, 'oh, a long time ago now. For my tenth birthday. My sister goes a lot: mother says that's why she has spots so often.'

'Spots?'

'Pimples. Zits. Facial eruptions.'

'Oh,' Tirla replied in a tone that expressed unenlightenment. Peter imagined a pimpled face at her. 'Oh! That sort.'

Surreptitiously she ran her hand over her face and Peter laughed.

'You may never get spots, Tirla,' Peter said encouragingly. 'They keep us on a healthy diet anyhow. Not subbie food.'

'What was Florida like?' Tirla asked.

Peter had learned a lot from watching Dave Lehardt answer difficult questions tactfully. So he told her about the flat land and the palm trees, the sand, the good food, the pool and the sunbeds and she seemed quite content that it implied that he and Rhyssa had been taking a holiday.

She assumed leadership as soon as they reached the right station and eagerly started running up the steps ahead of him before she remembered his disability. When she stopped, he was right beside her.

'Your vacation did you a lot of good, didn't it?' she said, and ploughed on upwards. 'See . . . there's the Parlour, just inside the mall entrance,' she added, pointing.

Neither youngster noticed that their progress was being closely observed by two men, just descending from an elegant private hopper, parked on the mall's heli-pad. The shorter man took a small black instrument from his pocket and pointed it at them.

'How exceedingly careless. Neither of them has been stranded! I want them taken! Especially that odious little boy! I want no slip-up, no excuses. You won't have too much trouble with the boy but his companion mustn't be allowed to spread an alarm. Do it as fast as you can assemble a crew. Have I made myself plain?'

'Yes, sir.'

40

Peter was able to shout just once, his cry more indignant than alarmed. Then an ominous silence despite Rhyssa's attempt to re-establish communications. She wasted no more time on the silence but broadcast on the widest band possible.

ALERT, ALL TALENTS, ALL LEO PERSONNEL. PETER REIDINGER MAY HAVE BEEN ABDUCTED. PRESUMABLY IN VICINITY OF OLD-FASHIONED PARLOUR. TIRLA WAS WITH HIM.

TIRLA! And Sascha's blast was nearly as loud as hers.

Complying! came Boris's calming bass tone. *All units in the area are to commence search procedures. Fax photos of the children are being dispatched to all vehicles. I'm proceeding immediately to question any possible witnesses. This is a TOP Priority.*

This is a G and H Priority! Sascha added with bitter vehemence. *Sirikit, what does Budworth have on the strand scanner?* There was a long and stunned pause. *Oh, my God. I never stranded Tirla. Rhyssa?*

Peter neither, was Rhyssa's horrified reply. *How could we have been so* stupid?

You weren't, Dorotea said in a bracing tone. *Their ID bracelets can be traced far more accurately than a stranded kid.*

The exchanges had taken bare seconds while Rhyssa, Sascha and Dorotea sped towards the Control Room where the monitoring equipment ought to give them some indication of where the children were.

Budworth was in front of the appropriate screen but tears were streaming down his face. 'Bracelets were cut off. Scanner has 'em in a sewer drain in the mall heli–lot.'

'Oh my God!' Sascha's exclamation came out in a sob, then he shook himself. *Carmen, get in here. Bertha, Auer, you come, too. Dorotea, any chance that you can reach Tirla?*

If you can't, I'm not likely to, and there was a quality of ineffable sorrow in her response.

'There's nothing, nothing there at all,' Rhyssa murmured, her voice breaking. 'I've always been able to hear Peter's mind.'

Dorotea said, 'Not if he's been anaesthetized, my dear. That's the only time he couldn't hear or answer.' Then, on a very tight band to Sirikit: *Phone Dave Lehardt and tell him to get here as fast as he can.*

Sirikit, her own eyes bleak, discreetly complied.

'C'mon, Bro, c'mon! How long does it take your squads to get moving!' Sascha demanded, pacing in his anxiety.

The Talents had to wait another five agonizing minutes before Boris contacted them.

The kids sat by themselves. Tirla's well known here and she introduced her friend, Peter, to her usual waitress. She saw them leave the place. She caught a glimpse of them entering a small hopper with the Talent Centre emblem. There were four men but she didn't see their faces. She didn't see anything odd except that the boy walked funny and then seemed to be assisted by one of the men. And no, she didn't notice the registration.

I've an APB on small hoppers with Talent emblems in Jerhattan, but it'd be helpful if your scanners have picked up their bracelets.

Sascha: *The IDs were cut off. Left in the sewer outside the mall.*

Boris: *That would be the first thing. So, can you pick something up yet on the strand scanners?*

Rhyssa, heavily: *Neither Peter nor Tirla were stranded.*

Boris, exploding: *In the name of all that's holy, why not? The two most important Talents? You have everyone running about like lunatics, stranding dumb subbie kids and pampered hive children and you don't strand Peter and Tirla?* The silence following his outburst was more eloquent that anything he could have added.

Rhyssa began to weep and Dorotea tried to comfort her, tactilely and telepathically.

Boris in a calmer tone: *All right, then. We have to assume the abductors are following their latest procedures. That's the only thing that would account for total telepathic silence. The kids were gassed. They're going to be stashed someplace and in those neat little cocoons. Sorry, Rhyssa. But I'm too angry to be diplomatic. Sascha, have you called Carmen in? My finders are all on the case. Somehow, we'll find 'em. Those kids are smart. Once they wake up, they'll be able to help us find them.*

Suz and Cass further dampened the spirits of the Talents by reporting that in excess of thirty children in each residential had been sold, or just taken. Ranjit, working covertly in Residential W, also confirmed rather more activity in the mall markets than could be discreetly ignored. Such scope and audacity was more than LEO or the Centre had anticipated. All had happened so smoothly and simultaneously that both Centre and LEO had been caught unawares.

'My sympathies go out to Rhyssa and the other Talents. It's incredible that two valuable young people like that could also be vulnerable to this despicable group,' the City Manager told Boris who passed her message on to Sascha and Rhyssa. 'This has top priority and all the resources of the City are at your disposal, Boris and Rhyssa. No effort will be spared. Is there anything I, personally, can do? Offer a reward? Trade immunity for information?'

'Get your department heads thinking,' Boris told Teresa Aiello, 'where such a significant number of children could be detained. I've got every available person on transport surveillance. They can't have been moved out of the Jerhattan area, not in a group or singly. I put a hold on all rail freight and every container is being examined. Any cargo of a suspicious size is being opened. They've got to be somewhere near by. For a while.'

'Everyone on this staff will start examining possibilities, unused warehouses, old buildings, underground stores, Boris,' Teresa Aiello assured him grimly.

Boris Roznine didn't have quite all his people on transport duty: he had a good third picking up as many ladrones and sassins as his teams found in mall or factory. LEO might just luck out and dislodge a clue from an apprehensive subbie.

'Peter is alive, isn't he?' Budworth asked, too concerned to be tactful in his wish to be reassured. Peter was a special friend of Budworth's.

'He's alive. It's not a dead silence,' Rhyssa said, wincing at her choice of adjective, her voice low with tension, 'but he's not conscious.'

'Nothing yet, Carmen?' Sascha asked the finder whose hands stroked the lock of Tirla's hair. She could not meet his eyes as she shook her head slowly.

'Christ on a crutch! How could we be so arrogant as to believe we could protect them with an ID bracelet!' Sascha demanded explosively, stalking around what free floor space there was. 'WHY on EARTH didn't we think to strand them?' He pounded one fist into the other hand. 'We've wall to wall Talents,' he said, gesturing almost scornfully at the various teams clustered about monitors or swiftly feeding programmes into the main frame. 'Where could they have got to? That many bodies are too hard to hide. The kids have to be fed. They can't have been whisked off to their . . . ' Sascha could not find the appropriate noun and grimaced, 'wherever. Boris had initiated transport surveillance within minutes. Damnit, the subways and cargo routes have been wired since the incident in G.'

Sascha, ease up, Dorotea said in his mind, her warning a very narrow quiet thought. *Rhyssa's feeling enough guilt as it is . . .*

Sascha: *And you think I feel none for not stranding Tirla, for encouraging her to go to the bloody mall? To that unmentionable bloody confectionery Parlour?* His response was loaded with derision. *She'd've been bloody safer if I HAD let Boris use her for bait!*

Dorotea: *Stop castigating yourself, Sascha. Tirla's been safely in and out of the mall and the Parlour for weeks now. I just can't imagine what factor made it such a dangerous journey this time.*

Rhyssa: *Peter's worked so hard. It seemed such an innocent thing to do.*

Dorotea, reassuringly: *We'll hear. We'll hear. The least whisper and we'll hear them.* Dorotea's mind was casting restlessly for a trace of Tirla's. After nearly five weeks of proximity with the girl, she was certain that she'd spot its consciousness.

MAY ALL YOUR ORIFICES BE CLOGGED WITH CAMEL DUNG, YOUR BELLY ETERNALLY FULL OF VOMIT! MAY YOUR TONGUE ROT AND YOUR TEETH FALL OUT AND YOUR GUMS SWELL WITH BOILS! MAY YOUR LIVER ROT AND YOUR BLADDER DRY UP AND YOUR GLANDS SHRIVEL AND PUTREFY!

'Good God!' Dorotea was jolted to her feet. 'Did you all hear that? It was loud enough!'

'Peter doesn't know that kind of language!' Rhyssa said, with a slight grin.

Beaming from ear to ear, Sascha replied, 'Tirla would. Pungent, isn't she? Damn, where's she got to? I can't hear her any more.'

'Well, I can and she's still in fine form,' Dorotea said. 'Neither of you hear her now? She can certainly broadcast when she's of a mind to.' She held up her hand, listening with every muscle taut. *Dorotea here, Tirla, can you hear me?* Dorotea's mental tone was tranquil and reassuring.

Tirla: *Dorotea? Where are you?*

Dorotea: *More to the point, where are you?* 'Can you hear her now, Sascha, Rhyssa?' Dorotea asked. A brief headshake confirmed Dorotea as the primary contact. She felt the light firm mind touches of Rhyssa and Sascha, listening in.

Tirla, savagely: *You tell me. I can't see a thing. I can't feel a thing. I can smell and the stench is worse than the bottom level of a factory bilge. Couldn't you guys track me?*

No, we couldn't, Tirla. Your bracelets were discarded right at the mall when you and Peter were taken. Is Peter near by? Dorotea spoke aloud for the benefit of those in the room. Sascha had motioned Carmen to her side but Carmen kept shaking her head at her continued inability to 'find' Tirla. *Can you remember what happened?*

Tirla's disgust was obvious to Dorotea. *I can't remember anything. Peter and I'd finished the new spectacular they just added to the menu. He paid for it himself. Said it was his treat this time 'cause he'd just had a vacation. We left the Parlour and were walking towards the subway when something covered my face and I don't remember a thing more. Awful stuff. Sweet icky smell. How come I can talk to you all of a sudden?*

Sometimes it's a case of need to, Tirla, Dorotea said, putting a smile of approval into her tone.

Tirla: *You needed me to? Or I needed you to hear me? Peter? Peter, answer me!* Dorotea caught the conflicting

281

emotions in Tirla's question but such competitiveness was not a bad sign.

You and Peter are not the only two taken today. Cass and Suz reported that a number must have been taken from E as well. A very well-organized affair. That's why anything you can tell us will help, Tirla. Anything, no matter how trivial.

Peter's not answering me in here. Maybe he's just not awake yet. My stomach's sour. I shouldn't've had that spectacular. Peter? Peeeeter!

Dorotea spoke gently. *Don't panic, Tirla. Peter will wake up soon enough if he was gassed the same time as you were. We're very relieved to hear from you, believe me.*

Tirla, mildly surprised: *I do believe you. You can't lie in your mind, can you?*

Not to me, you can't, Dorotea said, gesturing imperiously for Rhyssa and Sascha to stop trying to insinuate questions in her head. Tirla's voice was clear but, after the first burst of psychic outrage, neither as strong nor as loud. She could not risk losing the link. *Now, tell me what you can about your surroundings.*

They stink!

We've already established that. What of? Besides, I assume, the unpleasant bodily discharges of frightened children. What can you hear?

Tirla, disgusted: *A lot of crying.*

Even that tells me something, Tirla. Can you isolate the individual crying enough to estimate how many children are around you?

Dorotea could sense Tirla's concentration and did not interrupt.

Tirla: *I think there's a lot of kids: there's sure a lot of crying and moaning and someone's hiccuping. All around me, all sides, above, but none below. Why'd they blindfold us and tie us down like this? Most of these kids wouldn't even try to escape.*

Dorotea: *Yassim lost all the G children, didn't he?* Dorotea reminded her. *I think that, unfortunately, caused them to change their tactics. They're now employing a disorientation*

282

technique, sensory-deprivation, to reduce the children to com-
pliance when they are released. You're not afraid, are you?

Tirla, candidly: *I don't like it, but I'm not scared. I'm mad.*
Her tone strengthened. *I missed my maths class.*

Dorotea broke into relieved laughter. An angry Tirla
would be far more useful than a frightened one. Sascha
managed a relieved chuckle and the tension in Rhyssa's
stance eased.

*Stay mad, Tirla. Anger can be a valuable asset. Now what
I want you to do is to try and calm the children. Get them to tell
you their names and, if possible, where they came from. R was
not the only linear hit. We estimate that upwards of a hundred
children were taken.*

Including Peter and me?

*A hundred and two. Peter's not as physically strong as you
are, Tirla.* Dorotea gave Rhyssa a raised eyebrow at her
smothered protest. 'Well, she is. And a lot better able to
take care of herself in such circumstances.'

*Strong isn't much help right now with me blind and strapped
in like cargo? Hey, you lot! Shut up! Quit your grizzling,
stupid Neesters.* Tirla then dropped into languages which
Dorotea could not understand. *They prefer crying for their
mommies! Mommies who sold 'em!* Tirla suddenly dropped
into Basic again. *Some half dozen are from E, seven are from
W, and two from C. How they bleat! None of 'em's Peter.*

Dorotea: *Ask them their names.*

Tirla could give ten names of the estimated fifteen
children in with her. These were instantly forwarded to
Boris.

'Where can Peter be?' Rhyssa murmured softly. At
some point while she was concentrating on Dorotea's
conversations, Dave Lehardt joined the anxious group
in the Control Room. He linked his fingers in hers
and the physical contact was almost more reassuring
than the aura of encouragement from all the telepaths
about her.

'Ask her again about the various smells?' Sascha prompted

Dorotea. 'There may be *something* that'll give us a clue to where.'

Tirla: *Well, there's a sort of metal stink. And there's a mouldy mildewing rotten stink, that's stronger. There's another smell I can't identify. Oily. I'm stuffed into something . . . feels like plastic foam. Even my fingers are separated into slots. I'm bound at the wrists, ankles, waist and across my chest. If I was shorter, I'd be choking. There's a slit under my bottom so I can pee and stuff. Makes it breezy there. I think I'm near the floor. I just hope no kid's above me, that is all. That would be hard to take! Oh, cut the caterwauling! No-one's hurting you!* She roared out repetitions in other dialects.

'Her predicament is beginning to get to her,' Dorotea said grimly. *Tirla, I'm with you. Even if you can't hear them, Rhyssa, Sascha, Boris, Sirikit, Budworth, Dave, we're all there. We'll get you out of there, I promise.*

Tirla: *Soon, please. If I have to listen to all this crying and moaning, I'll Space out. What about that woman who wore my hair? Why don't you ask her where I am?*

Carmen is right here and reminds you that she needs light to find you! Remember? That's why she couldn't locate you in the linear: you were in the dark.

Tirla: *I'm a lot more in the dark now than I was then. What if they don't turn any lights on?* For the first time, Tirla's voice was tinged with fear instead of outraged anger.

It may be no consolation to you right now, Tirla, but they'll want you to be in good condition. They'll also have to feed you and keep you clean.

Tirla: *Yeah? When? Next week sometime?*

You were taken at approximately three. It's ten-thirty now. You can't be left without food and water much longer.

Tirla: *You're right. That's not much consolation. Dorotea, don't stop talking to me, will you? I don't care what you say. Just don't stop talking.*

I'm totally at your command, Tirla, and Dorotea imagined a flourish and a curtsey in her mind to Tirla. She was rewarded by a little chuckle. *Shall we start with the maths lesson you missed?*

Tirla: *In my head?*

Dorotea: *Write it on the board in my mind. I'll remember for you.*

'And also increase her telepathic facility,' Rhyssa said with a feeling but genuine smile. 'You are incorrigible, Dorotea.'

'Also very good at what I do,' Dorotea replied smugly.

Rhyssa? Rhyssa?

Rhyssa gasped with incredulity, her face stricken by the faintness of Peter's call. Dave wrapped an arm about her shoulders, supporting her as she held up her hand to stop all noise in the room as the weak voice reached her mind. *Yes, Peter. I've been listening for you.*

Peter: *I can't see. I can't feel. They gassed me. I'm going to be sick.*

Rhyssa, her mental tone calm and firm though she was clinging to Dave's hands: *Easy, Peter. Remember our drills. Reduce the nausea.*

Peter: *It's never been this hard before, Rhyssa.* There was an edge of despair in his voice. Rhyssa knew so well how he hated anaesthetics. He had reactions to most of the common ones. It was going to take time – which she didn't think they had – for him to shake off the residual disorientation and nausea and to bring his kinesis into use.

Rhyssa: *Focus your mind, Peter, just as you used to do in hospital. Focus your thoughts, ignore the extraneous.*

Peter: *There're other kids in here with me. Some of 'em are pretty scared.*

Rhyssa: *Call out for Tirla. She's somewhere! Maybe very near by.*

Dorotea, urgently: *Tirla, Peter's awake. Call his name.*

Neither heard the other.

'Christ! Fine team of Talents we are when our kids are vulnerable!' Sascha remarked in caustic anger.

Tirla, echoing Sascha's frustration: *Why doesn't Peter just*

glide out this contraption, Dorotea? And her own disgust.
He's the kinetic! When Dorotea explained Peter's problem
with the anaesthesia, Tirla gave a bark of laughter. *So
it's up to me again, I guess. Don't forget the answers to my
equations, will you, Dorotea?*

Dorotea: *Tirla. What are you planning to do?*

Tirla: *Get out of this coffin.*

How?

Tirla: *They made one mistake when they strapped me in
here. They strapped my fingers down, not up where I couldn't
reach anything. I should be able to dig out enough plastic to
free my hands.*

Dorotea felt the effort in Tirla's mind, effort and fringes
of pain. 'Could she do that?' she asked Sascha.

'According to the Bro, the kids retrieved in Manhattan
had been put into a foamed plastic cocoon, immobile,
blindfolded, and gagged. Designed, Harv said, to reduce
resistance.' Sascha grimaced.

You have made contact with Tirla and Peter? Boris's voice
was excited.

'Contact, Bro, but not release. Both kids are cocooned.
And Peter's having a bad reaction to whatever gas they
used.' Sascha made another face, mimicking the aggra-
vation his brother was mentally expressing. 'He'll need
a little time before he's any good.'

Boris: *Is there time? I've got the City Manager, AND all
her deputies on my back for action. Some of the other kids
were legal, too.*

Rhyssa was concentrating on strengthening her link
with Peter, helping him to dissipate the residue of the
anaesthetic which inhibited his kinetic abilities. Her face
mirrored his desperation and sense of failure, and she
leaned against Dave more heavily in her despair.

There! The triumph in Tirla's voice was evident to
Dorotea and she held up her hand, repeating the girl's
words. *Camel-gutted tripe! Miserable dung-eaters! Descend-
ants of snake offal. Scuzfarts! Maggots!*

Good heavens! How pungent. Tirla, how have you hurt yourself? Dorotea demanded, sensing pain.

Tirla: *Never you mind. I'm out of this cocoon. There are nineteen other kids stuck in 'em here, some of 'em still knocked out. Peter's not one of them. Tell Carmen not to fracture her skull finding me. This place is black as the bottom of an elevator pit. Ugh. I slipped in junk. Ugh! I've reached one wall. Faugh. It's slimy and gritty. Too smooth and cold for metal. Ah, an opening. A window. Plastic coated. I can't even scratch a sliver off. Look, I'm going to try something,* Tirla went on. *They always forget about ceilings. There's air coming in here from someplace.* She was silent for a long while, though Dorotea was aware of strenuous physical activity. *I am not hurting you. Just using you as a step-ladder. And I won't let you go, cry-baby. You're no use to me. Quit your grizzling.* Then another period of silence and Dorotea reported more physical effort, punctuated by inadvertent grunts of pain.

Tirla: *Well, I was right. There is a ceiling hatch. And I can see, a little. Well, whaddya know? I'm in a shunting yard. There are rows and rows of train cars, old ones. Can't have been moved in years. And some place down to my right there's light. Sort of around an edge, like of a window or a door. Any idea where I could be?*

From the moment Tirla mentioned a shunting yard, her description was forwarded to everyone concerned.

Tirla: *I'm going along the tops of cars towards the light. I can't hear anyone and no-one would be stupid enough to walk around this place without a light.*

Tell us how many cars have children, Tirla, Dorotea urged.

Tirla: *Peter! Peter! Answer me! Peter! It's Tirla! Answer me! Wow! I nearly fell off the edge of the car. Slippery surface, moist. Whole place is damp!*

'Try for yards by the river, by the sea. Along the sound,' Sascha said, prowling up and down the bank of monitors, checking patterns.

Peter, in an exultant mental cry: *Tirla!*

It echoed from Tirla's mind to Dorotea and lifted the anxieties of every Talent in the room. Rhyssa sank into a chair that Dave pulled out for her. Then he handed her a stimulant drink with an unmistakeable gesture to toss it down quickly.

Tirla: *So here's where they stashed you, huh? Now, I'll just drop in beside you. There! Sorry, the tape'll sting coming off.*

Peter: *Ouch! Isn't there any light in this place? Hey, don't take all the skin off my wrists! You're rough!*

Tirla: *Only the tan came off. You're free. Here! Don't go faint. Lie back. Stay easy. Get your breath. Now look, you'd better rest some more.* Dorotea could hear the nervous concern in Tirla's voice, a matter she did not impart to Rhyssa. Tirla went on: *I'm going to look around this place, Peter. You get your kinetics working again 'cause there's no way I can haul you up by myself.*

Peter: *I'll be OK, Tirla. I'll be OK. Just . . . just come back.*

Tirla: *Oho! Aircar! Big bugger. Expensive! No lights!* There was a long moment of silence. *That was too close.*

'Ask her if she saw a number, a description, anything!' Sascha prompted Dorotea.

Tirla: *I'd say that it's a metallic blue jetter, twelve seater, no lights but I got a glimpse – a 3, a dash and R I G . . . I think. Could have been a B but the I and G were clear enough.*

When Dorotea repeated what Tirla had said, Sascha exploded to his feet. ' . . . R I G! We couldn't be so lucky!' He slapped his right palm against his forehead to vent some of his excitement. 'Budworth, get through to Auer and Bertha, and see if they have any tickles about Flimflam.'

'Flimflam?' Rhyssa and Dorotea said together, both reaching into his mind for confirmation, but he was involved in a tight conversation with Boris.

'Boris is doing a search on the registration,' Sascha

said aloud, holding up one hand, his expression intent and eager. 'Dorotea, tell Tirla she's a star!'

Tirla, surprised: *Was that enough for you? Oops. There's another one coming in, from another direction. Also running dark. I'll see if I can get a better reading.*

Tirla, Dorotea replied hastily, *don't risk discovery. And Rhyssa says she'd rather have you stay with Peter.*

Tirla, blithely: *Peter's OK. Working on it. I'm going to find out who the other dark flyer is!*

TIRLA! Dorotea was momentarily stunned by the independence. *Tirla!* Then she turned to Rhyssa, hands outstretched in appeal. 'The little witch has cut me off! Oh, just wait til I get my hands on that child! The impudence of her.'

Rhyssa was also irritated. *Peter, stop her!*

Peter, on his dignity: *I don't need a minder, Rhyssa. I really don't. Just enough time to catch my breath. 'Sides, no-one could stop Tirla.*

'Rather admirable of the child, I think,' Sascha replied, staunchly defending his protégée. For a palpable moment he and Rhyssa locked wills. Then he continued in a gentler tone, 'I do realize, Rhyssa, that Peter's inhibited by the gassing he took. If Tirla can manage an ID on the second car, too, we'll maybe catch more than just the well-deserving Revered Pontis Prosit.'

'Has Boris confirmed the owner of that jetcar?' Rhyssa asked, only marginally appeased.

'Registered to Pontis Prosit, aka Flimflam,' Sascha said with a grin, 'complete with vanity plate – VRPP/2403/RIG, at a riverside address that is more palatial than reverential. Boris is sending out surveillance and stand-by teams. I'd like the Centre to muster Talent as of right now!' Sascha waited long enough for Rhyssa's assent and then pointed a finger at Budworth to punch the alert button. 'We can move once we've got a definite fix.'

'Neither Auer or Bertha have anything for us,' Sirikit told them.

'That's odd,' Rhyssa said with a frown. 'There should be something!'

'I find a pre–cog silence reassuring,' Sascha remarked, buckling on his utility belt and checking his trankgun. 'Flimflam is at least not going to trigger panic in the immediate future so we have a very good chance of catching him *in flagrante delicto*. Dorotea, is Tirla available again?'

Dorotea shook her head, her lips pursed in an aggrieved moue. 'Wretched little snip of a thing!' she said with a certain amount of reluctant admiration in her tone.

'Got it!' cried Carmen suddenly, jumping out of her chair, rushing to the map terminal, and punching co–ordinates that brought up the South Shore area. 'Tirla's come through again. There simply can't be two such similar situations. She's heading towards an old railway switchhouse. I can just make it out. There's a crack of light coming through a window that opens on to a platform. There seems to be hundreds of cars of old rolling stock rusting there. Here we are!' She pointed to the marked area on the map. 'Here're tracks. Acres of them. And obsolete railcars waiting to be recycled.'

Rhyssa, Dave, Sascha, Dorotea, and Budworth in his support chair, converged to look at the area magnified on the screen.

'It couldn't be better, could it,' Dorotea said slowly, 'as a place to hide terrified kids!' *Tirla! Answer me! We know where you are now.*

When she had no reply, Sascha gave Rhyssa a long look and then, with Dave Lehardt, they left the Control Room, jogging at quickstep to the stairs that would take them to the aircars and teams waiting on the landing roof.

41

Tirla's night vision had adjusted to the gloom, part mist, part lightlessness despite the angry red/orange glow of Jerhattan which lit the rim of the horizon on all sides. The upper levels of distant linears, majestic in the night, punctuated the city glow with their long silhouettes. From top storeys, with aerials and stacks, aircraft warning signals blinked their light patterns. She moved forward carefully on the narrow band of level surface on the top of the railcars. If she slipped, there'd be nothing for her to catch on to with such ovoid sides. The narrow surface was gritty with dirt and slippery in the moist air. She headed towards that thin band of light and the dark bulk of the building that framed it.

She had safely traversed five cars, two more with children moaning and weeping inside them, when she felt a pressure in her mind that she recognized as Dorotea trying to contact her.

Go 'way. I've got to concentrate.

She cursed softly as she slithered for a panicky moment between cars, waiting until her heart stopped thudding, fearful that her scrambling had been heard. Her sharp ears had caught the sound of muted voices from the building. The line of cars continued past a long platform and she debated slipping down and getting close enough to the building to overhear the conversations.

Conversations were useless tender: the registration number of an aircar undeniable proof. She crawled forward on her belly, conscious of every noise she made, and how dry her mouth was, that her fingers were painful and getting stiffer by the minute.

There was a sudden break in the murk and there, parked beside the less distinct blue jetter was an expensive sports jetcar, its hull a crisp white, its tail ID equally visible. The two cars were balanced on the one junction of rail that was free of rolling stock.

Tirla: *Peter, I got the second one. The number is CD-08-MAL, clear as day. And the other car is right beyond it. Peter?*

Peter: *I heard you, Tirla. I told them. You come back here. They're mad at you for closing Dorotea out. You're going to have to apologize to her.* Peter sounded fierce.

Apologize? Why? Tirla was so surprised that she slipped, banging down on the railcar. *Now you've done it!* She flattened herself on the far side of the car as light flooded out of the building, illuminating the platform to its edge and the slightly bulging side of the car on which she lay.

'I tell you I had heard something!' said the man silhouetted in the doorway. He peered around the doorframe and Tirla had a good view of the scene behind him, and two men, one of whom idly swung a short stick, clipping it against his boot with an air of indolent diffidence.

'Shut the door, you cretin!' The door abruptly closed. And then opened a much thinner crack. ' . . . a good look around. Up, over, under, in. Mess up once more, maggot. You can be eagle spread, too.'

The door closed a second time but not before Tirla thought the angry voice was familiar enough to freeze her guts. She heard the ladrone moving, his shoes crunching the grit on the platform. She heard him haul back one of the warped carriage doors, the plastic creaking as he looked in the carriage. He moved on down the platform, cursing softly under his breath, dropping down to flash his light beneath the car. 'Up' was next and Tirla could not take chances. She was just in time, for the red pinpoint of a filtered handlight shone briefly where she had just been. She held her breath lest the searcher notice her outline on the dusty top.

She watched as he cautiously opened the door and peered as hard as she could for details. As the stick swinger was nearest the door, she got another good look at his cruel and haughty face, with a beaked nose and thin plucked brows. And the table, piled with credits which two other men were counting: floaters by the size of them. One of the counters looked vaguely familiar though she had no time to identify him because the other man's face fascinated her. He turned his head, idly tapping his black boot with the stick: she caught the gleam of gold around the handle. Yes, he had a cruel face, and a hungry one. Only then did the significance of the pile of floaters dawn on her.

Tirla: *Dorotea! The pay-off's being made! Floaters. More than I've ever seen in my life!*

Dorotea, her voice hard-edged: *Tirla, don't you ever dare cut me out again.* There was no doubt of Dorotea's anger and disapproval. Tirla was momentarily dismayed and surprised. Wasn't she doing what they needed done? How could such a sweet old lady come on so tough and hard?

Tirla: *Well, if you crazy Talents don't move your asses, you're going to mess everything up and I'll have nothing more to do with you.*

Peter! Help Peter now! Dorotea didn't sound apologetic, but she did sound anxious.

Tirla knew very well that Peter needed help. So did all the other kids. As quickly as she could, she moved back along the line of cars. If the pay-off had been made, some of the kids might be shifted soon. She had to get Peter out. And free as many of the others as she could. If they all scattered and hid, it'd take all night to recapture them. That is, if she could stop them crying long enough to help themselves.

Tirla slipped and this time could not recover her balance, sliding down the dirt-encrusted side of the car and dropping to a painful stop on stones and cinders that bruised and cut her feet. Cursing her clumsiness and hoping that she had got far enough away so that the noise had not been heard, she made her way along on the ground. She could move faster this way even on sore feet but she cursed the bastards who had removed the beautiful purple boots that she'd bought on her first trip to the mall.

Crying had been reduced to whimpering in the first car. And in the second. Tirla winced. How much time did she have to get Peter out if the pay-off had been made? Could he make use of that special Talent of his now?

Yes, I can, said Peter and appeared out of the darkness between two cars. He touched her hand. *And I know exactly how. C'mon.* He led her along the track until she nearly stumbled over a big handle attached to one side of the track. *We're going to do a switcheroo.* And he laughed softly out loud. *Much faster than letting all those kids loose. There's a hundred of them.*

They heard a muffled thrumming and saw the whiteness of the aircar lifting slowly from behind the building.

Peter: *C'mon, I've got to get to that transformer box or my idea won't work! I need the gestalt for this. You know how to uncouple cars?* Suddenly the process was driven into Tirla's mind and she staggered a bit, stunned by the vivid intrusion. *Then go back and uncouple the last car with the kids in it. Stay there and warn me if anyone's coming.*

'You mean like, upstairs?' Tirla said in a hoarse whisper, pointing to the sky.

No, them! Peter pointed at the building.

'When are we getting some help?' Tirla said in an acid whisper, refusing to talk in her mind when she was nose to nose with Peter. 'My feet hurt!'

'Soon,' Peter hissed and then gave her a shove to help her on her way. 'Try walking my way!'

Grumpy because her feet hurt and her hands ached, and she didn't quite understand how he could possibly do what she thought he was going to do, she nevertheless obeyed instructions that she couldn't have refused. Railcars that hadn't moved in years were going to make the most awful racket. Peter was stupid! She hurried because the aircar hadn't cleared yet and that noise might cover some of what the railcars would make.

She identified the last car from the moaning inside it, and struggled with couplings encrusted with caked oil and dirt. *Peter, it's* . . . Suddenly the stiff coupling released itself and she was knocked off balance, staggering back into the end of the car. *Well, thanks!* A wail arose from within. *Shut your faces you stupid gits. I'm doing my best to save your innards and your virtue.* She banged her fist once, which hurt, against the side of the car and felt the pain worth it when the warning achieved an instant drop in the mewling. That did much to soothe her aggravations.

Nervously she glanced up to see the aircar's slow upward progress. Running dark like that, the pilot had to be careful not to get tangled in the wires that festooned the area around the building. If Peter could just get moving . . . He was! She heard the squeal, rattle and clanking as wheels long locked on rails reluctantly began to turn. She swung up to sit on the tongue of the coupling, watching the building for any sign that someone within heard the metallic protest. But the building was two hundred metres or so away and the aircar was whooshing and thrumming.

She peered at the skyline, yearning to see some subtle

movement in the air that hinted of the approach of help. Those Talents were so slow. How 'soon' was soon? Her car moved all too jerkily with rattlings and clankings, but was making progress along the track. The dark building with the telltale band of light was slowly receding. She felt her car clack across the junction, veering right, and experienced partial relief. If that ladrone looked outside and saw half the train missing . . .

She saw the white blur of Peter's face as the car inched past the transformer box and there was no disguise in the dark night for the audible hum emanating from it. What was Peter doing?

She jumped down from the coupling, wincing as her cut feet hit the stony, cindery ground. The cars continued to move obliquely away from danger, down an empty track.

'You can't leave just empty track. They'll know . . . ' Tirla put an urgent hand on his arm and then could not release it. She could feel him shaking from the effort he had already made, shaking and more. And she was also affected by his shaking and whatever it was racing through him.

'I'm trying. A gestalt's hard with all that anaesthesia slowing me down. Help me!'

'Gestalt?' Tirla stuttered over the unfamiliar word and then Peter put the explanation in her mind. Before she could ask how she could possibly help with that, she was. Her body seemed alive with the current racing through her, like the time she had caught a jolt from an exposed wire. Only this wasn't as painful as that shock had been. But it was . . . what was it?

The metallic protest this time was startlingly loud on the still air. The white jet had moved beyond visibility into the swirling mist. Tirla felt both stronger and weaker, clutching at Peter with both hands, wanting to help him make the gestalt and needing his support. Suddenly she was aware of movement behind her as

296

car after car began to slide past them, on to the track, clickety click, clickety click. Far too loud. Suddenly, with a resounding metallic clank, the new cars bounced against those near the platform. The shouts of alarm were quite audible as men piled out to investigate.

42

'Tell me! Did you let all those other kids loose?' Flimflam
said, his nose inches from Tirla's face. She wished he
would bend just a little closer so she could bite him. He'd
probably poison her, greasy, coarse, evil scuz.

Unfortunately before Tirla could help Peter to hide,
two of the faster ladrones had caught them. They had
been ungently hauled back to the building and into the
presence of a seething Flimflam, so enraged that foam
had gathered at the corners of his mouth. Screaming with exasperation, Tirla had been shoved in front
of the raging man as Peter collapsed on the floor,
groaning.

'We didn't see no others,' one of the ladrones said
anxiously. 'There wasn't a sign of them nor those cocoons
in the cars neither.'

'Tell me where the children are!' Flimflam repeated in
one of the more common Neester dialects, and squeezed
hard on her swollen fingers. 'Did you let them loose?'

Despite herself, Tirla let out a howl of pain, trying
to pull her hand out of his grasp. It hurt so much she

couldn't even think of a suitable malediction to fling at him. He let her go but scooped a stick off the table and began to slash it across her back.

'Hey, boss, the merch! Don't mark the merch!'

'Tell me where the children went!' he demanded in the most common Asian language.

Tirla let tears run down her cheeks as she glanced quickly around the room, as if seeking help. Then, in one of the most obscure languages she knew, she answered him, piteously appealing 'Don't beat me. I don't understand you! Don't beat me again!'

'Of all the . . . ' Flimflam roared, swivelling about to the ladrones and hitters in the room. 'What did she say? One of you must understand her? Just what I need! A dumb kid! Well?'

There were murmurs and shrugging as no-one there admitted to understanding.

Dorotea, reassuringly: *We're nearly there, Tirla. We have the yard on the nightscope.*

'Where . . . ' and Flimflam was making ludicrously broad, pantomime gestures, so unlike his polished performance as a RIG that Tirla nearly laughed even though he poked her with his stick to emphasize his words. 'Where . . . are . . . the others? Can no-one talk to her? Rouse the other one. We can't waste time. That bloody His Highness will be sending the transports. We must have the merchandise ready. Months of planning, everything goes without a hitch, we've got the money . . . WHERE ARE THE OTHERS?'

A ladrone poured water over Peter who did not even moan and Tirla watched him anxiously. He looked terribly pale, crumpled up like that. He'd been fine until they'd been recaptured. Perhaps the effort of moving those heavy railcars . . . She gasped as the stick sliced her again, right over the previous welt. Tirla tried to back away but hands clamped on her shoulders, holding her fast. She kicked backwards with sharp heels, jarring feet already sore, but her captor had heavy boots on and she only achieved more bruises.

'Let's really put some fear into her,' Flimflam said, gesturing, and she was flung face-down to the hard surface of the table where she'd recently seen piles of floaters. Cruel hard hands grasped her by wrists and ankles. Suddenly pain exploded across her already lacerated feet. She screamed and screamed again at the second horrific stab of pain, and fainted for the first time in her life.

So she missed seeing Flimflam violently propelled backwards to crash against the wall. She missed the explosive entrance of Sascha, Rhyssa, Dave Lehardt and the Talent teams. And she missed the other excitements that would have given her immense satisfaction.

43

'Commissioner,' Ranjit said, 'that's a diplomatic registration . . .'

'I wouldn't care if it was God himself, Lieutenant,' was the LEO Commissioner's answer. Law enforcement and order means just that from bottom to top, and right on down the line again. Or it's privilege, not law enforcement and order!' He measured the distance on the huge display map, from the South Shore trainyard to the riverside address. 'Assign the best driver we've got to shadow that CD. And I want that beehive – not just the penthouse lift or the domestic floors but that entire complex secured. Pack all entries with sensitives. Tell them to home in on any strong emotion – we may get a lot of wash on this. You know how hivers hate to have their privacy breached.' He turned to another aide. 'Barry, get me the City Manager and tell her this is a sensitive affair. You will not tell her the quarry but I want her forewarned so she can back us with the Corps. Feed the situation through the Judicial and get me four – no, make it five – John Does and a search warrant. And let's hope that Sascha's efficient.'

He shrugged on his tunic top, resplendent with the 'bravery bars' and braid, all necessary for this mission. He also strapped on sidearms. Now he gestured for Ranjit and his other aides to follow him to the rooftop garage. Jet-and aircars were spinning off, along usual routes, having been instructed to move circumspectly.

Sascha? Boris linked with his brother as his aircar took off.

Nearly there, Bro. It still takes time to drive a car from there to here. The other bird has not flown . . . holy hell, what's happening? Come back to you later.

Boris could feel the abruptness of the mental break and cursed under his breath as his aircar ploughed on to his destination. The pause lengthened, causing him some anxiety. Surely Sascha was competent enough? Should he have sent men with the Centre teams? If the child-dealers at the railyard should get a warning through to his own quarry, this whole operation might be jeopardized.

My God, Boris, and Sascha's voice burst in on him like a bellow, *if you let that Shimaz slime ooze out of this, Highness, Prince, Manager or whatever, I promise you that the Talents will handle him ex officio!*

The LEO Commissioner had never heard such vindictiveness in his brother's voice before.

Boris: *What happened?*

Sascha: *The Revered Venerable Pontis Prosit used a bastinado on Tirla's feet. Peter's collapsed!*

Boris: *Flimflam didn't get a message off, did he?* If the man had, they might lose the most important criminal.

Sascha, livid with rage: *No, not when he had a little girl to interrogate! Make it stick on that other bastard, will you? Or, by all that's holy, I will. Myself with no help from any other agency, dear LEO Bro.*

Boris: *LEO is on the move, Sascha. You hang on to your temper. Have you got the other children? Have we any proof of complicity?*

Sascha, sarcastically: *I don't suppose Tirla's bloody feet* count for more than assault and GBH. But we also took possession of a case full of many too many floaters, ready for a night deposit, complete with an account number I'll bet can be traced to the Revered Venerable.

Boris: *That should be enough to convict Flimflam. But is there enough to catch this – what did you call him?*

Sascha: *Shimaz, Prince Phanibal Shimaz, who seems to be a whiz at more than Josephson Junctions. Flimflam's spilling his guts. His Highness has rather an extensive operation: child labour in his rice paddies and mines, child prostitution, and a child farm where the healthiest are kept that way until someone can pay for the organ they need.*

Boris, growling: *Get me something to link him to that yard. Something that will stick!*

They were well on the way when the comlink heralded a connection from Commissioner Aiello. On the cabin screen, it was obvious that she was in formal attire. Hovering beside her was her protocol officer, Jak, who, for all his empathy, could, at times, be quite tiresome about details.

'Do you have incontrovertible proof, Roznine?'

'We have proof of a connection which is incompatible with any diplomatic occupation,' Boris replied, setting his jaw.

'Who? Surely not the Ambassador!' At that moment, Teresa Aiello was depressed with pessimism.

'We are not after his Excellency, so Jak can relax. Members of his Corps, certainly, and an Embassy vehicle has been identified and traced from the abduction site. There's no problem of proving involvement. Is the DA there, too? Well, give the old dog a comforting word in his shell-like ear. The Talents have cracked this abduction ring.' The last he admitted ruefully for, despite protests to the contrary, he and his brother were in constant competition.

The beehive was aptly nicknamed: a massive structure, its bottom levels along the block square bulk, where other buildings obscured views, housed maintenance, storage and worker accommodations. Where the hive rose above its neighbours, there were great curved plas-glas panels that were part solar-heating, part prestigious display of wealth. Each pie-shaped apartment boasted luxuriant gardens and views from the outer wall and, where the hive had an atrium core, rare plants and trees festooned the inner walls. Naturally the top apartments were the most exclusive and expensive . . . with one whole floor given over to private garden and garage facilities, swimming pools, game courts and whatever other amenities the residents expected to secure the ultimate of comfort.

Is the surround complete yet, Ranjit? Boris asked on his helmet comunit.

Just now . . . completely ringed, sir. No-one can get in or out without being observed.

'Commissioner,' Boris's pilot said, 'here comes the suspect vehicle now.'

The sleek white jetcar swooped to settle and deposit its passengers on the roof of the hive.

'Three men!'

'I can see that myself. Secure that jetter the moment it's garaged. See what you can get the pilot to say. Grab the log, and any garage records. And now,' Boris could not keep the satisfaction out of his voice, 'let's get the bastard.'

The LEO pilot put them down on the hive roof and Boris Roznine and his squad made for the ramp down to the entrance level of the penthouse. Seeing the formal and formidable attire of the LEO Commissioner and his aide, the door attendant hurried to open it. His bow was respectful and nervous.

'What are you doing, you naga? I'm not expecting guests!' exclaimed the man at the other end of the magnificent white marbled reception hall. A servant was just assisting the removal of his elegant blue suede long coat while a second man was also shrugging, unassisted, out

304

of his own outer wear. 'Exclude them immediately.'

'I think not, Prince Phanibal,' Boris said, stepping forward and giving Ranjit a quick thought about reinforcements.

The Prince's companion moved with astonishing speed out of the nearest of the many doors leading from the entry hall while the paralysed doorman gaped.

'Is his Excellency at home?' Boris asked, some glimmer of Jak's protocol lessons seeping through his anger. The doorman fearfully nodded before the Prince ordered him not to respond.

'How dare you – whoever you are,' Prince Phanibal demanded, his expression haughty and totally confident, 'enter a diplomatic residence without invitation?' His gaze ignored the lieutenant by Boris's side and the detachment standing just outside the door.

'Boris Roznine, Commissioner for Law Enforcement and Order in Jerhattan!' He turned to the awed and shaking doorman. 'Please beg his Excellency's indulgence and request an immediate interview on a matter of grave urgency.'

The attendant, ignoring the Prince's countermands and threats, opened a hidden door and disappeared. He had no sooner gone than all the other doors of the entrance hall swung open and a large number of large men, obviously a guard summoned by the Prince's elusive companion, filed in with military precision. Three immediately flanked the Prince, black-robed and turbaned, with silver mounted belts and daggers which were exactly the legal length permitted display guards.

Boris did not need to look over his shoulder to know that LEO reinforcements, carrying the weaponry legal for them, outnumbered the Embassy guards and were quite ready to force an entry. He waited a moment for the Prince to absorb that.

'I believe that we now await his Excellency's appearance,' he said with a grim and ungenial smile and, in studied insult to a 'royal' person, seated himself on the nearest decorative bench.

'Do you not understand the repercussions this unwarranted intrusion . . . ' Prince Phanibal began imperiously. 'I am not only a royal prince of my house but a Manager of the Padrugoi. I am due back on the Platform on the next shuttle.'

'That is why I, as LEO Commissioner, am here to explain personally to the Ambassador,' Boris replied. *Is this the guy who's been giving Rhyssa so much grief? Perhaps if we both try, we can probe his mind. It's not admissable evidence in court since it was under duress but it'll give us some clues. He's got a dense mind shield even for a Prince. He's had careful conditioning and I'd love to know where. No, we can't break it, not without breaking the law.*

The slightest of smiles tugged at the corner of the Prince's mouth and his eyes narrowed, hiding smug pleasure at deflecting the mental intrusion. He raised his left hand briefly, his fingers closing on some accustomed possession. Then he threw his fingers open in vexation and raised the arm indolently across his chest, the smile broadening.

'Perhaps you have mislaid you little stick,' Boris heard himself saying. Sascha was there! *Saving time and effort, brother?* Boris asked in his head.

Sascha, his mental tone savage: *The little stick which made raw meat of Tirla's feet.*

'I . . . what?' Prince Phanibal stiffened in surprise.

'The little switch that you are fond of carrying as an affectation for you don't own any . . . animals, I believe,' the Boris/Sascha link continued. 'The one with the ivory handle and the rather . . . unusual filigree design.'

'I do not have to account for my possessions to such as you,' Prince Phanibal replied as he angled himself obliquely from Boris, tilting his chin arrogantly to display what was probably considered a handsome profile.

At that point, the Ambassador, clad in a deep purple

velvet robe with exquisite gold designs, entered from the central door. He cast one startled look at the Prince and his pose, another at the group by the door and signalled for the guards to withdraw. Boris Roznine rose and walked forward to meet the Malaysian.

'Due to the gravity of this situation, your Excellency,' he said, speaking on his own although he knew Sascha listened avidly, 'you will permit me to dispense with formalities. This man,' and he gestured to the aloof Prince, 'and another have been involved in activities incompatible with any function in your Embassy. I must ask you to instruct His Highness and his companion to accompany me to the LEO headquarters.'

'With what could the Prince Phanibal be charged?' the Ambassador asked with great dignity.

'The charge is indeed grave, your Excellency, for there has been traffic in abducting minors and subjecting them to illicit bondage for the purpose of slave labour, unlawful intercourse, and organ removal.'

'You have proof of such a heinous crime?' The Ambassador drew himself more erect but to the LEO men he did not appear to be all that surprised.

'Yes, your Excellency,' Boris inclined his head with a nod of regret. The Ambassador was a fine old man to be saddled with this sort of scandal. 'There are witnesses!' continued the Boris/Sascha link, supporting Boris's reply. 'Talented witnesses.'

The Prince snorted his disbelief, his poise undisturbed. 'Such a claim tries all patience. You will dismiss these deceivers, Uncle.'

Sascha: *This bugger's clever.*

Boris: *He hasn't turned a hair or admitted a thing.*

Sascha: *Does he think all Talents are adults?*

Boris: *Tirla IS on the official register?*

Sascha: *Didn't you read the ID bracelet you got her six weeks ago? And there are four of the ladrones, spilling their guts to avoid being Spaced, confirming what we've got out of Flimflam for turning State's evidence — his mind took very little pressure when he regained consciousness. That was some scam they had going. We have all the details needed to implicate the Prince and that secretary of his. Returned from the religious institutions and a period of meditation in the Far East? He was planning the whole thing with Prince Phanibal's backing.* Sascha's snort of contempt was so strong that Boris grunted.

The Ambassador turned his head slightly over one shoulder in Prince Phanibal's direction. 'I will not dismiss them, Nephew. Talent cannot be forsworn.' Then he regarded Boris steadily for a moment and beckoned for the Prince to step forward. 'You will go with them.'

'But I cannot be arrested like a common criminal . . . '

'Oh, indeed, Nephew, you are an uncommon criminal, for diplomatic immunity does not shield pederasts,' the old man said in a voice that was leached of all emotion.

'You cannot permit such an insult to our name,' the Prince said, his manner altering abruptly, slapping his fists to his legs in his barely contained frustration and anger. 'My father will hear of this. You will hear of this. You will be disgraced! You will never return to your home. Your children and your children's children are dog meat . . . '

The Malaysian Ambassador ignored him as he strode to the nearest door and closed it firmly behind him. The guards now moved to cover each of the doorways, subtly removing official protection from the Prince.

Commissioner? Ranjit said politely. *The pilot has been arrested and we have the jetter's logs, the garage log, also Prince Shimaz's companion was apprehended, attempting to escape.*

'If you will come with us . . . ' Boris began formally, gesturing towards the roof landing steps.

The Prince suddenly erupted into action, his face contorted in rage, flinging himself towards the opening Boris had made. Ranjit, with great presence of mind, neatly tripped the man as he passed.

At that, it took three officers to subdue the raving man.

44

'So, despite appeals from his grieving father and protests from Ludmilla Barchenka that His Highness Manager Phanibal Shimaz *must* be released until the Station is completed,' Sascha told Tirla, sitting on the edge of her bed in Dorotea's house, 'that scuzball will spend the rest of his life at hard labour on the Moon.'

'And Flimflam?' Tirla's eyes flashed with anger and hatred that startled Sascha, though he could certainly understand it.

'Oh, turning State's evidence gave him a choice of occupations,' Sascha said with a grin. 'He elected to take a job as a sanitation engineer on the Big Station. Not exactly Spaced out, but near enough.'

'How many of the kids *were* illegals?' she asked after relishing Flimflam's future for a long and satisfactory moment. She and Peter had both been in court to give their evidence but had not heard the sentencing. She still didn't walk very far on her tender feet and, despite Peter's patient instruction in kinetics, she had been unable to levitate as he did. Peter maintained that he had been unconscious when some force had knocked Flimflam across the room just as the rescuers arrived.

'Eighty-seven children,' Sascha replied brusquely.

'In the hostels, huh?' Tirla gave a long sigh.

'Just think what you and Peter saved them from, Tirla. You had a taste of it.'

'And there haven't been any more deals or abductions?' Sascha shook his head.

The apathy that had settled over Tirla after the trial worried everyone in the Centre. Obediently she had worked with the physiotherapist to regain movement in her damaged feet: she had been more severely injured than had first been apparent. She had dutifully tried to improve her telepathic range but Dorotea and Peter were the only ones she heard at any distance, and Sascha only if he were within a hundred metres. She did test to an astounding degree of empathy, the source of her unusual linguistic feats.

She was assiduous in following her education programme, opting for a very wide variety of courses, some of which Dorotea was certain she couldn't yet comprehend. Her reports proved that she was more precocious than anticipated. She took no joy in the freedom of the Centre's grounds and played with no other children though they repeatedly attempted to interest her. She had even refused to go on shopping trips with either Sascha or Cass. She would become more animated in Peter's company but he and Rhyssa were deeply involved in his highly specialized training. She was virtually recovered from the abduction but her morale was extremely low so Dorotea had insisted that Sascha come for a visit.

'What does it take to strand a kid?' Tirla asked him.

'Look, Chip,' he said, laying a gentle hand on her knee – she felt no less fragile to him, though she'd noticeably put on weight and her eyes were clear, far too clear, Sascha sometimes thought. 'You can't save all the illegals. And for the moment the danger is over.'

'But not the appetites,' Tirla said, brooding. 'Like that scuzzy prince.' In the privacy of her room, her face took on an expression nearly as malicious as the man she thought of. '*Is* it difficult to strand a kid? Cass and Suz said they were stranding kids in Linear E. Have they improved the strand for a long-term use?'

'I know you're biologically twelve years old, Tirla, but you sound fifty,' Sascha was exasperated.

She tilted her head up at him, regarding his through slightly narrowed eyes, a little smile playing at her lips. 'In the linears I am. You surely don't want another scam like that RIG, do you? And like your brother said, even illegal kids have rights! I know Cass has had her baby and wouldn't want to go undercover so soon. But I'd bet my last credit . . . '

' . . . all of them are the Centre's now, remember?' Sascha teased and caught a sly gleam in her eye. So Dorotea was right about her squirrelling some floaters away. Old habits die hard.

'And the Centre also has to give me anything I want . . . '

'Within reason . . . '

'Well, I'll be reasonable. I'm good at languages – anyone's – but I can't keep sharp if I'm here,' and she gestured out the window at the lawn, 'and Teacher says I don't know all the languages of the world . . . yet. I'll do you a deal, Sascha Roznine,' and Tirla cocked her head at him, her 'haggling' manner, he was learning to call it. 'I'll strand illegals in every Jerhattan linear. I'll strand 'em, but I won't report 'em.' She gave a mirthless grin. 'If there're sweeps and I was blamed for it I'd lose my – what do you call it – credibility? I got ethics, too, you know. But I'd know when "trouble" was brewing, and that I would report. That'd help, wouldn't it? I'd be a better trouble-spotter than any of those LEO plants of your brother's!' The notion seemed to amuse her and certainly she had become more animated. 'I always knew who was LEO, even who was Talent.'

While there was no question of her affection for Sascha, she was never easy in Boris's presence though he had tried to be ingratiating. An ingrained distrust of all LEOs was Sascha's diagnosis, not wishing Tirla to be at odds with his twin.

'You really wouldn't consider staying here with Dorotea, and extending your Talents?'

Tirla wagged her head, grimacing. 'It's not that I don't like Dorotea. She's the best ever. It's just . . . I don't feel comfortable in all of this.' And her glance swept around the well-appointed room. 'I'm a linear brat. My Talent, as you call it,' and she wrinkled her nose in self-deprecation, 'works best in a linear environment.' Her eyes twinkled.

'You can't live all your life in a linear,' said Dorotea, entering the room, her expression worried. She radiated affection, reassurance and support.

'Why not?' Tirla demanded, lifting her hands in a quick gesture of exasperation.

'Indeed, why not?' Sascha echoed.

'Cass and Suz live on the high side of linears when they're undercover. I'd really like my own squat on say, Level 19 so I'd have a view and not so much smog.' Her grin was sheer impudence. 'In case he hasn't been listening in, ask your brother if I wouldn't be more use to him living in a linear.'

Sascha laughed. *Bro? Did you hear that?*

Boris: *Little bint! You'll never know where you are with that one, will you? It's demonstrable that she's superb as a pulse-keeper. There are far more squabbles and arguments in Linear G than it had while she was there. I could use a Tirla in all the big linears. If Rhyssa doesn't mind . . .*

Dorotea: *I mind!*

Boris: *Sorry, Dorotea, but Tirla's a Registered Talent and too damned vital to lay-about until she's of age. But there's nothing that says she has to live at the Centre while she's waiting for her eighteenth birthday to come round. If she'd be much happier in a linear, she could live in one. With Lessud and his family in Island K? Go to school properly and still keep her ears and eyes open for the general wellbeing of the community. With the scam dried up in Jerhattan, Long Island is the next logical pool to fish in for illegal kids. We could use a reliable pulse-keeper like Tirla.*

'Did you get any of that, Tirla?' Sascha asked her, grinning. Sitting beside her, he could feel her concentrating on 'listening' but her mind echoed nothing but the desire to hear.

She shook her head and gave a sad little sigh, with a look of apology to Dorotea who had been trying so hard to train her.

'The Bro wants to know if you'd prefer to live in a Long Island residential while you're waiting to grow up.'

'A residential in Long Island?' Tirla became animated at once, sitting up in her bed, her big dark eyes glittering, a delicate tinge of colour in her cheeks, a hopeful smile on her lips. 'That'd be living in high style!'

EPILOGUE

Three months later

Rhyssa?

The tone, apologetic but firm, roused Rhyssa from one of those intense sleeps where it is difficult to move the body even when the brain has become alert. She lay heavy in the bed and managed to open one eye to see the clock: then she heard the familiar sound of Dave singing softly to himself in the bathroom. Once again she had overslept. She really didn't know what was the matter with her these past few weeks: she simply couldn't get enough sleep.

Rhyssa! The tone was more urgent and then recognition came.

Yes, Madlyn? What's the matter? For Madlyn did sound anxious as well as tentative.

I didn't wake you, did I? I thought I had Earth times down pat.

I overslept. What's the matter?

It's her! Disgust, frustration, anger, exasperation and another emotion packed into that one pronoun forewarned Rhyssa. *She's at it again. Saying we Talents are*

NOT doing our job! We have only pulled her out of her midden and yet she has the gall to blame US for anything that goes wrong up here.

What is it this time? Rhyssa hauled herself up against her pillows and reached for the coffee thermos. Another elegant notion of Mr Lehardt's, and so civilized. She started to pour herself a cup and then stopped. The smell of it turned her stomach.

There's one last very critical shipment due to come up, Madlyn went on, *only it hasn't because Johnny says he won't ship it yet.*

Won't ship it? That blew the last of the sleep-fog from Rhyssa's mind. And what was Colonel Greene up to now? *And naturally it's essential for her to complete the installation?*

Vital! It's got the last of the internal mechanisms and remotes. Very delicate stuff, I know, and not something you want bounced about. And there's only a week more before the completion date. Then we can all come down to Earth! There was also heartfelt relief in Madlyn's tone now. *So we want to know why it's being held up. Because we are, too, you know.*

I know. I'll sort it out, Madlyn. Indeed I will.

Dave was singing louder now he knew she was awake. Dave might not be telepathic but he displayed a keen sensitivity where she was concerned that more than made up for it in ways she could never have anticipated. She grinned to herself and then recalled the task at hand. Eight-thirty was not too early to rouse Colonel John Greene out of his Floridian sack.

Johnny boy, phone me! He was too far to conduct an audible telepathic link with her but Rhyssa's call would reach him easily enough. She looked at the phone, counting down. It rang in exactly ten seconds.

'You wished parlance with me, Madame Lehardt?'

'I do indeed, Colonel Greene. What hanky-panky are you pulling on poor dear Ludmilla?'

Johnny's chuckle was drenched in malice. 'Only what

she deserves, petal. She conscripted us Talents to be sure she finished on time and finished on time she will be. Not one moment earlier, not one moment later. Why?'

'Oh, I see,' and Rhyssa chuckled because she did see. 'And you have it timed to the final hour?'

'Lance and me worked out the time it would take to install those controls and we've scheduled the kinetics needed. We know exactly how long it will take. Lance must have forgotten to clue Madlyn. I'm sorry she's getting some schtick, but she's well able for it. Soothe her down, will you, Rhys? We're doing it OUR way!'

'Oh, I quite agree. Not an hour early and not an hour late.'

As she hung up, Dave came in the room, a towel draped about his lean hips.

'I did try to wake you, Rhys,' he said with a rueful expression. 'You just don't want to get up in the morning.'

'I'm wanton enough to admit that I love being in bed with you, Dave, but preferably awake, not sleeping like the dead.' She lifted her arms and began to stretch, and stopped. 'And what's wrong with the coffee? The smell makes me nauseous.'

Dave grinned as he sat down on the edge of the bed, looking at her. His blue eyes crinkled. 'Figured it out yet?' he asked, glancing down at her abdomen.

'I thought. . .I mean, I haven't been ill,' Rhyssa said, with dawning awareness, '. . .just sleepy! Oh, Dave, could I really be pregnant?'

'Think about it a moment, oh wise woman!' He got up, shedding his towel as he began to dress. She loved looking at him, no matter what he was doing, and the intimacy of this daily act was something special for her. 'After all, I've been doing my best for several months now!'

Awed by the possibility, Rhyssa did start thinking about her body, placing her hands gently on her belly, intuiting the bio-feedback.

'Oh, Dave, I am pregnant. I am!'

'I think you're the last one to have copped on, then,' he replied, grinning broadly. 'Dorotea knows.'

'And she said nothing?' Rhyssa sat bolt upright again, startled and somewhat miffed that she'd been left in the dark . . . and by Dorotea!

'Well, there're some things it's more fun to find out by yourself,' Dave said, grinning as he stooped down to kiss her lovingly. 'There's a sort of glow about you, too. Everyone's noticed. They've been politely waiting for an official announcement.' He stroked her tangled hair, running fingers down her silver streak.

She sighed, then blurted out, 'Does Sascha know?'

Dave stopped in the act of pulling on his tunic, and ducked his head out of the folds to regard her with some alarm.

'Sascha? I know you're close but . . . '

'Well,' and Rhyssa paused. Here was one of the few drawbacks to Dave's lack of Talent. Sometimes she had to explain with far more detail than a Talent would require. 'Well, Sascha's got to wait, that's all, and he doesn't take waiting kindly.'

'Wait?' Dave pulled the tunic down. 'Wait for what?'

'For Tirla to grow up, of course,' she said, gathering herself to rise from the bed. She felt oddly protective of this new life, which was silly, since it was obviously well settled in.

'Tirla?' Dave's eyes nearly popped in astonishment. 'He's gone on her? Dirty old man!'

'Not so old and certainly not dirty where Tirla is concerned. Bolt out of the blue on him, right enough. He's never felt that way about any other female.' Rhyssa permitted herself a little knowing smile. 'But she's the one for him, and he knows it. He just has to wait a few years.'

'That wight's not even . . . '

'Tirla is twelve now, going on two hundred,' Rhyssa

317

replied with some asperity. Tirla was a very interesting personality, and she and Sascha would deal very well together. It was incredible really to have found two such diverse Talents during her Directorship: one macro who would shift worlds and one whose skill was a micro Talent, eroding language barriers. 'Neesters ripen a lot faster than we northern and occidental types. She'll be more than ready in four years to marry Sascha.'

'And that's decided?' Dave was sceptical.

Rhyssa smiled. 'Sascha's pre-cogged it. To his intense astonishment. Next time you see them together, notice how she looks at him. Quite proprietary that young lady is where Sascha is concerned. And she's better for him than Madlyn would ever be.'

'And they'll have Talented kids?'

'That's a very high probability.' Rhyssa smiled smugly.

Dave paused. In her presence he always allowed his emotions to show. He cleared his throat and asked briskly. 'What about us? When will we know?'

To reassure the man she loved, Rhyssa smiled as she nodded. 'No problem there.'

'You sound so sure?'

She put her arms around his neck, letting her gravid belly rest against him as she pulled his head down to kiss him.

'I am. He just told me so.'

THE END

THE ROWAN

BY ANNE McCAFFREY

The Talents were the élite of the Nine Star League. Their gifts were many and varied, ranging from the gently telepathic, to the rare and extremely valued Primes. On the Primes rested the entire economic wealth and communications systems of the civilised worlds. But Primes were scarce – only very rarely was a new one born.

And now, on the planet Altair, in a small mining colony on the western mountain range, a new Prime existed, a three-year-old girl – trapped in a giant mud slide that had wiped out the rest of the Rowan mining community. Every Altarian who was even mildly talented could 'hear' the child crying for help, but no one knew exactly where she was buried.

Every resource on the planet was centred into finding 'The Rowan' – the new Prime, the first ever to be born on Altair, an exceptionally unique Prime, more talented, more powerful, more agoraphobic, more lonely, than any other Prime yet known in the Nine Star League.

THE ROWAN – A NEW CONCEPT, A NEW LEGEND, FROM THE CREATOR OF THE DRAGONS OF PERN

0 552 13763 4

OTHER TITLES BY ANNE McCAFFREY
AVAILABLE FROM CORGI BOOKS

THE PRICES SHOWN BELOW WERE CORRECT AT THE TIME OF
GOING TO PRESS. HOWEVER TRANSWORLD PUBLISHERS
RESERVE THE RIGHT TO SHOW NEW RETAIL PRICES ON COVERS
WHICH MAY DIFFER FROM THOSE PREVIOUSLY ADVERTISED IN
THE TEXT OR ELSEWHERE.

All Corgi/Bantam Books are available at your bookshop or newsagent, or can be
ordered from the following address:
Corgi/Bantam Books,
Cash Sales Department,
P.O. Box 11, Falmouth, Cornwall TR10 9EN

UK and B.F.P.O. customers please send a cheque or postal order (no currency) and
allow £1.00 for postage and packing for the first book plus 50p for the second book
and 30p for each additional book to a maximum charge of £3.00 (7 books plus).

Overseas customers, including Eire, please allow £2.00 for postage and packing for
the first book plus £1.00 for the second book and 50p for each subsequent title
ordered.

NAME (Block Letters) ....

ADDRESS ....

....